Hello!

A quick thank you from me for picking up *A Cottage by the Sea*. I do appreciate it and am very lucky to have a band of dedicated readers. Whether you're a reader who's been with me since day one or if this is the first book of mine that you've tried, I hope this will get you in the mood for your summer holidays.

Haven't we all, at some time, wished we could escape to a lovely seaside retreat? I know it's at the top of my Lottery Win list. I could spend hours on property websites lusting after my very own cottage by the sea.

I've spent years doing long-haul holidays that leave me more exhausted when I return than when I left and have only recently rediscovered the joys of holidaying at home in the UK – although you do have to become an expert at weather-dodging! And, of course, packing for all seasons. No travelling light when you're going for a week in Wales, though I do highly recommend the beautiful rugged coastal areas of Pembrokeshire as a place to visit. I had such a lovely time there doing the research for this book – I'll definitely be going back.

I hope that you'll manage to find some time this year just to kick back and relax with a book or two. I wish you a happy and restful time whether you spend your holiday in Mexico or Margate, Puerto Rico or Pembrokeshire. May the sun shine on you!

Happy holidays!

Love Carole ☺ xx

Also by Carole Matthews

Let's Meet on Platform 8
A Whiff of Scandal
More to Life than This
For Better, For Worse
A Minor Indiscretion
A Compromising Position
The Sweetest Taboo
With or Without You
You Drive Me Crazy
Welcome to the Real World
The Chocolate Lovers' Club
The Chocolate Lovers' Diet
It's a Kind of Magic
All You Need is Love
The Difference a Day Makes
That Loving Feeling
It's Now or Never
The Only Way is Up
Wrapped up in You
Summer Daydreams
With Love at Christmas

A Cottage by the Sea

Carole Matthews

sphere

SPHERE

First published in Great Britain in 2013 by Sphere
This paperback edition published in 2013 by Sphere

Copyright © Carole Matthews 2013

The moral right of the author has been asserted.

A CIP catalogue record for this book
is available from the British Library.

ISBN 978-0-7515-4553-1

Typeset in Sabon by M Rules
Printed and bound in Great Britain by
Clays Ltd, St Ives plc

Papers used by Sphere are from well-managed forests
and other responsible sources.

MIX
Paper from
responsible sources
FSC® C104740

Sphere
An imprint of
Little, Brown Book Group
100 Victoria Embankment
London EC4Y 0DY

An Hachette UK Company
www.hachette.co.uk

www.littlebrown.co.uk

To Mike and Maureen Rignall,
who are dedicated to spending their
kids' inheritance on my books.
Thank you so much.

Chapter One

'*Destination*,' the dulcet tones of the sat nav announces. '*Destination*.'

Harry stamps on the brakes and stops dead in the middle of the road. There is nothing as far as the eye can see. 'Where, you bloody stupid woman?' he asks it, holding his hands aloft in supplication. 'Where?'

'*Destination*.' She is insistent. '*Destination*.'

The sat nav has the disdainful, upper-class tone of my old English teacher. She always hated me too. Normally, we call the sat nav Auntie Flossie. Today, neither of us is really speaking to her.

'Can you see anything, Grace?' he asks.

I gaze out of the car window. It's beautiful here. The road stretches ahead of us, unbroken, and there's not another car in any direction. The verdant green fields lie unspoiled beneath the unbroken acres of sky. There isn't a single man-made building in sight to mar the view. It's untamed, remote. And I guess that's the crux of our problem.

'Not really,' I admit. But it's fantastic and I hear myself sigh happily.

'Well, she says we're here.' It's clear that Harry is rapidly losing the will to live. 'Can you just look at the map, please?'

I scrabble at the road atlas on my knee. It's a tattered wreck and what remains of the front cover tells me that we bought it from a supermarket in 1992. Helpfully, inside it has a little red circle where all of their branches are – but none of the major roads built since that year, of course. Somewhat worryingly, there are no helpful red 'supermarket' circles anywhere in the area. According to this map, we are in total supermarket wilderness.

In fact, there's not very much near here at all. Currently, the only thing I can see are the miles and miles of rolling fields, hedgerows thick with flowers and sheep. Plenty of sheep.

'Fucking place,' Harry complains.

He is not a happy man. His hands are gripping the wheel again and his knuckles are white. His handsome face, however, is scarlet, becoming borderline puce. My husband, I know, would rather be in Tuscany or Thailand or even Timbuktu. Anywhere, in fact, rather than on our way to a cottage in Wales for a week.

'We can't be far away,' I offer, keeping my tone placating.

The polar opposite to Harry, I'm just thrilled to be here. My dearest friend, Ella Hawley, has invited us to stay with her and her long-term partner, Art. Ella's spending the rest of the summer in Wales and I just can't wait to see her. She's only recently inherited this cottage, but I've heard so much about it over the years that wild horses, never mind a grumpy husband, wouldn't have kept me away. Ella's also invited our friend Flick, but whether or not Flick will turn up is an entirely different matter. You can never quite pin Flick down. I hope she makes it as I haven't seen her in ages and it will be so lovely to catch up.

Outside the chilled atmosphere in the Bentley – only some of it due to the effect of the über-efficient air-conditioning – the sky is a blue more usually seen in the Mediterranean and beneath it, on the very edge of the horizon, a silver ribbon of sea shimmers invitingly. We can't be far away because Ella's cottage is by the sea and, if we drive too much further, we'll be actually in it.

'*Destination,*' the sat nav repeats.

She now sounds slightly weary with life. As am I.

'Get a grip, woman. We're not at the destination,' I tell her firmly. 'Even I've worked that out.'

'Grace,' Harry says, teeth gritted, 'do you mind? We can't stay here in the middle of the road all day.'

To be honest, Harry and I haven't really been speaking since we stopped at Magor Services just before the Severn Crossing. The service station was like a glimpse of hell with queues a mile long for everything and the place stuffed with families screaming at each other. Harry couldn't get anything to eat but a plastic ham sandwich on white bread and he's very much a smoked salmon on wholemeal man. His temper, already frayed by the amount of holiday traffic on the road, shredded to breaking point.

It hasn't helped that we've been on the road since silly o'clock and that there was a ferocious tailback to get over the bridge and into South Wales. On top of that, it cost us nearly a fortune to cross. Cue much muttering under Harry's breath that people should be paying to get out of Wales, not into it.

'We could have been halfway to the sodding Seychelles by now,' he mutters darkly.

In theory, I suppose we could be, but there's so much else to consider when flying somewhere. It starts with all the vaccinations – nearly the cost of the holiday in itself. Invariably we require malaria tablets too, which make me feel dreadful. The whole experience is just so stressful. All the glamour of flying has long gone. I always feel as if I need another holiday when I've flown for thirteen or more hours just to get back from somewhere. Your memories of the island paradise fade very quickly when faced with a four-hour-long queue for passport control at Gatwick or Heathrow followed by a week of hideous jet lag.

'I hate long-haul flights nowadays, Harry. You know that. For once, isn't it nice to throw the cases in the back of the car and just drive?'

I get a grunt in response.

Despite my husband's reticence, I'm so looking forward to this holiday and am so desperate for it. Work has been nothing but stress this year – the financial climate forcing everyone to tighten their belts, and where I work is no exception. I'm an accountant, the staff partner in a small but successful firm based in north London. We have only ten staff but, believe me, they're a full-time job to manage. I've just had a small mutiny on my hands after we told them that there will be no company Christmas trip this year. Normally, we take the staff and their other halves on a long weekend jaunt during the approach to the festive season. In the past we've been to Paris, Rome, Bruges. All very lovely. All on expenses. But this year we're going to have to do without. Every single one of our clients is watching the pennies and I think it looks right that we should do so too.

I feel the same about our own holidays abroad. More often than not, Harry and I go away at least twice every year. How can that be acceptable when so many people are struggling simply to pay their mortgages? I'm more than happy to have a summer staying at home, although I don't think Harry much likes the sound of it. So, when Ella asked us to come down and spend some time with her at the cottage, it seemed like the perfect solution. To me, anyway.

Harry wasn't keen, of course. Even as we set off he was bemoaning the fact that it would be more 'basic' than he prefers. My other half likes to lie on a sunlounger for two weeks and be waited on hand and foot. He doesn't care if there's culture or scenery. He just wants heat, a swimming pool and alcohol on tap. He likes a turndown service, a chocolate and perhaps an exotic bloom on his pillow every night. Those things don't really interest me. Don't get me wrong, I've enjoyed my fair share of luxury holidays too. But sometimes it can be just a tiny bit *boring*. Does that sound ungrateful? If you're typically British and fair-skinned, there's only so much sunbathing you can do if you don't want the boiled-lobster look. So this year I'm really looking forward to having a holiday in my own country for the first time in many years. I'll get to catch up with my dearest friends. Harry and

I will get to spend some quality time together without having to go halfway round the world. It'll be fun. I'm sure. Just the tonic we need.

'Shall we aim to get there before nightfall, Grace?' Harry says tightly.

So I pull my attention back to the map and try to work out exactly where we are.

Chapter Two

The fact that I get to hook up with my lovely friends is the icing on the cake for me. Again, I'm not sure that Harry feels the same way. My husband isn't overly fond of my friends. He says that I change when I'm with them. I think, half of the time, he doesn't like it when he's not the centre of attention and you know what it's like when old friends get together.

Ella, Flick and I all went to university together in Liverpool over ten years ago and, as such, go way back. We're more like sisters than friends and are inseparable. I feel as if we grew up together. Those formative years shaped us into the women we are today. Ella Hawley, Felicity Edwards and Grace Taylor. I smile to myself. We were quite the girls back then. A force to be reckoned with. Mainly due to Flick, I have to say. She was the one who dragged us kicking and screaming into the thick of student life. I'm sure Ella and I would have stayed at home in our skanky rooms every night, studying, if it hadn't been for Flick. Ella's the arty, thoughtful one. Flick is the fabulously pretty, fickle one. I, for my sins, am the steady and sensible one. Though we're ten years older now and, supposedly, wiser, our roles haven't changed that much.

We all took different courses at university, but found ourselves in the same halls. We hooked up at one of the events in Freshers' Week – I can't even remember what now – and have been together through thick and thin ever since.

After that first rollercoaster year when we struggled to get our studying to keep pace with our partying, we escaped halls and moved as a team into a totally hideous flat at the top of a draughty Victorian house in one of Liverpool's less salubrious areas. I only have to think for a minute how awful it was and it makes me shudder. The carpet had that terrible stickiness of a back-street pub and, as we were on the top floor, the windows had never been cleaned. They still hadn't when we left two years later. Learning how to exterminate cockroaches, mice and silverfish together is always going to be a lifelong bonding experience. Though it always seemed to be me, with rubber gloves and dustpan, who had the job of clearing up the resulting corpses.

Not only did we share the same hideous flat, but we also worked in the same hideous bar. Honkers. I don't have to say any more, do I? There's a fantastic, sophisticated nightclub scene in Liverpool. Honkers wasn't part of it. We used to run a sweepstake between the three of us – five pounds at the end of the night to the person who got the most gropes. One point for a bottom grope, two points for a boob grope. Flick had the dubious honour of winning most nights.

We put up with the groping, largely without complaint, simply to earn some extra cash to supplement our drinking – sorry, our studies. If someone got a feel of your tits they tended to give bigger tips. Oh, happy days. Our shared horror only helped to make our little team stronger than ever. Even though we had no money and lived in a fleapit, they were good times. We had fun together. Mostly. But there were heartaches too and we vowed then that nothing would ever come between us. Not men, not fame, not fortune. It's fair to say that it's just the men that have troubled us thus far.

Harry doesn't like it when we spend hours reminiscing about a life and a time that he wasn't involved with. I'll admit that when we get started on the 'good old days' we do get a bit carried away with ourselves. Once we get going, we can talk for hours. You can't help but do that with good friends, can you? It's not as if we have huge reunions every five minutes. We all have busy lives and often only manage to get together every couple of months for a catch-up. We normally go out for a glass of wine and a pizza, nothing more exciting than that. We haven't had a girls' holiday together since we all went to Prague on my hen weekend over seven years ago now. So, as reluctant as he is, I'm sure that Harry can't begrudge me a week with my friends.

'I'm dying of thirst,' Harry says sullenly.

My heart sinks. What he means is he needs alcohol. I think this interminable car journey is the longest I've seen him go without a drink lately. I don't quite know what's going on, but recently there have been far too many late nights at work, too much restorative red wine. When he does eventually come home, I can't prise him away from his iPad or his mobile phone. It seems as if he'd rather spend time doing who knows what on Twitter than be with me.

It pains me to say that I can't remember the last time we had a conversation that wasn't in raised voices. We've been married for seven years, but I can't see us making another seven at this rate. It's not so much the seven-year itch as the seven-year slump. The last few months in particular have been just awful and, as a couple, we're as far apart as we've ever been. We get up at different times, go to work, eat dinner separately. Sex is a distant memory as I'm usually in bed and long asleep by the time Harry climbs the stairs. The weekends are no better. Harry's taken to shutting himself in his office and I mooch round the house by myself until I too give up trying to have fun and resort to the distraction of paperwork. It's no way to live. It's barely half a life. We are living to work, not working to live.

If I'm honest, there are times when I've felt like walking out. The only thing keeping me from doing that is the fact that I remember the Harry who I married – just about. The man who was charming, sophisticated and great company. It's simply a phase, I keep telling myself. It can't be roses round the door all the time. But sometimes it's hard when I look at the stranger sitting next to me.

We're both desperate for this break and I'm so hoping that we can spend some time together, relaxing, having fun and getting back to how we once were. That's all we need, I'm sure. Time. Time to sort things out. Time to have a laugh. Time to work out where it's all gone wrong.

I glance across at him. He's still a good-looking man. Tall, once quite muscular, but now that he's drinking more there's a hint of a paunch as he's never been one to embrace the idea of vigorous exercise. We used to like walking, but now it's all I can do to get him out of the flat at the weekend to go for a stroll down the road. The distance between our front door and the pub is the only walking he likes to do these days. His blue chambray shirt is straining slightly at the seams. I daren't suggest a diet as that would only be another reason to argue, but I'm gently trying to introduce healthier options into our evening meals. Harry's older than me. At forty-four, he's twelve years my senior. Not a lot these days, I guess, but I wonder if it will become more of an issue as the years pass. Still, we have to patch up where we are now before I can worry about the future. I want to run my hand through his hair. It's cropped short, greying slightly at the temples. He hates it when I touch it.

This person was once the life and soul of the party. Harry only had to walk into a room to make it light up and I was in awe of him. He was always so confident, so assured, that it spilled over on to me and I blossomed in his love. We were great as a couple. We might never have had a wild passion as such, but we were solid. Or so I thought. We fell into step nicely. As a couple the whole was better than the sum of two parts. I sigh to myself. Now look at us. Two people circling each other, never quite in time. This holiday will do us good. It will bring us back together, I'm sure. Because, more than anything, I want my husband to fall in love with me all over again.

Harry's voice breaks into my thoughts. 'Found out where we are yet?'

'Yes,' I tell him. Though, if I'm honest, I'm not *exactly* sure.

Anxiously, I twiddle one of my curls as I try to figure out where we are on the lines and squiggles of the map. I wasn't blessed with the map-reading gene, hence our heavy reliance on the sat nav. 'It's just over this hill. I think.'

With a tut, he stomps on the accelerator and we set off again. A few minutes later, over the brow of the hill as I'd predicted, I'm mightily relieved to see a sign for Cwtch Cottage – pronounced Cutch, so Ella tells me.

'This is it,' I assure Harry and we turn into a narrow track.

We slow to walking pace as the lane is bordered by high hedgerows on each side, with a tall line of grass right down the middle of it, like a secret passage. We squeeze our way towards the cottage. Already I feel as if I'm entering a different world.

'I hope this doesn't scratch the paintwork,' Harry grumbles.

I feel stupid in this car. A Bentley doesn't fit with the scenery. Frankly, it doesn't fit with me at all, but it's Harry's new toy. His pride and joy. He treated himself to it a month or so ago when he had his annual bonus from work. Though I've no idea why anyone would feel the need to spend so much on a car. It's an insane amount of money to blow. To top it off, he bought a personal number plate too. He loves its gleaming black showiness. I just wish that we had something a little more anonymous. Something in beige, so that the local vandals won't feel the need to run a key down the side of it. This car is criminal damage waiting to happen. To me a man with a flash car is like him walking around, waving his willy. Though as I hardly ever drive now – who needs to in London? – I don't feel that I can really impose a low-key choice of car on my other half. If this is what Harry wants, then who am I to argue?

A profusion of wild flowers blooms in the hedgerow, glorious shades of pink, yellow and white. I open the window to let their colourful heads trail over my hand. The scent is heady.

'You'll get seeds and all sorts in the car,' Harry says. 'Next summer there'll be dandelions growing in the carpet and we'll wonder why. Shut the window.'

Reluctantly, I do.

Thankfully, a short and bumpy ride later, Ella's cottage comes into view. 'We're here!'

The sight of it takes my breath away. Cwtch Cottage stands in splendid isolation on a rocky promontory at the entrance to a small, secluded bay overlooking the sea. It's a simple structure, long and low, painted white, and I don't think I've ever seen anywhere quite so beautiful.

'Oh, look at it, Harry,' I say. 'Wasn't this worth that awful journey? It's stunning.'

Ella had shown me photographs of the cottage, but they just hadn't conveyed how spectacular the setting was. There's an unbroken view right to the horizon where the sea meets the sky.

Harry brings the Bentley to a standstill at the end of the bay and stares out of the window, open-mouthed. 'Christ, there's nothing here.'

'It's wonderful.'

The tight band that seems to be melded to my heart these days eases slightly. I think I can actually hear it sigh with relief. Tears prickle behind my eyes. You can keep your Seychelles and your Maldives, this is paradise to me. How I wish we were staying here for two weeks or even longer. A week seems barely adequate.

My husband is less moved by the surroundings. The expression on his face is bleak. 'Where's the nearest pub?'

'I don't know. Ella said that it was quite remote.'

'You're not bloody kidding.'

'Oh, Harry.' I kiss his cheek. 'It will be lovely, you'll see.'

'I haven't seen anything for miles.' He punches his digit at his mobile phone. 'No signal either.'

Smiling, I offer up a silent prayer of thanks. A whole seven days without having to compete with Twitter!

I put my hand on his arm. 'I'm really looking forward to this. We can have some time just to be together, to chill out, to put things right.'

'There's nothing wrong with us,' Harry says crisply.

But there is, I think. We both know that there is.

Chapter Three

We park up outside the cottage next to Ella and Art's cars. I climb out and massage my back. Even in a posh car all the hours of sitting have taken their toll. The breeze lifts my hair from my neck and I can taste the tang of salt in the air. The heat of the sun on my cold skin feels like a loving caress. Ella rushes out to greet us.

'Hey!' she shouts and grabs hold of me in as near to a bear-hug as someone who is five foot nothing can manage. We do a little dance while still holding tightly on to each other. 'God, it's so good to see you. I've missed you.'

'Well, now we've got a whole week to gossip to our hearts' content.'

'How lovely.' Ella looks as excited as a child at Christmas. 'Was it a pig of a journey?'

'It wasn't the best,' I respond wryly.

'The weekends are always a nightmare. Too many cars on the road.'

'We're here now,' I say. 'Let relaxation commence.'

Harry is hanging back, fussing with the cases and the gifts that we've brought.

She flicks her head in Harry's direction. 'Is he in a mood?'

'Frightful,' I tell her and we giggle together like schoolgirls.

'We'll soon get the old bugger sozzled,' she promises. 'That'll make him loosen up a bit.'

Ella's not to know that I'm worried about his drinking. Harry has always liked a drink and turns into a total party animal after a bottle or two. But, in the last six months, I feel that it's become a more regular habit and has tipped over the edge into something else.

'Liking' a drink has suddenly become 'needing' a drink, I feel, and I'm concerned about the amount of wine that he gets through in a week now. I've even been tempted to hide our recycling box so that the neighbours don't see the amount of empty bottles in there. Whenever I've tried to raise the issue with him, he's just snapped at me. But I'm frightened that Harry can't do without alcohol to get him through the day. I haven't yet mentioned my unease to either Ella or Flick. Somehow by keeping it to myself, I could pretend that it really wasn't a problem and I don't want to start the holiday on a negative note by voicing my fears, so I keep quiet.

Harry comes and takes Ella in his arms. 'Hello, darling,' he says. 'How's life with you?'

'It's good. Sorry that we're in the middle of nowhere,' Ella gushes. 'I know that you like having a multiplicity of bars and coffee shops close to hand. But just look at the view!'

'Fantastic,' he says in a voice that barely disguises the fact that he's disappointed that we're not admiring a white sandy beach in the Caribbean. He eyes the seagulls suspiciously. 'Brought my own booze. Thought I might need it.'

Harry flicks a thumb towards the boot of the car where there are two cases of wine nestling. Inwardly, I sigh. I couldn't persuade him that we didn't need to bring quite so much booze with us. Harry insisted that he needed it to 'get in the holiday mood'.

'Let's take a closer look at the beach,' I suggest. 'Coming, Harry?'

'I'll stay here,' he says. 'See if I can get a signal.' He waves his mobile at me.

Why? I wonder. *Why?* Can't he leave it alone for five minutes?

Ella leads me by the hand to the edge of the terrace. Away from the shelter of the cottage, a stiff wind whips in from the sea. But the breeze is warm and the cool spray spritzing my face feels wonderful, zingy. It's late June and summer is only just starting to live up to its promise. The weather for the last week has been sweltering, sultry, and it's so nice to be out of London and its oppressive city heat. I lift my arms and reach out to the sun. I should be in an advert for Ocean Breeze shower gel or something. No doubt my mass of brunette curls, untameable at the best of times, will take on a life of their very own here.

'God, this is brilliant.' I want to throw off my clothes and run barefoot in the sand. 'How do you stay away from this place?'

'It's increasingly hard,' Ella admits.

'I'm not surprised. I'd never want to leave.'

Ella inherited the cottage when her mum died a few months ago after a stroke. It wasn't entirely unexpected as Mrs Hawley wasn't in the best of health and had been in a nursing home for a few years prior to that, suffering from a hefty catalogue of illnesses. But it's never easy to lose a parent whatever the circumstances. Barely a year earlier Ella had helped to nurse her dad through terminal cancer, so she's gone through a rough time. Flick and I have supported her as much as we could but, as she was an only child, the weight of the burden had fallen on Ella.

'You look fantastic,' I tell my friend. 'You're positively blooming.' She blushes at that. 'The sea air must suit you.'

Ella favours the Goth look. Today she's abandoned her trademark black clothes for faded denim shorts and a fitted white shirt. Her dyed black cropped hair is messier than usual and it suits her. Her normally pale face has a smidgen of tan and the pinched look, from nursing ailing parents for too long, has all but gone. She's put a few pounds on her waif-like frame and – I'd never dare to tell her this – it sits well on her.

'I do feel like a different person when I'm down here,' she confesses. 'Perhaps I've found my spiritual home.'

'"Spiritual home",' I tease. 'You've been smoking those strange-smelling cigarettes again.'

'No,' Ella says, 'not me!'

'Well, whatever it is, it suits you.' I nod back towards the cars. 'I see that Art's already here.'

'He came down last night,' Ella says. She lowers her voice. 'He's a grumpy bastard too. He and Harry can sit on deckchairs and get pissed together.'

'Is he being supportive?'

She sighs. 'In his own sweet way. You know what men are like. Art doesn't *do* illness or death.'

'He probably doesn't know what to say for the best,' I offer. 'It doesn't mean that he doesn't care, sweetheart.'

'I know. Sometimes I feel I'm bottling things up for Art's sake when what I really want is a good blub. He's just so hopeless at dealing with emotion.'

'Tell me about it. After all these years of marriage, Harry still has no idea what to do if, on the rare occasion, I actually cry.'

'I've been down here for a few weeks already,' she tells me. 'Just making sure that the place is spick and span. With Mum having been in the nursing home for so long, it hasn't been used for a while.'

'How are you coping, generally?' I ask, giving her a squeeze.

'OK,' she says. 'Some days better than others. I miss Mum terribly, but she hadn't been herself for ages, so it was a relief in some ways. She hated living like that. She'll be happier now that she's with Dad.' We both start to well up. 'Don't start me off!' Ella cuffs away the tears. 'We're here to have fun this week, put all this out of my mind for a time.'

'And fun we will have,' I assure her. 'I've so looked forward to seeing you. We can have a good catch-up and relax.'

Cwtch Cottage has been in Ella's family for many years. I think it had originally been handed down to Ella's parents by an old spinster aunt of her dad's. Ella spent all her childhood holidays here and always used to tell us how fond she

19

was of the place. Then when her dad fell ill and couldn't travel, her mum didn't want to come here on her own without him. Ella used to bring her occasionally, but the visits were few and far between. Then, in turn, her mum became too frail to make the journey and the cottage was pretty much abandoned.

'The place needs a bit of TLC,' Ella continues. Much like my good self, I think. 'I've tried to get down at least a couple of times a year, but it hasn't always been easy. Thankfully, there's a lovely lady in St Brides who keeps an eye on it for me, makes sure it's not swallowed up by the sea or too overrun by spiders. Still, I'm going to have my work cut out getting it back up to scratch.'

'Well, it looks very lovely to me.'

'Thanks. Inside is a bit bashed and scuffed, but it's very cosy. We'll have a great week. I'm so excited to see you. I hope you like it, Grace. I've wanted you and Flick to come down here for ever.'

'Well, I'm glad we've finally made it.'

Ella tucks her arm into mine and steers me back towards the cottage. 'You're looking very tired, lovely lady. Everything OK?'

'Work, life.' We exchange a glance. She knows that Harry and I are having a tough time together, but not the specifics. 'Nothing that a glorious week by the seaside won't cure.'

'We'll have those roses back in your cheeks in no time.' She gives my face a friendly pinch.

I breathe in the fresh, salty air and wonder why I live in a flat in the city. Harry, standing behind the Bentley, is still trying to get a phone signal. He gives up when he sees us coming back and busies himself lifting one of the cases of wine out of the boot with a grunt.

'Can I give you a hand with that, love?'

'I can manage,' he puffs as he falls into step behind us.

'You look as if you've come well prepared, Harry!' Ella teases.

'I know what you lot are like when you get together,' he tosses back.

Ella grins at him.

'Is Flick still coming too?' I ask.

'Oh, you know what Flick's like,' Ella says, rolling her eyes. 'She's supposed to be arriving later. But, as we can't get a phone signal here, and there's no landline, I haven't been able to ring her and double-check. It's only a ten-minute drive to the nearest phone box, but I haven't had a chance to get there either. I told her she wouldn't be able to get in touch with me, but she's probably forgotten. I bet she's texting me like mad and wondering why I'm not replying.'

'I hope she hasn't forgotten altogether that she's coming.' Our friend isn't known for her reliability.

Ella laughs. 'I wouldn't put it past her, but I've made the bed up anyway.'

'I thought she couldn't make it.' Behind us, Harry sounds tetchy. He's not Flick's biggest fan. He finds her too loud, too attention-seeking. He thinks she's a bad influence on Ella and me. And he's probably right.

I shrug. 'She changed her mind at the last minute.' She could, however, just as easily change it back.

Harry tuts and stamps ahead of us. Ella and I exchange a glance and a giggle. 'He loves her really,' I say.

Flick doesn't like to commit to anything and, even if she's said that she'll come along to some get-together or other, is always liable to change her plans at the last minute. I think it comes with not having a partner to answer to. Ella thinks she's just naturally born selfish, but she says it nicely.

'Is she bringing anyone?'

'I think she must be resting between lovers,' Ella chuckles. 'She said she'd come by herself.'

'Either that or he's married, as usual, and can't get away from the missus.'

'Ah, yes. That's more likely.'

Ella has never really approved of Flick's preference for men who are already permanently attached to other women. Neither have I, come to that, but we've learned to live with it. Unfortunately, the concept of the sisterhood is an alien thing to Flick. Under sufferance, we've met a few of her married lovers over the years. They've always seemed unsuitable and shifty. They've never hung around for too long though. It would be lovely if Flick, for once, could meet someone nice, solvent and unattached.

'I've hardly heard from her in the last few months,' I confide. 'I've been texting and phoning, but she seldom replies. She's not avoiding me, is she?'

'Oh, you know what she's like,' Ella says with a shrug. 'She's probably up to no good somewhere.'

'Yes.'

If Flick's in a tricky relationship, she sometimes goes 'dark'.

Despite being in her thirties now, she's still exactly the same as when we were at university: flighty, fickle and very frustrating. But we both love her, nevertheless. Ella's right, I'm probably reading too much into it. I can't think of anything that I've done that would have caused Flick offence. She's not one to take anything too much to heart, anyway.

'We'll all have a lovely week,' Ella assures me.

'Of course we will.' I get a thrill of excitement. I'm going to put all my troubles behind me and just have fun. 'It'll be just like old times.'

Chapter Four

Ella, Harry and I swing through the front door of the cottage and into a porch filled with outdoor clutter. There are coats, abandoned shoes and a ragtag of sports equipment alongside a couple of tennis rackets that have seen better days. A slightly rusty Swingball leans up against the wall and, beneath it, lie a couple of mismatched golf clubs with a bucket of tatty balls.

'Daddy used to stand on the rocks and knock the balls out to sea, as far as he could,' Ella says when she sees me looking at them. 'Not exactly eco-friendly, but then he'd go and collect the ones that were washed up on the shore and do it all over again.'

'Good therapy.'

She laughs. 'It used to keep him amused for hours.'

The porch leads straight into the homely kitchen. It's roomier than I'd imagined from outside and is all stripped pine cupboards with a big, proper farmhouse table right in the middle. At the table, Ella's partner, Art Jarrett, has his feet up and is plucking absently at the guitar slung across his thighs. At his elbow stands a bottle of wine, already open.

Harry brightens as he sees it. 'Ah, a man after my own heart.' He instantly dumps the case of wine he's carrying and rubs his hands in anticipation.

My spirits sink slightly. I wish Art had been having nothing more potent than a cup of tea. That'll be Harry started for the day and, once he's begun, there's no stopping him.

Art stands up when he sees us. 'Welcome, one and all!'

'Hi, Art.' I give him a kiss and a hug.

'Hi, babe. Long time, no see.'

I like Art. He and Ella don't have the easiest of relationships, but he has a boyish charm that's appealing and seems to let him get away with murder most of the time.

The reason we haven't seen him for a while is because Art has been out in Romania or Bulgaria or maybe both. Art is a band manager, mainly for heavy metal bands, and he kind of looks like that's what his job should be. He favours the grungy image – ripped jeans or, for best, crumpled linen suits teamed with Guns 'n' Roses T-shirts. His dark hair is long, unkempt and currently appears as if a burgundy dye is growing out. Usually, as now, a couple of days' worth of stubble graces his chin.

Ella and Art have been together a long time and, after years of splitting themselves between two places, now share Art's very smart house in Notting Hill. Marriage is a banned word in their household although Ella makes no secret of the fact that she would very much like to be Mrs Jarrett one day. Most of their problems stem from the fact that Art is a 'free spirit'.

He hates to be tied down and, more often than not, they're not even in the same country. Ella is quite a renowned artist and she does her fair share of travelling, jetting around the world to create big installations of her work. Then, whenever Ella is at home, Art is usually away somewhere else. He can be on tour for months at a time. Heavy metal may not be the big thing here, but on the continent it's massive and Art has to go where the money is. Besides, he likes his life on the road. *Too* much, Ella would say.

Art claps Harry on the back and gives a thumbs-up to the case of wine that's now on the kitchen floor.

'There's another case in the boot,' Harry says. 'White.'

'Top man,' Art says.

The men, in many ways, are so different, but they rub along well together. My other half is as straight as the day is long. Harry is an actuary, specialising in pensions management for a huge global corporation. I'd like to say that his work isn't as dull as it sounds, but I'm afraid that it is. Even I, as a fully signed up and sensible accountant, can glaze over within seconds of Harry starting to talk to me of his working day. Art has absolutely no chance. Even the word 'pension' is a complete anathema to Art's life ethos. He's used to dealing with monumental egos who dabble in drugs or put televisions through windows of European hotel rooms or turn up late for photo shoots. He's not that interested in the minutiae of final pension schemes or the dwindling benefits of annuities. Can't say that I blame him. Thankfully, Art knows how to handle Harry and, once they get the drink flowing, they become great mates. I think it comes with Art having to manage tricky artists for a living that he can get along with anyone.

'Pull up a chair you two, get yourself some glasses,' Art instructs.

Only one of us lights up at the thought. Ella brings two glasses from the cupboard and puts them on the table.

'Not for me,' I say. So Art fills just one glass.

Harry grasps it gratefully. 'Devil of a journey,' he says. 'Need a bit of a snifter.'

'There's a load more stuff in the boot, Harry,' I remind him. Some of it is perishable and we'll need to put it in the fridge.

'Later, Grace,' he says dismissively.

Harry knocks half of it back in one swallow and smacks his lips gratefully. That'll be me getting the presents and cases out of the boot, then.

Sometimes when I look at him now, I'm not really sure quite how I came to be with Harry. We met at a function organised by a financial advisor who turned out to be a mutual acquaintance – so far, so boring. Over the champagne and canapés we chatted and, later, when the jazz band started up, Harry asked me to dance with him.

I liked his maturity. Compared to other men that I'd dated – and there were very few of them – he seemed so sophisticated, so urbane, so stable. Unlike Flick, I haven't had vast experience with men. At university, I hated the whole dating scene. I think I only ever went out with anyone because she cajoled me into it. I've never been Ms Popularity. I was an only child, terribly shy, who morphed into a swotty teenager and ever since then have preferred a good book to a man. Even in the thick of the college scene, I was a very reluctant dater. I could never have been like Flick, waking up with a different man every weekend, sometimes not even remembering who they were. She always had complicated relationships and, to be honest, some of the things that happened in our flat nearly put me off men for life. I think the wilder she was, the more determined I became not to go down that route.

When I first started work, I had two half-serious relationships – men that I dated for a few months rather than a few weeks. One was a teacher. One was a social worker. Both were entirely needy and in dire financial straits. They both needed a babysitter more than a life partner. I dated because I was expected to, rather than because I actually wanted to. I was actually a lot happier on my own.

Then Harry came along, my intellectual and financial equal. That sounds terrible, doesn't it? I don't mean it to, but it was nicer to be with someone who could afford to take lavish holidays rather than want to drag me round Europe in a tent. Someone who could afford to eat in real restaurants rather than McDonald's.

He was reliable and didn't play games. If Harry Lincoln said he would telephone, he did. If he said he would pick me up at eight o'clock, at five to eight his car would pull up outside my flat. He didn't grope me like the men my own age. He didn't rush me. He seemed to have got his life together. There might not have been giddy romance with Harry, but there was no high drama either. I was never swept away by passion for him. I didn't go weak at the knees when I saw him. I never felt the fevered heat of love stories. I'm not the sort of person who believes they need that as the foundation of a relationship. Harry and I simply got along well. We shared a love of the theatre and good food. We didn't argue. It seemed enough. When he asked me to marry him, I couldn't see a reason why I shouldn't and said yes. He loved me. He was solid, dependable. I assumed I loved him too.

My parents were delighted. They too had a quiet marriage – one without fireworks and falling out. I thought if I could be like them, it would serve me well. They were pleased with Harry. They thought we made a good match. They brushed over the fact that he'd been divorced and had two teenagers in tow. In their eyes, the fact that he had his own house and a good job more than made up for that. They were probably right. Though, with hindsight, I wonder if they were just relieved that I'd finally taken someone home to meet them and hadn't turned out to be a lesbian. They wouldn't have liked to explain that down at the golf club.

And I've been happy with him. It was a sensible decision. Harry has been a good husband. I've always tried my best to be a good wife. We're financially secure and have wanted for nothing. We have rubbed along well perfectly together. It's only now that the veneer is starting to chip, that things are unravelling. He's not the same man that I married and I wonder if he's having a mid-life crisis.

Now I watch him as Art pours him some more wine. Harry seems tired too. Perhaps both of us are simply exhausted and this break is long overdue. If we can just kick back and relax, maybe we can put these last few months behind us. Harry's blue chambray shirt is teamed with crisp jeans and trainers. He's put his jacket on for the journey from the car to the cottage and I'm not sure it's a look that I like, even though it's Harry's standard 'casual' attire. Particularly next to the laid-back Art, he comes across as far too buttoned up. But I'm being unnecessarily critical; this is how Harry has always looked. This is how he was when I met him, so I shouldn't start to complain about it now.

One great thing that has come out of our marriage is Harry's two wonderful boys. They're really great and I've never, not for one minute, regretted being involved in their lives. I've heard other stepmums beef about their partners' children and all the awful things they do and the problems they have. But I've never had that with Harry's kids. I've always treated them as if they were my own. Freddie's now twenty-two and Oscar is twenty. It was more difficult when Harry and I first got together as they were still teenagers and we had to fit our blossoming relationship round his access visits, but it wasn't long before we formed a unit. They were both so accepting of me that it was very easy to love them.

Now the boys are away at university and are so wrapped up in their own hectic lives that we hardly ever see them – on high days and holidays or when they are seriously short of cash. But I remember what it was like and even though I miss them terribly and phone them both regularly, I want them to have fun while they can, while they have no responsibilities to grind them down. Plus they do spend a lot of time on Twitter with Harry too – which, at least, accounts for some of the hours he spends on there. Not quite like sitting round the kitchen table together having a good old chinwag, but I guess that's the way of modern relationships.

'Look at those two,' Ella says, nudging me. 'Stuck in already.'

Sure enough, Harry has stripped off his jacket again and has settled down at the table next to Art. The second glass of wine also hardly touches the sides and he's pouring out his third. Harry sets the bottle down on the table next to his own elbow. It's practically empty already.

'No signal.' He taps forlornly at his mobile. 'How do you manage, mate?'

Art shrugs. 'I can just about cope for a few days at a time. Drives the office mad.'

'Mine too,' Harry agrees readily and, while they complain about the lack of technology, I take in the rest of my surroundings.

The kitchen has huge, full-length windows at the back – clearly a later modification – that look out on to the terrace and the magnificent sea beyond. The rhythmic ebb and flow of the ocean is mesmerising. It's like watching a constantly shifting painting. I feel that I could stand and look at this view for ever and never grow tired of it.

'Let's bring your cases in,' Ella suggests. 'Then we can join them for a natter.'

I was hoping that we might all go out for a walk on the beach while the weather is so glorious. It looks so enticing. After being cooped up in the car for hours, I'd love to stretch my legs, feel the sand in my toes. Who wouldn't want to? I'd like to feel that warm wind in my hair again more than I'd like a glass of wine.

So, leaving the men to their drinks, we go to unload the boot. I lift out our suitcases, but I'm going to leave the other box of wine for Harry to bring in. He can at least do something.

'I've brought you some of those cupcakes that you like so much from the bakery in Notting Hill.'

They're nestled safely on the back seat along with a bouquet of white lilies for Ella, which I know are her favourite flowers. I've brought a selection of nice cheeses too, which we can have after dinner. They're all in the cool box alongside a couple of tubs of really special olives, which I know Art has a soft spot for.

'Oh, Grace, you're always so thoughtful,' Ella says. 'Mmm. Those cakes look delicious. Perfect excuse to have afternoon tea now.'

I hand her the lilies too.

'Now you're spoiling me,' she says. 'It's a long time since anyone bought me flowers.'

'Me too.' We giggle at that.

We carry our booty back to the cottage. I don't think that Harry and Art even noticed that we'd gone. They're both laughing heartily, clearly in storytelling mode, and I'm relieved to see that Harry's bad mood has lifted. Ella and I roll our eyes at each other. She deposits the lilies and the cupcakes in the kitchen. When the cheese and olives are safely tucked away in the fridge, we tackle the cases. I lift mine and Ella takes Harry's. Together we lug them upstairs.

Thankfully, the narrow staircase to the first floor is short. There are three bedrooms up here, the main one with an en suite, and a nice bathroom shared between the two guest rooms. All of them have low ceilings as they're set into the roof. Big Velux windows have been fitted into the eaves in the bedrooms, flooding the space with light. The tiny, original windows have been left in place, though you have to bend down to look through them for a tantalising glimpse of the sea. It will be lovely to lie back on those soft pillows and hear the soporific sound of the waves crashing on the rocks.

Each room has been decorated in the same style, with the beds covered in plain white quilts, and coloured rag rugs on the sanded floorboards. It's elegant in its simplicity.

'Will you be comfortable enough in here?' Ella asks, showing me into one of the rooms.

I hug my friend. 'Of course we will. Thank you again for asking us.'

'I just wanted to see you,' she says. 'We don't spend enough time together.'

'I know.'

'I don't know where the years go,' Ella says and her voice is tinged with sadness.

'They just fly by.'

'We haven't changed much, have we?'

I shrug. 'I don't know.'

Am I the same woman that I was ten years ago? Perhaps I am. But I hope not.

'I'll leave you to freshen up,' Ella says. 'I'll get the kettle on. I'm sure you'd rather have a cuppa first instead of getting stuck into the booze. Plenty of time for that later.'

'Tea would be wonderful.'

'We can sample those fabulous cakes too. See you in a minute.'

'Ella,' I ask as she's ducking to go through the door. 'What does Cwtch mean?'

'It's like a cuddle. A loving embrace.'

'Oh, how lovely.'

She winks at me. When she's gone, I lie down on the bed, spreading out my arms and legs in a star shape, and look up at the blue sky through the window, letting the rhythm of the sea soothe me.

A cuddle. A loving embrace. I curl into a ball, wrap my arms around my chest and hold myself tightly. Just what I need right now.

Chapter Five

Ella and I sip our tea, watching Art and Harry from our armchairs by the fireplace in the kitchen. One bottle is already empty. Another is open and dwindling fast. I look away. I have to stop counting. That way madness lies. I should just loosen up and go with the flow. We're on holiday. Everyone drinks more when they're not at work, don't they? Though I can't, for the life of me, understand the reason for having to be completely drunk to enjoy oneself.

'Great cakes, Grace,' Ella says, massaging her tummy.

'You have buttercream on your nose,' I tell her.

'I might leave it there and lick it off later,' she laughs.

Ella has arranged the lilies in a vase and their sweet scent hangs in the air. Art, an accomplished guitarist, is strumming away, singing Black Sabbath's 'Smoke on the Water'. Harry is slapping the table with his hand not quite in time with the song. It's endearing and slightly annoying at the same time.

'Does anyone mind if I go for a walk?' I say brightly. The

tight band round my heart is back and I need to get out and fill my lungs with fresh air.

Harry waves his hand in acknowledgement. I don't think Art has even heard, he's so into his song.

'I'll come with you,' Ella says. 'It's windy but warm out there. You shouldn't need a cardigan.'

The only downside of not holidaying in St Lucia or Thailand is that for a break in Britain in late June, you still need to pack for every possible weather combination. The boot of the car was stuffed full of gear for any eventuality – just in case.

'I've brought half of my wardrobe with me. I'll get one just in case.'

At the back of the cottage, there's a small terrace but, in essence, you're straight out on to the rocks and then it's just a short scramble down to the beach. When we reach the sand, I unlace and tug off my Converse high-tops while Ella kicks off her flip-flops. Together we walk along the deserted beach, hugging the edge of the water where the band of smooth stones and shingle gives way to soft, pink sand. We link arms and wander through the edge of the freezing surf, letting it tickle our toes.

The breeze teases and tangles my curls, but I don't care. If I could simply spend enough time here, I'm sure my troubles would just float away.

'Oh,' I say, 'this is the life. No wonder you love it here so much.'

'I do,' Ella says. 'I'm glad you do too.' Then she's quiet.

'And?'

'Art doesn't.'

She looks at me under her dark lashes and smiles ruefully.

I think that Ella is the most naturally pretty of us all. Her hair is a spiky gamine crop, and only someone with a tiny, heart-shaped face could carry it off. I'm not exactly a strapping lass, but Ella's a little, elfin thing who looks as if a puff of wind would blow her away. Though it's a mistake to think that Ella is in any way a pushover. She's got a steely core of determination that has seen her climb from penniless art student to respected artist in ten short years. She's the type of artist who favours the bold, abstract school of art. Her paintings are generally large, almost like graffiti. She works with aerosol cans in vivid colours and splatters of silver paint. They're quite angry creations, slashed with vivid lines and jagged objects. You won't find any twee landscapes in Ella's portfolio. But there are enough people who enjoy paying high prices for graffiti and angry lines that she now commands a healthy five-figure sum for each of her paintings.

'We had a blazing row last night,' she says.

'Oh no.'

'I shouldn't burden you with this, Grace. You look as if you've got enough troubles of your own. But who else can I tell?' We walk along in silence until Ella is ready to speak. 'He hates Cwtch Cottage. With a vengeance.' A weary shrug of her shoulders. 'I adore it here, but Art can't stand it. You know what he's like. This is all a bit too low-key, too rural for him. Art likes the high life. Anything rustic brings him out in a rash.' She tries to make light of it. 'Five-star hotels are more his thing.'

'Harry too,' I sympathise. 'I can't see it myself. Why would anyone prefer that above this? Cwtch Cottage is like a slice of heaven on earth. Give Art time. He may come to love it,' I suggest. 'Is this his first visit?'

'Yes. You know that I've been trying to cajole him to come up here for years, but he always managed to wriggle out of it. It took all my powers of persuasion to get him to agree to spend this length of time at the cottage. If it was up to Art we'd have stayed one night and then would be on our way back again to the fumes and congestion of London. He says the air is too fresh here and it hurts his lungs to breathe.'

'Poor lamb. He's probably just one walking mass of toxins.' We both laugh at that. 'Well, you can only wait and see what happens. You're not easily deterred either. I'm sure you'll be able to grind him down eventually.'

'I don't think so.' Despite the carefree laughter of a few seconds ago, her voice wobbles and her words are snatched away by the breeze. 'Not this time.' She stoops to pick up a shell and washes the sand from it in the sea, holding it up for me to admire. It's creamy with whorls of raspberry pink, a minute universe of perfectly executed pattern. 'There's a lot of inspiration here. I could graduate from angry slashes.'

'Angry slashes are very profitable.'

She shrugs. 'So they are, but maybe it's time to move on. Try something new on the unsuspecting public. Not everything can stay the same.'

I'm only too aware of that.

Ella sighs. 'Art wants me to sell up here, put the money into a place in Spain. Marbella or somewhere.' We both wrinkle our noses. 'He says that we could go there in the winter, escape the relentless British rain and snow. I can't argue with that.'

'I'm struggling to imagine you in Marbella.'

'You know Art,' she says. 'Beneath that heavy-metal heart, he likes glitz and glamour. The things that go with it.' She glances at me again. 'But you're right, Grace. I can't picture myself there at all. I can think of nothing worse.'

'You must do what you want to do. This place has been in your family for generations. I've been here only a short time and I can see why you love it. Can't Art?'

'No. Not at all.' She scuffs her toes in the sand and I can just picture her doing that on visits to Cwtch Cottage as a child all those years ago. I bet it's hardly changed since. 'It makes you reconsider things when you lose both of your parents. Neither of them reached their seventies. That seems terribly cruel and so young, these days. What if I've got their genes? The Die Young gene?'

'Don't be silly.'

'It makes you think, though. I'm thirty-two. I could be halfway through my life and I haven't done hardly any of the things I want to do.'

'Oh, Ella.' I sling my arm round her shoulders and we touch our foreheads.

'I want to settle down,' she confides. 'I love the studio I have in the garden at Art's place, but the house belongs to Art, not me. It's never really felt like my home.'

Ella does have a small and very scruffy flat in Camden, which she's rented out since she moved into Art's fabulous place in Notting Hill. And, she's right, she has a great studio space in a specially built wooden summer house. It's lovely. She might struggle to give that up.

'I'd like children, Grace,' she confesses. 'I want to get married, settle down. Have the life that my parents did. They adored each other to the end of their lives. One day, I'd like to think that I'll come to the cottage for holidays with my own family and they'll love it as much as I did. We were always so happy here. It's such a simple place to be.'

I met Ella's parents only a handful of times over the years, but I remember them always holding hands and both grinning from ear to ear as they posed for pictures with her after her graduation ceremony. Both her mum and her dad were as tiny as Ella. Quiet, humble people who just got on with life without complaint. They'd run a haberdashery shop together and, as Ella said, they were so happy with each other until the day that her father died and her mother slipped into confusion. They pampered Ella, but didn't spoil her. A fine line that they managed to tread well as they turned out a beautiful, considerate daughter.

'Can you see Art wanting that?'

At the moment I can't, and my friend takes my silence as agreement. I think Art is far too rock'n'roll for the peace and quiet of Pembrokeshire.

'I know that he's unfaithful to me when he's away.' Ella lowers her eyes to the sand. 'I don't blame him. Not really. The temptation must be enormous. There are always groupies around happy to spend some time with anyone related to the group – even the manager.' She raises an eyebrow at that.

'In my twenties, I could put it to the back of my mind, turn a blind eye. What happens on tour, stays on tour and all that. But now it's different. I want a man who wants to be with just me. I'd like someone who can be in one place and doesn't hanker to always be on the move. I don't want someone who'd rather be in a hotel in Budapest or Berlin with some female with no name that he's picked up for the night. That's not good, is it?'

'No.'

I have to agree with that. I don't think I could handle it if Harry was cheating on me. He might have his faults, but that isn't one of them. It makes me feel bad that I get on to him about his attachment to red wine and Twitter. What harm is that doing, really, in the scheme of things?

'I want someone who adores only me as my dad adored Mum. They were so in love right to the end after more than forty years of marriage. His name was the last word that my mother spoke. Is that too much to want for myself?' Her eyes fill up. 'My body's changing, Grace. I'm having urges. Starting to look at babies in prams. Will Art want that when he can have a different nubile nineteen-year-old every night instead?'

'While you've got some time here together, you need to talk to him.'

'That's exactly what he's avoiding. He knows that I want something deeper and he's pushing against it all he can.' Ella's laugh is brittle. 'What Art really wants is uncomplicated sex. Even after all this time, I'm not sure he's convinced about the value of monogamous, lasting relationships.'

At the far end of the beach, we huddle on a rock, our chins on our knees, and stare out to sea. The ever-changing ebb and flow of the waves is mesmerising.

Ella's eyes fill with tears as she turns to me and says, 'Nothing stays the same, does it?'

Chapter Six

We scramble over some more rocks and carry on walking as far as we can along the next stretch of beach. Then the tide starts to roll in.

'We should head back,' Ella says. 'It comes in faster than you might think. We don't want to get cut off from the cottage.'

I hadn't even thought about that. So we set off, walking at a brisker pace. Ella links her arm through mine.

'It's been lovely to spend time together. We don't do it enough.'

'It's not because we don't want to,' I say. 'Life just gets in the way.'

'Sometimes I feel as if we'll be friends for ever,' Ella says, 'and sometimes we seem to be slipping away from each other.'

'We'll always be in touch,' I assure her. 'We've too much between us.'

'But that's not the same as being best friends, is it?'

'I'm supposed to be the worry-pot,' I remind her with a smile.

'You're right,' she says. 'Maybe I just need another of those excellent cakes.'

But, despite discussing my friend's fears, something in the back of my mind makes me wonder whether Ella might be right. As she said, nothing ever stays the same.

The sun is sinking lower as it's late afternoon when we return to the cottage. Harry has decanted himself from a kitchen chair into one of the armchairs, the second bottle is empty and the third is well on its way, but that's about it. Art seems to be working through the musical back catalogue of popular seventies rockers, which is fine by me as he's a talented musician, and Ella and I pull up chairs to listen. Eventually, we all join in, singing along – even Harry. There was a time when Art was up there on the stage rather than in the back room doing the paperwork or whatever it is that managers do. I don't know quite what happened to thwart that ambition; perhaps he just wasn't talented enough. Perhaps he simply didn't get the breaks. I guess not everyone can be the next Kurt Cobain.

Ella pours us both a glass of wine before this bottle is gone too. I sip the wine but it fails to hit the spot. The fact that Harry drinks so much now has taken the edge off my own enjoyment of alcohol. It no longer seems quite the benign aid to relaxation that it used to. There's a malevolence behind its ability to shape-shift personalities. Let's face it, very few people are better versions of themselves when they're drunk.

'Shall we get dinner going?' Ella says. 'Flick should be here before too long. Hopefully! She'd normally text and let us know. You just can't do that here.'

'I keep trying to get a signal,' Harry pipes up.

'There isn't one,' Ella reminds him patiently.

'Not ever?'

'No,' she laughs. 'Just live with it, Harry. You can do the supermarket shopping in the week if you like. There's a great signal at Tesco's in Haverfordwest. Four bars!'

My husband doesn't look particularly impressed by this revelation. Harry might hate remoteness, but he hates supermarkets more.

To deflect the conversation, I ask, 'What's on the menu?'

'Thought I'd just throw some bits on the barbecue while it's a warm evening and the wind has dropped now. We might not be able to do it every night. Art always likes to burn a few sausages. Makes him feel manly.'

'Harry too.'

Though most of what he cooks is generally burned to a crisp and inedible. Harry's forte is enjoying food, not producing it.

'Fancy chopping some onions for a barbecue sauce?'

'Sure.'

Ella and I make ourselves busy in the working end of the kitchen and soon the rich smell of cooking tomatoes fills the cottage. She adds some honey and Worcestershire sauce to the pan and already my mouth is watering. The windows are steaming up and the evening is drawing in.

'I could really see myself being here in the winter with the wind battering on the door and a log fire roaring in the grate,' I say.

'It's often like that in the summer,' Ella confesses in a voice that's too low for our menfolk to hear. 'I'm just praying that it stays like this while you're here and then we can all see it at its best.'

'We did bring wet weather gear, as a precaution.'

'Probably very wise,' she concedes.

While Ella removes chicken and sausages from the fridge, I make some garlic bread and wrap it in foil. Ella marinates the chicken in oil and herbs. Then we make a salad together, which Ella tosses in dressing. We cover it in clingfilm and slide it back into the fridge.

'I cheated on the pud,' she tells me. 'When I was at the supermarket yesterday, I bought a tarte au citron.'

'We'll just call it a lemon pie and then everyone will think you've made it,' I suggest.

'Excellent plan. We can finish up those cupcakes too. Yum.'

'Exactly how far is the supermarket?'

'Bloody miles,' she admits with a grimace. 'You can't forget a loaf here and pop out to Patel's on the corner any time of the night or day. Living out here takes planning. And a big freezer. There's three outhouses next to the cottage, one with a freezer. One of those giant American things that would take a lifetime's supply of fish fingers. When I first come down here, it takes me a few days to get into the swing of it and then I'm OK. You just need a different mindset and a large dose of organisation.' Ella glances at her watch. 'God, I hope Flick rocks up on time. I don't want to be giving her burnt offerings.'

'How long do you reckon?'

'Art needs to fire up the barbie now so that it's ready in about an hour or so. If I can prise him away from his guitar and that wine bottle for a few minutes, I'll get him on to the case.'

I look over at Harry who, glass in hand, appears to be struggling to keep his eyes open.

'Fancy a walk before dinner?' I ask him. 'Come and have a look at the beach before we start to lose the light. It's very lovely out there. I can speak from experience.'

He shrugs. I think he'd really like to say no, but I feel like digging my heels in. How can he be so uninterested in such fabulous surroundings and be happy to view everything through the bottom of a bottle?

'Come on, sleepyhead.' I tug at his hand.

'I thought we were all waiting for Flick,' he protests. 'Won't it be rude to be out when she gets here?'

'You know Flick,' I remind him. 'She could be here in half an hour or she could turn up at midnight with a coach party in tow. I'm sure she won't mind if we've gone to the beach. We won't be long.'

He still looks reluctant but I won't be beaten.

'Let's get you some fresh air or you'll be out for the count before nine.'

Harry sighs and lets me drag him from the comfort of his armchair. 'If we must.'

Art raises a hand, seemingly ambivalent that he's losing most of his audience. 'Laters.' He doesn't yet know that Ella has plans for him.

Harry puts on his jacket, which just doesn't seem quite right for the beach, but I say nothing. It usually takes him a few days to get in the holiday mood. Hopefully, he'll soon start to relax. I take a fleece from the coat rack in the porch by the door even though I don't think I'll need it.

'Can I borrow this?'

Ella nods, unable to talk due to a mouthful of stolen cheese.

'We won't be gone long.'

I lead Harry down to the beach. He huffs and puffs as we clamber over the rocks. I feel limber and light compared to him. There's not much left to walk on, now that the tide is in and all of the sand has gone. The sea shushes in and out on the shingle. Soon the entire beach will be under the sea, with the waves surrounding Cwtch Cottage on three sides.

Giving up on the idea of walking, I find a nice smooth boulder instead. Sitting down, I pat a place next to me for Harry.

'I could have sat down *inside*,' he points out. 'On a cushion.'

'That's not really the point, is it?'

'Perhaps I could get a signal out here,' he says and flicks out his mobile.

I bite down my irritation. 'Who do you need to call?'

'No one,' he says defensively. 'It just feels weird being out of touch.'

'Perhaps that's no bad thing.'

'Anything could be happening.'

'Like what?'

'I don't know. I like to keep up with Twitter. I haven't tweeted since the service station. They'll wonder where I've disappeared to.'

'Do you actually know any of these people that you follow?'

He looks perplexed.

'Only on Twitter?' I venture.

'The boys are on there.'

'So that's two real people that you know.' The two people who he'd never think to pick up a phone and call. They're lovely men and I find it disappointing that he pays them so little attention. 'Tweeting your sons every now and then is hardly the same thing as having a proper relationship with them.'

'I beg to differ,' he bristles. 'This is the modern way. I wanted to tweet them that we're away this week, in case they dropped in.'

'I spoke to both Freddie and Oscar last night,' I remind him. 'They know we're away. They're both fine and they send their love.'

He grunts at me. I have already told him all this.

'I just don't see the reason for all this "social networking". It feels as if you're hiding behind it. Can't you be happy to have a conversation with me? Or would it make this a better experience' – I jab a finger at the sea – 'if you could tweet it to strangers?'

'It's not just Twitter,' he grumbles. 'Or the boys. It's work too. What if they can't contact me? I like to keep my finger on the pulse.'

I don't remind him that pensions don't actually have a pulse. 'I don't think the big, bad world of high finance will grind to a halt if the office can't phone you for a week.'

'There's no need to be scathing, Grace.'

But I think there is. 'We're here on holiday, Harry. Let's try to enjoy ourselves. Watch the sea, admire the setting sun.'

He peers at the sun as if it is an alien thing. Then he stands on the rock and holds his phone aloft. 'One bar,' he says and there's relief in his voice. 'I think I've got one bar.'

I gaze out to sea, but the calm I felt out here before is eluding me. How can Harry be so enthusiastic about talking to people he doesn't know when he's not enthusiastic at all about talking to the ones he purports to love? How can he be so keen to keep in touch with his office, when I can't wait to get away from mine?

While Harry climbs up the rocks, hopefully holding his phone aloft, I try to block out my annoyance and attempt to find a serene place inside me. I sit, letting the noise of the waves send me into a trance, and allow my mind to wander. How did I come to be living a life that I no longer feel should belong to me?

I rack my brains for the millionth time, trying to figure out exactly why I'm working in a small accountancy firm, spending my days sorting out balance sheets and staff grievances. Of which there are many. They don't like working late, they don't like working early. They grumble that their access to the internet is restricted. They want the company to buy them iPads as their laptops are too heavy, too cumbersome, too last year. The office is too hot or it's too cold. Some of them complain that the windows are open, some that they are closed. Some of them complain that the air-conditioning is too cold, others that it is not cold enough. None of them seems to possess layered clothing. They would like paid overtime and longer lunch hours. They want to finish early on Friday and, preferably, take the whole of Friday afternoon off in the summer months. In fact, they rarely seem to want to work at all.

At the back of my mind, I wonder if they are all just terminally unsuited to accountancy. As am I.

I wanted to be a ranger. Of what, I'm not sure. And that was my stumbling block. I had no firm plan, other than that I didn't want to go to university or end up in an office. I thought that I'd like to work outside with nature, animals, the landscape. Perhaps in conservation. Digging out ponds. Repairing fences. Making bat boxes. My parents had other plans. Being outside in a vague capacity wasn't a real job. Going to university and becoming an accountant was. So, in the absence of anyone to steer or help me formulate an alternative plan, I went along with theirs. I was a good daughter and I didn't want to be a disappointment to them. To my parents' delight, I emerged three years later with a respectable 2:1 in something I hadn't the slightest interest in. I've been working in it ever since. Why? I can't limp on, using the excuse that I'm well paid, for ever.

I love nature, but when do I ever get to commune with it? I live in a flat in Muswell Hill, London, N10. Nothing wrong with it as such, but it's not exactly the wide open plains of the Serengeti or the towering peaks of the Alps. The odd ragged squirrel graces our scrubby patch of garden. If I'm lucky Harry and I walk up to Alexandra Palace or take a turn round Kensington Gardens on a Sunday morning, once a week. If I go out running, I pound the pavements, breathe in fumes and worry about getting mugged.

I look over at Harry, still trying to commune with Orange. He is not a nature type of bloke. On the beach in his smart jacket with his latest iPhone, he looks like a fish out of water. I give up waiting for him to come and sit on the rock with me in romantic and companionable silence and, instead, I get up and skim stones into the breaking waves. Harry steadfastly ignores the restless sea, the stunning sky, the plaintive calls of the seabirds that twist my heart, and yearns, instead, for Twitter.

After a while I wander away from him and spend my time alone, climbing over the rocks, checking out what treasures the isolated pools have to offer. I pick up shells and smooth pebbles and secrete them in the pockets of the fleece. I turn my face to the sun and think that I have found paradise.

My husband doesn't notice that I've gone.

Chapter Seven

I wander back towards the cottage, leaving Harry to his mobile phone dilemma and fuming quietly inside.

When I reach the little bay, there's a man standing in the edge of the surf, shoes in hand, letting the waves swish over his toes.

'Hi,' he calls out as I head for the terrace.

I stop and lift my hand to shade my eyes, trying to make out who it is in the blinding sunshine. He's tall, athletic, but beyond that I can't see very much at all.

He turns his back on the waves and walks towards me. 'The sea's lovely,' he says as he approaches. 'Cold, though.'

Then he's right in front of me and I see him properly for the very first time. I look up at him and feel as if all the breath has been knocked out of my body. I'm sure that my world rocks ever so slightly on its axis.

I stand and stare, when I know that it isn't polite. But I can't help myself. I'm quite simply mesmerised and I have no rational excuse for it. I'm losing myself in eyes that are the colour of dark chocolate. His face is kind, warm. The rays of the sun have flushed his cheeks and his mouth is full, luscious. His hair is brown, tousled by the breeze, and I have to stop my hands from reaching out to run my fingers through it. He's wearing khaki combats and a white linen shirt that's open and blowing in the wind. His chest is smooth, bronzed. I have never felt the urge to touch anything so much in my whole life and I'm not the sort of person who has previously had the urge to touch complete strangers. I ball my fingers into fists.

'Sorry.' His mouth turns up in a smile. 'Did I make you jump, shouting out like that?'

'No,' I say. 'No. Of course not.'

I don't know quite what you've done to me, I think. But I know that for the first time in my life I feel all lit up inside and I can feel a burning in my veins that is, at the same time, both pleasant and painful.

'Everything OK?' He frowns in concern.

'Yes. Yes. Quite all right,' I gabble.

What has happened here? I am sensible, level-headed Grace Taylor, not one moved to flights of fancy. But just look at me, I feel as if five thousand volts have shaken my body and I'm trembling like the proverbial leaf. My brain has been completely scrambled. I wonder if Cwtch Cottage is on an ancient ley line or something equally wacky.

'This is a beautiful spot,' he says, taking in the beach.

'Yes.'

But not as beautiful as this man standing before me. All the not inconsiderable delights of Cwtch Cottage and this idyllic setting have been swept from my mind.

I scour my brain for something to say, otherwise he'll think I'm an imbecile. And he'd be right. I could blame it on an excess of alcohol, except I've had one glass of plonk, a cup of tea and a cupcake. Perhaps there was a hallucinogenic drug in the cupcake. It would explain a lot.

'Are you here on holiday?' I manage to ask.

'Yes. I am.' The man holds out his hand. 'I'm Noah,' he says. 'Noah Reeves.'

I should take his hand, but I don't know if I can trust myself. If his smile can turn my legs to water, what will happen if I actually touch him? I look down at his hand and he does too. The fingers are long and strong. I feel my mouth go dry as I take them in mine. When I touch his skin, it feels like the strangest thing I've ever touched and, yet, also the most familiar. My hand fits perfectly in his.

We both laugh, uncertainly. Can Noah feel the powerful surge of electricity between us? Or is it just me going very slightly mad? Perhaps I've stayed out in the sun too long on the beach. His fingers tighten on mine and it feels so right.

'You must be Grace,' Noah says.

That takes away my breath again. 'I am Grace. How do you know?'

'Flick has told me a lot about you.'

That shocks me again. '*Flick?*'

'Yes. I'm here with her for the week.' He sounds flustered. 'I needed to stretch my legs after the long journey. Thought I'd have a walk on the beach for ten minutes while she unpacked.'

'Oh, right.' Oh, Lord. This is Flick's current man? Universe, you have got to be joking. 'You're with Flick?'

'Yes.' Now he seems embarrassed. 'It's nice to meet you.'

'Nice to meet you too,' I reciprocate, figuring that parroting is going to be easier than trying to formulate an original thought. 'Flick has told me a lot about you.'

'Really?'

'No.'

He grins at me, amused. 'I guess we should get back to the others,' he suggests. 'I said that I wouldn't be long.'

'I should find my husband,' I say, glancing back down the beach. 'I wandered off.'

'Ah, yes,' Noah says. 'You're married. I remember now. Harry?'

'That's right.' The husband who had been completely blanked from my brain for a brief moment there, along with everything else.

Noah lets go of my hand. He seems as reluctant as I do to break the contact. 'I'm looking forward to getting to know you better, Grace.'

'Yes,' I say, breathlessly. 'Me too.'

'I'll tell them that you're coming. We should get that barbecue going.'

'Yes.'

He holds up a hand as he moves away from me and his smile warms me more than the sun. I watch him climb effortlessly up the rocks and stroll into the cottage.

So, Grace, what exactly happened there? Whatever it was, I somehow feel deep in my bones that my life is never going to be quite the same again.

Chapter Eight

When Harry and I return to Cwtch Cottage, the lights are on. I'd found him just where I left him, on the rocks, surgically attached to his mobile. Still grumpy.

We walked back together in silence, which suited me as it gave me time to try to get my head round what had just happened with Noah. I still felt shaky inside.

As we enter, Flick barrels into us.

'Darlings!' she cries. 'I thought you'd got lost in this god-forsaken place!'

Behind her Ella rolls her eyes at me.

'I've been trying to phone, but this place is like outer fucking Narnia,' Flick expounds. 'I didn't think there was anywhere left in the world that didn't have mobile reception.' Flick sweeps me into her arms. 'Where the bloody hell have you been, woman?'

'On the beach,' I tell her from the depths of the crush.

'Good God, you could have been swept out to sea!' Her long blonde locks go flick, flick, flick, and that's partly how she got her nickname. Also because she was always quick to give her men the flick. And, of course, her given name is Felicity.

'I've been having a lovely time playing in the rock pools.'

'Really?' She wrinkles her nose, looking at me as if I'm mad.

'You still can't get a phone signal down there,' Harry informs her.

'That's because we're on the far edge of civilisation.' Then she says, 'Come here, you gorgeous thing,' and wraps her arms and legs round him. Already the calm and cosy cottage feels as if a whirlwind has blown through it.

Harry smiles at her indulgently. He knows the form by now. I'm just hoping that he lasts the week with Flick's excesses as he's normally twitchy in her company after ten minutes. She's brash and bossy and drives us to distraction, but Ella and I both love her dearly.

'Art says the barbecue is ready to cook,' Ella says. 'Shall we go outside and keep him company while he does man things?'

'My God, I'm famished,' Flick announces. Flick who barely eats a thing. Flick who can make a three-course meal out of lettuce.

'You might need a sweater out there,' Ella warns. 'The sea air can be cool at night.'

'Good journey?' I ask Flick as she slips her jacket back on.

'Dreadful,' she says. 'Thank Christ I didn't have to drive all the way.'

Harry frowns. 'You didn't?'

'No,' she says. 'Noah did.'

I exchange a glance with Ella and, behind Flick's back, she shrugs. As far as Ella was aware, Flick was coming alone. Although I've prematurely met Noah on the beach, he is yet another boyfriend on an ever-growing list who we haven't heard of.

'Who the hell is Noah when he's at home?' Harry asks.

Then a voice from behind me on the stairs says, 'I am.'

Spinning on my heels, I see him standing there, grinning back at me.

Harry's jaw drops open and stays that way.

'Harry,' Flick says eventually, 'you're catching flies.'

Flustered, he clamps his mouth shut, steps in front of me and shakes Noah's hand. Robustly. I don't think he plans to let it go. 'And you are?'

Noah shrugs. 'I'm Flick's ... er ... companion ... for the week.' He glances anxiously at our friend, clearly unsure quite what his status is.

Harry's head spins round and he stares at Flick. 'I thought you were coming alone,' he blurts out.

Now it's Flick's turn to shrug. 'Change of plans.'

Typical Flick.

Eventually, Noah extricates his hand from Harry's. 'Grace and I have already met on the beach.'

I feel myself flush at the memory. There's the crackle of electricity in the air between us again, so strong that I can almost see the sparks. Can no one else see this? Is it really just between me and Noah? I hope to God that it is.

'Everyone ready?' Ella says.

Which is just as well, because I feel I might have been

happy to stand and gaze at Noah, unmoving, for the rest of the evening.

'Darling!' Flick snakes her arm round Noah's waist and steers him away from me. The bubble bursts. 'Come outside, look at this place.'

I catch Noah glancing back at me as they leave.

On autopilot, I go to the fridge where Ella is lifting food out. I take a couple of dishes of chicken to carry outside.

'What do you think?' she whispers to me in a slightly breathless way. 'Is he not fifty shades of flipping fabulous?'

'Yes.' I can only agree. I'm glad that it's not just me and that Ella has been similarly struck by the presence of Flick's New Man.

'God, we are seriously going to grill her about him later. Has she said anything about this one to you?'

I shake my head. 'No. Not a word.'

'Hmm,' Ella says. 'Why the big secret? She told me she was coming on her own.'

'Perhaps she picked him up en route.' And all I got at Magor Services was a dreadful cheese sandwich.

'I wouldn't put it past her. Lucky bitch.' Ella rolls her eyes at me. 'More likely there's a Mrs Noah in the background who might have put the brakes on their little tryst at the last minute. That's probably why she kept him quiet.'

'It's a necessary side effect of dating married men,' I concur. 'They're unreliable.'

I must hold on to this thought. Noah is probably married and having a torrid affair with Flick and is, therefore, not a nice man at all, but a total ratbag.

We troop outside. The wind has dropped and it's a beautiful, balmy evening. Ella's made it really pretty out here, with candlelit lanterns all over the terrace and a string of white fairy lights stretching the full length of the back of the cottage. It's a truly magical setting.

Art starts to cook and the scent of smoky barbecue fills the air, competing with the tang of sea salt. Ella brings out an iPod and the sound of Caro Emerald's mellow voice wafts into the night.

There's much laughter as we all sit down together at the big picnic table. Someone pours me wine. I think Harry takes hold of my hand. Flick leans close to Noah and whispers in his ear. His eyes meet mine. I try not to stare. My mouth has gone dry and I gulp my wine and all I can think about is Noah's lips on mine and how it might feel. He gives me a slow smile and I know, instinctively, that he can read my mind. I feel as if I have to hold on to the edge of the table to steady myself, otherwise my whole world just might topple over.

I remember reading an interview with Johnny Depp in a trashy magazine – probably while I was at the hairdresser's. He said he knew he was in love with Vanessa Paradis when he caught a glimpse of the back of her neck across a crowded room. When she turned and he saw her eyes, he knew instantly that he was going to give up his hell-raising ways and devote himself to her. I thought it was total rubbish at the time.

'All right?' Harry asks.

I gulp. 'Yes.'

But I'm not and we both know it.

Chapter Nine

Having dinner with friends used to be such an easy affair. Pre-Noah. That's how I think my life will be from now on, split into two sections. The day Noah came and then the rest.

Art piles up the chicken and sausages on the table, all beautifully cooked. We tuck in.

Noah's sitting opposite me and I try very hard not to look at his fork as it travels to his mouth or at his lips as they curve to smile at something Flick says. Occasionally, he glances over at me and our eyes meet and his smile is just for me, I'm sure. I wonder to God how I'm going to get through this week without spontaneously combusting.

I can't move naturally any more. Every move I make seems amplified. I nearly knock over my glass. My fork clatters on my plate. My garlic bread hits the floor. My sausage, more than likely, will squirt grease in my eye.

'Everything OK, Grace?' Ella whispers.

My friend has noticed. Everyone has noticed.

I try a smile. 'Fine. Too much wine.'

'You've only had a glass.'

'Not enough wine.'

'Here, let me.' Noah tops up my glass.

Oh, Lord. I don't want to be crazy in love *and* pissed up. That is a dangerous, dangerous combination.

Flick slings an arm casually round Noah's shoulder and I feel hot coals burn inside my stomach. Jealousy. The first time I have ever experienced this emotion too. And, as well as irrational love, it's one that I feel quite uncomfortable with. This is not normal. I sneak glances at him and try to work out exactly what it is about his presence that's reduced me to this gibbering wreck.

He's tall. Possibly taller than Harry. Six-two? Broad shoulders, straight back. It looks as if he does something physical or works out a lot. I *really* hope he works out a lot as I hate gym bunnies. Thankfully, his shirt is now buttoned so I can't see the smooth, flat lines of his chest, his stomach. His hair is dark, mussed up, trendy. I'd guess that he's in his early thirties, about the same age as me. What else can I tell you? His mouth looks eminently kissable. His brown eyes are kind and smile as much as his mouth. He looks the type who would help old ladies to cross the road. He looks the type who would be happy to tear buttons from your blouse in the heat of passion. Oh, Christ. What is wrong with you, Grace Taylor? Stop it. Stop it *now*.

I don't know how we get through dinner, other than that most of us seem to sail through it on a sea of alcohol. I have more than my fair share. At least it has stopped me counting how much Harry has to drink. I notice that Noah doesn't have any wine and that Ella sticks to water as well. Should have made that my policy too. Everyone's laughing and joking, but I feel as if I'm floating above everything, disconnected.

When we've eaten the shop-bought lemon tart and polished off the last of the cupcakes, we all compliment the chef on his excellent cooking, and Ella and I begin to clear the table. The breeze has picked up again and it's time for us all to retreat inside.

Harry and Art retire to the sitting room to light the fire. Flick follows. She's never been one for tidying up after other people. On the other hand, Noah hangs back and helps Ella and me clear the table and stack the plates in the dishwasher. I go outside and blow out all of the candles. I stand there, with the only light coming from the moon and the glow from the fairy lights. There's a footstep behind me and I turn to find Noah there.

'I'm not disturbing you, am I?'

'No. I was just taking a moment to be still.'

'Me too,' Noah says. 'I wanted to listen to the sea. I can't get over what a fabulous place this is.'

'Yes. I love it here too. We could sit on the rocks. It's nice there.'

He nods and follows me off the terrace. I climb over the rocks, looking for a suitable place. 'Here looks good.'

I try to act normally and, of course, end up turning too fast and he bumps straight into me. My life has descended in an instant from disgruntled order to a cheesy *Carry On* film. He holds out his arms to steady me, but I duck away from his touch.

'I'm fine. Thanks.'

It's clear that Noah can sense my awkwardness at being alone with him. When we sit down together, I'm thinking that this was really a bad idea. Why didn't I just retreat to the safety of the kitchen as soon as he came out and leave him to it? I hug my knees and, at Noah's proximity, a shiver runs through me.

'Cold?'

'No. Just a shiver.'

'I'd offer you my jacket . . .' He laughs and indicates the thin shirt he's wearing.

In an attempt to deflect attention from my embarrassment, I say in a voice that sounds too bright and half-strangled, 'So, how did you meet Flick then?'

Ignoring the fact that I'm talking like Beaker from *The Muppet Show*, he says, 'A film company were using my estate as a location shoot. It happened to be one of Flick's authors.'

Flick works as a film agent for a big literary agency in London – though, in reality, she's rarely there. She jets all round the world – LA, Cannes, wherever there are film festival-type things going on. As well as a pretty chi-chi place in London, she now even has her own apartment out in California, she's there so much. Flick keeps saying that we three girls should go out there together, but, well, we never quite have.

'David Stevens,' Noah adds. 'Do you know him?'

'I don't.'

Ella and I know all about Flick's work – she tells us enough. But we've never got to go to any of her authors' events or anything.

'Well, it's his book. *The Best of May*.'

'Who's starring in it?'

Noah shrugs his ignorance. 'I have no idea. I'm afraid that I'm no celebrity watcher, but I don't think there were any big names. It seemed like a pretty low-budget affair to me.' He winces. 'Just don't tell Flick I said that.'

Already, he has the measure of my friend.

'I won't. Your secret's safe with me.'

He looks at me as if to say he knows that.

'Flick came up for the day to see how the filming was going and well …'

Noah doesn't need to say any more. Most red-blooded men who see Flick fall instantly at her feet. That's pretty much where she likes to keep them throughout her relationships.

Flick is tall, willowy and extraordinarily pretty, although she's not got Ella's endearing looks. Flick is glamorous, stunning and damn well knows it. Her face is a perfect oval, flawless, her mouth pert. She's blonde – naturally – with wide baby-blue eyes. Only the hardest of hearts could resist her. Only the most confident of men can keep up with her. And, though she could have her pick of them, Flick invariably goes for ones who are married or 'complicated'. She likes alpha males and actors. Men who are either too young for her or twice her age. Multimillionaires, commitment-phobes or penniless spongers.

Given her track record, Noah looks way too normal to be one of Flick's boyfriends. I do hope he's not in the multimillionaire, commitment-phobe category.

'So you have a country estate?' I enquire, sounding as casual as I can.

'No.' An easy laugh. 'I'm the operations manager for one. That's corporate-speak for dogsbody. I do everything from fixing their leaky cisterns to cooking breakfast for shooting parties.'

'Which house is it?'

'It's just a small place. Relatively speaking. If you call seventeen bedrooms and six reception rooms small.' Another laugh, which clearly comes more readily to him than a frown. 'It's not one of the famous grand houses, though. We open to the public only on high days and holidays. Just enough to secure our government grant. Melbray Hall, in the Midlands, not far from Birmingham. You probably won't have heard of it.'

'You're right.' I give him an apologetic smile.

'It's a charming place,' he adds. 'The grounds were designed by Capability Brown.'

'Then I'll have to come and visit you one day. We could go out for lunch or something.'

Oh, good grief, what am I saying? He'll think I'm flirting.

'I'd like that,' he counters. 'I could show you round the estate. You'd love it there.'

Oh, good grief. So is he.

This is my best friend's man. Remember that! I hate it when Flick comes on to other people's husbands. I must not do this.

Then we're awkward with each other, so I pick up a couple of pebbles and toss them, half-heartedly, towards the sea.

'It was a last-minute arrangement,' he adds. 'To come here. Flick asked me just yesterday. We've had only a handful of dates. We hardly know each other really.'

'I'm sure we'll all get on just fine.'

'I hope so. I don't want to intrude.'

'Oh, I'm sure that you won't do that. We're a pretty friendly bunch.'

Then Ella opens the back door and comes out on to the terrace. 'Coffee's ready,' she shouts at us.

'I guess that's our cue to go back inside and join the others,' he says. But, again, Noah seems as reluctant as I do.

'Yes.'

We stand and Noah holds out his hand to help me, but I don't take it. I can't. Instead, I wobble my way back towards the terrace.

'Have you two been putting the world to rights out here?' she jokes.

'Something like that.'

'Well, you both look very cosy.'

Too cosy. 'I should get back inside,' I say hastily. 'Harry will be missing me.'

And, without even glancing in Noah's direction, I scurry back indoors.

Chapter Ten

We all troop through to the sitting room, which is spacious, but just as comfy as the kitchen. The fire is roaring away, flames licking up the chimney and giving the room a soft glow. There are three sofas, all of them ancient and covered with a pretty, floral print that is nothing like Ella's taste, but somehow they suit the room. I wonder how much of this stuff she will get rid of and how much she will keep for sentimental reasons. I get the impression that she loves it just the way it is and I can't say that I blame her.

The brandy is open and Art, Harry and Flick have already started without us. Harry and Flick are on one of the sofas together. Flick is laughing outrageously. Her earthy cackle splits the air.

'Your husband is a rogue,' she cries out as we appear.

But she doesn't make a move and stays settled where she is. She and Harry have always been good drinking buddies. It's only when they're both sober that she gets on his nerves.

Ella curls up next to Art, who picks up his guitar again and starts to pluck it.

Noah sits on the remaining sofa, which leaves me no choice but to sit down next to him. So I do. I fold in my clothes so that they're not touching him. This is a stupid crush, I admonish myself, and I should just get a grip now. He's a bloke. A nice one. Nothing more. All this waves-crashing, sparks-flying nonsense is a product of my imagination.

'We should drink a toast,' Flick says effusively. 'I've got champagne in the boot of the car, but I can't be bothered to go outside for it now. We'll have that tomorrow instead. Charge your glasses!'

I'm not sure that another glass of wine is a good idea, but I have one anyway. Noah seems to drink nothing stronger than orange juice and Ella, again, refuses a drink. I'm not sure that she's had anything alcoholic all night.

'To us,' Flick proposes. 'To friendships old and new.' A suggestive glance at Noah.

'To friendships old and new,' we all echo.

'Here's to a lovely holiday,' Ella proposes.

'To the holiday!' More drinking.

When the toasting is done, I sink back into the sofa. All attention is on Art who's softly singing Coldplay songs. Noah turns towards me. We're very close. I can feel his breath on my neck, as warm as a caress. I resist the urge to fan myself in the style of a woman having a hot flush.

'So how do you know Flick?' he asks quietly so as not to interrupt Art's playing. 'I think she said you were all at university together?'

'Yes. Many moons ago.' I toy with my glass, then realise I'm being coquettish and stop. 'We were all on different courses. I was studying accountancy, Ella was at the art school and Flick was doing media studies. We were in the same halls and we all used to work in the same dodgy bar to earn some extra cash. At the end of the first year, we decided to rent a flat together.'

'And you've been friends ever since?'

'Sounds corny, doesn't it?'

'No. I think it's nice that you've stayed so close.'

The others are laughing loudly and I try not to lean my head in towards his so that I can hear him better.

'You seem like very different people.'

I'm sure he means that Flick is a total drama queen whereas Ella and I are not.

'I don't know. We're not so different really.'

We're all women who have been successful in business, yet seem to have totally messed up our love lives. With the latter, Flick has certainly done it in greater quantity than the two of us.

She was a nightmare at university. We never knew who we were going to wake up to find in the flat. Going into the kitchen in pyjamas was a definite no-no. There'd always be some strange man at the table, nursing a cup of coffee. Occasionally, there were even two. They always looked the most sheepish. At one point we considered making her split the rent four ways, with her paying two parts, as she was rarely without an overnight guest. It was exhausting – even as a casual observer. There was a constant parade of college lecturers, minor popstars, footballers. We used to call them the

Breakfast Club. Even the postman didn't escape her attentions. He was a nice enough man, but it was always disconcerting to find him in his regulation uniform in the kitchen, eating toast. Still, after that we'd always get more than our fair share of free samples of soap powder or hot chocolate or shampoo when he was delivering them.

We used to tolerate her excesses more than we perhaps would have done those of another flatmate. She'd arrived at university a very messed-up young woman and, frankly, Ella and I were left trying to put the pieces back together. Sometimes, I look at Flick and wonder whether we could have done a better job. She's a year older than both of us and is still showing no signs of giving up her wild child ways. The things you can get away with as high jinks in your twenties start to become slightly more difficult to accept as normal behaviour as you hit your mid-thirties. By forty, it leaves you generally out of step with your peers, who have all grown up, settled down, started families. If you're the one still dancing on the tables at parties and taking home random men, people start to pity you. I don't want that for Flick. I want her to be loved.

The summer that Flick finished her A levels, her plans – to backpack around South America, or volunteer to work with elephant conservation in Thailand, like everyone else – suddenly changed. Out of the blue, she packed a bag and ran away to Las Vegas to marry her music teacher, a friend of her father's, a middle-aged stalwart of the Rotary Club who drove a top-of-the-range Mercedes and played golf every weekend. By all accounts it sent shock waves of scandal through the small and highly affluent village where she lived. The teacher,

Mr Tavistock, or Brian if you knew him intimately, left his long-term partner and two very confused teenage children for her.

It transpired that the affair with Flick had been going on throughout the sixth form, right under everyone's noses. It didn't last. Of course. Before the ink was dry on the marriage certificate, they'd split up. As soon as he could, Brian Tavistock filed for divorce, citing her adultery with a person or persons unknown. Perhaps Flick *had* started another breakfast club. Perhaps he was just being bitter and twisted. Perhaps it was the pot calling the kettle black. Who knows? But it was like a pebble being dropped from a great height into a still pond. The story didn't end there and the ripples continue to spread out, exerting their influence, even now.

Her parents, who have barely spoken to her since, packed her off to university in disgrace. She became estranged from her only sister and has never seen her to this day. It seemed as if it was easier for them to get Flick out of the way, sweep it all under the carpet and pretend it never existed, rather than examine in cold, hard daylight what had really gone on. Every few years Flick might get a Christmas card from her family, but that's pretty much it. Her younger sister is now the golden child – married with two toddlers and a husband in data management. So Ella and I have pretty much stepped into the void left by her abandonment. We're all the family she has now.

She arrived at university already completely off the rails – a hard-drinking, hard-partying, good-time girl. Ella and I spent a lot of time trying to protect her from herself. We were the ones who made sure she got home safely, didn't get into cars with strangers, didn't wander off into the night with men she'd just picked up. We were the ones who wiped away her tears when it all went horribly wrong with yet another man. We recognised the build-up to each emotional fall-out – from our many all-night conversations round a bottle of Jack Daniel's – but didn't have the tools to deal with it.

Ella came from a stable and very happy background. My own was pretty good too, if a little repressive. I was a Good Daughter, who always strove to please others. My parents weren't exactly progressive in their parenting style. When Flick was having sex on a daily basis with her teacher in the back of his Ford Escort, I wasn't officially allowed to date boys or even wear eyeshadow.

But along with the self-destructive tendencies, she was such fun too. The only scrapes I have ever got into in my life were with Flick. The times I've cried so hard with laughter that my face hurt have all been with Flick. I need her in my life to show me how to enjoy myself. She taught me how to let my hair down, kick off my shoes – something that I seem to have forgotten again. She could get us into any nightclub free and rounds of drinks would always miraculously appear. How she ever managed to complete a degree is a mystery. It pains me to see that Flick still bears the scars of her emotional crises, but she's just better at hiding them now. Mostly.

Since university her relationships have all been very much short-term. The ones that last longer than a few nights are, more often than not, with married men. I don't think that I can remember a single one who has been appropriate for Flick. Ella and I have long stopped bothering to remember their names and, to be honest, Flick rarely remembers them herself. I don't know what she's searching for, but she hasn't so far been able to find it.

Noah seems different. As far as I know he's actually single. Though I can hardly at this juncture ask him if he's married, can I? Or even if there's a significant other. There isn't any evidence of a wedding band, though, or the tell-tale pale skin where one might have resided until recently. And sometimes you can just tell if a man is married, can't you? Just by looking at him you know. You know that his wife has chosen his tie, his suit, whether his watch was a birthday gift. If men have children too, they bear that permanently harried look. I glance at him again. Noah looks like a down-to-earth, what-you-see-is-what-you-get, honest chap. No subterfuge lurking behind his countenance as far as I can tell. There's an openness to his face, a clarity in his eye that says it doesn't wander. I don't think he's the sort of man who'd cheat on his wife. But what do I know? Men always have been, and remain, a total enigma to me.

Flick's flirting outrageously, as always, monopolising Harry – who doesn't seem to mind – but I can still feel her eyes constantly straying this way. Is Noah more of a challenge than her usual flings? I don't know. He certainly doesn't seem to be hanging on her every word as her normal conquests do. Perhaps this guy knows how to handle himself. Maybe that's what Flick sees in him. This time she might be having to do all the running.

Or that could just be sour grapes on my part, I think. And I'm not being fair on Flick. She may have had more than her fair share of men in the past, but she's a beautiful and bright lady, who's a lot of fun to be around. Why shouldn't she make the most of that? I really hate to admit this but there are times – more of them recently – when I wonder why I was happy to settle down with the first man who asked me to. If I'd had more experience of men, would I have married Harry? Should I have played the field more, like Flick? Except that I'm not like Flick. Never have been, never will be. I'm a one-man woman and I've always rolled that way.

Starting with Ella, a Mexican yawn goes round the room. I slide down into the sofa, contented.

'No way are we all falling asleep this early!' Flick declares. 'There's no one going to bed before dawn on the first night!'

I can't see me lasting past midnight.

'We need to do something to get this party started!'

It makes me smile. In some ways, Flick is still that crazy, mixed-up kid.

Chapter Eleven

'Art, crank up the music,' Flick instructs. 'You're sending us all to sleep with that "meaning of life" stuff. Play us some songs that we can sing to.'

'Name your poison,' Art says.

'Have you got any Abba in that old guitar of yours?'

'I think there's a cheese setting here somewhere,' Art counters and pretends to fiddle with the tuning keys.

'Well, turn the dial to Full Cheese then!'

'What about "Dancing Queen"?' he suggests.

'It's our anthem,' Flick assures him. 'That right, girls?'

I haven't had nearly enough to drink to be doing this, but Flick pulls me up from the sofa, nevertheless. Our drunken get-togethers nearly always end up with a karaoke session. Except we never need a Singstar as we always have Art to supply the music.

Flick isn't a great singer, but she makes up for it by being loud and enthusiastic. She also has all the moves down.

'Come on, you.' Now Ella is yanked up unceremoniously. 'You're looking far too comfortable sitting there.'

Flick grabs three bananas from the fruit bowl and hands us one each to use as our microphones.

So in the middle of the living room, we join Art and belt out our very favourite Abba number. We are the girls who have watched *Mamma Mia!* together ten times. On one occasion, three times in the same day. If you are tired of Abba, then you're tired of life.

We sing and dance, kicking up our heels and using our bananas to full effect. Flick does a Freddie Mercury circle with hers.

It makes me realise how long it is since I've sung. I used to be in a choir, but could never keep up with rehearsals because of work commitments. Another part of me that I've let slip away.

Art slides seamlessly into Kylie's 'Can't Get You out of my Head' and we follow. Flick swishes all the newspapers off the coffee table with her arm. She kicks off her shoes to mount it and then pulls us both up with her. Thank goodness our impromptu stage is made of solid pine with tiles on top, so it has a chance of holding our weight. We sway together, giggling.

I remember Flick having a tiny pair of gold hot pants just like Kylie's that she'd bought from Topshop or somewhere. We were always inundated with free drinks on the nights she wore them. The bar where we worked might have been horrible, but we used to select a few of our favourite customers for a lock-in afterwards. The manager would turn a blind eye while we lined up the shots, put our favourite tunes on the sound system and danced on the bar counter. It makes me smile to think about it. But for Flick, my life would have been a lot more grey.

Now we dance on the coffee table, 'la-la-la-ing' our hearts out into our bananas, and I feel as if I'm right back there. Our bottoms might hang lower, our midriffs thicker slightly, our clothing less revealing, but, underneath it all, those girls are still inside us.

'This takes me right back to Honkers!' Flick cries, giving voice to my thoughts. 'Those were the best days of my life.'

I wonder if that's why she's still like she is, trying to hang on to her youth, her wild child days. While Ella and I are moving on, is Flick still stuck firmly in the past? Maybe she thinks that if she relives it enough times, one day she'll get it right. Part of me can see the attraction of living in the past. Perhaps it's the passage of time or the fact that memories viewed from a distance are always more golden, but it seems that they were simpler times then.

Harry and Noah clap their appreciation as we work our way steadily through the cheesy song catalogue of the eighties. We throw in a bit of Britney Spears and the Pussycat Dolls. I'm always amazed at the range of Art's skills and how he's just as happy playing our karaoke favourites as he is Black Sabbath numbers.

To redress the balance, Art sings Eminem's 'Slim Shady' and the Libertines' 'Can't Stand Me Now' with aplomb.

'Come on, you two,' Flick urges. 'Sing something.'

'You know that I'm completely tone deaf,' Harry laughs.

'My talent lies more in providing applause. I'll leave the performing to you lovely ladies. You should audition for *The X Factor*.'

'We would storm it,' Flick says.

'I'll sing,' Noah says quietly, surprising us all.

Flick's eyes widen. 'You can sing?'

He shrugs. 'A bit.'

'Name your tune, man.' Art readies his guitar.

'What about Will Young's "Leave Right Now"?'

'One of my favourite songs,' I say, even though no one asks me.

'I don't have to stand on the table or use the banana, do I?' Noah looks worried.

'No,' Flick says. 'Not as you've asked so nicely.'

So Art plucks the introductory chords and Noah starts to sing. His voice is strong and clear. He's hesitant at first, but soon gains his confidence. The lyrics are heartbreaking, poignant, and I feel as if he's singing them just for me. I try to tell myself I'm being ridiculous, but I can't help feeling as if all the air has been sucked out of the room. When he finishes, my heart is pounding.

Flick flops back in her seat and says, 'Wow. What a voice. You're not just a pretty face.'

Noah sits down, smiling shyly. His eyes meet mine.

'How are we going to top that, ladies?'

Ella yawns. 'I don't want to break up the party, but I'm going to call it a day.'

'It's all the sea air,' I offer, suddenly stifling a yawn myself.

'You are all such lightweights,' Flick complains. 'Just one more song.'

It's gone two in the morning.

I hold up a hand. 'I'm done.'

Flick pouts. Then her eyes light up. 'Though an early night might be nice.' Full of meaning, they laser past me and fix on Noah.

He meets her gaze steadily. 'I'm ready when you are.'

I feel myself flush. Certainly no lack of chemistry there.

'We might as well all go up,' Harry says.

'I'm going to play for a while longer.' Art pulls the bottle towards him. 'Plus there's still brandy in here.'

'Oh,' Harry says. 'Might just stay and have another little snifter.'

'Don't be too long,' I warn.

What I mean is, 'Don't you think you've had enough to drink?' But Harry has long since started to ignore my coded words, my school-marm looks.

Ella stands up first. 'Night, then,' she says. 'It's so lovely having everyone here together. I'm sure we're going to have a great week.'

She heads upstairs.

'I'm struggling to keep my eyes open too,' I confess. 'I can't do late nights any more. And I certainly can't do late nights and too much alcohol.'

Noah stands and Flick comes over to join him, slipping her hand in his.

'Night, all,' he says. Then he turns to me. 'Night, Grace. It's been nice talking to you.'

Flick follows him up the stairs and I trail behind, trying to stem the flow of misery that's threatening to engulf me. Halfway up, she turns back to me, winks and licks her lips lasciviously.

This could be a long week, I think. A very long week.

Chapter Twelve

Oh, God. I can't believe that I'm going to be sleeping in the room right next to Noah and Flick. I sit on the bed and don't move. I can hear every creak of the floorboards. Supposing they're *at it* all night? Every night? Of course they're going to be *at it*! This is Flick, remember. And I know just *how* they're going to be *at it*, as she's regaled Ella and me with tales of her bedroom antics often enough. Not that she needed to. In our shared flat with paper-thin walls, you could hear her halfway down the corridor, let alone in the next room. Flick always liked to make sure everyone knew that she was having a good time. Oh, no. I wish I'd brought sleeping tablets. Or industrial-strength ear defenders.

I open the Velux windows in the ceiling and listen to the soothing sounds of the sea. It's going to have to be a darn sight louder than that to drown out the sounds of passion from next door. Perhaps there'll be a convenient Force Nine gale or storm overnight with howling winds and crashing waves. I might be in with a chance then. I sigh to myself. All my visions of a relaxing week are crumbling before my eyes. With Flick and Noah being here and all loved up, it's only throwing into sharp relief the weaknesses in my own relationship. Of course it's made ten times worse with me going goo-goo-ga-ga over Noah when I am really not that sort of person at all. I could count on one hand the amount of times I've even done a double take at a man over the last ten years. I just want to put a pillow over my head and die.

At this end of the cottage, the four of us are sharing the bathroom, so I listen carefully, trying to work out when both Noah and Flick have finished their ablutions in there. I promise myself a shower in the morning, as I don't want to keep everyone awake with the noise at this hour, and I slip into my pyjamas. As it's hot, I'm wearing a strappy top and shorts. I wish I'd thought to bring a dressing gown with me, but I have only a winter-weight one, nothing light or floaty or remotely sexy enough to make me happy about bumping into strange men on the landing.

I sit and sit and sit, blanking out the soft giggling, the creaky floor, the opening and closing of doors, the running of taps, the flushing of the loo. Eventually, I can hear no noise. Nothing. I wait a bit longer. Still nothing. Then, when I think the coast is clear, I creep out of my bedroom, across the hall, and slip silently into the bathroom. I close the door with the quietest of clicks and stand with my back to it, breathing heavily. Made it. I'm not sure my heart will stand all this tension.

'Hey,' a voice says and I nearly jump out of my skin.
'Noah!'

'I'm nearly done,' he says, clearly unfazed by my presence. 'Just a minute.'

'I'll come back.'

'No need.'

But there is need. The man I most hoped to avoid in all the world in my pyjamas is currently standing at the sink wearing a small white towel and a winning smile. I've come over all hot and silly again. I'm trying not to acknowledge the fact that he is half naked and that I'm in a very small room with him, but I can't help it. Noah seems to be filling more of the space than he physically should. He has muscles. Lots of them. Everywhere. There are thighs. Lovely strong thighs. Shoulders. Big shoulders. And abs. Abs on abs on abs. Abs that make you want to touch them. Did I mention the thighs? Touchable, too.

His body is bronzed, toned. A result of working outside, I'd say, now that I've had the opportunity to examine it more closely. Those are muscles that come from wielding an axe and lifting very heavy things. The only hair on his torso is a dark line from his waist that disappears tantalisingly below his towel. Stop looking at it, Grace. Stop looking.

A toothbrush is sticking out of the corner of his mouth and he shifts it, which brings me back into the real world.

'Oh, my. I'm sorry. Very sorry.'

'Don't apologise. I guess we're going to have to get used to being up close and personal this week.'

'Yes,' I say. 'Yes.'

My nipples are showing him just how much they like being up close and personal. Surreptitiously, I try to position my hands over them in a foldy-arm sort of way.

'I'm done now,' Noah says.

The bathroom is small and there's not much room for manoeuvre. He puts his hands on my hips while he eases around me to the door. There is just one thin layer of cotton between our flesh. I gulp. He smiles as he shifts me. Now I'm at the sink.

'Sleep tight, Grace,' he says and then, with a backward glance and a wink, he's gone.

I look in the mirror. My normally pale face is red with embarrassment. It looks as if I've run a marathon – and not one of the people who train regularly and finish in respectable times. No. One of those at the back who wear Superman costumes and have to be helped over the line an inch away from death. Bugger.

I need to get a grip. I *so* need to get a grip.

Chapter Thirteen

Back in the bedroom, Harry has finally come upstairs too. He's currently standing on the bed in his underpants, waving his phone at the windows in the roof.

'Thought I might get something up here,' he slurs.

It's obvious that Harry is very drunk. But why wouldn't he be? He hasn't had a glass out of his hand from the minute we arrived here.

I look up at him. His body is white as it hasn't seen the sun for some time. Because he drinks so much now and never exercises, other than to lift his drink to his mouth, his stomach has gone slack and flabby. Where is the man I once knew? I wonder. We may not have had a marriage based on high romance, but we've had our moments. Harry has done his fair share of romancing me over the years. He would, occasionally, whisk me away to Paris for the weekend, organise a beautiful dinner at my favourite restaurant or buy me a diamond as a surprise. And I loved it. I loved to feel so cherished. But that man seems to be long gone.

'Get down,' I say as if I'm speaking to a child and not a responsible adult. 'It's nearly three in the morning. You'll wake the whole house. Twitter can surely live without you for one night.'

What has he got to tweet about anyway? Or is it that his life is so dull now that he has to live it vicariously through a bunch of people that he doesn't even know?

Harry topples on to the bed with an 'ouf' and I bite down my irritation. Within seconds he's asleep. With an ease that has come with years of practice, I turn him on to his side so that he doesn't snore, and I cover him with the duvet. I climb in beside him. There was a time when I'd cuddle up, spoon into his shape. Now I lie on my back and listen to the ocean crashing against the rocks. It sounds lonely.

Then, ten minutes later and even though I'm trying to tune out every noise except the sea, I hear Flick moan with pleasure through the wall from the room next door. Wonderful. Then comes the rhythmic creaking, slow, slow, deliciously slow. More soft gasps from Flick. My imagination is too good. I can picture exactly what is going on next door now that the little white towel has been removed. The vision of those muscles burns itself inside my eyelids. I can even feel those strong hands on my skin. Next to me Harry snores and I kick him. *I* want to be making love – with someone, *anyone*. Another pleasured moan. Flick is clearly in the throes of ecstasy. The movements from next door, become faster, more urgent. My hands start to move on my body of their own accord, echoing the rhythm. They move over my breasts and down, down. My hands reach between my legs. Then I stop dead. What on earth am I doing? I want to touch myself because I can hear Flick and Noah having great sex? That is *so* wrong. Too pervy by half. Instead, I slap my own traitorous fingers and fold my pillow round my head. But that's not good enough, as I still can't block out the noise. After a few more minutes of torture, I can stand it no longer and I get up.

Pulling a cardigan from my suitcase, I slip it on and then add some socks. I look at Harry's face, puffy in the moonlight, and know that I won't be missed. Flick's gasping is becoming more regular. Time for me to leave. I certainly don't want to be here for the finale. I pad downstairs, being as quiet as I can.

In the sitting room, a few embers are still glowing in the fireplace and I huddle as close as I can, but it's not emanating much warmth. I pull the cardigan around me and cuddle myself. What am I going to do? I'm having lustful thoughts about a man who's not my husband. And murderous thoughts about the one who is. Harry and I need to sit down and have a serious talk while we're here. He's turning from a person that I used to love so stoically into one that I don't actually like very much any more.

We've been married for only seven years and we had a year together before that. I wonder how it can all have gone wrong in such a short time. Is it me? Is it something I'm doing? I'm not normally a demonstrative person. Is that what Harry's problem is? So, again, that leaves me wondering, what is it about Noah that's sparked such a strong and instantaneous attraction? I have to put my feelings for him into context. I'm unhappy at home: that can be the only rational reason he's turned my head. In all the years I've been with Harry, I've never looked at another man. I've had no reason to. But lately?

Because my job is soul-destroying, I'm always tired, run-down and, as I need my wits about me to stay one step ahead of my staff, I like to go to bed early. Harry doesn't. He prefers to stay up until the early hours, drinking wine and tweeting to God knows who. We have to put a stop to that. If we actually went to bed at the same time and Harry wasn't too pissed to . . . respond, then we might have a chance of regaining some intimacy. Should I perhaps think about changing my job? Should Harry perhaps think of changing his? If our careers are dictating what goes on in our lives, that can't be right. Whatever happens, something needs to be done. We can't go on like this.

I sit in the dark, mulling it all over. I'd like to have a cup of hot chocolate or something, but I don't want to make a noise and wake everyone up. Time ticks by. I've nothing to read as I forgot to bring my book downstairs, and thinking too deeply about the meaning of love and life is starting to give me a headache. Eventually, my toes – even in socks – are starting to get cold and the fire has died. If I don't want to die of hypothermia in Ella's sitting room, I should go back to bed.

Tiptoeing up the stairs, I quietly let myself into the bedroom. The moon is shining full through the window. Harry has rolled on to his back and is snoring loudly. I climb into bed next to him and roll him over. He stops. When I lie down, I put my ice-cold feet on him as a punishment. Still he doesn't flinch. All I can hear is the sea. Thank God.

Then, just as I'm starting to feel myself drifting off, I hear an ecstatic moan from Flick and the rhythm starts up again. Oh, fuck. Fuckity-fuck.

Grabbing Harry's shoulder, I pull him on to his back. He grunts and grumbles and, mercifully, starts snoring again. I lie there with my eyes screwed shut and my fingers in my ears and try to sing la-la-la in my head.

Chapter Fourteen

In the morning, the sun is high in the sky. Harry's fast asleep. I lie still, listening to the waves and trying to prise my eyelids from my eyeballs, which feel as if they've been superglued together.

I can hear the sound of women's laughter coming from outside so, eventually, with much huffing and puffing, I haul myself out of bed. Standing under the shower, I let the hot water run over me and turn me into a human being again. I must have dozed off before dawn, but I don't think I slept for more than a couple of hours last night. But then neither did Flick or Noah. More's the pity. Sigh.

Pulling on the nearest clothes to hand, I head downstairs. In the kitchen, there's no one about, so I try the teapot, which is nestling under its cosy. Sure enough, it's still warm and I manage to squeeze out enough to fill a mug. Out on the terrace I find Flick and Ella sitting at the picnic table. It's another glorious day. The sea is blue, sparkling, and its white foam tips tickle the rocks below the cottage. There's nothing else to see but the immense, unending sky. The air, sharp with the tang of salt, is warm, comforting.

I let out a long, lingering sigh. 'It's so beautiful out here.'

'Morning, sweetie,' Ella says. 'There's tea in the pot.'

I hold up my mug. 'Already done.'

Flick has her knees hugged up to her chest on one side of the bench, so I sit down next to Ella. Nursing my tea to me, I come to the realisation that I'm going to need about ten cups to get me going this morning. Every time I blink, my eyes want to close again. It's been a long time since I've partied until past midnight. Today is going to be a struggle.

Opposite me, Flick lights up. Not surprisingly, she doesn't look as if she's slept much either. Her hair is tousled and she still hasn't put her make-up on, and Flick is not usually one to be seen without her full slap. Both of them are still in their dressing gowns. Ella in fluffy, pink and white polka dot. Flick in a silky, sexy, Chinese-print kimono that barely covers her thighs. It falls open at her breast, showing that she's wearing nothing beneath it. I feel overdressed in my jeans and T-shirt.

Flick drags her cigarette smoke deep into her lungs.

'I thought you'd given up,' Ella says.

Flick looks accusingly at the cigarette. 'So did I.'

'I could hear you both laughing,' I tell them as I sip my tea. 'I just wanted to see if I was missing anything.'

Flick leans in conspiratorially and lowers her voice. 'I was just telling Ella that I have been shagged ragged all night.' She takes another drag on her cigarette as if she's trying to kick-start herself. Which she may well be. 'I hope we didn't disturb you.'

'No,' I say disingenuously. 'Didn't hear a thing. Slept like a baby.' God strike me down dead for lying.

'He's something else,' Flick adds, letting out a contemplative breath and a long stream of smoke.

'You say that about them all.' Ella shoots a look at her. 'I seem to remember you telling me exactly the same thing about someone else not too many months ago.'

Flick looks away from her. 'I am trying very hard to untangle myself from that particular person, believe me.' There's a sadness in her voice that I've never heard before. 'Sometimes relationships are *too* complicated and you have to move on.'

Must have missed the lowdown on this one, but from the undercurrents there's no doubt that means he was married again with no intention of leaving his wife. Flick's flings follow very much the same pattern. She's madly in love one minute and then forgets them as quickly the next.

'Did I miss something?'

Flick waves a hand dismissively. 'It's over,' she says. 'It never should have begun.'

'Amen to that,' Ella says and fixes Flick with a cool stare.

I'm definitely missing something.

'Noah's different.' Flick is suddenly serious. 'This one's a keeper.'

'You've only just met him,' I point out. My voice sounds crisper than I intend. But, in my defence, I've heard this a dozen times before from Flick.

'You've seen him, Grace,' she counters. 'Look at him. He's handsome. He's got a body to die for.'

I use all my strength to push away the image of Noah in the

bathroom, clad only in his small white towel, which springs immediately to mind.

'That's not all it takes to make a lasting relationship.' Why do I want to turn this into an argument with my friend?

'I know.' Flick shrugs away my concerns. 'He's funny, caring, bright. *Fantastic* in bed.'

My heart lurches. Is it my fertile imagination or does she stare directly at me when she says that? Does she know that I was listening to them? I'm sure she must.

'I think you've mentioned that already,' Ella chips in.

'Did I?' Ella and Flick cackle together and I can tell that she's only trying to wind us up. 'He can cook too. Did I tell you that?'

'You didn't,' Ella confirms, 'but that's not nearly so interesting.'

'I haven't seen much evidence of it,' Flick adds. 'But he tells me he can. And who knew that he could sing like that?' She looks pleased with herself that she's managed to land such a catch.

'So, how long have you known him?' Ella asks.

She's thoughtful for a moment. 'Long enough to know that I'd like him to stick around.'

'*Must* be love,' Ella coos.

'I hate to say this, girls,' Flick continues, 'but he could be The One.' She gazes out to sea. 'I know that I haven't got the best track record when it comes to commitment, but I'm serious this time. Look at me. All this isn't going to last.' She points at her face. 'I'm already thinking of getting Botox. I can't still be running around like this when I hit forty.

Everyone else has moved on and I haven't. I'm stuck in party mode.' She knocks ash into the saucer next to her. 'Sometime soon, I need to think about settling down and what else would I be looking for in a man? Noah's the real deal. Even I, who can't spot a decent guy from fifty paces, can tell that.' She shakes her head as if admonishing herself. 'I can't let this one slip through my fingers. Believe me, they don't come along that often.'

I wonder if the main attraction is that Flick is having to do all the chasing this time. There's no doubt that he likes her and, clearly, there's a lot of sexual compatibility between them, but Noah certainly doesn't look as besotted as her usual men.

Flick takes the last puff of her cigarette and grinds the butt into the terrace. 'Don't tell Noah that I smoke,' she says. 'He hates it. I'm going to give it up.'

This we have also heard before.

'He's a total nature freak,' she continues. 'That's why I thought he'd love this place. No offence, Ella, but it's a bit too bloody middle-of-nowhere for me. Where can you buy Jo Malone toiletries up here?'

'Nowhere,' Ella admits.

Flick looks appalled. 'I like a coffee shop on every corner and you never want to be too far from a branch of Zara.'

'You sound exactly like Harry,' I note with a laugh.

'There's nothing for it,' Flick adds, 'I'm going to have to get Noah seriously into five-star hotels and spas.'

We all chuckle at that. But underneath the laughter I can feel myself quietly seething. It's clear that Noah and Flick are totally mismatched. Why can't she see that? Why can't she see that this relationship will go the same way as all the rest of them? Hasn't she worked out that opposites might attract in the first place but they rarely grow old together? But who am I to pour cold water on her happiness just because my hormones are convinced that they fancy the pants off her man? I need to get my own house in order first.

What happens if when you get together you have a lot in common and then, slowly but surely, you grow apart? How do you go about starting to fix that?

'You're not thinking of whisking him off to Las Vegas at short notice?' Ella enquires.

We rarely mention Flick's short-lived and ill-fated marriage these days. Or the trouble it caused. And all for nothing. It broke up two families, left two vulnerable teenagers with a weekend daddy, and cost her briefly wedded husband his reputation and his standing in the community. Flick might have moved on quickly to the next man, but I fear the experience has left her with lasting damage when it comes to her ability to form healthy relationships.

'I've done Vegas,' Flick jokes, though her voice is tight. 'This time I'm thinking of a beach wedding. You'll be my bridesmaids.'

Ella and I both roll our eyes and together say, 'Thanks.'

'The thing is,' Flick worries at a beautifully manicured fingernail, 'there's just one small flaw with this plan.' She looks at us both squarely. 'I don't think Noah feels the same way about me.'

Ella reaches out and takes Flick's hand and squeezes it.

'I'm sure he thinks that I'm fun to be with. But I get the

impression that it's a relationship that's just for now with him. I have to show him that there's more to me than that.' She looks anxiously at us. 'I've spent so long with men I don't give a toss about that I can't remember what I'm supposed to do any more when I do care.'

'He's come here,' Ella reminds her. 'That must mean he likes you a lot. You wouldn't go on holiday with someone if you didn't.'

'I'll be content with "like a lot" for now,' Flick says affably. 'Come on, Grace. You're the fixer. Can't you sort this out for me?'

'You just need to turn on your charm,' Ella chips in, rescuing me.

'I am on a full charm offensive. I'm surprised you haven't noticed.' More laughter. 'But it's going to take more than that,' she admits. 'I'm going to have to work really hard to make him love me.'

And she's perfectly capable of doing that. I know. She can make any man she wants fall in love with her. Perhaps I should ask her for some tips on how to get Harry to fall in love with me again. Because, frankly, I don't have a clue.

Chapter Fifteen

Ella yawns as we both make another pot of tea and a big cafetière of coffee.

'Tired, honey?' I ask.

'Always, at the moment,' she says. 'Don't think I've ever been as sleepy. If it was an Olympic sport then I'd get a gold medal.'

'You do look a bit pale. Take it easy. Don't be running round after everyone. We're all grown-ups, we can look after ourselves.'

'I just want to make sure that everyone has a nice time while they're here, but I am feeling a bit queasy today.' She laughs. 'Too much rich food.'

We take the tea and coffee back outside. Then Art appears and, when Flick budges up, plonks himself down on the bench next to her. He looks remarkably spry for a man who consumed an inhuman amount of brandy last night. He does, however, pour himself a very large mug of strong, black coffee and, after grunting a cursory 'Good morning' at us all, says very little as he stares unmoving at the waves.

The sun is climbing higher in the sky, the sea glitters invitingly. The chill has long gone from the morning air and it looks as if it's going to be another scorching day in Pembrokeshire. The golden crescent of the beach is deserted. I've got the map and the guide books out of the bookcase in the sitting room and I'm trying to get my bearings. I didn't know that there was anywhere left in this country that was still so undeveloped.

Cwtch Cottage is pretty isolated. According to the guide books, there's a coastal hamlet nearby called St Brides that has a few pubs and a couple of streets of houses, but not much else. The biggest town within driving distance is probably St Davids. What the area lacks in major metropoli, it makes up for by having lots of rugged coves and deserted beaches. I can't wait to get out and explore.

'I've put some croissants in the oven,' Ella says. 'We can have breakfast out here.'

'I may never eat again,' Art mumbles.

'It's the drinking you should never do again, sweetheart.' Ella kisses the top of his head.

'I'm an old-school rock'n'roller,' he points out. 'That is what I do.'

I wonder what Harry's excuse is. He still hasn't surfaced yet and, do you know, I simply don't have the inclination to wake him.

Instead, I go back to my maps. There are some fabulous walks around here and, again, I can only wonder why I live in

99

London. Or why we don't come away to places like this at the weekend. It's a bit of an effort, for sure, but we could do it if we wanted to. I used to like nothing more than going hill-walking. When did I last do that? My thighs burn if I have to walk up a staircase now. When we do have time off work, we always do what Harry wants to do, which seems to involve not much more than sitting in a pub or, at best, a cinema. It's only when you have time to stop and think that it brings it home to you. I can't believe that I've got so out of touch with what I actually want to do with my life.

Ella brings out fresh, buttery croissants and puts them on the table along with creamy butter and some plum jam that she's bought at a local farmers' market.

'The supermarket might be miles away, but they have all the necessary requisites for the good life,' she says. 'Croissants, coffee, chocolate, champagne.'

As the rest of us tuck in hungrily, I notice that Ella doesn't eat anything herself. But, before I can ask her if she's all right, Noah arrives. I hoped that listening to him and Flick having sex for the best part of the night would make me feel more ambivalent towards him. But no. No such luck. The minute I clap eyes on him, my hormones go into overdrive once more.

It's not helped by the fact that he's wearing cropped combats that hang low, low on his hips and black leather flip-flops. That's it. Sum and total of attire.

'Hey,' he says. His eyes travel first to me and he smiles. All coherent thought goes out of my head and my mouth can't form a reply. Then he sees the true object of his affections and his gaze moves to Flick. 'Sorry I slept in.'

'That's what holidays are for,' Ella assures him. 'Help your-self.'

'Thanks.'

He passes behind Flick, who tucks a finger into the top of his combats and pulls him down to sit next to her. In his hand, he has a short-sleeved white shirt, which he pulls on, but doesn't button.

'Here, let me,' Flick says. 'What would you like to drink?'

'Tea,' he answers. 'White, two sugars.'

Flick makes a big fuss of pouring it out for him.

'Want a croissant?' she asks. This is the most solicitous I've ever seen her.

'Hmm. Sounds good.'

'You need to eat,' she purrs in his ear. 'Keep your strength up. You were busy last night.'

Noah flushes and looks down at his plate. As well he might.

'What does everyone want to do today?' Ella asks. 'There are some lovely beaches and some fabby places to go for a walk. We could head out to Trevallen and walk along the coast there. The views are spectacular and I know a nice coun-try pub where we could go for a late lunch halfway round.'

'Sounds great,' Noah says.

'Great,' Flick echoes. 'I love a long walk.'

Since when? Button it, Taylor.

'Grace?'

'I'm up for that,' I add. 'Are you sure you are?'

'I'm fine,' Ella says, waving away my concern. 'Think Harry will be keen?'

'I'm sure he will.'

I'm not actually at all sure that he will be, but as he's not appeared to give his vote, I'll put my own slant on it.

Plus I want to be occupied today. I want my body and mind to be busy enjoying themselves so that I don't really have time to think about how unhappy I am.

Chapter Sixteen

When we've eaten all the croissants and drunk all the tea and coffee, Ella and I clear up. In the kitchen, she says to me, 'Want me to warm some croissants for Harry?'

I shake my head. 'He doesn't usually eat anything in the morning.' These days he's normally too hung-over to eat and doesn't have anything until after his first lunchtime glass of wine. 'I noticed that you didn't have anything.'

'I'll have a bit of toast in a minute,' she assures me. 'I'm feeling fine now. The fresh air must have done me good.'

'Glad to hear it.' I glance at the clock on the wall. 'I thought Harry might have put in an appearance by now. I'll go and get him up in a minute.'

'There's no rush,' Ella says. 'We'll probably hang around in the house for a while yet. We're all here to do nothing more than relax,' she assures me. 'No pressure.'

I lean against Ella. 'You're a good friend.'

'No, you're better.'

'No, you're the best.'

We laugh with each other and I realise that I don't hear that sound often enough.

'Struggling with Flick doing her "love's young dream" act?' Ella asks.

'Do you think it's an act?'

'Yes. Isn't it always?'

'Maybe she's changed. She certainly seems smitten.'

'Think Noah is?'

I shrug. 'That I don't know.' Even though I do nothing but think about it. 'They kept me awake all night banging.'

Ella giggles. 'What *is* she like?'

'I wasn't going to give her the satisfaction of finding out that I knew she was having a good time while I wasn't. Is that mean of me?'

'I would have done the same thing.'

'Then you're mean too.' We giggle like schoolgirls.

'Want to swap rooms?'

'No. But if we go near somewhere that sells earplugs, then I'm going to get some. Big buggers!'

'Hopefully, he'll wear her out and she'll sleep like the dead from Monday onwards.'

'I can't bear to think about it.'

And I can't. Not even in a teasy way. Not for the reasons that Ella thinks.

She lowers her voice when she turns to me and asks, 'Do you think that Flick ever thinks about what happened with her teacher?'

'Yes,' I say, honestly. 'More than she'd admit.'

'That was years ago now.'

'I don't think that scars like that ever heal.' I lean against the cupboards and my mind goes back to our days in the flat, the parade of unsuitable men, her preference for ones she couldn't have, her reckless promiscuity. 'I'm sure it's the reason she chases after married men. Get her on a psychotherapist's couch and they could have a jamboree with her.'

Ella folds the tea towel and leans against the Aga. 'We're all pretty messed up just underneath the surface,' she concludes. 'Look at me and Art. We're not exactly a textbook couple.'

'But you've made it work,' I say. 'In your own way.'

'It's not ideal, though, and I don't know how much longer I can put up with it.' Ella tries a laugh. 'Scratch me and you'll reveal a seething mass of resentment. Why do you think I paint such angry pictures?'

'And all along I just thought you had Short Person's Complex.'

We both giggle at that.

'Please tell me that you and Harry are doing better now. I'm worried that you look so sad.'

I thought I was hiding it so well.

'I know that everything hasn't been great,' she continues. 'Let at least one of us out of the three be holding it together.'

I'd already told Ella some months ago, over a glass or two of wine, that we were having a bit of a rough time, without going into too much detail. She doesn't know that we're rapidly spiralling apart, haven't made love in months or that, to add fuel to the fire, I'm currently yearning for another man.

'We're still not right,' I admit. 'I'm hoping this week will help us to sort things out a bit.'

This would be a good time to tell Ella how I feel about Noah. She would offer some sensible words to stabilise the situation. She would warn me that no good could come of it. But I don't. I keep quiet. I keep my guilty secret to myself.

Ella comes and hugs me and, suddenly, I feel like crying. 'You deserve to be happy, Grace. We all do. Whatever that takes.'

Then she gives me the tea towel and I sob silently into it.

Chapter Seventeen

We all pull up in a line together at the car park in Trevallen. I refused to let Harry take the Bentley as I'm sure he'd still be over the limit. Plus the car is such a stupid, ostentatious thing that I can't bring myself to drive it. Instead, Harry and I piled in with Flick and Noah for the short journey over here. Now we clamber out of the back of Noah's ancient Range Rover. It's rusting, covered in dents and scratches, and needs a bloody good wash. It looks like a car that's used for day-to-day business on the estate, not a car that marks you down as a pompous prick. I may have read Flick wrong as, previously, she wouldn't have been seen dead in a car like this.

'Harry, you should have let Noah drive the Bentley,' Flick says.

No, I know my friend well.

'Not bloody likely,' Harry says. 'That car is like a child to me.'

'This is good, healthy dirt,' Noah teases Flick. 'You came all the way down to Wales in it and didn't catch anything.'

'I'm sure I have flea bites,' she protests. 'And I keep finding bits of straw in my Prada.'

'*Prada.*' Noah rolls his eyes at me and I give him a sympathetic shrug.

'I'll have to fumigate everything.' Flick brushes herself down with a shudder.

'Operation Make Noah Love Me?' I whisper in Flick's ear.

'Oh, yes.' She grimaces as she whispers back. 'Forgotten about that.' Then, out loud, 'It does have a certain rustic appeal, though.'

Noah laughs. 'Too late now,' he teases. 'You've been rude about my wheels.'

'Fuck,' Flick whispers to me through gritted teeth. 'This is going to be harder than I thought.'

I can only smile at that.

Ella has devised a long walk for us, taking in the clifftops, a pretty village and then a return route along the beach. I'm ready and raring to go. In preparation, I'm sporting denim shorts, red Converse, a white T-shirt and have brought a jumper in case the forecast day-long sunshine is a lie and it turns chilly. In the boot of Noah's car, I have walking boots. I had to dig them out of the back of the cupboard in our flat as they now rarely see the light of day. It will be good to get them back on again.

In contrast, Flick has on silk harem pants and a gypsy top teamed with wedge-heeled sandals. She's wearing Prada aviator shades. I look as if I am going on a hike. She looks as if she's going on to a film set. I'm wondering if she misunderstood the 'walk' part of today's activities. But, knowing Flick,

108

some unsuspecting male will probably offer to carry her all the way round. It could well be Noah. Thankfully, the man in question is wearing a T-shirt now, which doesn't show any of his skin at all. Something I'm very grateful for. Except his forearms and just a tiny peek of finely honed bicep. Gulp. If he peels the T-shirt off later, I'm a goner. As it is, I might just accidentally walk off a cliff. All I have to concentrate on is putting one foot in front of the other, nothing else.

Harry is very reluctant to go on this walk. He muttered darkly about the perils of exercise all the time while we were getting ready. This morning, even though he lay in bed for most of it, he still looks like death warmed up. Even by Harry's standards, he had an awful lot to drink yesterday. Now he looks terrible and I know I should feel sympathetic, but I'm finding it so hard to be kind when it's all self-inflicted. We've hardly spoken a word yet because everything I want to say sounds so judgemental that I'm better keeping my mouth shut. Then I feel awful. His drinking is clearly damaging him now and I can't just stand by and let that happen. But what can I do to stop this? Should I take the bottle away from him? Treat him like a naughty child instead of the responsible adult he's supposed to be? As I'm his life partner, is his excessive drinking my responsibility too? Do I become the difficult wife, if I monitor every drink he takes? Is that my role?

His face is puffy, his eyes red. He's grumbling a lot. He's only forty-four. That's a man still in his prime. Once I used to think that was a measly twelve years older than me – hardly even classed as a May to December relationship now. But suddenly Harry is acting as if he's twenty years older or more.

Or am I the only one who's suddenly noticed it? He comes up next to me.

'Are you OK?' I ask.

'Yes, why?'

'You don't seem to be very happy.'

'I'd rather be sitting in a deckchair with a newspaper than going for a walk.'

'It'll be nice,' I assure him. 'Ella's working hard to make sure we all have a lovely time. Please try to enjoy it. For me.'

His face softens. 'I'll love every minute of it. Just for you.'

I smile at him. 'Thank you.' I slip my hand into his.

Ella and Art jump out of their Mercedes. 'Right,' Ella says. 'This is where I'm planning to go.'

We all gather into a group and, on the bonnet, Ella opens the map.

Only Noah and I take any great interest as she outlines the route. Flick and Harry have wandered off already and are huddled in the corner of the car park, gossiping, no doubt.

'Does that suit everyone?' Ella asks.

'Looks great.' Noah seems keen. 'Want me to take the map?'

'Lead on,' Ella says.

'Ready, everyone?' Noah says and we all set off walking along the edge of the cliffs.

I wave Harry and Flick to rejoin the group while we all fall into step behind Noah to leave the car park and head into the fields that lead down to the cliffs. It's nice just to be tagging along for once and not be the person who's doing all the organising.

The breeze is strong, refreshing. The epitome of the word bracing. But it's the kind of day that makes you feel happy to be alive. We stride out – as much as we can with someone in wedge-heeled sandals and someone nursing a monumental hangover. We're strung out now along the narrow path. Flick and Harry are already at the back, lagging behind.

The path, worn in the grass by the feet of the many walkers who have been here before us, follows the contours of the rocky cliffs. The sheer drops are dizzying, not a good place to be if you have vertigo. I stop to admire the view and fill my lungs with the dizzyingly fresh air. The coastal scenery is stunning, rough and untamed. I want to go as close to the edge as I can and lean out, feel the wind in my hair, the chill sea spray on my face. My hair is whipped into a wild frenzy and I give up trying to control it.

We wait for Flick and Harry to catch up, then Ella balances her camera on a rock and sets it up to take a photograph of all six of us.

'Say cheese,' she instructs.

'Cheese!' we all shout and the camera clicks. She shows me the snap. All friends together. We're all beaming widely and it looks as if none of us has a care in the world. And they say that the camera can't lie.

'For posterity,' Ella notes and I wonder if she's had the same thought as me.

We set off again and Noah ushers Flick up next to him, so I drop back to be with Harry.

'OK?' I ask him.

'Fine.' He shrugs. 'It's all very ... *wild* ... out here, isn't it?'

What he means is that there's no Starbucks or Costa Coffee.

'It's beautiful,' I say.

'Yes,' Harry agrees. 'In its own way.' He peers reluctantly over the edge of the cliff. 'Not sure I need to get quite so close to it.'

We carry on. I notice that Noah stops to hold out a hand to Flick to help her wherever he can as she minces along behind him in her ridiculous footwear. I get a pang of jealousy as Harry is only wrapped up in his own misery, stomping along at the back, determined not to enjoy himself. Even Art, who is far more at home at a rock gig than on a clifftop, is having a great time. He chases after Ella with aeroplane arms and picks her up, throwing her over his shoulder. She squeals with delight. I've never been a rough-and-tumble person, but I suddenly get a pang of regret that no one has ever thrown me over his shoulder to run along a clifftop with me. Again, I get the feeling that there's a different person inside me just dying to break out.

I look at Harry. I want us to run together, roll in the fields, splash in the surf. Do crazy things. Harry looks as if he wishes he was anywhere else but here.

Birds of prey balance on the wind high over the sea.

'Kestrels,' Noah tells us. 'I've got my binoculars if anyone wants a closer look.' He pulls them from his rucksack and passes them around.

When it's Flick's turn, she declares, 'I never know how to use these bloody things,' and Noah instantly comes to her aid. She snuggles in close to him while he adjusts them for her and helps her to focus on the swooping birds.

'Grace? Want a look?'

'Yes, please.' Then he does the same for me, standing close behind me, arms over my shoulders, pointing out the birds. I resist the urge to snuggle.

'Look,' he says. 'There's a kittiwake too.'

A dainty white gull with a bright yellow beak and black beady eyes hangs on the wind while we watch it. Its cry of 'kitt-ee-waaayk' leaves you in no doubt where it got its name from.

'I'd forgotten that I like to watch birds,' I tell Noah as I return his binoculars. I don't think that the few scruffy city pigeons that visit my office windowsill count. 'I haven't done it for a long time.'

'I could sit here for hours,' he says with a contented sigh. But, of course, we can't because Harry is whining and Flick now says that her feet are hurting.

We follow the cliffs some more, then turn inland, our backs to the sea. In a line we hike through fields where swallows swoop close to us, buzzing around our knees, and even Harry is momentarily transfixed.

'They don't normally come so close,' Noah tells me. 'We're very lucky.'

'I do feel lucky,' I say. 'I feel lucky to be out in the open air, in the sun, away from the office and spreadsheets and twelve-hour days.'

He smiles at me and I feel luckier still.

We pass lily ponds replete with fat, waxy flowers floating on the water. Then we come out of a wood into a pretty, quintessentially British village. The sun is high, trying to burn us with the best of its rays. Harry is hot and sweating.

Feeling guilty about my lack of sympathy, I drop back again and walk next to him. 'Are you OK?'

'You don't need to keep asking me that, Grace,' he snaps. 'I'm here, aren't I?'

Then we turn a corner and Ella shouts out, 'Lunch stop!' and a thatched pub, bedecked with flowers, comes into sight.

Harry brightens. 'I'm OK now,' he says, his smile broadening. 'Just what the doctor ordered.' He completes the next few hundred yards with a spring in his step. 'I bet I could even get a phone signal here.'

Now I'm wishing that I'd pushed him off the cliffs while I had the chance.

Chapter Eighteen

We sit in front of the pub in its charming garden filled with summer flowers, bees buzzing lazily from one to another, and have lunch. Harry, Art and Flick get a bottle of red wine to drink between them, but the rest of us abstain and have soft drinks instead. We sit and eat our sandwiches, and I nick a few of Art's chips as I find out what he's up to on his next tour.

'It's going to be a long one,' he says. 'I've got a new band that's making a big impression on the metal scene and they've got a string of festival bookings in the Far East and then across Europe. I can't wait.'

'That's great.'

And while I'm genuinely pleased for Art that it's all going so well for him, I'm also worried that it looks as if Ella will be home alone again for some considerable time.

Momentarily distracted by good food and wine, Harry has forgotten all about Twitter, and he and Flick are enjoying a bit of jovial banter, which is nice to see. But, the minute he's eaten, he wanders off from the rest of us in search of a wretched phone signal. A few minutes later, Flick's phone beeps.

'Looks like Harry's in luck. I've just got a text for the first time.' She fishes it out of her pocket and reads the message, before quietly slipping it back.

By the time Harry returns, a few black clouds have appeared above us. 'It's going to rain,' he says.

Noah surveys the sky. 'Just a summer shower.'

But, as soon as the words are out of his mouth, a big, wet splot hits the table.

'Shower, my arse,' Harry says cheerfully. 'There's no way that I'm walking in the rain. Who says we retreat to the bar?'

'Bar sounds bloody good to me,' Art agrees. 'Too much fresh air makes me dizzy.'

'No,' I say. 'I can't sit inside on an afternoon like this. Noah's probably right. It's just a shower. It'll blow over quickly, I'm sure.'

'Let's sit in the bar until it does,' is Harry's solution. But I know what he's like. Once he's in there, on a comfy sofa with another bottle in front of him, there'll be no shifting him.

'I'm for walking too,' Noah says. 'That was a long drive yesterday and I want to stretch my legs.'

Flick looks disappointed. 'My feet are killing me,' she says. 'I think I'd rather stay here.'

'You don't mind if we carry on, do you?' Noah asks her. 'I've enjoyed my lunch, but I want to get moving again before I seize up.'

'I'd rather you stayed here.' She does her best coquettish look.

'We won't be long,' he promises, oblivious to the batting of her eyelashes. 'A couple of hours at the most.'

She tries a pout, but it looks as if Noah has made his mind up not to spend the afternoon in the pub. I see Flick glance at her shoes, and there's no way that she wants to get those wet.

'Free wi-fi inside,' Harry says, as if that's a clincher.

The rain is coming down a bit heavier now. Still a shower, but more insistently so. We huddle under the big umbrella over the table that had, not a few minutes earlier, protected us from the sun.

'Ella? Are you up for walking or drinking?'

'I think I'll stay here with Art,' she says reluctantly. I know that she'd love to join us really, but she still looks a little bit peaky to me, so it's probably wise. 'I can show you the rest of the route, Noah.'

So Noah spreads out the map on the table while she goes through it with him.

'We can go and pick up the cars at the other end,' Noah suggests. 'Come and collect the rest of you. Then you don't have to walk back at all.'

Harry and Flick clearly think that this is a marvellous idea. Ella hands me the keys to the Merc.

'Trust me with it?' I joke.

She kisses me. 'I'd trust you with my life, sweetheart.'

'Looks like it's just me and you that are the stalwarts, Grace,' Noah says.

The rain's so fine that I don't even bother to put on my

jumper or take my light waterproof from my rucksack. I'm sure there's an umbrella tucked in the depths of it too if I get desperate.

Noah goes to kiss Flick on the cheek, but she takes his head in her hands and gives him a lingering smacker. He pulls away, slightly embarrassed.

I kiss Harry too, on the cheek, and with less enthusiasm. 'Watch how you go with that,' I warn, nodding at the bottle. 'I don't want to have to pour you into the car.'

'Don't be a nag,' he grumbles. 'We're on holiday, aren't we? I thought the idea was that we'd have fun.'

That's what I intend to do. And I realise it's what Harry intends to do too. It's just that our idea of fun isn't the same any more.

Noah stands and hoists his rucksack on to his back. 'Ready, Grace?'

'Ready.' My mouth has gone dry. Looks as if it's just me and Noah blazing a trail. 'Got the map?'

He holds it up. 'Got the map.'

So, waving to the others, we stride out of the pub garden and set off down the path that will lead us back to the coast.

Chapter Nineteen

Noah and I fall into step, side by side, as we walk along the road and away from the pub. We say nothing until we're out of sight of the others. The few spots of rain have eased off already and the sun has come out all guns blazing again, so it was just a fuss about nothing.

Then he turns to me and says, 'Are you OK about this?'

'Leaving our reprobate friends in the pub?'

'Yeah. I'm the new boy here, I'm not sure how they'll take it.'

'I'm sure they'll be fine. They can cope without us for an hour or so.'

'I'm not really one for sitting in a pub all day. I'd rather be out doing something. Drink doesn't really interest me.'

Music to my ears. 'Me neither.'

'As long as they're all happy.'

'I think Ella would really have liked to come with us. But she's a bit tired today and it's good for her and Art to be together as they spend a lot of time apart.'

'That must be tough.'

'I think they've found a way to make it work.' I sound convinced and can only hope in my heart that it's true.

We continue on the road out of the village, hugging the hedge. I'm struggling to keep pace with Noah and I notice that, almost imperceptibly, he slows his speed slightly. Must have heard me huffing and puffing alongside him.

'He manages rock bands?'

'Heavy metal mainly. But yes, he's a manager. One of his bands is becoming quite successful. Sacred Days?'

'Never heard of them,' he admits, 'but then my knowledge of heavy-metal music is negligible. I'm into more soulful stuff.'

'Oh, really? Me too.'

'So Art's away a lot, travelling?'

'Most of the time. He goes all over the world. It means that Ella gets a lot of painting done.'

'I looked at some of her stuff on the internet when Flick told me about it. I thought it was great.'

'She does really well. Lots of commissions for big corporations and she always seems to be doing exhibitions or installations.'

'Ever go to them?'

'As often as I can.'

The truth is that I don't support Ella as much as I should, as work, as always, gets in the way. She had an exhibition a couple of months ago and invited me to the opening night. I ended up having to work late and missed the entire thing. That was wrong of me. I should have been there. Ella was understanding, of course. But I still felt terrible about letting her down. When we get home I'm going to make much more of an effort to work shorter hours and claim my life back.

'We have some of her paintings in our offices.'

'Flick told me that you're an accountant.'

'Yes.' And I bet that she made it sound as dull as dishwater. Which, essentially, it is. 'I'm a partner in a small practice in north London.'

'Enjoy it?'

'Loathe it with a vengeance,' I admit with a rueful smile.

'Then why do it?'

I shrug. 'Stuck in a rut, I suppose.'

'It's never too late to change.'

'No. But sometimes ruts can be difficult to climb out of.'

I don't intend to tell Noah that my hidden agenda for this week is to discover exactly what Harry and I are going to do with the rest of our lives because I certainly don't think I can spend it at Hoskins, Framling and Taylor Associates. Even though that's exactly what I find myself doing.

'I'm hoping that I'll come up with a new life plan after this holiday,' I confess, 'if that doesn't sound too grand. I'd love to live somewhere like this, but I don't know if I've got the bottle to leave the convenience of London.'

'Places like this are good for the soul,' Noah agrees.

'It's so hard to uproot once you've got settled into a partic-ular place, a particular way of life.'

'Perhaps you just need a bit of a jolt,' he says.

I don't tell him that the biggest jolt I've ever had in my – so far – mundane life was meeting him yesterday. Without mean-ing to, or even knowing that he has, he's sent my emotions into a tailspin. But that's something that only I will ever know.

We turn on to the coastal path. Noah stops and holds out his hand to help me over a stile. I take it and try not to think how good it feels when his fingers wrap round mine. I jump down and he catches me round the waist, steadying me. Is it my imagination, or do his hands hold on to me a moment longer than is strictly necessary for me to get my balance?

'Thanks.'

My voice is as wobbly as my knees. Maybe this was a bad idea. Maybe I should have stayed safe in the pub with Harry. Maybe Noah should have stayed safe with Flick.

He picks a delicate fern frond from the wall and then stoops to pick some wild flowers in the field – a sprig of pink wild campion and a tiny piece of cow parsley. He fashions them into a posy for me and then tucks it into the top of my rucksack.

'What's that for?'

Noah shrugs. 'For nothing in particular.'

'Well, thank you. It's lovely.'

'You're welcome.' Then he grins. 'Come on, last one to the sea is a cissy.'

So we run down the steeply sloping field, laughing together. Noah far outclasses me. Within seconds, he's streaked ahead and I'm puffing and panting behind. He stops and waits for me, hands on knees. It's good to see that he's out of breath too. Then I trip on a bump or a dip or over my own feet and, suddenly, I'm barrelling headlong into Noah's legs in a good impression of a rugby tackle. I take him out and we both end up in a giggling heap on the ground.

'I'm sorry, so sorry,' I say and, laughing, we lie flat on our backs. Then, just as suddenly, a wave of sadness threatens to engulf me. I can't remember last when I laughed like this with Harry, when we threw back our heads and let joyous noises come out of our mouths, our lungs, for no good reason. This is what I want to do. Be silly in a field with someone who loves me. Is that so much to ask?

Eventually, our laughter dies down and we lie next to each other in silence, staring up at the shifting sky. Dark clouds are rolling in, gathering over the sea.

Noah props himself up on his elbow and looks at me. 'Are you OK now?'

I blink away the tears that have welled up again and nod.

'I think that rain might be back,' he adds. 'We should get moving.' So he helps me up but, before we set off, he catches my hand and holds it tightly. 'That was fun.'

'It was.'

I think the unspoken message is that neither of us could imagine doing that with our respective partners.

'And you were the cissy,' he reminds me, which breaks the moment and starts us off laughing again.

We work our way down to the beach as the rain increases steadily. Our pace increases steadily too and we hit a small, secluded bay just as the rain sets in.

'Let's shelter here for a minute,' Noah suggests. 'The rain might pass.'

We both look at the gathering clouds out at sea and know that it's unlikely.

'I think we're going to get very wet.'

Noah consults the map. 'We're nearly halfway round the walk. Want to press on or make a dash back?'

Our eyes meet. 'I don't want to go back.'

'Me neither,' he admits.

In that split second, I feel that I can see into his soul and that mine is bared to him. My heart is banging so hard that I fear it will jump out of my chest. Then a thought shocks my addled brain. Is this love? Is this what it feels like? Is this what's happening to me? I have never felt like this with Harry. I'm sad to say it but my husband has never made my hands tremble.

I don't know this man, yet all I want is for Noah and me to be alone together. As if sensing my feelings, he takes my hand and it feels so right and yet so wrong. But I don't pull away. Our palms, slick with rain, burn together.

Noah leading me, we press on and the strength of the shower increases. The fine pitter-pattering soon turns to pelting rain. The sky blackens and the temperature drops.

'In here,' Noah says. 'Let's shelter.'

We find a rock tucked into an overhang by the cliffs and, hip to hip, settle on it. Pointlessly, I shake the rain from my hair. It's just a tangled mass of madness and there's not a thing I can do about it. Noah turns and he's so close that I can feel the warmth of his breath in the sudden chill. He reaches out and tucks one of my curls behind my ear.

'Should you put your sweater on?' he asks. 'Don't get cold.'

Untying my jumper from my waist, I pull it on, though I'm not actually cold at all. I feel almost feverish.

I tear my eyes away from him and stare out to sea, trying to marshal my scattered thoughts. In the swell there are three intrepid surfers, still catching waves that either toss or glide them back towards the beach.

I nod my head in their direction. 'That looks like great fun.'

'When I was at college, I always used to spend my summer breaks down in Newquay. The folks had a bit of a shack down there on Tolcarne beach. All I did was surf all day and work in a bar at night to pay my way.'

'Sounds idyllic.'

'I have only good memories.'

'Do you surf now?'

'Rarely,' Noah admits. 'I'm too far from the sea to make a dash there and back in what little time I have free. But I still love it and my parents are living down in Cornwall now, so I try to surf whenever I visit them – even when I'm on a quick turnaround.' He nods out at the raging ocean. 'There are some good surf beaches round here too. Less well known, but they'll still give you a good buzz. Perhaps we could give it a go later in the week?'

'I'd love that.'

He grins at me. 'Let's see what we can do then.'

I don't like to remind him that I can't see his girlfriend as a surfer chick and I wonder again what it is that they see in each other. Then I remember how busy they were all night. Apart from the obvious, of course.

'Any other family?' I ask. Not that it's any of my business.

'A brother in Chicago and a sister living the good life out in France. She has a couple of great kids, a host of pigs and chickens. The whole thing. We're close but don't see a lot of each other. My parents brought us up to be independent spirits. I think they'd be disappointed if we'd all ended up living in the same street. I never know where they're off to next. They're in their late sixties, but they're always travelling somewhere. I guess that adventurous streak never leaves you. They're out in Kathmandu for a few months, helping out at a small orphanage they support. We all try to get together at Christmas, but sometimes we don't even make that.'

I think how different that is to my parents whose interests still revolve around me and *Cash in the Attic*. They have led a quiet and unassuming life. My dad wanders down to the local Conservative club for half a pint of beer most evenings and my mother trots along to her WI meetings. I wonder who I'd most want to be like in my dotage and, as much as I love my parents, I think that I could quite easily give *Cash in the Attic* a miss.

'What about you?'

'Only child,' I say.

'Keen reader. Bound by duty.'

'That pretty much sums me up,' I admit.

Noah laughs. 'I'm sure there's so much more to you than that, Grace.'

'Really, I'm very straight. Very boring.'

'No, you're certainly not that.'

I flush under his intense gaze and, for sanity's sake, turn my eyes back to the sea.

We watch the surfers ride in on the waves for the final time then run up the beach towards us, laughing and joking.

They're young, late teens, and they all have straggly, bleached hair and toned torsos. They tumble over each other like excitable puppies. It must be nice to be so carefree. If this is how surfing makes you feel, then I should definitely try it. They have their whole lives ahead of them and I envy them their freedom. They are not yet entrenched in guilt, responsibility and Doing the Right Thing.

'Hey, man,' one of them hollers over to us. 'Want tea?'

By their pile of clothes and paraphernalia, I notice a Primus stove.

Noah looks at me for approval. 'Sure,' I say.

'That'd be great,' he shouts back.

'It'll be ready in five!'

So we watch the surfers pull on fleecy tops and fuss with their boards and make the tea. They bring it over to us in tin mugs and we budge up so that we can all sit down on the sheltered rocks together.

Within seconds the men are talking about surfing. I have no idea what half of it means as every sport has its own unintelligible jargon unless you're a disciple, but it's clear that they share a passion. Noah asks them about the beaches round here, which are the best for beginners, and, too soon, our tea is finished.

'We should press on, Grace,' Noah says. 'Unless you want to stay here all night.'

Right at this moment, that sounds like an appealing option.

But, instead, we thank the boys for our tea and then we all high-five each other. How very surfery! I feel as if I've joined a little club that, previously, I'd been excluded from. We watch them grab their boards and head back into the swell of the sea.

'Oh, to be young again,' he says wistfully as he watches them go.

'My sentiments exactly.'

Then Noah and I move on, climbing back up from the beach to the cliffs once more. He reaches out his hand and, with only a moment's hesitation, I take it.

'I don't think the weather's going to be kind to us at all,' Noah adds.

And I'm not sure that fate will be either.

Chapter Twenty

I hadn't realised how effectively the cliffs were sheltering us as, now that we've left our sanctuary, the rain seems to be coming in much heavier. The sky and the sea have both turned battleship grey and it's hard to tell where one starts and the other ends. The wind is driving the rain clouds towards us. I scrabble in the bottom of my rucksack for my waterproof, but by the time I find it, my jumper is already wet through, so I give up and leave it where it is.

'Stand on this side of me and tuck in,' Noah says. 'It'll shelter you a little bit.'

It's a lovely thought, but even the comforting bulk of his body does nothing to shield me from the onslaught of the elements. Then a thought hits me like a hammer blow.

'You know,' I say to Noah, 'I don't care that I'm getting wet. I haven't been this soaked through in years and I'm quite liking it.'

He shrugs. 'I work outside in all weathers, so I never mind it.'

We walk on, me embracing the rain, letting it run down my face, licking it from my lips. Soon we come to some grassy sand dunes and we work our way down towards Barafundle Bay. Before we descend too far, I stop and look out over the bay. This has to be one of the loveliest places on the whole earth: miles of golden sand stretch ahead of us, deserted because of the rain. Seems that we're the only people foolish enough to be out here.

'This is stunning.'

I want to fix this image in my mind for ever. Remember this as a very special day indeed. Close, so close, we just stand and look at it through the mist and rain. A rumble of ominous thunder rolls across the sky and the black clouds scowl down at us. But I've never felt lighter.

'OK?' Noah asks.

I nod. He takes my hand in his and helps me down the steep stone steps ahead of us, which are slick with water. Rivulets run down the sides like mini-waterfalls.

When we reach the beach a moment of insanity grips me. 'I want to paddle.'

Noah laughs. 'Today?'

'We're already soaked through.'

'Sure,' he says, good-naturedly. 'Let's paddle.'

So we sit on a rock and tug off our boots and socks. We leave them where they are and run down to the edge of the sea. The sand is freezing and, when the waves reach our toes, they're like ice.

I gasp and dance in the water. I can't decide whether I'm experiencing pleasure or pain.

'It was your idea,' Noah reminds me as he shivers with cold. 'Brrr!'

'So it was!'

I run into the sea up to my knees and splash and splash. Seconds later, he joins me and, holding hands for balance, we jump the waves together as the rain pours down on us. Then I remember my umbrella in my rucksack on my back and I pull it out.

'Bit late for that,' Noah notes.

'I don't think so.'

I open the umbrella and swirl it round. I start up with the opening bars of 'Singin' in the Rain'.

'Da-da-da-da-da-dah. Da-da-da-da-dah.'

I twirl and whirl and splash at the edges of the waves. Noah runs alongside me and I pass the umbrella to him. He spins expertly along the breaking surf – singin' an' dancin' in the rain. We stamp on the surf, one foot at a time, then both together. I drop the umbrella and we link hands and spin round and round together, in and out of the sea, until I shout out with joy. I let my head go back and cry out to the wind, 'Yeeeeee! Haaaaaaa!'

When we're all twirled out and breathless again, we link arms, leaning on each other, giggling.

Me, 'Just singin'.'

Noah, 'And dancin'.'

Big finale! 'In the rain!' we shout out at the sky together.

One last crazy spin and we chuckle at each other. Then we collapse in a heap and lie back on the wet sand, letting the rain sleet down on us, breathing heavily.

When we've finally composed ourselves again, Noah helps me up. He starts to brush sand off me and then, with a resigned grin, gives up. We pick our way softly along the edge of the surf, walking along the whole length of the beach and back. We both collect pretty shells as we go, comparing our treasures.

The question that I don't want to answer pushes into my brain. Would Harry do this with me? Would he be here with me on the beach being stupid in the rain? Would he dance like Gene Kelly just for the sheer fun of it? Would he spend time picking up shells?

The answer is no. He'd rather be in the warmth of the pub with a drink. I look over at Noah whose hair is plastered flat to his head. He has red, weather-worn cheeks and a broad grin, and I think that Harry doesn't know what he's missing.

Eventually, when we both start to shiver in earnest, we reluctantly go back up to the rocks on the beach and find our boots and socks.

'That was brilliant.' I feel as if every fibre of me is more alive than it's ever been before. My skin tingles as if it's been scrubbed all over. Now to practicalities. 'How on earth are we going to get our feet dry?'

'Here,' he says. 'Sit down.'

Noah takes my feet in his hands and rubs them down with the dry inside of his fleece. He doesn't take his eyes from my toes or look up at me at all while he does it, which I think is probably a good thing. And I'm glad that he's doing it briskly and that the sand is scratchy.

When he does look up, he asks, 'Better?'

'Thank you.'

I pop my socks back on, which, unfortunately, are wet and then my boots, which are wet too. Clearly I need some new, more waterproof ones. While I do that Noah brushes the sand from his own feet and puts on his boots.

'I daren't get the map out,' he says. 'I think it might disintegrate in this downpour, but I'm pretty sure there's a treat waiting for us just around the bend.'

'I don't think that I can cope with any more ecstasy,' I tease, but neither of us laughs.

Noah looks as if he's about to say something but, instead, he presses his lips together and turns away.

So we set off again, crossing the empty beach, and there's a silly, stupid giddiness in my heart that I can't ignore.

Chapter Twenty-One

There's also a heavy sogginess in my bottom that I can't ignore either, so when we come to a tiny harbour with a tearoom, I do nearly spontaneously combust.

'Hot chocolate?' Noah suggests.

'Lead me to it.'

We run the last few hundred metres towards the Boat House Tearoom, laughing. The doorbell clangs our arrival as we burst in through the door, still giggling. The torrential downpour has kept away all but the hardiest of tourists. In one corner there is a family wrapped up in serious waterproof gear but, other than that, we have the place to ourselves.

They look up at us. 'You sound happy,' the father notes.

'We are,' I say. 'We've been playing on the beach.'

It's clear from their faces that they think we're barking mad and it only makes us laugh more.

Noah orders hot chocolate for us both with whipped cream and marshmallows. He has a piece of chocolate cake and I opt for the yummy-looking millionaire's shortbread. We take them to a table by the window where we can still watch the rain and the restless sea. The family, their tea finished, fuss with zipping up their coats. With a cheery wave to us, they head out once again into the deluge. The children look as if they'd rather be at Disneyworld.

Now that we're alone in the tearoom, we sit quietly, our silliness spent. My fingers are red raw with cold. I wrap them round my mug, trying to encourage some feeling back into them. Slowly, they tingle back to life. Noah fiddles with a sachet of sugar, tapping it gently on the table, waiting for the grains to fall softly from one end to the other, gazing out of the window, watching the slow, reluctant progress of the sodden family as they clamber back up the cliff.

While I'm spooning melted marshmallow into my mouth, Noah leans in close.

'I'm thinking of giving up my work at the estate and moving to the coast,' he confides in me. 'It was one of the reasons I agreed to come here with Flick.' I feel myself flinch at the mention of her name. It sounds ridiculous but, for a few hours, it was almost possible to pretend that no one else existed except Noah and me. 'I've had my eye on this part of the world for a while.'

'Would you look for a similar job?' I'd imagine that posts like that are few and far between.

'Ideally, I'd prefer to do something for myself,' he tells me. 'I'm not sure what yet. Something outside.' He looks up and smiles. 'You've seen how much I like being out in the elements.'

'Yeah, I should say so,' I joke. Then I look round the bright, welcoming café. 'I wouldn't mind throwing everything in and running a little place like this. When it's not pouring down, I expect it's very popular.'

'I was thinking just the same thing. It's in a fantastic location.'

Noah hunches over his hot chocolate in contemplation while he stirs and stirs it. I'm just content to sit here and watch the movement of his long, strong fingers, his fringe flopping over his forehead, the drips of rain still on his cheeks.

'Could you do it?'

'I don't really know,' I admit. 'I used to be quite the cake baker at one time.'

Something else that I don't get time for now.

'Would Harry be interested in this kind of business?'

I shake my head sadly. 'Not a hope in hell.' He might just about be interested in running a bar, but I'm sure he'd end up drinking away the profits. 'I think he's happy where he is. Well, not exactly happy, but I can't see him ever wanting to leave his job.' He likes the status it confers on him, the money, the endless business lunches.

'Would you ever do it on your own?'

I recoil at that. On my own? It's not something that I've previously considered before. Could I do that? Leave Harry and strike out in a new life by myself? And, to be honest, it's a question that's struck at my core and is way too big for me to answer.

'I'm sorry,' Noah says, obviously reading the expression on my face. 'It's none of my business.'

'No. It's fine.' I brush crumbs from the table while I find the right words. 'Harry and I are going through a difficult time.'

Now I look up and risk a half-hearted smile. 'I'm sure you've noticed.'

He nods.

How could he *not* have noticed? He'd have to be blind.

'I'm sure we'll come through it.' As much as I hate to admit it, in my heart I'm not at all sure that we will. We're supposed to be bound together for ever, but I feel those bonds fraying with every passing day and, instead of Harry and I being the ones to pull them together, we're the ones who are tugging them apart. 'But I'm not sure the solution lies in running a tearoom though.'

We both laugh at that.

Then Noah lets out a long breath and says, 'I love my work on the estate, but I want something more. For me. I can't always be at the beck and call of someone else. The people that I work for are great but, essentially, they call all the shots. I don't want to be always beholden to someone else. On the plus side, I have very little in the way of outgoings there. Everything's provided for me. I live rent-free in a cottage in the grounds, eat in the café. I'm on call twenty-four hours a day, so I'm not out spending cash every night. It means that I've been able to save quite a bit of money. I'm not rolling in it, but there's enough to give me a start or to mean that I don't have to work for a year or two.'

'That's an enviable position to be in.'

'If I don't do something this year, seize it now, I'm frightened that the moment will pass me by.' Noah laughs softly. 'I don't know why I'm telling you this.' He's suddenly shy. 'I haven't even mentioned it to Flick.'

I'm not sure that my friend would be happy to hear these plans. They certainly don't fit with hers.

'In fact,' he adds, 'I haven't told anyone else.'

I reach out and my hand covers his. 'I'm glad that you did.'

'Will we both get our dream?' he says.

'I hope so.'

The problem is that I really have to figure out what mine is.

Chapter Twenty-Two

'Have you seen the time?' Noah says with a worried frown. 'They'll think we've fallen off a cliff.'

'I'll ring and let them know ...'

'No phone signal,' he reminds me.

I smack my forehead. 'Of course not. I keep forgetting.'

'It's amazing how quickly we've become dependent on all this technology.'

I think of Harry and his overriding addiction to Twitter. There are times when I'd like to grab his iPhone, hurl it to the floor and grind my heel into its smug, shiny screen. But I can definitely see the benefit of being able to make a quick phone call at this moment.

'We'd better get back,' Noah says.

Sadly, it feels as if the time that Noah and I have spent alone together is drawing to a close and, already, the others are beginning to encroach. He is my best friend's man, I remind myself. He belongs to someone else. As do I. Still, I can't deny that there's a connection between Noah and me. I've never felt that with any other man. I thought it was the stuff of fairy tales. If it was a different time, a different place, who knows what could happen? I think we would have had the potential to make a great couple. As it is, we've shared a few lovely moments together. Nothing more. Noah may, or may not, end up with Flick. And I have a failing marriage to sort out.

The Boat House Tearoom is closing up as it's five-thirty and the staff are making it clear that they have homes to go to, even if we haven't. We've been here for hours. The rain hasn't eased at all. But now we have to leave our welcome oasis of hot chocolate and cake and head back to the car park. Just as well, as I might be tempted to sit here for the rest of my life.

Noah checks the map one last time before we brave the deluge. 'It's not far now,' he assures me. 'One last big push.'

So we go out in the rain and, our heads down, we stride out. No more pleasant dawdling for us. No splashing in puddles or kicking at the surf. No silly twirling with the umbrella. I cast a longing glance back at Barafundle Bay. This place, this afternoon, will stay long in my heart.

Half an hour of solid trudging later and with heavy, aching legs, we finally hit the car park at Trevallen. Noah's Range Rover and Art's Mercedes are the only two cars left. There are deep puddles all around them.

'How am I going to drive Art's car like this?' I look down at my sodden clothes. 'He'll kill me.'

'I might have something in the boot,' Noah says. 'Let me look.'

So he opens the boot of his car and rummages inside. Sure

enough he finds a blanket. 'It's rough,' he says. 'We use it for the horses.'

I don't ask in what capacity. 'Nice.'

'Needs must.'

'Even my pants are wet. I'll ruin his seats.'

'Rub yourself down.'

Which is easier said than done when the rain's still coming down like stair rods. I take the blanket and rub myself with it.

'You'll have to put more elbow behind it than that. Strip off your jumper.'

I do so, but I'm standing shivering now. Noah tries to help me, but I get a fit of the giggles. He takes the blanket and rubs it over me like a towel. I've never had a man rub me down roughly with a horse blanket before. I quite like it and I laugh even more.

'Stand still, woman,' he instructs, trying to sound stern while I collapse in hysterics. 'I think that there are some black bin liners in the boot too,' he says, struggling to keep control of the situation. 'I'll make two holes in the bottom. If you take off your shorts and ... stuff ... and slip it on, that'll keep Art's seats dry. Stand in the lee of the open door. I won't peek.'

Now I'm completely convulsed with laughter.

'Grace,' he says, 'you're really not helping.'

While I fall about helplessly, Noah finds the bin bag, muttering to himself. I watch him rip two holes in the bin bag with his teeth and he measures it up against me.

'I think you'll find that's the perfect fit, madam. Now, clothes off.'

More cackling from me.

'Do it!'

So, hiding behind the open door of Noah's car, I take off my waterlogged shorts and pants in the car park. The wind whips round my bare bottom and the giggles grip me again.

'Come on, Grace,' Noah pleads. 'Get a wriggle on before you catch your death of cold.'

I slide into the bin bag. It looks like a huge black plastic nappy. More hysterics.

'I've found some string to tie it up with.'

I step out from behind the car door, tears of laughter streaming down my face. 'Ta-dah!'

Noah turns towards me with his serious face on, holding said string. As soon as he sees me striking a pose in the black bin bag, he dissolves into fits of laughter too.

'Don't,' I say, guffawing. 'What else can I do? I can't sit in Art's Merc in my wet pants and we have to get back to the pub.'

Noah is doubled up.

'You need to tie it tightly,' I say.

But he can't bring himself to stop laughing, so I snatch the string from him and wind it round my own waist.

When he is finally able to look at me properly, he says, 'Oh, Grace, you're never going to win any fashion prizes in that.'

I look down at myself. It's bad. 'You promised me couture,' I joke.

'You'll do. I can't imagine what the others will think. Maybe you need to take off your wet T-shirt too and put your water-proof on.'

That'll be my waterproof which is almost dry, in the bottom

of my rucksack. It's so light that it never would have kept this rain out anyway, so it might as well have stayed where it is.

'Good idea.'

I duck into my car-door changing room again and, already used to being naked in a public car park, peel off my wet T-shirt and my equally sodden bra. Slipping on my waterproof jacket, I zip it up tightly.

I stand out in the middle of a parking space and hold out my arms, giving Noah a twirl for his approval.

'You look beautiful,' he says and we both crack up laughing again.

'Stop it,' I chide. 'Or we'll never leave.'

'I'm ready when you are,' he says.

'Not sure that I can face the others in this get-up.'

'Truth be told, Grace,' he says with a sigh, 'I don't actually want to go back at all.'

Then our laughter dies and we just stand in the deserted car park, facing each other.

My throat tightens. 'Me neither.'

'This has been a good day.'

'The best,' I agree.

I want to reach out and stroke Noah's face, feel the graze of his stubble beneath my fingertips, the dampness of his skin against mine. I jam my hands deep in my jacket pockets so that I don't.

Standing there in my makeshift bin-bag hot pants and waterproof jacket, I know that it's a day that I'll remember for the rest of my life.

Chapter Twenty-Three

It's gone seven o'clock when Noah and I finally walk into the pub. It's true to say that our friends look mightily relieved to see us. Only Harry is stony-faced.

'We were about to send out the bloody coastguard,' he splutters crossly.

'Sorry, Harry,' Noah says. 'That was my fault. The weather that came in was horrendous. We had to seek shelter.'

In a lovely tearoom with hot chocolate and cake. Neither of us 'fesses up to that bit. We are both trying to be suitably penitent, but I still want to laugh.

'We knew you'd be all right with Noah,' Ella says.

Noah and I avoid looking at each other.

'What the hell are you wearing?' Flick narrows her eyes.

Again, it's hard not to dissolve.

'This year's collection of emergency rain clothing.' I do a twirl in my bin-bag ensemble. 'We got soaked through and I didn't want to get the seats wet in Art's car.'

Ella comes to hug us both. 'Well, I'm just glad that you're

both safe and sound. Despite the foul weather, was the walk good?'

Try not to gush too much, I tell myself. Don't mention the 'Singin' in the Rain' bit. 'It was very nice.'

'Yes,' Noah agrees. 'Very nice.' I hear a gulp in his throat and hope no one else does.

'Though the wise call was probably to stay in the pub,' I offer.

A smug look crosses Harry's face at that.

'Yes, very wise.' Noah again.

'We were just about to order dinner,' Ella says. 'Would you rather go home and change, Grace?'

You know, I wouldn't. I'm quite happy as I am. A little shared joke just between me and Noah. 'I'm fine like this,' I insist. 'As long as you don't mind being seen out with me.'

'You look ridiculous,' Harry comments.

But I don't mind at all. I want to stay in this idiotic outfit and, strangely, I feel quite sexy wearing nothing but a waterproof jacket and a bin bag. Only Noah knows that I'm going commando underneath and that sends a thrill to places that it shouldn't. That man definitely brings out the Little Miss Mischief in me. I probably do look a complete state, but who cares? I realise that I can't compete with Ella and Flick, who still look unutterably immaculate, but did they dance in the sea? Did they drink tea with cool surfers? Did they discuss their hopes for the future over hot chocolate and cake with a lovely, lovely man?

No. They did not.

'I'll get some menus,' Art says and he jumps up.

'Come and sit here, darling.' Flick pats the vacant seat next to her and Noah goes to her side.

A bit of my happy bubble bursts. There's an empty chair next to Harry, so I sit down too. 'Miss me?'

'I've been trying to phone you,' he concedes. 'But it was just dead at your end.'

'Never mind. We're here now.' I'm hot in my waterproof jacket and I unzip it a bit. 'Did you have a nice afternoon?'

'Few drinks,' he holds up his glass. More than a few, I'd say. I might look ridiculous, but at least I'm sober. 'Read the paper. Tweeted a bit.'

Of course.

'Everyone else OK?' I ask.

'Why wouldn't they be?' Bit bristly.

I shrug. 'No reason. Just asking.'

Flick is playing with Noah's wet hair, smoothing his fringe from his eyes, treating him as if he's been gone for a week. Flick smiles at me and winks as she pulls Noah closer to her. She's happy to have him back. Why wouldn't she be?

I look at her with mixed emotions. I know in my heart that she'll never have an afternoon like that with him and I feel so sorry for her. But then I'll never have the nights with him that she does and I feel sorry for me too. Noah laughs at something she whispers to him. Seems as if he's forgotten me already. Which is exactly how it should be.

Chapter Twenty-Four

We eat an excellent dinner. For a few hours, all the tensions disappear and we're just good friends having a laugh together once more. I wolf down my chicken casserole as if it's my last meal. All that exercise has given me an appetite. I even have a couple of glasses of red wine and barely glance at what Harry's drinking. Art makes us all guffaw by telling us stories of the many and varied forms of bad behaviour that his bands indulge in. Flick tries to out-anecdote him with tales of her troublesome authors. We all tease and joke. For the rest of the evening, we forget our niggles and are just having fun on holiday as a group.

It's closing time when, happy and full of good food and wine, we finally drive back to the cottage. Art reclaims the keys to his Mercedes, but Ella drives it home as she's the only one who's not been drinking all day. I sit with Harry in the back of Noah's Range Rover, still with my black bin-liner pants on. Flick keeps her hand possessively on Noah's thigh all the way back and, somewhat overtly, I think, slides it up and down on the denim of his jeans, caressing him. When I can bear to watch it no longer, I lean against Harry and spend the rest of the journey staring resolutely out of the window.

When we get back to the cottage, it's gone midnight and, frankly, I feel dead on my feet. All I want to do is fall into bed and, hopefully, get more sleep than I did last night. More importantly, I'm hoping that Noah is tired too after our long walk and he'll also fall asleep before his head hits the pillow.

While Art goes through to light the fire in the sitting room, Ella stays in the kitchen to make hot drinks for us all. The others make themselves comfortable on the squashy sofas while I slip upstairs to change out of my bin bag into my jeans and a sweatshirt. It would take very little persuasion for me to climb straight into bed. But, having been missing for most of the day, I feel I should be sociable now. So, reluctantly, I go back downstairs and join Ella in the kitchen.

'That looks better,' she says when she sees me.

'Think so?' I pose so that she can check out my new ensemble.

'I'm not saying that the bag-lady look didn't suit you but . . . ' We giggle.

'Everyone's ordered coffee,' she says. So together we set about making it. Ella spoons the fresh coffee into the cafetière. 'How did you get on with Noah today?'

'Great.' I keep my voice as steady as I can. 'He seems lovely.'

'Certainly better than any of Flick's other boyfriends.'

'The ones that we've seen, that's for sure.'

'Think they'll stay together?'

I aim for a disinterested shrug. 'I've no idea.' If Flick has anything to do with it, then I'm sure they will.

'I think she's right,' Ella whispers. 'He doesn't seem as keen to me.'

'Who knows what's going on in his head? He's a man.' Be flippant. Be light.

'You like him, though.' Ella gives me a searching look.

I wonder exactly how much she has seen. I wonder, does she realise that my heart is banging in my chest simply because we're talking about him?

'What's not to love?' I say as non-committally as I can muster.

How can I even begin to voice the fact that I think I have fallen head over heels for my friend's man? How would that sound, even to Ella, who is possibly the most tolerant and non-judgemental person on the planet? Even she doesn't like it when Flick parades her married men around. How would she feel if she knew that, in my heart, I'm betraying Flick? I don't know how I can even be thinking like this when Flick deserves happiness as much as anyone. They say that you can't help who you fall in love with, but I firmly believe that you can help what you do about it. And I am going to do nothing. Except quietly wonder to myself, in dark moments, what might have been.

I line up the mugs and try to divert the conversation away from Noah. 'How did you enjoy today? Sorry to leave you in the pub.'

'I think the rest did me good,' she admits. 'But I was bored out of my head. I so wanted to come with you guys. That clifftop walk is one of my favourites, but I just felt that I needed to stay with Art. Let's face it, he did jolly well to walk so far!'

'Everything OK between you?'

Ella sighs. 'It's fine. I think. I love being with him, Grace, but sometimes I wonder if the feeling's entirely mutual. Even after all these years we've been together, he still likes his space, his freedom.' She fills the cafetière with hot water and stirs it with a melancholy air. 'I just like being with *him*, whereas Art always likes an audience. He's never happier than when we've got a house full of ragtag musicians draped over the sofas and he's holding court.'

The strains of his guitar drift through from the sitting room and Ella rolls her eyes as if to say that proves her point.

'I want to settle down, but I'm frightened even to discuss it with him. I'm tired of not knowing where he is or who he's with. Sometimes if I ring him late at night when he's away, I can hear that there's someone else in the room, but I never like to ask who. Being kind, it could be one of the band members but, more often than not, I think it's another woman. It tears me up inside even now.'

'Oh, Ella.'

'What will it be like in ten years' time, Grace? Am I still going to spend most of my time at home alone, wondering what he's up to?'

'You need to talk to him.'

'The sad thing is, I know in my heart that Art is perfectly happy with the way things are. He won't see any reason to change. What makes it all so stupid is that part of me loves his "rolling stone" nature. That was one of the qualities that first attracted me to him.'

Art and Ella met when she got her place in Camden, scraping a living as an artist and topping up her income by working as a receptionist in a gallery. The pub on the corner of her street was a rowdy, biker place – it now serves deli-boards featuring houmous, chorizo and complicated dishes involving beetroot to the trendy young things from the music television station near by – and Art used to play guitar there in a band on Saturday nights. Ella pretended that she liked their music, but they were truly awful. I think Art was the only one with any talent. Pretty soon after that, he gave up playing professionally and moved into management. They've been together for about the same time as Harry and me, eight years or so, but I bet they're lucky if they've actually spent three of those together.

'What if we bring children into the equation?' she continues. 'Will I be left bringing them up on my own? Who would want that?'

'Is it likely?'

Ella turns away from me. 'He says that we can't afford them. That his work is too unpredictable.' Now she's cross. 'We have two flats between us and two top-of-the-range Mercedes in the drive, for heaven's sake.' Art bought her car for her as a birthday present for her thirtieth birthday in a typically grand gesture. Nice but, like me, Ella would probably be happier in a battered, old runaround. 'Exactly how much money do you need?'

'Everyone who has kids says that if you thought about it

too much, you'd never be able to afford children. Or, indeed, find the right time to have them.'

'I had such a happy childhood, Grace. My parents were wonderful people. They were nothing but supportive and loving throughout my life. We were never a wealthy family, but I wanted for nothing. It was a great sadness to them that they were never able to have more children. I think they would have made their very own Waltons family if they could. They always let me know that I was cherished. I'd love to be able to do that for kids of my own.'

'You were very lucky.'

'That's all I want, to settle down with a proper husband, one who's around every night, have a couple of freckle-faced kids. Maybe even a dog. Is that too much to ask? Why have our generation of women made it so hard for ourselves to do that? When did we stop regarding that as a good and noble thing to do? Why do we have to push ourselves to be successful at something else, rather than being happy to be defined as a home-maker and mother?'

'Maybe it was at the same time that men became unreliable and were as likely to dump us for a younger model when the fancy took them.'

Perhaps our mothers were the last generation who were able to rely on their men as the breadwinner and protector of the family. Since then the traditional family unit has become much more fractured. To the detriment of everyone.

Ella sighs. 'Makes me glad that I am a successful artist with money in the bank in my own right.'

At that moment, Art comes through to the kitchen,

rubbing his hands together. 'What are you two gossiping about now?'

If only he knew.

'Nothing much.' Ella shrugs dismissively and we exchange a glance. 'Girls' things.'

Art gives a mock shudder and I thump him. 'Where's that coffee got to?'

Ella smiles at him. 'Just coming, baby.'

'Any more brandy?' He pokes about on the big dresser, shifting around the range of half-empty bottles.

'I think you and Harry polished off what was left last night. We'll have to restock when we do the next supermarket run. Have a rummage in the cupboard underneath and see what there is. There are all kinds of random bottles at the back. I think there are a few bottles of spirits, too. There might be some of Dad's whisky. Though it will probably have an inch of dust on it.'

He twines his arms round her waist and hugs her, and at the same time that Ella's hands go, protectively, to her stomach, I notice that her waist isn't the skinny little thing that it was. And then I twig: the not drinking, the urge to settle down. Is Ella pregnant? I look at her again. I'm sure she is.

'Here.' I take the tray of coffee cups from her. 'Let me carry that.'

We exchange another glance and she knows that I know. But it's clear that someone else in the room doesn't. All she has to do now, I guess, is break the news to Art.

Chapter Twenty-Five

Flick is all over Noah like a rash. They're on the sofa together and she's snuggled into him with her legs slung over his. She can't stop touching and stroking him. It seems as if she's trying to prove that she's all loved-up. Is this for my benefit? If it is, I can hardly bear to look.

Even if Flick is annoyed with me, I can't stop thinking about today and how Noah and I got on as if we'd been friends for years. I wish I could stop. There's no doubt that I should just put him firmly out of my mind and not be thinking about ways that we can be alone together again. That way madness lies.

'What shall we do tomorrow?' Ella pipes up. 'Anyone fancy going to the beach? The weather forecast is good.'

'The forecast was good for today,' I remind her. 'But we got soaked.'

Noah and I exchange a furtive glance and we both break into a smile.

'Only some of us,' Flick says crisply.

'Well,' Ella intervenes, 'it's *supposed* to be a sunny day.'

'Why don't we go up to Portgale beach?' Noah suggests. 'I was talking to a couple of surfer guys today who said you can rent gear there. If anyone fancies trying their hand at surfing.'

'I don't think so . . .' Flick says and then tails off.

'I'd like a go,' Art says. 'I haven't been on a surfboard in over twenty years.'

'Me too.' Might as well put in my vote.

'Harry?' Ella.

He shakes his head. 'Count me out. I'd rather be in the pub.' That goes without saying.

'No one has to surf,' Ella offers. 'It's a lovely beach. The perfect place just to sit and watch the sea. And there's a pub right on the front, Harry.'

'Sorted! Let's all go to the beach,' Flick says decisively. 'I might want to give it a go myself when I see that surf.'

'The beach it is, then,' Ella says.

An hour later, we're all in bed. I'm tired down to my bones and all I want to do is sleep. I'm under the duvet, drifting off to the soporific shwooshing of the ocean.

Harry, against form, hasn't even tried to get on to Twitter and is lying next to me. He must have tweeted himself out in the pub. My eyes grow heavy and I'm really knackered after all my walking today.

Lovely, lovely sleep is coming, coming, coming.

Then I feel Harry's hand on my breast. He starts playing with my nipple and it's really annoying. I want to bat his hand away. All night, he's hardly exchanged two words with me and now this? A second later I realise that the rhythmic sounds are coming from next door again and I'm sure that's what's getting Harry aroused. This is all I need.

'I'm sorry, Harry,' I mumble, 'but I'm really tired.' And I want to bury my head in the pillow.

'Come on, Grace,' he wheedles. 'When did we last have sex? I can't even remember.'

That's usually because you're pissed or on Twitter or both and have no interest, I think, but I bite my tongue. This holiday is supposed to be about us getting back to where we used to be in our relationship, not about arguing.

He starts to kiss me, and he tastes of red wine and whisky and, for the first time ever, I find myself repulsed by my husband. I'm shocked to my core, but Harry is oblivious. The muffled pleasured moans from Flick only seem to serve to make him more determined and he pulls down my pyjama shorts. I pull them back up.

'Harry, no,' I say. 'Not now. Someone will hear us.'

'They're all too busy themselves,' he says with a grunt and carries on regardless. 'I love you, Grace. Why don't you show me that you still love me?'

'Not like this, Harry. Let's put the light on and sit and talk.'

His hand is between my legs and I'm dry, unwilling, but he's rubbing, rubbing, rubbing anyway.

'Harry, you're drunk. Stop it.'

But he doesn't stop. He pulls up my top, sinks his head on to my breasts and nuzzles. His stubble is rough, scratching my skin.

'Harry, no.' I push him away and he falls back on the bed.

Then I realise that nothing is going to happen because Harry is incapable of making it happen. He sits there looking dejected, broken.

All the fight goes out of me and out of him too.

He flops next to me on the pillow and wrenches his hands through his hair in frustration. 'I want to love you again, Grace.' He's almost crying now.

'Hush,' I say. 'It's all right.'

'It's not all right,' he counters and his voice is bitter, crushed. 'Nothing is.'

I curl into him and stroke the tears from his cheeks. 'Maybe not now. But it can be again. We just need to try.'

He wipes his eyes with the back of his arm. 'I'm such a fuck-up.'

'You're not,' I whisper. 'We just seem to have lost touch with the people that we once were.'

From the back of my mind the thought pushes through that I'm only just beginning to think about the person that I want to be and I can't go back to being Grace the good girl, Grace the accountant, Grace the dutiful wife.

'I'm an idiot if I lose you,' he says.

'I'm not going anywhere,' I promise. 'But things have to change, Harry. We can't go on like this.'

Perhaps the best thing for us to do is pack our bags and go home. I love this place, love being here. I know that Ella would be so disappointed, but we should leave. I have to put some distance between Noah and myself so that I can concentrate on my husband.

'I'll do anything,' he says. 'Anything.'

This would be the time to raise the issue of his drinking and make him realise the detrimental effect it's having on us both, but I don't. Instead, I squash it down as I always do as I just don't have the energy to face it now.

'We have a lot to talk about. Let's not do it when we're tired and emotional. Things always look better when you've slept on them.' I rest my head on his shoulder and his arms twine round me as he pulls me close.

'We'll be OK, Grace,' he assures me. 'I just have to get my head round some stuff.'

Me too.

He kisses me again and this time it's tender and I don't protest when his hands move over me. The kiss deepens and I close my eyes as he moves above me. This time we make love almost like we used to do, but as Harry comes I feel as if he's trying to lose himself in me. I know it because that's exactly what I'm trying to do too.

Chapter Twenty-Six

Another sleepless night. I lie awake until dawn, going over what has just happened between Harry and me, wondering whether I actually still love my husband at all. At the moment, I sometimes struggle to like him. But last night I believe there was a glimmer of hope that we could rescue our marriage. I may be clutching at straws, but I feel that I need to.

When I hear the clink of cups and the running of the tap in the kitchen, I pull a sweatshirt over my pyjamas and go downstairs.

As I thought, it's Ella in the kitchen, brewing up as usual. I pause at the foot of the staircase, forming sentences in my head. I should tell her that Harry and I need to go home and sort out the mess of our marriage in private – away from here, away from Noah, away from everyone. I know how disappointed Ella will be and I'd love to stay here more than anything but I think it's wise if we leave. But, before I can speak, she leans over the sink, holding her stomach and retching drily.

'Morning,' I say. 'Not well again?'

'Still a bit pukey,' Ella admits. 'Flick's already up. She's out on the beach. I'm just making tea for us.' She straightens up and wipes her mouth on some kitchen roll.

'Better now?'

A nod. 'Come out with us, we can have a good gossip before the boys get up. Will you be warm enough?' She indicates the jumbled rack of coats by the door. 'Put my fleece on if you're not.'

I stroke her hair from her face. 'Is this sickness happening every morning by the way, Ms Hawley?'

Ella looks up at me. 'Pretty much.'

'You know, you'll make a lovely mum,' I say.

Ella folds her arms protectively across her tummy. 'I knew you'd guessed.'

I nod. 'Only last night.'

'I don't know for sure myself yet.'

'Really?'

'Oh, Grace,' she says, a sob in her voice. 'I haven't even dared to take a test. What if I *am* pregnant? How the hell am I going to tell Art?'

'This wasn't planned then?'

'Not by a long way.' She massages the little mound pressing against her jeans and then regards it with despair. 'It might just be bloating.'

'Bloating?' We both laugh at the ridiculousness of her statement. 'I've heard it called some things before.'

'What am I to do?'

'First thing is to make *absolutely* sure,' I offer. 'You say you haven't done a pregnancy test yet?'

She shakes her head.

'We should get you to the nearest chemist straight away and buy one.'

Ella grimaces. 'That would make it all too real. I'm happily in denial at the moment.'

'Not knowing for certain isn't going to hold it back. Forewarned is forearmed.'

'It's not that I don't want it. I do. Desperately. I couldn't wait to be pregnant.'

'But?'

She looks stricken. 'I know that Art won't feel the same.'

'You might be surprised.'

'Yes,' she says, but she doesn't sound convinced.

'You're not going to be able to keep this from him for ever,' I point out, unnecessarily.

'I know. I just need to find the right time.'

I think that the right time is now, but there's no point in pressing home the point. 'Are you going to tell Flick?'

Ella shrugs. 'I should do. I hate it when we have secrets from each other.'

I don't know if that remark is aimed at me in any way, but it makes me blush nevertheless.

'Why don't you break the news to her and then we'll all take a trip to the nearest chemist's now?' Besides, it might look odd if just the two of us scuttle off together on a mission.

'You're right.' She sighs resignedly. 'I need to get it over and done with.'

'It'll be a weight off your shoulders when it's out in the open. Then we can all celebrate together.'

Ella brightens. 'We could run into St Davids, perhaps grab a coffee while we're there for cover. What'll we tell the boys?'

'I'll think of something. We'll leave a note. If we get a move on, we can be there and back before they're up and notice that we've even gone.'

'I don't really feel well enough to drive,' she admits. 'I'm still a bit wobbly.'

'Don't worry. We'll take the Bentley,' I say. I hate it with a passion, but I'll drive the bloody great lumbering thing if it helps my friend out. 'Harry's left the keys on the hook over there.' I nod towards them.

Ella smiles weakly. 'Thanks, Grace.' She eyes me properly. 'You look as bad as I feel. I'm betting that you didn't sleep a wink again.'

'I didn't.'

'Did Flick and Noah's nocturnal activities keep you awake?'

'No.'

I can't even begin to tell her what it was that left me feeling bleak and staring at the ceiling until first light broke. How can I burden Ella with that when she has so much else to contend with? Harry and I might be struggling, but there's no way that we can leave now. I need to be here for Ella. It doesn't matter what's going on in my life, I'm going to be at her side until she gets through this.

I manage a smile. 'Just thinking.'

While Ella pours out tea for Flick, I take my own. The heat has gone out of it and I knock it back quickly so that we can get going.

'Put your shoes on, Ella. I'll get Flick. We can tell her that we need to go into town to get something for your "bloating".'

She laughs at that and some colour comes back to her wan face.

'Don't worry,' I say. 'We'll make sure that it's all right. You know we will.'

'What would I do without you both?' she says.

I slip my arm round her tiny shoulders and hug her to me tightly. 'You'll never have to worry about that.'

'Thanks, Grace.' Ella wipes a tear from her eye and I do the same.

'We can't stand here blubbing. We'd better get a move on.' Finding a Post-it note, I scribble on it, 'Popped into St Davids for urgent supplies. Back as soon as we can! E, G & F XXX.' That should be suitably cryptic.

Outside, Flick isn't on the terrace, but has wandered down to the beach where she's sitting cross-legged on the sand. Without her make-up and her skyscraper heels, she looks ten years younger than her thirty-two years. My heart squeezes with love and affection for her. We've been through a lot together in all the years that we've known each other – since we were wide-eyed and reckless teenagers, filled with anticipation for life and all that it promised. How can I think of betraying her trust and friendship, even if only in my heart?

'Hey,' I say.

She starts when I speak.

'I'd gone into a trance,' she says. 'It's nice to have some time to stop and take stock. I never have time to do that.'

Like the rest of us. But now I don't have time to find out

what's on Flick's mind or what's making her frown with worry. I hand her the tea. 'Ella needs to run into St Davids. Coming with us?'

Flick shrugs. 'Sure. Right now?'

'Drink your tea as quickly as you can.'

'What's the rush?' She glugs it despite the question.

'Ella can tell you herself while we drive. Are you ready?'

She looks down at herself. 'Will I do like this?'

Flick is wearing cut-off denim shorts that show off her toned, tanned legs – a result of the obligatory Pilates classes in LA – and a crisp white shirt.

'You look beautiful,' I tell her truthfully. 'As always.'

'You've always been the diplomatic one, Grace,' she says as she stands and brushes the sand from her skin.

'I'm not being diplomatic, I'm being honest.'

She puts her arm round my shoulders and together we walk back up the beach to the cottage.

'I don't see enough of you,' she says. 'When did we last get together?'

'Ages ago,' I concede. 'You know how it is. You're busy. I'm busy.' The last few times we've all tried to hook up it just hasn't worked out. This isn't the time to say to Flick that I thought she was trying to avoid me. 'It's not for lack of trying.'

Flick stops suddenly and turns to me. 'I love you,' she says, and there's a terrible underlying sadness in her voice. 'I love you and Ella more than you'll ever know.'

'I know. And we love you.'

Then we walk back to the cottage, me feeling wretched and guilty for the dark thoughts in my heart.

Chapter Twenty-Seven

I swing the Bentley out of the drive and into the lane. The gravel crunches loudly as we turn. At Flick's behest, we've got the roof down and our hair is blowing wildly in the breeze.

'Woo-hoo,' she shouts as we hit the main road. 'This is the way to travel. Woo-hoo!'

The Bentley purrs along, eating up the miles. Two Lycra-clad cyclists puffing up the hill stop to stare at us, slack-jawed. I hate this bloody car.

'Christ, this is like a road trip,' Flick expounds. She's in the back seat, arms reaching up to the sky. 'We're like Thelma and Louise and . . . someone else!'

'I don't like to remind you that Thelma and Louise's road trip ended very badly,' I say.

'Oh, shit,' Flick says. 'You're right.'

And she's the one who's the film agent.

'I'm hoping this excursion will end with nothing more than good news and a celebratory cup of tea.' I look over at Ella, offering up her cue.

Ella turns in her seat. 'I've got something to tell you, Flick.' She takes a deep breath. 'I think I'm having a baby.'

Flick's head snaps up. 'You're kidding me?'

I laugh. 'I think that's the same as congratulations, Ella!'

'Omigod,' Flick continues. 'I'm just so shocked.'

'I'm not sure yet,' Ella continues, 'so that's what we're going to St Davids for. Grace has press-ganged me into getting a pregnancy test.'

'I had no idea you and Art were even trying for a kid. Why do I not know this?'

'That's the one snag,' Ella admits. 'We weren't "trying". Far from it. This little one sneaked in when we weren't watching.' Her fingers rest on her barely-there bump with affection.

'Fuck,' Flick says, pointlessly trying to smooth her hair against the best efforts of the wind. 'How long has Grace known?'

'I guessed last night,' I offer. Flick's clearly annoyed, thinking she's been left out of the loop. 'I asked Ella only an hour ago. Just before I came to get you from the beach.'

'Oh.' She's slightly placated now, I think.

'I haven't even told Art yet,' Ella explains. 'You can't breathe a word yet, Flick. This *definitely* wasn't in his life plan.'

'He'll be cool,' Flick assures her. 'Art can cope with anything. You know he can.'

'I'm not sure.' Ella's fingers fiddle with the seat belt. 'I'm terrified to tell him.'

'Have a few stiff drinks and spill the beans. It's the only way. He'll come good.'

'I'm quite probably pregnant,' she reminds Flick. 'No more "stiff drinks" for me for a while.'

'That's all a load of bollocks,' Flick says. 'My mother says she smoked like a trooper and drank gin all the time she was up the duff with me. What harm did that do?'

Ella and I laugh. It's not hard to see that Flick is the product of a chain-smoking, hard-drinking parent.

'What?' she says, feigning hurt.

We all giggle and, suddenly, it's like going back ten years when we were girls together, before life had started to weigh us down. I'm glad that Flick is here with us. She always adds some much needed levity to a situation. We sweep into the car park in St Davids, still laughing.

'God, I hate parking this thing,' I say. 'It's such a monster.'

I find the biggest space that I can – frankly, they all seem small when you're in a car this size – line myself up and put the car into reverse. The girls become quiet while I start my manoeuvre.

'Want me to get out and guide you in?' Ella offers.

'I'm fine,' I assure her. The parking sensor beeps calmly.

As I'm carefully reversing back, tongue out in concentration, totally focussed on getting this bastard parked up, Flick says, 'I've got some news of my own.' She takes a deep and shuddering breath. 'I'm going to ask Noah to marry me.'

At that point, I let out an involuntary gasp, my foot – also involuntarily – hits the accelerator instead of the brake and I shoot backwards at high speed. The beeping of the parking sensor goes into total overdrive. Then there's an almighty bang and a disturbing, crumpling sound. The Bentley comes to an abrupt halt.

Chapter Twenty-Eight

We're all out of the car in seconds. 'Oh,' I say. It's not good. It's not good at all. 'I didn't see that post.'

There's a bollard at the back of the parking space. It's two feet high and painted in such an eye-watering shade of bright yellow that you can probably see it from the moon. It's now firmly embedded in the bumper and boot of the Bentley. The metal of the car is crumpled like a tissue around it. Harry's personal number plate is bent beyond recognition.

I would like to lie down on the floor and cry. Or die.

'You hit the accelerator, you daft cow,' Flick says as the three of us stand and stare at it, stunned. 'What were you thinking?'

'I don't know,' I mumble in the face of her exasperation.

But I *do* know what I was thinking. I was thinking about Flick's announcement that she was going to propose to Noah, of course. How can I tell her that? My face turns bright red.

'It's not that bad,' Ella says.

Flick whirls on her, open-mouthed. 'You're not going to

hide that with a dab of nail varnish. That'll cost thousands to put right.'

'I'm not sure that Grace needs to hear that just now,' Ella points out.

I manage to shake myself out of my daze. 'Are *you* all right?' I ask Ella.

'I'm fine,' she assures me. 'It's you I'm worried about.'

I'm worried about me too. Flick's right. This is going to be one expensive bump to fix.

'I'm fine too,' I reply.

'So we're *all* fucking fine,' Flick says. 'Harry, unfortunately, *isn't* going to be fine. You know how much he adores this car.'

Indeed I do. More than me, that's for sure.

'She couldn't help it,' Ella says. 'Who would think to put a bollard at the back of a parking space?'

'A man. Who else?' Flick snaps. 'If women designed car parks, the spaces would be twice as big and there'd be no posts.'

'I don't know what happened,' I offer pathetically.

Flick's right. Harry will not be fine *at all*. He probably would have preferred it if *I'd* been badly damaged and the car – his shiny, shiny, expensive, status symbol of a car – was all right. I can hardly bring myself to look at it.

Even after our discussion last night, I'd say that it looks as if the chance of my husband falling in love with me all over again on this holiday has become extremely remote. We are starting to attract a crowd. Men who have parked their Ford Fiestas in the more time-honoured fashion come to gloat at our misfortune.

'Let's get out of here. There's nothing we can do about the car,' Flick concludes. 'Just pull it forward, Grace. We'll have to face the music with Harry when we get back.'

'I'm sorry, Ella,' I apologise. 'I didn't mean for our mission to turn out like this.'

'Don't worry, Grace. It's not your fault.'

But I'm very much afraid that it is.

'It's still drivable,' Flick says. 'It'll get us home all right. As long as Grace can keep it on the road.' She throws me an exasperated glance, which I let bounce off me. 'Let's go into the city centre and get your pregnancy test. Hopefully, we'll have something to celebrate in a minute.'

'I feel sick just thinking about it,' Ella confesses.

Thankfully, Flick doesn't mention her intention to ask Noah to marry her again, because I feel more than a bit sick myself.

Chapter Twenty-Nine

I park the Bentley properly, miraculously not hitting anything at my second attempt. The crowd, disappointed that there isn't a better show, wanders off. I put the roof up again before we walk into the centre of St Davids.

It's a pretty city with a more cosmopolitan feel than I'd expected. The beautiful cathedral stands proud on top of the hill as we make the steep climb up from the car park. I take Ella's arm and help her up the steps. Now that I know that she's more than likely with child, I want to wrap her in cotton wool.

Amid the traditional tourist trappings, there are chi-chi little shops and coffee bars. Frankly, I could do with a double espresso right now; at least then I could blame my jittery feelings on an excess of caffeine.

Ella leads the way, while I fall into step behind her and Flick. I feel sick to my stomach. It's possibly a good thing that I haven't yet had time to eat breakfast. Is Flick serious? I wonder. Does she really think that Noah will marry her? She must be pretty sure as you wouldn't do that on just a whim, would you?

This is the first time I've heard her talk like this and I'm shocked to my core. Trust Flick not to do it the usual way and wait for the man to ask. Or even to wait until they've known each other for more than a couple of weeks. Did she learn nothing from her last failed marriage? Clearly not.

We find a chemist's and stop outside.

'Wish me luck,' Ella says and she pops inside while we stand on the pavement in the sunshine. Despite the warmth of the day, I feel cold inside.

'You sure you're all right?' Flick asks.

I realise that I'm shivering. 'I'm fine. Just a bit shaken.'

'You're a bloody idiot,' she says, not unkindly. She assumes I'm referring to the car crash, whereas I'm not. 'It'll be OK.'

'You don't really think that, do you?'

'No,' she concedes and we both risk a weak smile.

An age later, Ella finally comes out. 'Queue,' she says, but in her hand she's holding up a pregnancy test.

'Coffee shop,' Flick pronounces. 'We need a loo and fast.'

With that we dash along the high street and into the nearest café we can find. We choose badly. This is, quite probably, the only place in St Davids that has failed to move with the times. It's cramped but doesn't seem to have embraced minimalism as a concept. Surrounding the chipped tables and scuffed chairs are racks and racks of beach equipment for sale, including inflatable toys, flip-flops, body boards, wetsuits and swimsuits that were possibly last fashionable in the 1950s. In fact, there's so much stuff that we can hardly get to the tables. We are, currently, the only customers. There's not even any staff in sight.

'Euww,' Flick says, wrinkling her nose. 'I'm not staying here.'

'It'll do,' I insist. 'It has a loo.'

'We can find somewhere else.'

'I need to know now.' Ella is surprisingly firm. 'I'll be back in a minute.'

'Good luck,' I offer, even though I think it's a foregone conclusion. I hug Ella to me tightly.

'Thanks.'

Flick hugs her too.

Ella hesitates. 'Come with me,' she says. 'I don't want to do this by myself.'

So we all follow the sign – a woman in a crinoline on a little brass plaque – and squash into the tiny ladies' room.

There's barely room to move and Ella struggles to open the cubicle door with us huddled in here. Flick and I are jammed together by the sink. The owners might not have lavished much care on the café, but this is sparklingly clean. Thank goodness.

Ella, still clutching the pregnancy test, disappears into the loo.

'We'll sing,' Flick jokes, 'so that we don't listen to you pee and put you off.' Flick starts up with Katy Perry's 'I Kissed a Girl'.

'I don't think it was kissing a *girl* that got Ella in this situation,' I point out.

I join in anyway, even though my heart isn't in a singing

mood. A few minutes later Ella emerges triumphantly, stick in hand.

'Want to sing something else while we wait?' Flick asks.

'We're nearly done,' Ella says and, with a deep breath, checks the test. The colour drains from her face and she looks up at us teary-eyed. 'I am, indeed, about to become a mummy.'

We both hug her and jump round in the crowded space. Soon we're all crying.

'That's fantastic,' I say to Ella.

'I'm going to be an auntie,' Flick crows.

'I'm going to be sick,' Ella says and we both step away from her slightly.

'Let's get out of here,' Flick says. 'We should go somewhere nicer to celebrate.'

'Are you well enough?' I ask Ella.

She nods. 'I could do with some fresh air. Why don't we pick up something from the deli across the road and go to the beach for half an hour? I could do with a bit of breathing space, some time to get my head together before we go back and tell Art.'

'Good idea.'

Then the door bursts open and a woman stomps in wearing a waitress outfit that could have come from a fancy-dress shop. Even her lacy apron is bristling with indignation.

'Would you mind telling me what's going on in here?'

'Pregnant lady coming through,' Flick says, matching her imperious tones. 'Pregnant lady!' She ushers Ella past her.

'These toilets are for customers only!' she shouts after us. But we're already out on the street and giggling again.

Chapter Thirty

In the tragically crumpled Bentley, I drive us to the beach at Caerfai Bay. Perhaps I shouldn't voice this to Harry, but I like it a bit more with its dent in it. It adds more character to it. No, better not say that at all.

'Shall we stop here?' I say as I slow down. I am going to have a lifelong phobia of parking now.

'This is fine,' Ella says.

As it's still early in the day, the car park is quite empty and I slip, uneventfully, into a vacant space overlooking the sea. Thankfully. I do make sure that the handbrake is firmly applied, though, as I don't want to go shooting straight over the cliff if Flick decides to make any more momentous announcements.

We've bought bagels and Danish pastries. I have a tray with hot coffee in it for me and Flick, peppermint tea for Ella to try to settle her tummy.

The journey here has been subdued. We climb out of the car and walk down to the empty beach in silence. This is another idyllic spot and it will be hard to settle back into London life again after this break. I know in my heart that Harry and I should go home together now but, to be honest, I'm grateful for the excuse to stay here. Despite all that's going on, I feel a real connection to this place. Ella's a lucky lady to have Cwtch Cottage and I hope that Art doesn't persuade her to sell it.

The sun is climbing, gathering warmth, and it looks as if it's going to be a beautiful day. Flick sets the tray on the golden sand to mark our place. Ella and I flop down next to her so that we're all in a line, backs to the rocks, looking out at the glittering sea. Opening the bag of goodies, I hand a pastry to each of my friends, along with a serviette. I do the same with the drinks. Flick takes the polystyrene cup that I offer her.

'Thanks.'

We eat our belated breakfast without speaking. I think the shock of Ella's pregnancy is really starting to sink in for us all. In my own quiet way, I'm still reeling from Flick's announcement too.

We all nurse our drinks, sipping thoughtfully in unison, and stare out to sea in comfortable companionship, watching the ebb and flow of the waves. Eventually, the mesmerising swell of the ocean starts to soothe me. If Flick wants to ask Noah to marry her, then who am I to argue against that? She must really love him. More than I thought. I'd imagined she was just being her usual self and that she'd tire of him in the blink of an eye. Seems I was wrong. She's clearly more serious than I've seen her before.

Plus I have my own issues to worry about. So much has

gone on already this morning that I'd almost forgotten about my own troubles. All that racing around has let me push to one side the drama of the night. Now it floods back. Everything should look better on a sunny day, shouldn't it? But it doesn't. Harry has said that he wants to work things out between us, so why are my spirits not lighter? Ella is pregnant and we should all be rejoicing.

'All girls together,' Flick says, eventually, as she wipes a flake of pastry from her lip. Her voice sounds melancholy. She leans her head on Ella's shoulder. 'How long have we been doing this?'

'Longer than I care to remember,' Ella says.

'We've been through a lot together.'

Ella and I nod in agreement.

'It seems only yesterday,' Flick continues, 'that we were young, free and single.'

'You still are,' I point out.

'Young, free, single and not complicated,' she tries.

'You've never had a life that hasn't been complicated, Flick.' Mostly of her own making.

'You're right.' She sighs at that. 'Sometimes I feel as if I've lived three lifetimes already. What I need is a new start.'

'And you think that's what you'll get with Noah?' Ella asks and I'm glad that she did as I wouldn't have been able to voice it.

'I hope so,' she says. 'I've got to try. I feel like I'm stuck in my twenties. There's a time when we've all got to knuckle down and grow up. Look at you ...' She nods at Ella. 'You're going to be a mummy!'

Ella leans back on her elbows and sticks her tummy out. She looks down proudly at her burgeoning bump. 'So I am.'

Flick hugs her. 'You clever, clever girl. Perhaps you're the first of us to discover the meaning of life. I thought eternal partying was the way to go, but I know now that I'm wrong. I'm so happy for you that I'm going to have to have a celebratory fag.'

Flick lights up and, as a concession, blows the smoke away from Ella. And towards me. I cough.

'I want you both to be godmothers,' Ella says. 'What better start could my baby have in life than to have two fabulous aunties like you?'

'Oh, Ella, that's lovely,' I say. 'I feel very honoured.'

'Obviously, I don't believe in God,' Flick says, 'but as long as that's not an issue then I'm in too.' She hugs Ella. 'I can't wait to buy all those fabulous kids' clothes. When she's older I'll take her out and teach her all my bad habits.'

'Now what have I let myself in for?' Ella laughs. 'Can I change my mind?'

'Truth is, I'm fucking *green* with jealousy,' Flick says, puffing out again. 'I'm desperate for a kid.'

Ella and I sit up straighter. This is also news. I think we'd both assumed that Flick wanted everything in life, *apart* from children.

'You never said.' Another announcement to be stunned by.

Flick smiles. 'I don't tell you *everything*, Grace.'

'There's plenty of time yet,' I assure her.

'What about the abortion?' she says, lowering her voice. 'What if that was my only chance of having a kid? I should never have done it. What an idiot.'

'You were young,' I offer as comfort.

'And stupid. What sort of chump gets knocked up on her honeymoon?' Flick continues. 'By that no-hoper, Brian. How ridiculous was that? On top of everything else.' She sucks smoke deep into her lungs. 'What could I do? I'd come back to England in disgrace. I'd got no money. My family wouldn't take me back. I'd just started university.'

I remember it well. Ella and I came home from our lectures to find Flick drunk, with two black tracks of mascara down her face from crying. She poured it all out to us while I cuddled her and Ella made tea and toast.

'What would I have done without you both?' She rubs her face.

We took Flick to the clinic. Waited while the terrible deed was done. What else could we do? We were young and, with the best will in the world, we couldn't possibly have taken on a baby, even if Flick had managed to get maintenance from Brian Tavistock. She hadn't even told him about the child and she certainly didn't want to tell him about the resulting abortion. We all worked extra shifts at Honkers to get the money together. We cried with her for days afterwards and have rarely talked about it again since.

'I gritted my teeth, got rid of the baby, moved on. Except you don't, do you? Not ever.' She looks at us both bleakly. 'I didn't tell anyone. It was the worst thing I've ever done. Some things you just have to keep to yourself. You can't ever say them out loud.'

I feel myself flush. That I can identify with.

'What if I've messed up my chance of having kids? I've been

reckless with contraception over the years and have never fallen pregnant again. What if I've got fucked-up tubes or something?'

'They seem to be able to fix anything these days, Flick,' I say softly. 'I'm sure it won't be a problem even if anything did go wrong. There's no reason to think that you can't have a baby.'

'But you don't know, do you? You don't really know what's going on inside your body. Sometimes until it's too late.' She takes a drag on her cigarette again. I could tell her what *that's* doing to the inside of her body, but this isn't the time. 'I think of the baby all the time. What it would be like now. Whether it was a boy or a girl. It would be thirteen.' Flick laughs bitterly. 'Imagine me with a teenage kid! How different my life would have been.'

'You've just got to look to the future,' Ella says. 'There's no point regretting what happened back then. You made what you thought was the best choice at the time. We all did. No one can blame you for that.'

'That's also why this relationship with Noah has to work,' Flick says. 'He'd make a great father. He's the first person I've ever thought that I really could do this with. I can't mess up this chance.' Then she laughs, trying to make light of it. 'Think of what great-looking kids we'd knock out.'

I really had no idea that Flick felt like this. I always thought she was happier with the one-night stand, the married man. When did the idea of motherhood start to creep into the forefront of her consciousness? Why has she never mentioned it to us?

'Have you never wanted a baby, Grace?' she asks.

'No.' I shake my head.

'Harry's got a couple already. He'd be great,' she presses on. 'At least one of you would know what you're doing.'

'It's never even been an option,' I tell her. 'His view is that he's already done the baby thing with Freddie and Oscar. He's never wanted to start over again with another family. He's always been very firm about it.'

She looks taken aback by that. 'Didn't that bother you?'

'I just accepted it.'

'And you've never gone round, looking in prams and wondering "what if"?'

I can honestly say that I haven't and now I wonder why that is. Have I pushed down my own maternal instinct in deference to Harry's views? I've loved being a stepmum to Freddie and Oscar, but have I been fooling myself all these years that it was enough for me? Given the chance, would I want more?

'If it was me, I'd have been putting a few holes in those condoms, missing a few pills.'

Is that, I wonder, what she's doing with Noah? It would simply never occur to me to let my plans trample over someone else's. As a partnership we've worked out something that suits us both. But something uncomfortable pricks in my brain. It actually suits Harry more than it suits me.

'Everyone wants kids,' is Flick's verdict. 'It's only natural.'

Do they? Do *I*?

When I examine it, I think the main problem is that I've never really seen Harry as wonderful father material. So perhaps that's why I've never had the urge to procreate with him.

When I first met Harry, the boys were already teenagers, so I used to stay away from his place when he had his access visit once a month. Then, gradually, I got to know them. Now, of course, I love them to bits. They were great as kids, but I'm not sure that most of it is down to Harry's input. His first wife left him when the boys were only five and two, so he didn't have a lot of influence on them as he didn't push for regular access. I don't know why that was. They just never figured very highly in his life. We used to take them out for pizza and on bicycle rides – the things that part-time parents do to fill the time – but he never felt truly involved in it. His style of parenting was very much hands off and still is.

Now, they're both lovely young men with their own lives to lead. I think if I didn't call them regularly to see how they were, Harry would have very little to do with them other than exchanging tweets. They're a credit to their mother rather than to Harry, I suspect, and I feel blessed that they still want contact with me.

Perhaps if we'd had them as younger children, it would have influenced me more. But sometimes dragging round two teenagers who clearly would prefer to be somewhere else made it seem like so much hard work. Harry used to say that I was lucky as I'd had the benefits of kids without enduring the sleepless nights and the stretch marks. But I'm not so sure that he was right. I've loved the brief glimpse of family life that I have had. Wouldn't I love it more if I had children of my own?

What would happen if I did suddenly start to feel broody? I'm thirty-two. Hardly past it. There's still time for me to have a baby. Haven't I just been telling Flick the very same thing? But is that ever likely to happen with Harry? The answer, quite probably, is no. Coming out of nowhere, that hits me hard. As well as always being an accountant, am I also going to stay a child-free zone? The thought shakes me more than I'd like to admit. Am I happy to spend the rest of my life doing what everyone else thinks I should do rather than what I want to do myself?

'Well, I'm done with waiting around for married men,' Flick says. She grinds her cigarette butt into the sand. 'There comes a point when late nights and one-night stands become a chore. I've had more than my fair share of cocktails and high heels. Noah has turned everything upside down. Now I want to give it all up and have something more meaningful in my life. I'm ready to play house and babies,' Flick admits. 'Bring it on.'

I had no idea that Flick felt quite so deeply about Noah. He would make a great father, there's absolutely no doubt about that. If this is really what she wants – husband, children, roses round the door – then who am I to resent my friend having some happiness?

'This *has* to work with Noah,' she reiterates. 'It has to.' Flick smiles at us both ruefully. 'I've messed up so many times. I can't do it again.'

'Does he love you?' It's out of my mouth before I can stop it and I want to bite off my tongue.

'I think he does. He just needs convincing.' She throws back her hair. 'Wish me luck, ladies. This one has to stick around. I'm even going bloody *surfing* in an attempt to show him that

I'm his ideal woman.' She laughs. 'What do you think about that, Grace? Me on a surfboard. It must be bloody love.'

'It must be,' I agree. And I feel guiltier than ever.

'When do you think you'll propose to him?' Ella wants to know.

'On this holiday,' she says, decisively. 'No time like the present. I'd like to end this week with a clear vision of my future and, more importantly, a ring on my finger!'

There's a rushing noise in my ears that's not the waves and, though I'm still sitting firmly on the sand, I feel as if the ground has suddenly fallen away from beneath me.

Chapter Thirty-One

Later than we'd planned, we pull up in front of Cwtch Cottage. It's time to face the music. I kill the engine and we all sit in silence.

'Please don't say anything about the baby,' Ella makes us promise. 'I need to find the right time to tell Art. Until then mum's the word.'

'Well, that's bloody funny, woman. "Mum's the word." That's exactly what it is!' Flick says and we dissolve into giggles. I feel that there's a touch of hysteria in my own laughter.

When we've calmed down again, Ella says, 'We'd better go inside. They must be wondering why we've taken so long.'

'Wish me luck,' I say. 'I'll need it. Harry's going to go ballistic.'

Heavy of heart, I follow the others through the cottage. As we expected, our men are outside on the terrace. It looks as if Art and Noah are just finishing breakfast at the table. Harry is out on the rocks. He has one of the golf clubs and the bucket of balls and, like Ella's dad used to, he's knocking them out into the sea.

'Hello, ladies. Where have you been?' Art says when he sees us. 'We thought you'd got lost.'

Ella kisses his cheek. 'I had an errand to run in St Davids and it took much longer than I thought.'

Noah looks up. I'm sure it's not my imagination, but his eyes search for me before they search for Flick. His face lights up in a smile.

Flick goes over to him and kisses him passionately. 'Hello, darling. Did you miss me?'

'It was very quiet without you,' he teases. Then he studies me closely. 'Are you all right, Grace?'

'We had a bit of an accident,' Flick says. 'Grace has pranged Harry's pride and joy.'

'I thought you looked pale.' His face is lined with concern. 'No one hurt?'

I shake my head. 'Not yet.' I look again to Harry who is, at this moment, blissfully unaware, and I sigh to myself. He is not going to be happy. The tentative truce we came to last night is, I feel, not going to survive this. 'I'd better get it over with.'

So while Flick fills in Noah and Art on the dastardly details, I walk out to where Harry is. He doesn't pause in his activity.

'Nice shot,' I say as another ball disappears into the ocean beyond the rocks. He stops and turns to me. I clear my throat. 'Harry, I need to have a word with you.'

'Not now, Grace,' he says, not meeting my gaze. Clearly he thinks a talk is on the cards about what we said to each other last night and he is, obviously, not keen to revisit it. 'Can't it wait?'

'You'll want to know about this.'

He stops and leans on the golf club, expectantly.

'I've had a bit of a bump in the car,' I explain calmly.

That makes him jump like a scalded cat. 'What? In the Bentley? Is it bad?'

'You'd better come and look.'

He throws down the golf club and is already racing ahead of me. I haven't seen Harry move this fast in years. I trudge after him. The others, very wisely, stay where they are and I shoot them a rueful glance as I pass.

I hear Harry cry out. Well, it's more of a despairing howl. It's clear that he's seen the damage that the Bentley has sustained during its brief skirmish with the post. And, as I round the corner of the cottage, I see him on his knees at the bumper. He is rocking backwards and forwards, hugging himself.

'Have you seen this?' he splutters as I approach.

'Of course I have, Harry. I'm the one who backed it into a post.'

'How the hell did you manage to do that?'

'I lost concentration for a second,' I explain. 'Just a second.'

'Oh my God.' Harry rends his hair. 'Oh my God.' He crawls forward to stroke the crumpled metal, lovingly.

'It's a car, Harry,' I say, flatly.

'It's barely a month old!'

'We can fix it.' My lips are tight. 'I'll organise everything.'

'This will cost thousands! Thousands, Grace.'

'I know and I'm really sorry.'

Again I have to wonder why Harry has seen fit to spend so much money on a car. The chances are that, these days, it's going to get dented. Will he be hysterical when we park it on the street anywhere? Surely this kind of car is a prime target for vandals. Our old car was much more modest and he wouldn't have created like this if I'd bumped it. Who does he think that he's trying to impress with this ostentatious show of wealth? Certainly not me.

'It's only money and the insurance policy will cover most of it,' I reiterate.

'That's hardly the point, is it?' he says.

'It was an accident, Harry.' I'm surprised that I sound so calm. I was worried about what he'd say but, frankly, now I don't give a flying fuck. There are far more important things in life to worry about than a bit of a dent in your car. 'No one was hurt. Which is all that matters.'

Harry looks at me as if he wishes it was me lying crumpled on the road with a still-pristine Bentley embedded in my brain. He shakes his head.

'I'll say nothing more about this,' he says crisply. 'For the sake of harmony. My instinct is to get straight in it, drive back to London and put it into the garage to be repaired right away.'

'If you want to leave, Harry, then you must do that.'

'I thought you wanted to go too,' he counters. 'That's what you said last night.'

'I can't leave,' I tell him. 'Ella needs me here. We should put our differences aside and stay for the rest of the week.'

He doesn't know yet, but I hope we will all be celebrating her and Art's good news – as soon as she tells him.

Harry pouts. 'The salt air will make the exposed metal rust.'

'Not in a few days,' I point out. 'It's not going to make it any worse than it is now, for heaven's sake.'

He speaks to me as if I'm a naughty child. 'I want you to pay for this, do you hear?'

I wonder if he means in money or emotional torture. To be honest, I don't care either way. For the hell of it, I feel like kicking in one of the panels too. Or maybe pouring red wine all over his leather seats. And just last night I hoped that we might have turned a corner.

'I don't know that I can ever forgive you for this, Grace,' he warns.

I say nothing. He seems to think that this gives him the high moral ground, which may be so. But all I feel is that it's another nail being hammered into the coffin that has become our marriage.

Chapter Thirty-Two

Commiserations about the injury to the Bentley are passed around. Harry drags Art and Noah outside to examine the damage and no doubt tells them what a complete idiot I am. When they come back, Ella says, 'Let's go off to the beach. That'll cheer us all up. It's a beautiful day and we don't want to waste it.'

So, with Harry still grumbling, we all head off to Portgale beach as we'd agreed last night. We leave the Bentley behind because my husband announces that he needs a drink and I refuse to drive it. Never in my lifetime am I going near that car again.

Today, I've vowed that I'm going to try to give Noah a wide berth, so we hitch a ride in Art's Mercedes even though the back seat is considerably more cramped. As we're heading for the cars, Noah catches my arm.

'Are you OK?' he says. 'There's been much talk about the car, but I'm sure you're shaken up too.'

'I'll live,' I say to Noah, more crisply than I should.

His hand falls from my arm. 'Good.'

The atmosphere is terrible between me and Harry. I'm trying to be jolly – too much so – but Harry is morose, unspeaking. So Ella and I sit in the back together and I notice that my friend's unusually quiet on the journey. I take her hand and hold it and she smiles at me gratefully.

When we arrive, the sun is already high in a sky unbroken by clouds. The beautiful weather has brought everyone out and the beach is busy. But as it's broad and wide, there's still plenty of space for us amid the sandcastles, the beachballs and the buckets and spades. I stand and breathe in the salt air, feeling it clearing my head. We set up camp on the shingle slope near to one of the surf shops and the pub. Ella has brought some of the beach towels and cushions from the cottage and makes a comfy seating area for us all.

The sea shimmers invitingly and already there are plenty of surfers out, bobbing on the waves. Kite surfers with their brightly coloured canopies scoot along the edge of the surf in the wind. The warm breeze lifts the hair from my neck and I pile up my curls and secure them with a scrunchy.

Harry has finally divested himself of formal clothes and is in his shorts, a T-shirt and a pair of crocs. He's absolutely ruled out any chance of having a go at surfing and asked Art to stop off at a petrol station on the way so that he could buy himself a copy of *The Times*, which he's now manfully trying to read. The wind, however, is making it difficult for him to keep the newspaper open and he keeps shaking it as if he's trying to get rid of an annoying wasp. If I were him, I'd give up and join in with the chat, but Harry is clearly determined to sulk.

'Grace?' he asks. 'Have we got any suntan cream?'

'Yes.' I rummage in my beach bag and then take it over to him. I don't want to spoil the day for the others with our squabble. 'Do you want me to put some on for you?'

'I can do it myself, thank you,' he says. Clearly, Harry is not so keen to forgive and forget.

Ella has, very sensibly, decided to opt out of the surfing too and sits next to Harry with a magazine.

'Will you be OK here?' I ask.

'Yes, fine,' she assures me. 'You go off and have fun.'

'I'm quite happy to sit here with you.'

'Nonsense,' Ella says. 'I won't hear of it. I'm just going to chill out, read my mag and do a bit of sea gazing for inspiration. I've brought the binoculars so that I can watch you all.'

Noah comes over. 'Hey,' he says. 'Ready to go over to the Surf Shack and get our gear?'

'Sure.' I peck a kiss on my husband's forehead. 'See you later, Harry.'

I get a grunt in return. So I go over with Noah to join Flick and Art and together we all head along the beach to the equipment shop to get kitted out.

The Surf Shack, it turns out, is beyond trendy. It's a cool place full of guys with bronzed bodies in board shorts sporting blond dreads. I feel a hundred and thirty-two years old. There's a little café at the back that seems to specialise in smoothies, falafel and wraps. It looks as if they have a couple of rooms upstairs, catering for bed and breakfast guests too. They offer surf lessons and kayaking as well as gear hire and also coasteering trips. I have no idea what that is. But I know someone who will.

'Noah, what's coasteering when it's at home?' I ask.

'It's great fun. You swim, dive, jump off rocks, explore caves. Whatever floats your boat.' I knew that he would know. He was bound to.

'Wow.' Flick raises her eyebrows at me to say that it sounds like anything but fun. 'I've never heard of it.'

'We could try that later in the week,' Noah suggests. 'If anyone's up for it.'

Behind his back, Flick makes a chopping motion across her neck to suggest that she's not. She nods towards the stacked surfboards. 'Let's see if we can do this first without killing ourselves, shall we?'

Noah laughs. Clearly, he thinks that she's joking.

'This is a great place,' I remark, still looking round in wonderment.

'Yeah,' he agrees and I wonder if I detect a wistful note in his voice.

We all troop to the equipment hire desk and, along with the young assistant, Noah helps us to select wetsuits and boards. As another act of conciliation towards Harry, I get him and Ella a cup of tea each from the takeaway hatch and pick up two Crunchies for them. I feel truly awful now. Harry is extraordinarily proud of that car and it is very dented. I know that tea and a Crunchie hardly constitute a massive apology, but it's a start.

Noah has to carry my equipment as my hands are full, which means that Flick has to carry her own and she doesn't look too thrilled by that.

Back on the beach, I hand over Harry's tea.

'Thanks,' he says, a cursory attempt at politeness, and returns to his paper.

We all struggle into our wetsuits. Flick giggles and wriggles and flirts, while Noah laughs as he helps to squeeze her into it. It's fair to say that she's the only one of us who looks good in tight rubber. Even Harry lowers his newspaper to get an eyeful. Her suit is snug, barely containing her voluminous breasts, and, even done up to the neck in rubber, she looks incredible. No wonder men can't help themselves when it comes to falling for Flick. I'm absolutely sure that, in my own wetsuit, I won't be creating the same impression. Still, I'm more concerned about not being chilly when we're in the sea than being a femme fatale. Perhaps that's where I'm going wrong.

Then, duly equipped, we trot down the beach and hit the surf.

The sea is mind-numbingly cold. It takes my breath away as the waves swirl round us. The surf – according to the information board in the shop – is 'choppy'. I bow to those who have greater knowledge than me. To my eye, it looks just plain scary. The waves aren't high – don't think *Hawaii Five-O* – but to me it looks as if there's quite a swell and they're more than enough to strike fear into the feeble heart of a mere novice.

After we've swum out, Noah shows us some of the basics, how to look for a good wave and, to get us started, how to lie on the board and ride the surf into the beach.

Art and I split off, moving further down the beach, and

leave Noah and Flick together. I'm trying very hard to stick to my promise to myself of staying out of their way. If their romance is to blossom, Flick doesn't need me around like a lovelorn gooseberry.

'I did this years ago,' Art says to me as we swim further out. 'I wonder if it's something that you never forget, like riding a bike.'

'I don't know,' I tell him. 'Let's give it a go.'

So we try to catch the waves and, every now and then, hit it right and are whizzed up on to the beach on our boards, flat on our bellies, which feels just fantastic. Art and I high-five each other, as that's what surfers seem to do. We swim out and do it over and over again, until I'm totally knackered and panting.

'You go ahead,' I say to Art. 'I need to rest for a few minutes.' So while he tries to catch a wave, I hold on to my board and bob in the sea.

While I take a second to get my breath back, I glance over to Noah and Flick. My friend seems to be faring less well, disappearing under the waves more often than is pleasant. Each time I see her pop up again she's coughing out sea water.

It looks as if all she wants to do is wind her legs round Noah's waist and indulge in some ocean-based foreplay. But, from where I am, he seems much more intent on teaching her to surf. Whereas Flick doesn't seem all that intent on learning how to do it. Oh, well.

I see Harry watching us and I wave, but only Ella waves back. Minutes later, I see Harry get up and wander off. I assume he's exhausted the delights of the beach and is already going to sample the wares of the nearest pub.

The next stage of surfing is to try to catch a wave while you're kneeling up. It seems that Art's muscle memory kicks into action, as he's up on his knees on his board after a few attempts and roars in delight as he's carried along. I catch a glimpse of the future and I can really see Art doing this with his son or daughter in years to come. I'm so excited for them both and I hope that Ella tells him soon, so that we can dissipate the tension and get on with the job of celebrating with them.

After a couple of successful rides on his knees, Art manages to stand up for a few seconds before being dumped in the water. I give him a jubilant round of applause. Noah and Flick swim over to where we are and Noah high-fives Art in congratulation.

'This is great, man,' Art shouts above the rush of the ocean. 'I'd forgotten what a buzz it is.'

Flick, standing forlornly next to me, says, 'I'm hating every minute of this. I'd rather poke out my own eyeballs. Are you enjoying it?'

'I am,' I admit. 'I'm not very good at it, but it feels fabulous when you get it right.'

'All I'm doing is drinking vast quantities of sea. I feel like puking up,' she mutters. 'I'm done. You lot can stay but I'm going to hit the bar with Harry.'

'See you later,' she says to Noah and stomps out of the sea and up the beach.

He looks as if he's in two minds as to whether he should

follow her or not. In the end, he turns back towards me and Art.

'Have you tried kneeling?' he says when Art paddles away from us.

'I haven't even mastered riding the board on my stomach yet.'

'Here. Let me show you.'

And I must hesitate or something, as he peers at me over the top of his sunglasses and says, 'We are OK, aren't we?'

'Fine.'

'There was no problem with Harry last night, was there?'

My mouth goes dry. Did he hear us arguing through the wall? I wonder.

'He wasn't annoyed about how long we were out yesterday?'

'No. He was fine,' I assure him. Even though I know he wasn't fine at all. That, to be honest, is the least of our problems. 'He was less happy about the dent in his car this morning, though.'

'Oh.' Noah acknowledges his misplaced guilt. 'We can follow the others,' he says, glancing back at the beach. 'If you think that's a good idea. I don't want to upset anyone.'

I contemplate abandoning my attempts at surfing and hitting the pub instead, but, do you know, that really isn't what I want to do at all. I don't want to bend to the will of others, I want to stay here with Noah, learning some more about this sport, and try, at least, to get a bit better.

'No,' I say. I meet his eyes squarely. 'We've got the boards rented for another hour. I'd rather stay here.'

He grins. 'Good. Me too.'

So, for the next hour, Noah shows me how to time the wave right so that I can jump up on to the board. I wobble and bash my shins and skin my knees. I go off the board backwards, sidewards and splat flat on my face. I swallow more water than a whale. My whole body is aching, but time and time again he helps me up and gets me going once more. And we laugh and laugh. We laugh until my sides ache as much as the rest of me. It shouldn't make me feel so happy to be alone with Noah again, but it does. All my plans, to stay out of the way and let him focus on Flick, have gone right out of the window.

Art keeps whizzing by. He's managed to stand, albeit very tentatively, but at least he's cracked it. Eventually, he comes to join us and is, rightly, very pleased with himself. 'I'm going in now,' he says, puffing from his unaccustomed exertion. 'This is the most exercise I've done in years, I probably won't be able to move tomorrow.'

'Looked like you were having fun,' Noah notes.

'Brilliant.' More high-fiving. 'And now I need beer.' He jerks a thumb towards the pub. 'I think Harry and Flick have abandoned Ella, so I'd better get back to her. We'll see you in the bar soon?'

'Yeah,' Noah says.

Art swims back towards the shore.

Then Noah turns to me. 'Sure that you're happy to hang out a bit longer, Grace?'

More than happy. My heart is banging in my chest simply because we're alone again. 'I'm going to master this if it kills me,' I tell him.

'I don't think we need to go that far,' he assures me.

So we splash about in the sea some more and every time I fall off my surfboard, Noah helps me back on.

I forget about Harry and Flick, Ella and Art. There's just me and Noah and the sand and the surf and the sea. And, when I finally manage to kneel on my board and ride the surf all the way to the shore, I feel as if I've conquered the world.

Chapter Thirty-Three

'I'll cook for us all,' Noah offers. There's been much discussion while we're still in the pub about what to do and where to go for dinner tonight. 'Curry suit everyone?'

'Christ,' Harry mutters over his glass of wine. 'You can cook as well? Is there anything you *can't* do?'

While I wish the ground would open up and swallow me, Noah chooses to ignore Harry's snide comment.

'We can run to the supermarket on the way home and pick up the ingredients. Are you happy with that, Flick?'

Since we came back from the beach and joined the others in the pub, Noah has been very attentive towards Flick. So much so that she looks like the cat who's got the cream.

'Sounds great.' I wonder if I'm the only one who hears her whisper to him, 'I hope you're as good in the kitchen as you are in the bedroom.'

She pulls Noah to her and squeezes him around the waist. I go and sit next to Harry, who is already three sheets to the wind. He's busy tweeting, so ignores me, and I stare into space, going over in my mind the things I learned about the art of surfing and trying not to be self-conscious about how bedraggled I must look. Although my husband and I are here together on holiday, we seem to be in totally different places altogether.

Finishing our drinks, we leave the pub. Harry, Ella and I climb into Art's car and head back towards Cwtch Cottage, while Noah and Flick turn in the other direction, in search of the nearest supermarket.

Back at the cottage, Ella stifles a yawn and says, 'I'm going to have a quick nap before dinner. All that sunshine has made me sleepy.'

'Mind if I join you?' Art asks.

'That'd be lovely.'

They kiss each other deeply. Art is relaxed, happy. Maybe this is Ella's moment. Surely this would be a good time to tell him that it's more than fresh air that's making her tired?

'Give me a call when Noah comes back,' she says as they disappear upstairs hand in hand, 'and I'll help him with the preparations.'

A nap sounds like an excellent plan, but I don't want Harry to get the wrong idea and offer to join me too. Our lovemaking was weird last night and I don't think I could do that again.

'I'm popping up to have a bath,' I tell him.

That will buy me an hour on my own. I feel that what I should be doing is addressing with Harry how I felt after our conversation last night, but I can't bring myself to do it. Harry's acting as if nothing has happened.

I sigh to myself. 'See you in a short while.'

'He's bloody annoying,' Harry says, apropos of nothing. 'That fellow of Flick's. She might think he's a superhero, but it won't last. The all-action chap isn't her type.'

'She's had enough men to know what she does and doesn't like,' I suggest. 'The only "type" she usually prefers is married. Noah's a definite improvement on that.' Why does Harry even care what Flick thinks about him? What's it got to do with him? 'She seems pretty smitten to me.'

'Pah,' is his verdict.

'She's going to ask him to marry her,' I put in. 'She said that she wants to settle down and start a family with him.'

Harry recoils. 'Flick said that?'

Why is he suddenly taking such an inordinate amount of interest in my friend's love-life? He's not even that bothered about his own. 'Yes.'

My husband looks shocked to his core. 'I can't believe it.'

'Well, that's what she said. Only time will tell, I guess.' I pick up my beach bag and wet towel. 'I'm going for my bath before they come back.'

I lie down in the bath, letting the hot water soothe me and wash the crusted sea salt from my skin. Closing my eyes, I drift away. I'm envious of people who live by the sea, I think. Not in a popular resort, somewhere heaving with tourists, or with a pier, like Brighton or Bournemouth, but somewhere still wild and remote like this. How different my life could be if I didn't have to sit in an office all day long, poring over company accounts, trying to pretend that I care.

Ella is one very lucky lady to have Cwtch Cottage as a bolt-hole.

Does this have to be my life? I wonder. Could I get out of my partnership at work? It would mean the other three partners buying me out of my share or bringing someone else in to do so. I've worked there for years and am generally so busy that I don't have time to consider whether I'm discontented or not.

And what about Harry? Where are he and I going? Do we have a future at all? If he knew how desperately unhappy I was, would he be able to stop his drinking, get help perhaps? I don't think Harry would consider counselling. He'd probably see it as admitting to a weakness. I try to think back to when his drinking became a problem. Is there something at work that he hasn't told me about? We're not short of money, so there's no particular financial pressure. Not that I know of. I don't think he has a secret gambling habit or a second secret family tucked away somewhere. So, if it's not money, what is it? He's always enjoyed a social drink – perhaps too much – but now it seems to have got out of control and in a relatively short space of time. Has something happened to trigger it that he hasn't shared with me?

There's too much to consider and even exploring the edges of it makes my brain ache. If I left Harry, where would I go? What would I do? I promised that I'd love him for better, for worse, forsaking all others until death us do part. What if I can't do that any more? Can I consider throwing in the towel on our marriage already? What would people think of me? I'm the steady one. The one who sees everything through to the end. I'm not one to run away from difficulty. It would feel like such a failure.

Hearing Noah's Range Rover pull up outside the cottage makes my heart skip a beat. Another complication that I could do without. But perhaps the fact that I've got on so well with Noah and had so much fun with him has made me realise even more what's missing in my own relationship. Harry and I certainly don't have any fun together any more.

I listen to Noah and Flick giggling, as they lift the shopping out of the car, and then I hear the front door of the cottage bang.

Reluctantly hauling myself out of the bath, I rub myself down and, hoping that Ella doesn't mind, slather myself in some of the body lotion that's on the shelf. My skin feels dried-out from the sun and the surfing. Time to put my face on for the evening ahead.

I have a lot to think about and, at this moment, like Harry, I can see the joys of embracing the oblivion of wine.

Chapter Thirty-Four

Noah is already busy frying chicken in the kitchen when I come downstairs. Ella is standing next to him chopping onions. There's already a growing pile of prepared vegetables next to her – carrots, green beans, tomatoes.

I take the knife from her. 'Sit down now, woman.' I try to sound as if I mean business.

'I've just been having a lovely nap,' she protests.

'And now you can have a lovely chill out with Art until dinner's ready.'

Art has his guitar out again and is playing some great soulful tunes that are drifting in through the windows from the terrace – Adele, Will Young, Nerina Pallot. He seems really relaxed and I wonder if he too has finally fallen under the spell of this magical place. Like me, if he's taken a break from the treadmill of his life, will he start to wonder why he's on it in the first place? I do hope that Ella has been able to tell him her news ... *their* news.

I shoo her out of the kitchen to sit with Art on the terrace and I take her place next to Noah chopping onions. 'What's on the menu?'

'Noah Reeves's special chicken biryani with vegetable curry and aubergine bhajee.'

'Sounds incredible. Do you do this kind of thing often?'

'Sometimes I cook at the estate.' He grins at me. 'Usually knocking out hearty breakfasts for shooting parties. I'm a dab hand at afternoon tea and sometimes I even wander into the outer reaches of fancy food.'

'Oh, really?' I look suitably impressed.

'Yes, really.' He grins at me as he mixes all manner of spices together.

'I'm more of an open-a-jar sort of person myself.'

'Then you are missing one of the great joys of life,' he informs me.

'At least I discovered another one this afternoon.'

'You enjoyed the surfing?'

I nod. 'Very much.'

'Aching now?'

'A bit. I had a nice long bath. I'm hoping that will stave off the worst of the pain.'

'You did really well,' Noah says, generously.

'I think that might be stretching it, but I did enjoy myself.'

'You've caught the sun.'

'That means that my nose has gone all freckly.'

His eyes soften. 'It suits you.'

'What are you two up to?' Flick breezes in from the terrace. 'Can't have you getting all cosy in here together.'

206

Guiltily, I take a step away from Noah. 'We could do with an extra pair of hands,' I say lightly.

'I'm just here for more wine,' Flick informs us. She picks up a piece of peeled carrot and pops it into her mouth. 'You should know by now that I don't do kitchens.' She twines her arms round Noah's waist. 'Looks as if you have it all under control.'

'Sure do,' Noah agrees.

Flick raises an eyebrow at me and nuzzles his neck. I chop my onions faster. She drifts off to get another bottle of white wine out of the fridge. 'Smells divine,' she says and disappears again.

'Nearly done with the onions?'

'Yes, thank goodness. My eyes are starting to smart now.' Tears squeeze out and flow down my cheeks.

'Hold your hands under the cold water,' Noah advises.

I do as he suggests, but still the tears run down my face and I blink furiously to try to stem the burning. Then suddenly the tears that were onion-induced turn to real tears and, unbidden, I find myself crying.

'Here,' he says and rips some kitchen towel from the roll. As I hold my hands in the stream of water, he comes close. He turns off the tap and turns me towards him. His hand goes into my hair and he tilts my face towards him, then dabs gently at my eyes for me, blotting my tears.

This is what I would call getting too cosy. His face is above mine, very near, and he's gazing at me intently. My tears dry to a trickle and, with a few noisy gulps, stop.

'Better?'

'Much,' I gulp.

He gazes down at me, frowning in concern, and I sniff again. Noah rests his forehead against mine and the mere touching of our skin makes me tremble inside. We stand there, immobile. I know I should pull away, but I can't. Someone could see us. All it would take is for Harry to turn his head this way. Or Flick could come back inside at any second. Then what would we do? I close my eyes and try to steady my breath, but the heady scent of Noah fills my senses. He still has the fresh tang of the sea air layered with a musky, oriental spike of aftershave that makes my head swim. Eventually, when there are no more tears, he moves away and I gulp in air that doesn't taste of Noah.

'OK now?'

I let out a shuddering breath.

'I don't like to see you sad,' he says.

'Just onions,' I assure him, shakily.

'I don't think so, Grace.'

I shrug as my voice simply can't be trusted.

'Have it your way. Shall we move on to less distressing vegetables then? There are some aubergines to slice.'

I try a teary laugh. 'I can do that.'

So I distract myself by taking a knife and hacking vengefully at some innocent aubergines.

Noah takes the onions and tips them into the pan with the chicken. He adds the spices and stock, stirring all the time. 'Want to talk about it?' he asks, not looking at me.

I shake my head. 'It's something I've got to deal with.'

'I know that you're struggling,' Noah says softly. 'I'm not blind.'

'No.' I look up at him and smile ruefully. 'But perhaps *I* have been for too long.' Before I can say any more, Ella comes in. Which I think is a good thing.

'That's it,' she says. 'I can't just sit there and vegetate. My bottom's going numb. I've spent all day doing nothing.'

'Ella!' I admonish.

'I can, at least, set the table, Grace,' she counters. 'Find me a little job to do before I go mad.'

Rooting in the drawer, I pick out the knives and forks and hand half of them to Ella. Together we move over to the table. I lower my voice when I ask her, 'Did you find the right moment to tell Art yet?'

'I didn't,' she admits.

'Oh, Ella.'

But what can I say when I'm no better myself? Seems that both Ella and I are happy to ignore the elephants in our rooms.

Chapter Thirty-Five

We all sit round the big kitchen table and Noah serves the curry. Harry, Art and Flick are already in hearty, ebullient mood. The wine is flowing and, do you know, I've decided that if you can't beat them, you should join them. I'm tired of being disapproving, always feeling as if I have to watch what I drink myself, so that I can be Harry's conscience. Tonight, I want to lose myself too, to squash down the emotions that are battling for space in my head and float on a fluffy cloud of alcohol-induced bliss. It seems to work for everyone else.

The wine is flowing and I hold out my glass. Barely looking at me, Harry fills it. But I don't care. Tonight he can sulk all he likes, I'm just going to let it wash over me. To add to the ambience, Noah's curry is sensational and everyone tucks in enthusiastically.

'This is delicious, darling,' Flick gushes. 'Really heavenly. You're *so* clever.'

'Very bloody Jamie Oliver,' Harry grumbles. But he eats a massive plateful, nevertheless.

I swig my wine, but it tastes bitter in my mouth and I acknowledge without regret that I've completely lost my enjoyment of alcohol. Putting my glass down, I realise that the answer to this isn't to be found in getting drunk. If only I could persuade Harry to feel the same way. So I sit on the sidelines and watch the others getting totally plastered. We seem to have fallen into two camps – Harry, Flick and Art are the heavy drinkers while Noah, Ella and I are the abstainers. Despite the excellent food, the former all seem to be determined to get as drunk as possible.

Over dinner the banter gets louder and louder. Before long, Harry and Art start to trade insults.

'You want to get a real job, you long-haired layabout,' Harry jokes. 'Band manager? What the hell is that when it's at home?'

'Yeah, old man,' Art says affably. 'Money for nothing and my chicks for free.' I see Ella flinch at that. 'If I wanted to be a boring fart like you, I'd have gone into pensions.'

And, of course, the more wine that is consumed, the more the jovial insults start to take on a more spiky tone and become point scoring, particularly when it's Harry aiming them at Noah.

'What do you do for work, Noah?'

'I'm an estate manager.'

'Council estate?'

'Country estate,' Noah says patiently.

'Not your own?'

'No.'

'By the time I was your age, I'd had two kids and a house in Hampstead, another on the south coast, and a boat.'

211

By the time he was a year older, he also had a divorce under his belt. One of those homes had been sold to pay maintenance to his ex-wife and the boat had gone too. But I don't say that out loud.

'I think that says something about a man,' Harry says smugly.

It says that he's a plonker. I'm seething silently.

'Perhaps it does,' Noah agrees.

'Harry, shut up,' I say.

But he doesn't. Instead, he gets worse. A lesser man would be riled, but Noah deflects all Harry's jibes with good humour.

As it carries on, even Flick is beginning to get annoyed. 'Put a sock in it, Harry,' she says, regarding him over her wineglass. 'You've made your point.'

My husband falls silent and stays that way.

Ella is looking panicked as well she might. Harry is behaving like a petulant child and he's spoiling the evening. The good-mood vibe has seeped away and there's a tension round the table that's palpable. I don't know why he's quite so against Noah.

'Let's go and play ping-pong,' Ella suggests as soon as we've eaten. 'There's a table set up in one of the outhouses.'

'I'm game,' Art says. He's looking very laid-back and has started rolling a joint.

'Let's clear the table.' I start to collect the plates and Noah does the same.

'I need a breath of fresh air,' Flick says. 'I'm just going to walk on the beach for five minutes.' She motions to Art to follow her outside. What she means is that she needs a puff of his joint and knows that Noah will disapprove.

'I'll come too,' Harry says and, taking one of the half-empty wine bottles, he heads out after them. I don't think that Harry has ever used drugs, so perhaps he does just want some air. Perhaps he's just trying to make amends after picking on Flick's boyfriend. Usually Ella would have a smoke with Art, but I notice that she hangs back instead and fiddles about, tidying the kitchen.

I stack the dishwasher and pile the pots and pans up in the sink. With much therapeutic clanging, I start to wash them. Noah comes alongside me.

'That was great,' I say to Noah, aware that no one has thanked him properly for his efforts. 'Really great.'

'You're welcome.' He takes up the tea towel and starts to wipe.

I clang some more, then Noah puts his hands on my arms and stops me. 'You'll give yourself a headache on top of everything else,' he says with a smile.

'Sorry.' My anger ebbs out of me and I can't help but laugh.

'Harry's not my biggest fan, is he?'

'I don't know what's going on there,' I admit.

I'm beginning to think that Harry is aware of the amount of time I'm spending with Noah. Is that why he's like he is? If so, I have to make sure that I put some space between us. I don't want to antagonise the situation further and spoil the holiday. Already we're walking on eggshells with each other.

'He's being a total prat. I'm sure it's nothing personal. It's just the drink talking. I'm really sorry.'

'There's no need for you to apologise,' he says.

Before I can say any more, Ella comes into the kitchen and starts to rummage through the cupboards. 'I'm sure there are some more ping-pong balls in here,' she says. 'I bought some last time I came down.' Then, 'Ah. Here they are.'

Perhaps if we all run round and blow off a bit of steam, it might help to clear the atmosphere a bit. I can only hope.

Chapter Thirty-Six

The outhouse that holds the table-tennis equipment is the biggest one of the three that lie alongside Cwtch Cottage. It's dusty and clearly hasn't been used for years. There are cobwebs in every corner and it smells of pipe tobacco. Ella and I are the first to arrive.

'I should come and give this a good clean-out,' Ella says. 'It would look so much better.' She runs her hand fondly over the well-used green table that dominates the room. 'This is what Dad and I used to do on rainy days when we were up here on holiday. We could spend hours playing each other. Even though I never seemed to get any better, he always used to let me win.' Her voice is wistful. 'I do miss them both.' Her eyes fill with tears. 'I can't believe that I'm going to have a baby – their first grandchild – and that neither of them is here to see it. They would have loved to be grandparents. I'm just sorry I never did it when they were around.'

I take Ella in my arms and give her a hug. She's such a tiny little thing that I always want to protect her from the knocks of the world, but this girl is tougher than she looks. 'They'd be very proud of you, Ella. You know that.'

'I'd have liked their help too. It must be so much easier if you have your family supporting you.'

'We're family,' I say. 'Flick and I. We'll be here for you.'

She squeezes my hand. 'I'm not sure I'm brave enough to do this by myself.' Ella smoothes her T-shirt over her bump. 'It might not look much, but I think I'm already three months gone.'

I had no idea that was the case.

'That doesn't leave me much time to prepare. If I'm honest, Grace, I'm frightened.'

'You *have* to tell Art.'

'How can I?'

I put my hands on her tummy. 'He's going to figure it out soon enough, Ella. That bump's going to get steadily bigger. You can't keep wearing baggy jumpers and blame it all on an increased appetite.'

Then Noah arrives and we abandon our chat to pick up the table-tennis paddles. The rubber is worn and puckered, the colour faded.

'Come on, Ella, I'll take you on,' I say.

So my friend and I play together while Noah takes up a seat and watches us. Like the girls we are, Ella and I hit the ball to each other. I don't want to make her run around in her condition but, as I haven't played this since I was about twelve years old, it's all we can do to get it backwards and forwards across the saggy net. I feel self-conscious with Noah's eyes watching us intently.

Just like her dad, I let Ella win. As we finish our match, Harry, Art and Flick arrive, presumably drawn by the light on in the outhouse. The mood is a lot more mellow now, probably due to the influence of the wacky-baccy. Only Harry is still crotchety.

'Who's on next?' I hold out my bat.

Noah and Flick take up the paddles and it's clear that Noah lets her win too, but it's equally apparent that Flick is bored within seconds. Obviously, the delights of table tennis are failing to enthral her. She might say that she wants to give up the wild life of hard partying, but the reality of the alternative is, perhaps, harder to swallow.

Then I play Flick and give her a good thrashing because, if it's humanly possible, she's even worse than I am. In fairness, my opponent isn't helped by the fact that she's as drunk as a skunk and swaying like a ship on the ocean. It's also clear that she's been enjoying Art's pot and that hasn't improved her game either.

It's the turn of the men. Art takes Harry on, but smoking a joint or two hasn't improved his hand-to-eye coordination either and, even though Harry is drunk and lurching about, he runs rings round Art who concedes gracefully.

'Come on, Noah,' Harry says. 'Show us what you've got. See if you're as good at this as you are at everything else.'

'Harry,' I warn, 'it's table tennis.' You'd think he was challenging Noah to a duel.

'It's fine, Grace,' Noah says. 'I'm happy to take Harry on.'

With the first serve, the tone of the match is set. Harry smashes the ping-pong ball across the net with all the force he can muster and it whizzes straight past Noah at hip height.

'Not so clever now,' Harry snarls.

So Noah serves and spins it back across the table expertly. So it continues.

Ella keeps score. As the points fall, the game gets more tetchy. 'Come on, boys,' she says lightly. 'Play nicely.'

The angrier Harry gets, the more extreme his play. The more extreme his play, the more Noah ups his game and returns every ball. Harry is getting redder and redder in the face. I fear he might have a coronary. He couldn't be more aggressive with a table-tennis paddle if he tried.

'Harry,' I say, 'this is ridiculous.'

Flick is watching them both with narrowed eyes and a half-smirk at her lips. Surely she can't be enjoying this? Or is it just me who's embarrassed by Harry's behaviour?

Inevitably, being sober and so much better, Noah beats him with ease. Harry is fuming.

'Great game,' Noah says, staring levelly at Harry. 'Another one?'

Harry throws the ping-pong ball to the floor and stamps on it.

'I guess not,' Noah says affably.

'Oh, Harry!' I pick up the squashed ping-pong ball. 'For goodness' sake.' I remember him upending the Monopoly board one Christmas when we were playing the boys and he was losing. This takes me right back.

'Shut up, Grace,' Harry mutters, throwing down the paddle and retreating to top up his glass again. Clearly he's had enough of a pasting for one day. It's ridiculous, he doesn't need to compete with Noah. What does he suddenly feel he's got to prove? If he wants to impress me, he just needs to stay sober for once.

'I think we'll call it a day, anyway,' Ella says. 'Before someone loses an eye.'

'I'm sorry,' I whisper to her.

'There's far too much testosterone flying around for me,' she says. 'Come with me, Grace. I want to show you something.' She links her arm in mine. 'We'll be back in a minute,' she calls over her shoulder as we head to the door. 'Someone be a love and put the kettle on for coffee.'

Goodness only knows they need it.

So, as the others troop back towards the house, with Harry hanging back miserably, Ella and I head in the other direction.

Chapter Thirty-Seven

We negotiate the rocky path in the dark as my friend leads me down to one of the other outhouses. The moon is high in the sky and the stars are shining brightly. It's a fantastic night and it makes me realise how much light pollution there is in London as I hardly ever seem to see the stars any more. Perhaps later I'll get my jacket and come out to sit and stargaze on the beach. Perhaps Harry, if he's got over himself, can be cajoled into coming with me too.

Apart from the rush of the waves, the silence is overwhelming. It's like being cut off from the rest of the world, being here. I could quite easily believe that my accountancy practice has simply ceased to exist. If only.

'Ta-dah!' Ella says as we reach the door and she flicks on the light. 'Welcome to my humble studio.'

'Oh, wow!'

This outhouse is smaller than the games room but, in contrast, it has been thoroughly cleaned and newly painted. It's now a very smart home to some of Ella's paintings. There's a big workbench in the middle, stacked with her paints and jars of brushes. Her current work in progress is up on an easel.

'You've been busy since you got here.'

'I couldn't wait to get started,' she confides. 'It just felt like the right thing to do.'

Round the room are ranged various paintings, the like of which I've never seen Ella produce before.

'These are really yours?'

She nods, proudly. 'What's your opinion of my new style?'

'They're fabulous,' I tell her honestly.

'Not an angry slash in sight,' she says. 'I've found such inspiration down here. All this has come from the landscape.'

The new artworks are very clearly Ella's in that they're strong and colourful. But in place of the completely abstract images that she usually specialises in, these are based on patterns from nature. Swirls from seashells, curling waves and rugged rocks feature heavily. It looks as if she's been very productive. A rack of completed canvases leans up against the walls.

'I'm doing an exhibition of them in London in three months' time, so I've got a long way to go yet, but I'm brimming over with ideas.' Her eyes are glittering with excitement. 'I've had great feedback so far. Providing the public like it, this could take me to another level altogether.'

'I think this is your best work yet, Ella.' Rather than being angry and striking, like her previous paintings, these are warm, vibrant images. 'This baby is clearly bringing out the Earth Mother in you.'

'I think it is,' she agrees. 'I'm seeing nature as I've never seen it before. If this is a result of my hormones, then bring it on.' She sighs contentedly. 'I've been churning out the same kind of thing for years – and have been happy to do it. But this is liberating. I had no idea that I was capable of such things. The whole landscape is just so inspiring. Can you see why I want to stay down here?'

Yes. I can very much see.

'I feel so much closer to my parents when I'm here too. It's as if they've not really gone.'

'Oh, Ella.' I hug her again. 'I guess it doesn't matter where you are, if Art's away so much. You have to be happy. That's all that matters. But it's very isolated,' I remind her. I think of the lack of phone signal or landline, the fact that it's a good drive to the nearest supermarket. Where is the nearest doctor's surgery? With a new baby she'd need close-to-hand amenities that she currently takes for granted. 'Would you really be content down here alone?'

'I won't be alone, Grace,' she reminds me as she massages her bump affectionately. 'It'll be me and Baby Hawley.'

'How could I possibly forget?'

We both giggle at that. But I wonder how Ella would manage way out here on her own. It's remote enough in the summer months, but she could be cut off completely in the winter. I can imagine that it would be really bleak. Still, there's time enough to talk about that. For the moment I just want to revel in her reawakened creativity.

Then there's a commotion outside, much shouting and yelling.

Ella and I exchange a weary glance. I sigh. 'What now?'

Chapter Thirty-Eight

Art has found a rusty old tandem. He and Harry are currently riding it up and down the sandy track that runs along the back of Cwtch Cottage and eventually leads to the road. They're distinctly wobbly, but are clearly enjoying themselves as they're giggling like schoolboys.

'Good grief,' Ella says as we both stand and watch them, open-mouthed. 'I chucked that old thing out of the outhouse when I cleared it. I'd completely forgotten about it. I don't think it's moved in twenty years. I'm surprised it hasn't rusted away.'

'Looks like it's enjoying a new lease of life.'

'It's only here because I couldn't work out how to get it in the car to take it to the nearest tip.'

The chain creaks and the gears or something are clonking alarmingly. Art is at the front, pedalling like crazy, while Harry is at the back. He doesn't seem to be doing a lot of work, just hanging on with his arms and legs flailing. They zoom up and down like lunatics and we're all doubled over laughing at them.

It's the first time I've seen a smile on Harry's face in weeks – possibly months – and I get a brief glimpse of the man I used to know and love. It's nice to see.

'You're not getting me near that thing,' Flick says. She's still clutching her glass of wine.

'I wouldn't mind a go,' I admit. But not with Art or Harry in control.

Art and Harry skid to a halt in front of us, breathless and tittering.

'That was fun,' Harry says, out of puff. 'I haven't been on a bike in longer than I care to remember and I've never been on a tandem before.'

'Noah?' Art indicates that he should hop on the back and Noah does. They go even faster this time as Noah actually does some pedalling. That thing looks lethal.

'Mind the ditch,' Ella shouts as they do a juddering turn.

A tall hedge borders the track with a shallow drainage ditch in front of it. Art and Noah narrowly avoid it.

The night is chillier now and a breeze has picked up. But, despite the clouds gathering in the sky, a lot of the earlier tension has ebbed away again. Thank goodness. If only Harry could stay this good-natured, life would be so much simpler.

Art and Noah do a few more runs and then stop sharply in front of their audience, showering our feet with sand. We all clap.

Noah climbs off and pretends to stagger. 'I wonder how fast we could get that bike going out on the road? It's brilliant fun.'

'Come on, Ella,' Art says. 'Get on.'

She and I exchange a glance.

'Not on your life,' she says, holding up a hand.

'Don't be miserable,' Art says. 'It's great fun.'

'I really don't fancy it, Art,' she reiterates. 'Leave it.'

'I'll get on,' I say, even though it's probably the last thing on earth that I want to do.

'No.' Art's face has darkened. 'Get on, Ella. Stop being such a miserable cow. You're no fun any more.'

Ella looks as if he's slapped her.

I step forward. 'Art, let it drop. I'll have a go with you. What does it matter?'

'Stay out of this, Grace,' he says. 'Everyone else is having a laugh, Ella. Why are you always such a killjoy? You won't drink, you won't surf, now you won't get on a fucking *bike*. What's wrong with you, woman?'

I look at Ella. It's not the right moment, but she has to say it. She has to say that she's pregnant.

Instead, she says, 'OK. If it's so important to you.'

I put my hand on her arm. There's no way that I want her to do this. 'Ella ...'

'I'll be fine, Grace.'

Noah can tell how worried I am and he frowns at me, but what can I say? How can I tell him that every fibre of my being is willing Ella not to allow herself to be bullied by Art? Noah comes and stands next to me and, lowering his voice, says, 'Is there a problem?'

'She shouldn't be doing this,' I whisper back. 'Please stop it.'

'Maybe it's time to call it a day,' Noah ventures, glancing

up at the sky. It's black, glowering. 'The weather's on the turn. We've had the best of the evening. Why don't we all go in for a coffee instead before the rain comes in? I'll put the kettle on.'

'Butt out, Noah,' Art mutters. 'She'll do this.'

Noah stands in front of the tandem. 'Come on, Art. We've had our fun. I'll get on with you again, if you've got the energy.'

'Stand out of my way, Noah,' Art says tightly. 'Ella's going to do it. For me.'

'It's fine, Noah,' Ella assures him. But she knows that it's not.

With an apologetic glance at me, Noah stands aside. I hope that my returning look says, 'Thank you for trying.' What could he do? He couldn't forcibly stop Art without punching his lights out.

Reluctantly, Ella climbs on to the tandem and my heart goes into my mouth. Her feet can barely reach the pedals.

'Be careful,' I warn Art. 'Take it slow.'

But, of course, he doesn't listen and Ella is barely settled before he sets off at breakneck speed. The wind whips up and only serves to make them go faster.

They shoot off down the track, Ella clinging to the handle-bars. At the end they spin round and whizz back. Ella's face is white as they come rushing past.

'Enough now, Art,' I shout.

'One more run,' he insists.

'Quit while you're ahead,' Noah calls. 'You've made your point. It's going to pour down in a minute.'

The storm clouds are mustering and the wind, out of nowhere, is steadily increasing in speed. But Art pays us no heed and speeds down the track again. At the bottom, we hear the brakes squeal. They overshoot the point where they should be turning and instead head off into the rough grass. While Noah and I are standing with our mouths agape in terror, the wheel of the tandem hits a rock and over it flips.

I gasp out loud.

Art and Ella tumble from it into the ditch, the tandem on top of them.

'Not good,' Noah says and simultaneously we sprint down the track to where they've crashed.

Art is lying on his back, legs in the air, laughing, laughing. I think the amount of alcohol he's drunk must be anaesthetising any pain. Ella, on the other hand, isn't moving. She's also on her back in the ditch and has landed awkwardly. The bulk of the tandem has fallen on top of her.

Noah, who is first to reach them, jumps into the ditch and, with my help, hauls the tandem off Ella. I climb down and kneel beside her, stroking her hair.

'Are you hurt?' There's a cut on her forehead that's bleeding profusely. I fish a clean tissue out of my pocket and wipe the blood away. The first fat spots of rain start to hit us. 'You've just got a little cut. Nothing to worry about. Are you in pain anywhere?'

She tries to get up. 'My back,' she wheezes.

'You've probably just winded yourself,' Noah says soothingly. 'That was a fair weight on you. Take it easy.' Slowly, he helps her to a sitting position. 'OK?'

My friend nods uncertainly.

'Look after her, Grace,' Noah says tightly, then moves along to see to Art. 'I should go and dump his skinny arse into the sea,' he mutters darkly.

Ella looks up at me, her eyes filled with terror.

'You'll be fine,' I say as levelly as I can, even though I too am shaking with shock. 'You'll be absolutely fine.'

Her hands go protectively to her stomach.

'We'll get you back to the cottage and then you need to go and lie down. I'll bring you up some tea.'

'Thanks, Grace.'

'I shouldn't have let you go on that bloody thing in the first place.' I could kick myself. I just knew it was going to end in tears. 'What kind of a friend am I?'

She grips my hand. 'A good one.'

'Shut up with that or you'll make me cry.'

We both laugh shakily, but I see a few tears squeeze from Ella's eyes. Bloody Art! I could wring his neck.

Noah moves back towards us. 'Art's fine,' he says. 'A few cuts and bruises for his trouble. Feeling a bit shamefaced now he's sobering up, I should think.'

'Let's get Ella into the cottage.'

It's starting to rain more persistently now. This could well set in for the night. So, without hesitation, we lift her between us and half carry her back up the track.

Art limps along behind us, head hanging. I have no sympathy whatsoever. Not so funny now, eh?

'We could do with another pair of hands to wheel the tandem back,' Noah notes.

As the rain gets heavier and we struggle towards the door, it suddenly occurs to me that there's no sign of Flick or Harry. I look around, but I can't see them at all. I frown in the darkness. Where have those two disappeared to while all this has been happening?

Chapter Thirty-Nine

In the kitchen, Flick and Harry are standing by the table. They spring apart guiltily and, if I'm not mistaken, Harry was holding her hand. My husband's face is thunderous and Flick looks as if she's been crying, but I don't have time to ask what's going on now. Instead, I say, 'There you are! We wondered where you'd got to.'

'Look lively, we need a hand here,' Noah says, shaking the rain from his hair. 'Pull out a chair for Ella.'

Without question, Flick does as he asks, and Noah and I lower Ella into it gingerly. She's covered in dirt and there's sand in her hair.

'What the hell happened?' Flick wants to know when Ella's settled.

'Isn't it obvious?' I get some kitchen roll and wipe the dirt from her cheeks.

'Art crashed the bike,' Noah supplies. 'It fell on top of Ella.'

On cue, Art follows us through the door. He eyes us all

sheepishly, then goes straight to kneel at Ella's feet. 'I'm sorry, babe,' he says. 'Are you OK?'

Ella looks to me as if she's going to be sick. 'I've felt better.'

'Let's get you straight up to bed,' I say. 'Flick, will you put the kettle on and make her some sweet tea?'

I must have said it in a very authoritative voice as, for the second time tonight, she does as she's told without argument.

'Can you make it upstairs, sweetheart?' I say to Ella.

She nods at me.

Unbelievably, instead of helping, Art makes a beeline for the whisky bottle that's on the dresser.

'Don't you think you've had enough?' I snap. 'It's all the booze sloshing about that caused this accident in the first place.'

'I'm in shock too,' he says weakly. 'It was just a little medicinal snifter.'

'Have a bloody cup of tea.'

His hands fall to his sides.

'Put your arms round my neck,' Noah tells Ella and, with a sharp intake of breath, she does so.

Noah lifts her from the chair as if she's a feather and carries her up the stairs. I follow him up, close on his heels. At the top, I open her bedroom door and he lays her down on the bed.

'You don't think we should take you to the nearest hospital and get you looked at?' Noah asks.

'It's miles away,' Ella says. 'I think the journey would make me feel even worse. I'm sure I'll be all right if I just rest.'

'I'll go and get a cloth and some antiseptic to tend to that cut.'

'Thanks, Grace.'

Noah follows me into the bathroom and sits on the side of the bath while I rummage in the cabinet, looking for some cream to put on Ella's wound. At least it's not big enough to need stitches, just a nasty graze. I think the hedge must have caught her or perhaps part of the bike.

'Here.' Noah hands me a towel. 'Dry your hair. We don't want you catching a cold.'

I take the towel and give my hair a cursory rub. 'Thanks.'

'Is she going to be OK?' Noah asks. 'I'm happy to drive to the hospital.'

'I'll keep an eye on her.'

He pauses, weighing up his words. 'Is there something else going on with Ella?'

Hesitantly, I nod. 'I can't tell you, Noah. It's a secret.'

He shrugs. 'I can hazard a good guess.'

'You can't say anything. Not to anyone.' Most of all Art, I want to add. But I bite my lip. 'Not anyone.'

'If that's what you want.'

'The situation is ... difficult.' Then I sigh. 'I'm so sorry, Noah. I bet you thought you were going to be coming on a lovely, relaxing and romantic holiday with Flick. I'm sorry that it's not turning out like that.'

Noah purses his lips. 'Grace ...'

Before he can say any more, Flick sticks her head round the bathroom door. 'I've brought Ella's tea up. Shall I take it in to her?'

232

'Yes.' I've found some cotton wool and antiseptic cream.

'I'll leave you to it,' Noah says. 'Just let me know if Ella needs anything else.' He hesitates. 'Or if you do. Anything.'

'Thank you.' His kindness nearly moves me to tears.

I trail after Flick into the bedroom. Gingerly, we both help Ella out of her clothes and into her pyjamas. Tucking her up in bed, I pull the duvet around her.

'You'll make someone a lovely mum,' she teases.

'And so will you.' I wipe her wound and put some cream on it.

'Ouch,' she says pitifully.

'You're probably going to have a nice egg-shaped lump there tomorrow.'

She touches it tentatively. Let's hope that's all that's wrong. Then we will have had a lucky escape.

'You've got to look after yourself now, Ella,' I tell her. 'Lie as still as you can and try to get some sleep. If you have any pain – a twinge or anything – then let me know straight away. Just shout out. Don't be brave. Noah says that he'll drive you to the hospital.'

Flick shoots me a look, but I ignore it. If she thinks I'm spending too much time with her boyfriend, then hard bloody lines. Noah has been a rock. I don't know what I would have done without him. Besides, where had she and Harry sloped off to when we needed them?

Chapter Forty

Flick leaves and I stay for a few more minutes just to make sure that my friend is comfortable. I stroke Ella's hair and kiss her cheek.

'Sleep tight, sweetheart.'

It's a terrible night outside now and the rain lashes against the window. I go and close it, but already the windowsill is wet. The sea is raging against the shore.

The benign scenery has changed to a frothing, angry monster, as if echoing the mood of the cottage.

'Thanks, Grace.' Ella rests her pale cheek on the pillow.

'Do you want Art to come up?'

'Not really,' she says. 'I think I'd like to be on my own for a while.'

Can't say that I blame her. 'I'll take him a duvet downstairs and he can kip on the sofa as his punishment.'

'There's a spare one in the airing cupboard on the landing. Will he be comfortable down there?'

'He'll have to be,' I tell her. 'Don't you dare worry about him.'

Ella smiles wanly. 'I'll try not to.'

'Remember, all you have to do is call out if you want me. I'll come straight away.'

'I know.'

'Love you,' I say.

'Love you too.' She blows a kiss at me.

Reluctantly, I leave her alone. Ideally, I'd like to sit and watch her all night, but I know that she wouldn't let me.

As soon as I'm outside the bedroom door, Flick pounces on me and whispers, 'She looks like shit.'

'Is that a medical opinion?' I ask crisply.

Flick looks chastened. 'I'm just saying—'

'Then don't. It's not helping anyone. Least of all Ella.'

'It was just a silly accident.'

'She could have lost the baby,' I remind her. Opening the cupboard door, I get out a duvet and pillow for Ella's stupid, selfish boyfriend. 'It was a ridiculous thing to make her do. I'm just sorry, as one of the few sober people present, that I didn't prevent it.' I puff out an angry breath.

'Art doesn't know that she's up the duff,' Flick hisses.

'Would it have mattered? From where I was standing, he was too far gone to care. She didn't want to do it, that should have been clear enough to everyone.' I resist the urge to bang the door. 'All this drinking has to stop. I don't know what's going on. Why does everyone feel as if they need to get pissed to have a good time?'

Flick fidgets uncomfortably, but says nothing. So I give up with my lecture and stomp downstairs.

Art is sitting at the table, having the prescribed cup of tea, head in hands. He looks up, bleary-eyed, as we come into the kitchen. 'Is she going to be all right?'

'Yes.' No thanks to you. 'She just needs to rest.'

'Can I go and see her?'

'No. Leave her alone. I don't want her upset.' I throw down the duvet and pillow. 'You can sleep off your excesses on the sofa. It will all look better in the morning.'

I sink into a chair. This is one of my few weeks off a year. At this rate, I'm going to go back to work more exhausted than when I left. 'A quick cup of tea and then I'm going straight to bed.' I can hardly keep my eyes open. Then I look around. 'Where's Harry? Has he gone up already?'

Now everyone scans the room. I see a look of panic flit across Flick's features.

'What?'

She shrugs. 'I don't know where he is.'

'He's not in the sitting room, is he?' Knowing Harry, he could quite easily have sloped off and fallen asleep on the sofa.

Flick jumps up and puts her head round the door. 'No,' she says. 'He's not there.'

I didn't see him go upstairs while we were putting Ella to bed, but I suppose it's worth checking. I haul myself out of my chair and tiptoe up the stairs, trying not to disturb Ella, and peep into our bedroom. No Harry. And the bathroom's empty too.

Back in the kitchen, I say to the others, 'He's not in the cottage at all. That's weird.'

'Perhaps he's gone out for some fresh air,' Art suggests helpfully.

'In this weather? What would possess anyone to venture out on a night like this?'

The wind is whipping round the cottage; the rain and spray pound at the windows.

Flick's expression is very cagey.

'Any ideas, Flick?' I look levelly at her. They seemed to be having some sort of altercation when we came in earlier. Wonder what that was all about ...

'Maybe we should just have a quick look outside for him.' She nibbles at a perfectly manicured fingernail. 'Just in case he's wandered off by accident.'

'Why would he do that?' I ask her. 'Is there something I should know?'

She glances shiftily at Noah. 'No,' she says. 'Nothing at all.'

'It's a filthy night out there,' I point out. 'Why would he go out in this from choice?'

'Flick's right,' Noah intervenes. 'If he's not in the cottage where else can he be? We should go out and have a hunt for him. We'll check the outhouses first. He might just be brushing up on his table-tennis skills.'

I know that Noah's trying to make light of the situation and we all attempt a laugh, but it doesn't entirely take away my feeling of foreboding. What can Harry be playing at?

'OK.' I can't hold back my weary sigh. Tonight has been far too traumatic already without this. 'Let's go and find Harry. Flick, are you coming?'

She looks as reluctant as I feel. 'Perhaps I should stay here and listen out for Ella.'

'Art could do that.'

I don't want Art lurching about outside drunk. He'd be more of a liability. I think it's the lesser of two evils that he's here for Ella. I'm hoping that she's sound asleep by now. Flick is definitely the more sober of the two, but that's not saying much.

Art nods his agreement. 'There are some waterproof jackets on the coat rack, if you dig deep. Best to wrap up.'

He's not kidding. You can hear the rain pelting against the cottage. The wind is whistling round the eaves.

I'm taking it as given that Noah will put himself out for Harry and, sure enough, he's first to the door to search out coats for us all. When he locates them, he hands the waterproofs to me and Flick, then slips one on himself.

'Before we all get wet through, let me go out first,' he says. 'I'll check the outhouses. Hopefully, he'll be there.'

'If I remember rightly, there should be one of those great big torches hanging up too,' Art adds.

Noah rummages around some more under the coats before he eventually finds it nestling on top of the bucket of golf balls. It has a reflector the size of a dinner plate, which hopefully will throw out a lot of light, as I don't much fancy scrambling about on the beach in the pitch darkness in a storm.

Noah checks the battery and then, with a grimace, goes out into the night alone. Time seems to pass interminably slowly. I pace the floor in the kitchen. Flick, unusually for her, looks on the verge of tears. Eventually, he comes back. Still alone. It's all I can do not to rush to his side.

He shakes his head. 'Nothing.'

Both Flick and I realise that it means we'll all have to go out and so, without speaking, we don our waterproofs.

'We'll take an extra one for Harry,' I say, 'in case he's gone out without one.'

I really hope that he hasn't, as Noah has been out for just a few minutes and he's soaked through.

'I'll carry it,' Flick says and she tucks it under her arm.

'Ready?' Noah asks.

We nod in unison.

As soon as we open the door, the wind tries to batter us back in. The pleasant sun-soaked day is but a distant memory, replaced by a black, malevolent night. This is going to be tough. We push outside and the wind hurls needles of rain and sea spray in our faces. Now I'm worried. If Harry is out in this, I have no idea what he was thinking. What if he did just want a bit of fresh air and he slipped somewhere and hurt himself? We would never have heard him shouting.

'Watch your step,' Noah warns, shining the torch ahead of us. 'These rocks are lethal.'

Was it only this morning when we were all sitting out here with a cup of tea, basking in the sunshine? It feels like a different time and place entirely. On this outing there'll be no singing' and dancin' in the rain on the sand.

Slithering and slipping over the rocks, we carefully make our way towards the beach. The tide is high, the waves crashing angrily against the shore.

'Harry!' Noah shouts out. 'Harry!' His voice is whipped away by the noise of the wind and sea.

Huddled together, we make our way along the top of the

beach, keeping well clear of the treacherous sea. My mouth goes dry. What if Harry has been swept away? It would be so easy. What if he'd walked out on the rocks, perhaps slipped and banged his head? If he'd fallen into the sea, he'd be dragged under and we might never find him. Oh God. My heart starts to thump in panic. I've had such unkind thoughts about him recently. I thought, I was so sure, that I didn't love him any more. But now I'd give anything just to see him again, to have the chance to hold him in my arms.

Tears stream down my cheeks, mixing with the rain.

'Harry! Harry!' We all call out in unison, trying to make ourselves heard.

Noah scans the rocks with the torch, but the beam scarcely penetrates the rain. We could cover more ground if we searched for him separately, but it's so dangerous out here that any one of us could slip and fall. I think it's best if we stay together. I have no desire to go wandering off on my own on this filthy night and, again, I wonder why Harry would.

We're clambering across the rocks now, further away from the safety of Cwtch Cottage. Surely he can only have gone this way? If you go in the other direction, there's quite a steep climb behind the cottage and I don't think Harry, even in his inebriated state, would have tried that. He could possibly have headed down the road, but why would he do that when it would take him nowhere?

The clouds are dark, shouldering into each other just above our heads, weeping. If we didn't have this big, fuck-off torch, we'd never see anything. We trudge further and further, facing into the rain.

Then, just as I'm beginning to abandon all hope of finding him, Noah says, 'There!'

I look up and, sure enough, Harry is sitting on a lone rock, staring out to sea. My heart races and I hear myself whisper, 'Thank God.'

Together, we pick up our pace and hurry forwards. He's not wearing a jacket and his shirt is soaked, stuck to his skin. The waves are swirling just below his feet and we have to wade in the water up to our knees to reach him. The tide is coming in fast.

'Harry!' Noah shouts out. But he doesn't hear us.

We're right upon him, splashing heavily through the waves, when he turns and finally notices us. We climb on to the rock and I kneel down next to him. He looks as if he's in a trance and I'd say that he's been crying, but it's hard to tell with the rain. I don't think that I've ever seen Harry cry and I wonder what on earth can be wrong.

'Come on, love,' I say. 'You'll catch your death of cold out here. Come back to the cottage with us. I'll get some hot chocolate on the go.'

He doesn't move, and Noah and I exchange a worried look. Flick is hanging back. When Noah moves to the other side of him and we lift him together, Harry doesn't resist.

'Let's get you into this nice warm jacket.' I try to sound jovial, as if it's the most natural thing in the world to find my husband out in the blackness, being lashed by the fierce rain. If we don't get him off here quickly, then we'll soon be up to our thighs in water. 'Come on, love.'

Flick steps forward and helps me to feed his arms into the waterproof.

For the first time, Harry looks up. 'You came,' he says, sounding choked.

'Of course we did,' I answer.

'I knew you still cared.' He seems to have aged ten years in the last few hours and I feel frightened for him. With Noah's help I lead him gingerly, slowly, down the rocks. We support him as we wade back through the ever-encroaching waves. Any longer and we'd have been cut off from Cwtch Cottage, I'm sure. We might never have found Harry at all.

Flick thrusts her hands deep into her pockets and marches along beside us, head down. She doesn't deal very well with overt displays of emotion and I think, at this moment, she'd rather be anywhere else. My friend falls into step next to me.

'Are you all right, Harry?' she asks quietly.

But I don't think he hears her as he mumbles, 'I'm sorry. I'm sorry for everything.'

'It doesn't matter now,' I assure him. 'You're safe. That's all that matters to me.'

The wind and rain are at our backs now, making the going slightly easier. Nevertheless, when Cwtch Cottage comes into view, I could lie down on the sand and cry with relief.

Chapter Forty-One

Harry is lying back in the bath, eyes closed, the suds piled around him. I found some muscle-relaxing foam bath in the cabinet that must have belonged to Ella's parents. I hope she doesn't mind me using it. As this rate, I'm going to have to replenish all of her bathroom supplies.

'Better now?' I feel as if I have to treat him with kid gloves.

I've made him hot chocolate and am sitting on the loo seat, studying him, while he lies there. He looks weary beyond his years. His face is grey and he could easily be in his sixties. I remember a time when I would have stripped off my clothes and slipped into the bath with him for a romantic cuddle. Part of me really wants to do that now, but I don't know how. We seem to be strangers to each other and I can't seem to cross that chasm. Particularly unaided. If only Harry would reach out to me too.

He opens his eyes and nods. 'Yes. Thank you.' His eyes roll shut again.

'Want to tell me what that was all about?'

His eyes stay shut. 'Not really.'

'Harry, if there's anything wrong we can work it out. Whatever it is.' I squash down my sigh of frustration. 'If I don't know what the problem is, then how can I help?'

I slide down and sit next to the bath, toying with the hairs on his damp arm that lies along the side, making whorly patterns this way and that.

'We can get back to how we were. I know we can.'

At this moment, I feel that I'll do anything to try. Our marriage is worth saving and I realised, as I saw Harry sat out there alone in that terrible storm, that I'd be devastated if anything happened to him. What if we hadn't found him? What if it had been a cold, lifeless body we were bringing home instead? The thought convulses me with a shiver and I feel sick to my stomach. There's no doubt that I desperately want things to change, but I'm equally sure that I don't want to be a widow. I might not like Harry much at the moment, but I do believe that, underneath it all, I still love him. We're going through a rough patch, that's all. Nothing more. All marriages have them. The couples that stay the distance are the ones who can push through the painful times until all becomes well again.

He lifts his hand to stroke my hair and I shift so that he can cup my face.

'What's happened to us?' Tears prickle my eyes. 'We used to be in love.'

Nothing from my husband.

'Is it work?'

He shakes his head. 'No.'

'The kids? Your ex-wife?'

'No.'

'Me?'

'No.'

'Mid-life crisis?'

A vague smile at that. 'Perhaps so.'

'People having a mid-life crisis don't put themselves at risk by wandering off on to dangerous rocks by themselves. They buy sporty motorbikes, wear inappropriate clothing and chase younger women.'

'I might do that too,' he offers weakly.

Perhaps he needs some antidepressants, to take up some exercise, give up drinking. I know that it's not the right time to raise any of this now. But when is?

'We need to sit down and have a good talk, Harry. Clear the air between us.' I take a deep breath. 'You may not be happy with the way things are, but it's no bed of roses for me either.' I dip my fingers into the bathwater. The heat has gone out of it. 'Let's go to bed now. Everything will seem better in the morning.'

'Will it?' he says despondently.

I hold out a towel for him. It's warm from the radiator. 'Want me to dry you?'

'I can manage.' So he stands up, gets out of the bath and, somewhat lethargically, rubs himself down.

A few minutes later, we're lying next to each other in bed, Harry on his back, staring at the ceiling. I cuddle up to him, with my arm across his chest.

'That Noah,' he says flatly. 'He's a solid chap, isn't he?'

My traitorous heart pitter-patters, even in these circumstances. Is that what this is about? Am I right? Has he noticed that I seem to be drawn to Noah like a moth to a flame? If he has, then it has to stop. I need to save my marriage, not keep thinking how much better Noah and I get on together than I currently do with my husband. Harry and I were good for each other once. Surely we could recapture that again?

I keep my tone neutral when I reply, 'I couldn't have found you without him tonight.'

'He and Flick aren't suited,' is his opinion. 'It won't last.'

With that he turns his back to me and goes to sleep.

Chapter Forty-Two

'God, what a night,' Flick says. She drags on her cigarette and blows the smoke into the wind. 'Noah and I were so exhausted by the time we got to bed that I didn't even get a shag!'

There are some things I should be grateful for.

I too was exhausted when I got to bed. I slept fitfully, with nightmares of being chased, scratched and hurt by creatures unknown. I feel just as exhausted this morning.

Flick, Ella and I are sitting on the picnic bench on the terrace, our regular morning spot. It's nice for just the three of us to spend time together. We're all nursing tea and there's a rapidly dwindling plate of toast in the middle of the table. I'm taking plenty of carbs on board in the hope that they'll give my energy a quick lift.

Of the terrible storm last night, there's hardly a sign. The day is clear, bright and, though there's a sharpness to the air, it looks as if it's going to be beautifully sunny again. The sky is cloudless, tranquil. The raging sea, now a veritable millpond.

Very much the calm after the storm. The only indication that there had been any trouble at all is that the beach is strewn with detritus thrown up by the petulant waves: seaweed, shells and pebbles, as well as the much more human waste, a litter of plastic bottles, bits of rope and even a single shoe.

'How are you feeling today?' I ask Ella.

'I'm fine,' she says, nursing her little baby bump. 'Nothing to worry about.'

'Good.' Though I do think that she looks a little pale this morning and maybe there are slight shadows under her eyes.

'Art?'

'He crept in beside me in the early hours,' she admits with a rueful smile. 'I expect he was getting cold on the sofa.'

'I hope he apologised.'

She nods. 'He did feel like a bit of an idiot.'

'Also good,' I say. 'I don't know what got into him.'

'Well, it was a shock, but no harm done. Here ...' She takes my hand and places it on her tummy. 'I'm so excited now that I know it's really going to happen. Thanks for that, Grace.'

I rest my hand gently on her bump. I'm thrilled by the thought of new life beneath my fingers. 'How lovely.'

'I feel like a benign Earth Mother,' she confesses with a self-conscious laugh. 'Just like you said.'

'Art still doesn't know?'

Ella shakes her head. 'I was going to tell him last night, but well ... It was nice just to cuddle up instead. There's time enough yet.'

I let my hand fall away. Subconsciously, it goes to my own

flat belly. Nothing in there but a gnawing feeling that I'm living the wrong life.

'Noah and I cuddled up too,' Flick chips in, wistfully. 'Somehow it was even nicer than torrid sex.' A frown creases her perfect brow. 'How is that possible?'

Clearly this is an alien concept for Flick and I try to push the image out of my mind. It's actually ten times worse than my image of them getting down to it.

It's fair to say that my own internal storm has also left its own kind of debris. Scattered across my heart are remnants of promises, fears, hopes and tears. I'm still just not feeling the calm after *my* storm. I'm hoping that it will come and, instead of feeling racked with trepidation, I'll see the future full of sun-filled possibilities.

'How's Harry?' Ella wants to know.

'He seems OK,' I tell her. 'Still no idea what's going on in his head, but at least we all got him home safely.'

'Thanks to Noah,' Flick throws in.

'Yes.' Can't argue with that.

I sigh inside. Despite his ordeal, Harry seemed to sleep like a baby. Whereas I did not. It doesn't matter what domestic strife we've had, Harry can be fast asleep and snoring moments after his head hits the pillow. I'm the one who tosses and turns, fretting about all that was said, as well as what wasn't that should have been. I still can't get out of my mind that image of Harry sitting alone on the beach in the teeth of the storm. What had driven him to that? I'm no closer to knowing.

'I don't know what I would have done without Noah last night,' I say candidly. 'He was a hero.'

I can imagine Noah in one of those disaster movies where one ordinary man is required to save the world. That would be him. And he'd acquit himself admirably. And get the girl. And the world would be saved. And Noah Reeves would look very fine in a ripped and dirtied vest too.

'Yes,' Flick agrees. 'I thought they'd broken the mould that made men like Noah. Seeing him in action has made me even more resolved in my determination to propose to him.'

'Isn't Noah the sort of man who would want to do the proposing?' I suggest gently.

'Oh, Grace.' She sighs with exasperation. 'You're so old-fashioned. I could wait for ever and I just don't have the time.'

'There's no hurry, Flick. It's better to get it right than rush in.'

'How do you know? Anyway, *you're* married. Why not me? Surely you can see why I fully intend this one to be a keeper?'

I do. Noah Reeves's charms are so very, very apparent to me. And I'm going to have to turn my face and my heart away from that, as one of my vows in the deep, dark night was that I'm going to be a better wife from now on. Whatever is going on in Harry's head or life that is making him like this, I'm going to devote myself one hundred per cent to helping him through it. Isn't that the role that I signed up for?

'God,' Flick says. 'I could write a book about all the crap boyfriends I've had.' She sighs.

'It would be a best-seller,' Ella agrees with a laugh. 'Though you'd have to change the names to protect the guilty.'

'It could run to several volumes,' she acknowledges.

'You had a veritable parade through our flat at university,'

I add. One or two of them are captains of industry now or famous sportsmen. But most are probably still signing on.

'I was young and foolish then,' Flick says. 'I didn't know what I was looking for.'

'Other than great sex,' Ella says.

'Yes,' she admits. 'I had plenty of that. And more than my fair share of terrible sex. But that's all behind me. The new me is looking for a man who can put up shelves and be reliable through life's ups and downs.'

'And, presumably, one who hasn't already got a wife,' Ella notes.

'I've always envied you two, you know,' Flick continues. 'Able to stay with one man. Up until now, I've never found anyone who's been enough for me.'

'Or you've run rings round them,' Ella adds.

'We had fun, though, didn't we?' she chides. 'When we were all in the flat together? I might remind you that I wasn't the only naughty one. You two had your moments in the sunshine or the squalor too.'

Ella laughs. 'I suppose we did. There were several blokes that I brought home to that flat that I've tried very hard to erase from my memory bank.' She shudders. 'What was I thinking?'

'I was never "naughty",' I protest. I was the one who made sure we paid the rent, dealt with the bills, bought food, exterminated the vermin.

'You had some great boyfriends off me, Grace,' Flick recalls.

'I had two or three of your unfortunate cast-offs,' I correct. 'Briefly. Poor saps who dated me a couple of times –

unenthusiastically – just so that they could stay near you and torture themselves a bit.'

'That's not my version of it,' she cackles. 'Just try to keep your hands off this one. He's mine. All mine.'

Underneath that joviality, is there really a veiled threat? As it's closer to the truth than I'd like, I let it pass.

'Remember that terrible bar we worked in?' Flick says. 'The manager used to try to grope us at every possible opportunity. Why did we put up with it?'

'We needed the money,' I point out. 'To pay the landlord who also used to try to grope us at every opportunity!'

That raises a titter from all of us.

'His hands were as damp as the walls in the flat,' Ella says. 'Yuck.'

Me: 'And he used to try to press us up against the cooker.'

'Oh, happy times,' Flick concurs. Then she's suddenly subdued. 'I don't know what I would have done without you both,' she says. 'I thought I had it under control, but I was such a mess after the whole thing with Brian. I look back on it now and can see that it was so tawdry. At the time it felt like a big adventure. Until it all went wrong, of course.'

In Vegas, while still on honeymoon, Flick's new husband, Brian, had proved that he didn't have eyes for just one young pretty girl. Despite his having abandoned his family for her, every time Flick moved from his side she'd come back to find him chatting up someone else.

'I knew it was a total cock-up the day I married him,' she says, sounding bitter. 'What a fool I was.'

'You were young,' I counter. 'He took advantage of you.'

252

'It just seemed so exciting. I thought I was so sophisticated, that I had it all sorted. Now I wonder just how long he'd had his eye on me,' Flick muses. 'Probably too long for it to be legal. Tosser.'

When Flick had told him that she thought they'd made a mistake, the lovely Brian had thrown her out of the hotel room without her bag, her airline ticket or her passport. She'd had to call the police to the hotel to get them back for her. It wasn't quite the dream ending to her affair that she'd hoped for. She returned to England, alone and penniless.

Then Flick shrugs. 'He was shacked up with another teenager within months. He didn't exactly grieve over me for long. Men!' She puffs out an unhappy breath. 'I let him divorce me. For adultery. What a laugh. I should have exposed him for what he was. You'd have thought that I'd learned my lesson.'

But we don't, do we? Something like that can shape our future and not in a good way. We so often repeat destructive behaviour learned at an early age.

'It's all water under the bridge.' Flick forces a laugh. 'Look at us now. Who would have thought that ten years later we'd still be firm friends?'

Ella stares out to sea.

'We've all turned into strong, successful women,' Flick declares. 'We should be proud of ourselves.'

'It's only love that we're unlucky in,' Ella counters.

Another shrug from Flick. 'You make your own luck. If you want something badly enough, you should let nothing stand in your way.'

'Not even friendship?' Ella asks quietly as she turns to look at her.

Flick stands, clearly riled. Did I miss something here? She shakes herself down. 'Let's go and find those lazy bastards, see what they want to do today.'

Flick strides ahead while Ella and I trail behind – much like it has always been. I help Ella over the rocks. But somehow I feel that the sun has gone behind a cloud and I don't know why.

Chapter Forty-Three

Harry, it seems, is determined to stay at the cottage, moping. After his theatrics last night, you'd think that he'd be in a conciliatory mood. But no such luck.

He's on the sofa, fiddling about with his redundant phone. I crouch down in front of him.

'It's a beautiful day out there,' I cajole. 'We're thinking of going to the beach again.'

'I'm not overly fond of sand,' Harry retorts. 'It gets everywhere.'

'You can't stay here all day by yourself.'

He looks up at that. 'Is everyone going out?'

'As far as I'm aware.'

'Huh.'

'We're taking a power kite or there's talk of going coasteering.'

'What on earth is "coasteering" when it's at home?' he grumbles. 'That, no doubt, will be one of Noah's bright ideas.'

I sigh. I thought that perhaps Harry was softening towards Noah a little.

'Without Noah, I would have struggled to find you,' I remind him. 'Who knows what could have happened? A bit longer and you could have been swept out to sea and ended up as fish food. You owe him your thanks, Harry, not your snide comments.'

But he turns his face away. It looks as if my little pep talk still won't encourage him to join the Noah fan club.

'Do you want to do something, just the two of us?' I ask.

I'd rather be with everyone else, but if it's the only way that I can get Harry out of the cottage, then so be it. Is it bad that I don't want to be alone with Harry any more? Once I used to value the precious times we had on our own. Now I'm more likely to dread what will fill them. This time it will no doubt have to involve going to the pub as usual and that's the last thing I want to do.

Then Flick bursts through the door. 'Come on, you two,' she says. 'Look lively. We're leaving in ten.'

'Harry's not coming,' I say.

'Don't be such a miserable bloody bastard,' she tuts. 'If it all gets too healthy, you and I can go and get pissed together.'

At that, he brightens and almost springs off the sofa.

Sometimes, Flick's blunt way of getting to the crux of the matter can come in very handy.

Half an hour later, we're setting up camp again on Portgale beach, in much the same place as we did yesterday. Harry and I came down in the Merc with Art and Ella, so I haven't had much chance to talk to Noah. Despite the sun being set on scorchio, the beach is a bit quieter today and we can spread ourselves out. The school holidays haven't started yet, so the only families are the ones with toddlers and they seem to be few and far between. The delights of Pembrokeshire seem to be overlooked in favour of Devon or Cornwall. Or Corfu.

While we're shaking out blankets and unloading picnic hampers, generally making a lot of fuss about getting settled, Noah comes and stands next to me.

'You're quiet today,' he says.

'Tired,' I offer weakly. 'Too much drama last night.'

He nods at that. 'All well now?'

I shrug. 'For the moment.'

We both glance over to where Flick and Harry are laughing together on a blanket. If only I could elicit such hilarity from him, I think meanly. Then I notice that they already have a bottle of wine open between them. It's not yet noon, for heaven's sake. Harry's going to be having Merlot with his muesli at this rate.

'Thanks again for last night,' I say. 'You were great.' My voice cracks slightly on the word. 'Two crises narrowly averted, I think.'

'All in a day's work,' he teases. 'Now we're going to put all that behind us and have some fun together.'

Personally, I feel like lying down on the sand and having a lovely long doze. After a few sleepless nights, I think I'm still running entirely on fumes.

'Everyone's up for coasteering,' Noah says. 'Except Ella. She's going to stay and look after all the gear.' He lowers his voice. 'Is she all right?'

I match his tone. 'Yes. Thank goodness.'

He looks relieved, as am I.

'What about Harry and Flick?' I ask. 'They're already stuck into the hard stuff.'

Noah frowns at that. 'They both said they were coming along. I'll have to keep an eye on them. You don't want to be jumping off rocks and stuff while you're drunk.'

I'm rather surprised that Harry and Flick want to be jumping off rocks at all, but I say nothing. Then, while we're talking, Flick jogs over to us.

'We're going to fly the kite,' Flick says with a nod towards Harry. 'How long have we got?'

'A good half-hour,' Noah says. 'I've booked us all in for noon. I thought we could work up an appetite and have something to eat later. Know how to set the kite up?'

'We'll work it out,' she says, then goes back to the rug and tugs Harry by the hand. With a mock grumble, he allows Flick to tow him along and they head off on to the sand together.

Ella and Art are lying on a blanket, curled up side by side. Art is stroking her hair and it's good to see that they're looking quite loved-up again. I don't want to disturb them, so I go to sit on the bank of shingle that borders the beach and hug my knees to me. Eventually, Noah drops down beside me, lying back, propped up on his elbows. I should turn my face away, cross my arms, hum a little tune, anything to avoid being close to him. I have promised that I will keep my distance and I should damn well stick with it, even though it's taking every shred of willpower not to chat amiably with him.

In silence, we watch Harry and Flick running about on the

sand. They've both kicked off their shoes and Harry has rolled up his jeans. He's untucked his white linen shirt and it's flapping loose – a look that he doesn't normally embrace. Harry prefers to be buttoned up and tightly knotted. For the first time in ages, he looks relaxed. Flick has on the shortest of shorts, which show off her long, tanned legs. Her white-blonde hair streams behind her in the breeze. It's very easy to see why she usually has a queue of men waiting for her.

Noah's eyes follow her every move, a contented smile on his face.

The canopy of the bright red and yellow kite billows high into the air in front of them. Harry and Flick hold the lines together, arms entwined, laughing as the wind lifts it and pulls them this way and that at the edge of the surf.

'They're doing well,' Noah says. 'That's a whole lot of kite to handle.'

And Flick, I think, is a whole lot of woman to handle.

The kite dips and dives and scuds sideways across the sky, while Harry and Flick hang on for dear life.

'It looks like great fun.'

'You've never flown a kite?'

'Not like that,' I admit. 'I had a little one as a kid, with a string of bows as a tail.'

'This is a bit different. Want to have a go?' Noah asks.

I shake my head. 'We should leave them to it while they're happy.'

I'd like to join in, run about on the beach with Harry, but I know that if I went and took over from Flick, he'd sink into sullen moodiness. What does that tell me about our relationship?

Chapter Forty-Four

I've made sure that Ella is settled and happy. I can leave her now that I know she has plenty of water, snacks and magazines to keep her company. Noticeably, Art does nothing to challenge her decision to dip out of the activity.

Kissing her cheek, I say, 'See you later. We won't be long.'

'Don't worry about me, Grace,' she says. 'I'll be fine. All I'll be doing is some extreme sunbathing.'

'Well, don't get burned.'

'Clear off,' she chides amiably. 'Just relax and have fun.'

We cross the road, go to the surf shop again and get kitted out for our coasteering experience. Harry and Flick are stumbling and giggling more than I'd like them to be. Noah and I exchange a worried glance.

'Are you guys going to be OK?' he asks. 'I don't want you hurting yourselves.'

'Chill out, fusspot,' Flick says, hanging on to Harry. 'We're gonna kick your sorry ass.'

'Oh, you think so?' Noah teases. 'Well, bring it on then.'

She comes and wraps her arms round him and, knowing my place, I drop back next to Harry.

In the surf shop, we're given rubber slip-on shoes to enable us to grip the slippery rocks for climbing, wetsuits and knee-length baggy board shorts, which are, quite worryingly, on a par with my black bin-bag knickers in the fashion stakes. An orange buoyancy aid and matching safety helmet top off our lovely ensemble. Flick and I go to the ladies' changing rooms to put them on. We strip off our clothes and don swimwear, then all the gear required for our adventure.

'Ohmigod,' Flick stares at herself in the mirror. 'There's no way I would have agreed to do this if I'd known the outfit was so bad!'

'You look fine,' I assure her. 'Well, no worse than the rest of us.'

At least Flick's shorts seem to fit her. Mine seem to be about three sizes too big and dangle somewhat unattractively round my knees. They're also in clashing shades of pink and orange and patterned with bold flowers. It's fair to say that if they were hanging on a clothes rail in a shop, I'd pause briefly to poke fun at them, then walk right on by.

'That is small comfort, Grace,' she says, turning every which way to find an angle that doesn't look so grim. Eventually, with a disheartened sigh, she gives up. 'I should have stayed on the beach with Ella.'

I link my arm through hers. 'It'll be fun. You'll see.'

'My idea of fun is finding a great bar in the sun that does a nice bottle of something chilled, not freezing your arse off in the sea in Wales. I can't for the life of me see why Ella would want to leave London to move down to this godforsaken place.'

'I love it here too.'

'You're both mad,' she says. 'I could do it again for a long weekend. Probably. But be based here permanently?' She shudders.

Clearly, Noah hasn't yet told her about his plans and dreams.

'Come on. They'll be waiting for us.'

'Lip gloss,' she says, rooting in the pocket of her shorts. 'At least I can add a *bit* of glamour.'

So I wait while Flick fluffs her hair, tries a dozen different ways to put it up under her safety helmet and slicks on lip gloss. Finally, she's ready and we join the others, who by now must have been standing there for ten minutes.

The owner of the shop, an affable chap called Callum who's probably in his forties, doubles up as our coasteering guide. We follow him out of the shop and over the shingle bank, making our way along the sand to the far end of the beach. My stomach's twisting with anxiety and excitement.

Then we all come to a standstill.

Flick looks up. 'Oh, fuck.'

We've clearly reached our destination as we've run out of beach and nothing but a big wall of rock faces us.

Chapter Forty-Five

'We're going up *there*?' My voice comes out high-pitched and more shaky than I'd hoped. I want to sound confident and assured, as if I do this every day of the week and not as if I'm some sort of soft Southern townie who's lost touch with what she really likes in life.

Next to me, neck craned back and staring up the sheer face of the cliff, Flick has gone as white as a sheet.

Only our menfolk are looking galvanised by this challenge and I think most of that is bravado on Harry's part. He truly hates this kind of activity but he seems intent on turning the whole holiday into a competition with Noah.

Callum laughs at my concern. 'Don't worry. We can take this as easy as you want to. Don't feel pressured into doing anything you think you can't manage. There are always easier routes. Keep within your comfort zone.'

'And what if my comfort zone is propping up a bar?' Flick whispers in my ear.

'If you need help, just stay close to me,' Callum continues, unaware that already there is dissension in the ranks. 'We're going to be climbing, scrambling, diving, swimming and exploring some caves. This is meant to be fun!' Then he adds, 'With a bit of terror thrown in for good measure.'

It's the terror part that's bothering me most.

Callum gives us a safety briefing, warning us sternly about reckless behaviour and not putting ourselves in danger. No one mentions that Harry and Flick have already been drinking, but I feel that someone should have.

The sun is high in the cloudless sky as we start to climb the jagged rocks of the headland. What's the saying about mad dogs and Englishmen going out in the midday sun? No one thought to mention them climbing up cliffs. Taking a deep breath, I hitch up my lurid shorts and, in turn, we all follow in Callum's footsteps, taking handholds where he does. I make sure that Noah isn't directly behind me. While I don't mind having my bottom directly in Harry's eyeline, I'm not sure that I want it in anyone else's.

We climb higher and higher, working our way along the rocks, away from the beach, until there's nothing below us but the crashing waves of the Atlantic Ocean. My knees are knocking, but there's an exhilaration in it too. This is far higher than I would ever have dared to climb by myself. In fact, I can't remember the last time I went rock climbing. Probably when I did my Duke of Edinburgh award when I was a teenager. The roughness of the rocks on my hands feels good and, at this height, the breeze is refreshing on my face. And to think that I could be sitting at my desk and working on an Excel spreadsheet instead. It's only the fact that I'm having to concentrate so much that's stopping me from shouting out, 'Woo-hoo!'

Soon we're strung out in a line. Callum is leading, followed by Art, then me and Harry. Flick is close behind my husband and Noah is bringing up the rear. So far, so good.

There's no time for chatting or banter as we're having to focus hard on our footing and handholds. Which is nice as it gives my mind time to clear. We scramble down now towards the sea and along a ledge that has the waves tugging at our legs, threatening to suck us away. I cling on to the rock, my knuckles white from the exertion. I should be good at this. It's what I do all the time – cling to my life by my fingertips.

As we crawl along a spine of rock on our hands and knees, the water washes over us and I feel as if it's cleansing me. All the unpleasant events of this week seem to be floating away on the foam-tipped waves. I could do this for hours and hours.

We work our way up again until we reach a broad, flat outcrop of rock. We're all soaked through and panting by the time we arrive. Harry flops on to his back. Noah holds out his hand and helps Flick with the last few steps. Already, she's looking as if she's seriously regretting her decision to sign up for this. Whereas I feel more alive than I have in years. The world of balance sheets and bank overdrafts is far behind me.

'Fuck,' she mutters to me. 'That was *totally* hideous.' It seems that her moment of being Action Girl has quickly passed.

From the rocky overhang, there's a breathtaking sheer drop below us. Art and I peer over the edge, nervously.

'That's high,' Art notes, unnecessarily.

'Who's going to be the first to jump?' Callum asks.

My eyes widen. 'Down there?'

The others join us to have a look at our next challenge. There's a collective intake of breath.

Callum laughs. 'It's not as bad as it looks and I promise that you'll get the most *amazing* adrenaline rush.'

When we all cower back from the edge, Noah rubs his hands together briskly and says, 'I'll give it a go.'

'OK,' Callum says. 'Make sure that your helmet is on nice and tight. Take a run at it, jump out as far as you can and, before you hit the water, cross your arms over your chest.'

We move out of Noah's way as he backs up against the rocks. He adjusts his safety helmet and takes a deep breath. Then with three bounding steps and the cry of 'Geronimo!' he launches himself off the edge of the rock and into oblivion.

My heart is in my mouth until, seconds later, Noah hits the water with an enormous splash and shouts out, 'Woo-hoo!'

I look over the edge and he's waving madly at me. 'Come on in,' he shouts. 'The water's lovely.'

'I can't,' I say.

'You can do it!'

Then, just as I'm summoning up courage, Harry says, 'I'll go.'

With that, he leaps from the edge and into the sea. I watch him plummet into the depths and it seems like ages before he bobs on to the surface again. He too shouts out with joy.

With the only announcement being, 'Oh, fuck!' Art follows suit, leaving just me and Flick staring over the edge in terror.

'No,' Flick says. 'I can't. This isn't my bag at all.'

'I want to,' I tell Callum.

'Just take a deep breath and go for it. You've heard how much the others have enjoyed it.'

I too tighten my helmet before I back away from the edge and lean against the rocks behind me in preparation. My breath is ragged and I can hear my heart pounding in my chest.

'Come on, Grace,' Noah shouts from below. 'You can do it!'

That's the spur that I need. Without further thinking, I run and launch myself out from the cliff and into the blue sky. I'm rushing, rushing, light and free. And I realise that I want to feel like this for ever.

Chapter Forty-Six

I plunge down, down into the ocean. The ice-cold water of the Atlantic swallows me up. I'm a tiny, insignificant speck in the infinity of the waves. Just when I feel that my lungs are about to burst, I'm rising again and I pop up like the cork out of a bottle, my head bobbing above the waves. I add my own yelping to the shouts of delight from my friends.

'That was fantastic!' I yell. My helmet is skew-whiff and my buoyancy aid is up round my nose somewhere. I can hardly contain my excitement. 'Let's do it again!'

'I'm up for it,' Noah says. 'Anyone else?'

'Oh, yeah,' Art punches the air.

'Harry?'

He holds up a hand, coughing and spluttering. Perhaps drinking before coming out wasn't the best idea. 'Still getting my breath.'

I should stay with him. I know I should, but I can't. Something inside me feels that I don't want to miss out on this experience. I may never get the chance to do it again. It's as if

I can feel life rushing through veins that have got all clogged up with city living.

So Art, Noah and I all swim to the rocks together and climb back up to the platform. Flick is still standing there with Callum. She's shivering and looking miserable.

'Want to jump with me?' Noah says. 'It feels fabulous. Honestly.'

Flick shakes her head. 'It's too high for me. I might try it lower down.'

I feel giddy with adrenaline. Before I can catch my breath, Art has launched himself off the cliff again. So I run after him and do the same, shouting as I fall. All the tension of the last few days leaves my muscles and flies free on the wind. Moments later, Noah splashes into the sea beside me. We burst through the surface of the water, giggling like loons.

Harry has got out and is now sitting on the rocks with Flick who has climbed down to him.

When we're all treading water again, Noah says, 'One last time?'

I nod.

Art says, 'I'm done. We've hardly started yet. I should conserve my energy.'

'Just me and you, Grace,' Noah says and, despite my having swallowed a gallon of salt water, my mouth goes dry.

'OK.'

So we swim to the shore in tandem and climb the rocks, Noah helping me all the way. At the top, we stand close, looking out over the sparkling sea.

'Together?' he says.

My face breaks into a grin. 'Hell, yes.'

He takes my hand in his and the strength of it makes me feel as if I could conquer the world. We back up against the rocks behind us.

'Ready?' he asks.

I nod and then, as fast as we can, we take a run at the edge. As we fly out into nothingness, as one, shouting at the sky, with fingers entwined, our eyes meet. And I know that, at this moment, I've never ever been happier.

Chapter Forty-Seven

Sadly, we leave behind the adrenaline-junkie jump and Callum leads us scrambling and crawling over the rocks, working our way round the coast. For the next hour we're bashed and crashed, tossed and twirled by the waves. The reward for braving the maelstrom is that we swim deep into cool, dark caves and lever ourselves along narrow ledges until we're right inside secret caverns. The rugged landscape is just so spectacular.

Harry and Flick have done really well. Callum has kept us quite low to the water and he's taken it at a pace that we could all manage. We haven't done any more of the high stuff, but we've jumped from lower outcrops of rock and Flick has given that a go. She didn't look entirely enamoured of the experience but, all credit to her, she did it.

Now we're up against a sheer face of rock on a narrow ledge, negotiating a particularly slippery area. We're strung out in a line, pressed tight against the cliff, making our way round a sharp headland.

'Careful, guys,' Callum warns. 'When the waves come make sure you hold on tight.'

Callum has already turned the corner when the sea washes over me. The powerful wave takes away my breath and threatens to dislodge me, but I hang on to the rocks for dear life. Seconds later, it recedes and I brace myself for the next onslaught. As it hits, I grab the rocks again and cling on.

The next thing there's a cry and, when I look round, Flick has been pulled from the ledge and into the sea. She's being buffeted by the waves, arms flailing. Without a moment's hesitation, Harry and Noah jump in and swim to her aid. In a dozen strong, swift strokes Noah reaches her first and, grabbing hold of her buoyancy aid, he tows her back to the rocks. Between them, Harry and Noah haul her out.

Coughing and spluttering, Flick sits on the ledge.

Noah's arm goes round her and he says, 'You're OK. You're OK now.'

Flick nods, but she doesn't look convinced. I make my way back to her. 'Are you all right?'

She's so shocked that she doesn't even think to make a drama out of it. She must be bad. 'I'm OK.' Her voice is raspy, her breathing uneven and shallow. 'But I think I've had enough now.'

'You've done really well,' Noah says.

'I'll get Callum,' I say. 'See if we can take a break.' In a few brisk steps, my heart in my mouth, I catch up with him. 'Flick's just taken a dunking and it's shaken her up.'

'Is she OK?'

'Noah and Harry went in for her. Can we stop for a while?'

'There's a small beach just round the next rocks. Make your way there. I'll go back and help her round.'

I inch my way forward, following Art, and, a few minutes later, we make it to the safety of the beach. It's a beautiful, sandy cove with no one else in sight. Art and I take off our helmets and, side by side, lie on our backs, trying to catch our breath.

'This is fantastic,' Art says, staring up at the wispy clouds. 'I wish Ella had come along. She used to love this kind of thing.'

What do I say? Do I tell Art that there's a very good reason why his dearly beloved doesn't want to be flinging herself off rocks into the sea? Should I keep Ella's secret or should I give some kind of hint to help Art along?

'Is she OK, Grace?' he asks. 'She doesn't seem quite herself at the moment.'

Look at her closely, I want to scream. *Can't you see the tell-tale bump she's sporting?*

'Talk to her, Art. She's got a lot going on at the moment.' I settle for neutrality. 'You guys should take some time to be alone together while you're here. It won't be long before you disappear off on your tour.'

'She loves it down here, doesn't she?'

'I can't say that I blame her.'

'I guess Ella has an emotional attachment to the cottage that I don't.' He rolls on to his stomach and glances over at me.

'I thought you were beginning to love it too. You seem to be having a lot of fun.'

'This is great.' Art nods towards the others who are just clambering down from the rocks. 'The sea, the surf. I haven't been so energetic in years. I could do a couple of weeks a year, at a push. But move down here permanently? No way. It's too remote from the real world.'

'Isn't that supposed to be the major appeal?'

'It would drive me to distraction.'

'All that peace and quiet?' I tease.

Art laughs. 'Can't help it if I'm a rock'n'roller at heart.'

I trace my fingers in the sand and avoid looking at him. 'Do you think there'll come a time when you're tired of being on the road?'

'Maybe.' He shrugs. 'I might look like a raddled old druggie' – Art looks nothing of the sort – 'but I'm still young and I still love it. The new band I've signed could really go places. I want to take them as far as I can. There's still life in the old dog. This game used to be for the fresh-faced youths, but age is no barrier now. You only have to look at Jagger and Richards to see that. I could go on until I get my free bus pass.'

It looks as if Ella may be right. Art isn't showing any signs of wanting to slide into the slow lane and settle down. She may not get her dream of them both moving down here any time soon.

'I like somewhere with a bit more life, a bit more sun,' he concludes. 'She could get rid of this place and we could buy somewhere in Ibiza or Marbella.'

I can't think of anything worse and I know that Ella feels the same. Perhaps if we were twenty again, it would be a different story. But I can see that Ella is growing up, moving on, whereas Art isn't. What she wanted when they met isn't what she wants now. Ella could never part with Cwtch Cottage, I'm sure, and I don't know why Art can't see that.

But, before we can talk about it further, Harry, Flick and Noah hit the beach and walk across to us. Flick flops down with a heartfelt sigh.

'I need a good glass of chilled white or three after that torture!' she declares.

'Hear hear,' Harry says and sits down next to her.

'You're not hurt?' I ask.

'Scraped my hand,' she says. There's a gritty and bloody graze on her palm. 'And I've broken a fingernail!'

Typical Flick. 'A well-known sporting injury.' I smile at her. 'You did really well.'

'There's plenty of time left,' Callum assures us. 'We can rest here for as long as you like.'

'I'm done,' Flick says, throwing up her hands in resignation. 'The trauma of a broken fingernail has put paid to my coasteering career. I need to get this gear off and head to the nearest bar for a serious recuperation session.'

'Sounds good to me,' Harry agrees, rubbing his hands together.

I can't even bring myself to argue against him. If Harry really wants to go to the pub rather than do this, then that's his choice. I'm not going to persuade him to stay.

'You can walk back to the surf shop from here,' Callum says. 'Although we've come a long way around the rocks, it's only a five-minute stroll across that field.' He points out the route. 'Then you're there.'

I sigh inwardly before I say, 'Shouldn't we all go back together?'

It's fair to say that Art and Noah don't look too impressed by this suggestion.

'The route after this is easier,' Callum tells us. 'And you've got options. There's nothing you *have* to do.'

'I think I've given coasteering all I have to give,' Flick says. 'Now I need to show a bar what I can do.'

'You've got another hour that you've booked and paid for,' Callum points out. 'I can tailor it however you like.' He's obviously trying to be as helpful as possible. 'It would be a shame to waste it.'

'Of course it would,' Flick says quickly. 'Don't change anything for us. We're happier to opt out. Harry and I will be fine. We can totter back together.'

Harry nods effusively.

Flick is already unclipping her helmet and peeling off her buoyancy aid. 'You lot should stay and enjoy it. Masochists.'

Glances all round. Shrugged agreement from Noah.

'I'm going to go back too, see if Ella's all right,' Art says, stripping off his buoyancy aid. 'She might be getting lonely without me.'

I wonder if our brief talk has made him think about things. I hope so.

It looks as if it's going to be just me and Noah again. Is that wise? I wonder. I should insist that we join the others. As much as it hurts my heart, I can't resist the lure of having some time alone with him.

'We'll see you later,' Flick says. 'Have fun, the two of you.'

With Harry and Art in tow, she turns away from the sea and the three of them head up the beach, leaving us behind.

I stand and watch them go.

'OK?' Noah asks.

'Yes. I'm fine.'

There's no way that I want to give up on the coasteering and go off to sit in the pub. This is the most alive I've felt in years. It seems no matter what I do, I'm destined to be thrown together with this man. And, do you know, I'm happy not to fight it.

Chapter Forty-Eight

Flick, Harry and Art are already at the top of the cliff by the time Noah and I set off with Callum again. They turn and wave at us. My heart feels lighter now that Flick and Harry have left us. I know it shouldn't, but it does.

We both fall into step alongside Callum and soon we're climbing on rocks again, the warm sun at our backs, being splashed by the cool waves, forgetting everything but where to put our feet and hands to keep us moving safely. The dark cloud that covered us briefly has lifted. Our guide leads us round another outcrop of rocks. Perhaps worried that I'm going to be swept away like Flick, Noah grips my hand as we go.

When we reach our next destination, Callum stands with his hands on his hips and nods towards the ocean crashing wildly below us. 'This is called the washing machine!' He has to shout above the roar of the pounding waves. 'Ready to take a tumble?'

We go to the edge of the rock. Below us the sea is a frothing maelstrom. The waves rushing into the jagged mouth of a huge, yawning cave are meeting the riptide coming out, creating a swirling whirlpool. It looks fabulous. And more than a little frightening.

'There's nothing to it,' Callum assures us. 'Just jump in and hang on for the ride!'

'I'm up for it, if you are,' Noah yells.

I nod my agreement. With a deep breath, and before I think better of it, together we plunge feet first into the roiling sea.

When I hit the water, I'm instantly thrown this way and that. In seconds I can't tell which way up I am. First I'm whooshed forwards towards the cliffs and the gaping cave. Next I'm dragged back, spun round and tossed like a salad. There's a terrible noise above the waves and I think it's me screaming at the top of my lungs.

Noah bobs up next to me. He shouts over the din, 'OK?'

'Fantastic!' I yell back, getting a mouthful of water for my trouble and coughing it out again. We both twist and turn. When the wave catches me again, Noah grabs my hand and we're thrown forwards together, rising on the crest of the breaker.

'Woo-hoo!' he cries out.

Then, with a strength that's awesome, the sea drags us away again and spins us as if we're on a fairground waltzer. I can hear shouts of encouragement from Callum on the rocks, but I can't make out a word he's saying.

'Aargh,' I cry. 'My shorts!' Ahead of me I can see that, somehow in the chaos, I've become parted from my brightly coloured board shorts and they're floating away from me on the waves.

'I'll get them!' Noah says and he strikes out towards the pink and orange fabric.

Thank goodness I've still got my wetsuit on and this hasn't left me overly exposed.

Effortlessly, he catches hold of them. My hero! As he swims back towards me, we're both caught by the next onslaught of waves. I'm hit by one with a force that knocks the breath from me. The second is even bigger and, when it reaches us, it picks us both up and pelts us headlong towards the mouth of the cave.

For the first time, the wave doesn't abate, dashing me into the cool darkness of the chamber. Ahead of me, I can see Noah and he's still hanging on to my shorts. 'Grab them!' he instructs.

So I lunge forward, trying to swim against the current, and make a lurch for my shorts. Somehow, I manage to catch hold of the material and Noah pulls me towards him. The wave retreats and we're left treading water together next to a smooth slab of rock just above waist height.

'Let's climb up,' he says, panting. 'We can have a look around the cave. Catch our breath.'

He clambers out first and half lifts, half drags me up by my buoyancy aid. I flop on to the rock in front of him, laughing hysterically.

'That was such a rush,' I puff out. 'I think it's scrambled my brain.'

I'm sure if I tipped my head to one side, gallons of sea water would pour out of my ear.

We're giggling and breathless. I haul myself upright and try to shake off the water. Then I realise that we're alone in the darkness and we're both suddenly still.

Noah breaks the tension. 'You might want these back,' he says, holding up my ugly shorts.

'I probably should.' I take them from him. But as I try to put them back on, I'm hopping all over the place. Putting on soggy shorts over a tight wetsuit is not something that should be attempted single-handed.

'Here,' he says. 'Let me help.' He stands close by. 'Lean on me.'

So I put my hand on his shoulder and he steadies me while I feed my feet into the hideous things and wriggle them up to my waist.

'There. Looking lovely again.'

We both take in my appearance and laugh. 'Not so sure about that.'

Self-consciously, I drop my hand from his shoulder, but Noah catches hold of it and squeezes tight. 'It doesn't matter that you're wearing extremely bad shorts,' he says and runs his fingertip softly over my cheek. 'You do look lovely.'

If it wasn't for the crashing of the waves, I'm sure he'd be able to hear my heart pounding. I lick my lips nervously. Noah touches his thumb to them.

This is the situation I have both dreamed of and dreaded.

'Can you tell how I feel, Grace?' he asks.

I don't answer. What can I say? I search for the right words but nothing will come.

'Do you feel the same?' He tilts my chin, so that our faces

are close together. If I lifted my mouth just slightly, so slightly, our lips would touch. I know that Noah's would taste of salt and sweetness. There'd be the cold from the sea, the heat of his tongue. I feel myself shiver with desire.

Oh, it would be so easy. So easy to slip into Noah's arms, surrender to his strong embrace. In the short time that I've known him, this very scenario has flitted through my brain far too often. It's taking every ounce of control not to run my hands over those hard muscles that I've imagined only too well. I want to reach out and touch the contours, the smooth skin of his handsome face. One step. That's all it would take. One step to cross the line.

'Tell me, Grace,' he pleads. 'Am I wrong?'

In the small, dark hours I've vowed that I would do all that I could to salvage my marriage, but here, alone in this cool cavern with Noah, do I have the strength to turn away from what I want so much to happen?

'Grace?' His dark eyes search my face, my soul.

'I'm married,' I offer weakly. Tears well up and my throat closes.

'I don't want to cause you any trouble,' he says. 'That's the last thing on my mind. But I've never felt like this before. When I first saw you, I felt as if ... as if I'd come home.' His expression is anxious. 'Does that sound ridiculous?'

No, I think. Because that's exactly how I felt too. As if the other half of me, the half that I hadn't even realised was missing, had somehow been found.

'I know you feel it too. Tell me that I'm not wrong, that I haven't misread this.'

Of course he hasn't misread this, but how can I admit it? Where would that confession leave me? If I say yes to Noah, then I betray my husband, my marriage vows, my best friend. What sort of person would that make me?

'You're my friend's partner,' I breathe. 'She loves you.'

'I don't think so,' he counters baldly. 'Flick might think she loves me, but I'm not the one for her. I know that. You know that. And, in her heart, I'm sure that Flick knows it too.'

How can I tell him that not only does she love him, but she's also planning to marry him?

'Grace, talk to me. Tell me what you're thinking.'

'What can I do?' I murmur.

'You're not happy where you are. I know it.'

How can I argue against that? But I've always hated the fact that Flick has had relationships with married men. I've always felt that fidelity, monogamy, are paramount in a relationship. Yet this has shaken me to the core. Could I really be selfish and destroy everything I have to be with Noah?

I can quite honestly say that all the time I've been married, I've never looked at another man. Yet here I am, feeling like a teenager again with someone I barely know, who, conversely, I feel I've known all my life. But can I bring down destruction on everyone I care for? Harry would hate me, I know that. How will Ella feel? If I explain to her fully the way things are with Harry, she might well understand me leaving. But if I do this to Flick she might never forgive me. This is the one man she's ever found who she feels she can truly love. Does it matter that I feel exactly the same way too? It might be what I want with all of my heart, but I don't think I can be that person.

283

'I can't do this to Flick,' I say. 'Or to Harry. They've done nothing to deserve it.'

I push away some of the pictures, imprinted in the forefront of my brain, of my husband in recent days. Those are not the things I want to think of now.

'But you do feel the way I do?'

Then, as the words are formulating in my thick skull, Callum's voice rings out. 'Are you two OK in there?' he shouts.

The moment is broken.

Noah looks at me, eyes filled with pain and regret. 'We're fine,' he calls back. 'Just taking a breather!'

'Do you need help getting out?' Callum comes back. He's standing just beyond the mouth of the cave. 'You can walk along the ledge to the right, which will bring you out to the rocks.'

Our eyes follow the path.

'Talk to me, Grace,' Noah begs.

I swallow the emotion that's tightened my throat. 'I think I'd like to go back now,' I say.

Sadly, Noah lets go of my hand and I trail after him. Seconds later, we emerge from the darkness into the bright light once more.

Chapter Forty-Nine

In silence, we make our way out of the cave and, in the blinding sunshine, rejoin Callum.

'Enjoy that?' he asks.

'Yes, brilliant!' Noah and I answer in unison. Both too bright, too forced. I can't bring myself to look at him.

'Cool,' Callum says, looking slightly puzzled.

We make our way back towards the beach where we left Flick, Harry and Art. Noah and I have spent so long in the sea and in the cave together that our coasteering experience is nearly over.

Fifteen minutes later, we're back on terra firma again. I'm tired and I'd like to say happy, but my emotions are in more turmoil than the 'washing machine' of water that we've just escaped from. For the first time since we set eyes on each other, there's an awkwardness between Noah and me. Something that I bitterly regret. But what can I do? If I have any hope of salvaging what I have with Harry, I'm going to have to cut this dead.

How could I consider walking out on seven years of marriage for someone I hardly know? That's the sort of thing that Flick would do, not me. Racked with guilt, I think of my friend. She adores this man. She wants to marry him. I can't deny her that. But, if you can commit adultery in your heart, then that's exactly what I'm doing.

'Ready to head back?' Callum asks.

'Yes, sure.' Back to the others, back to the pub, back to reality, I think.

'That was great,' Noah says to Callum, shaking his hand.

'Awesome,' I agree.

We're making a valiant attempt at joviality, but I think Callum can tell that for some reason we're more muted than we were. We'll have to be back to normal by the time we join the others, that's for sure. I might be completely wrong, but I feel that both Harry and Flick are watching us like hawks.

We both fall into step alongside Callum as we set off on the return journey.

'I really envy you your job,' Noah adds. 'I'd love to do something like this on a permanent basis.'

'I've had ten good years here, but I'm planning to go out to Australia,' Callum tells us. 'Do the same kind of thing, I hope. My good lady wants us to start a family and she says she'd rather do it with guaranteed sunshine.' He glances up at the cloudless sky and says wryly, 'It's not always this glorious in South Wales. The beach life is very addictive, though.'

'I could see myself somewhere like this,' Noah confesses.

'I'll be sorry to turn my back on it. I've made a good living here. Enough regulars to keep me going and, despite what the

newspapers say, the last few holiday seasons have been busy.'
Callum shrugs. 'The business is going on the market soon. I want a quick sale, so someone will get themselves a bargain.'

Noah turns to me and I can see the excitement shining in his eyes. This would be his dream come true, I know it would. There's a spring in his step as we make our way back to the surf shop.

When we're offloading our gear – glad to hand back these shorts! – I can see that Noah is taking everything in.

As soon as we're dressed again, we both shake hands with Callum and thank him profusely. When he's gone, Noah takes my hand and pulls me to one side. We're in the back of the shop surrounded by wetsuits and surfboards.

'What do you think?' he whispers. 'I can't believe he's thinking of selling. Does it look like a good business to you?'

'Yes.' From what little we've seen, it seems to be thriving. 'There certainly seems to be a lot of potential too.'

'It would suit me down to the ground,' he confesses.

'I can just see you here,' I tell him. 'You seem so at home.'

'I feel it. This would be perfect. I've got to give it some serious thought,' he continues. 'A place like this is all that I've ever dreamed of.' He looks at me. My hand is still firmly clutched in his. 'Well,' he adds with a rueful smile, 'not *quite* everything.'

'Noah . . .'

He holds a finger gently to my lips. 'You don't need to say anything, Grace.' He sighs. 'I'm sorry for what happened between us. We're just friends. Nothing more. I got a bit carried away. You're a married woman and I should have respected that. I apologise and we'll say no more about it.'

I nod mutely and he lets go of my hand.

'This afternoon has been fun,' Noah says. 'I'll always remember it.'

'Me too.' I can hardly get the words out.

'We should go and find the others. Flick and Harry will be wondering where we are.'

Noah takes one last longing look at the surf shop and then one last longing look at me.

Chapter Fifty

After a few drinks in the pub, we spend the rest of the afternoon on the beach. I'm pleased that everyone seems to be getting on. We all play an unruly game of beach volleyball that stops only when Flick breaks yet another nail.

'The first thing I'm going to do when I get home is get a manicure,' she says with a tut.

Ella and I roll our eyes and grin at each other. Flick doesn't do outdoors.

When we've dipped into the picnic baskets for a late lunch and basked in the sun, Art and Ella lie down together and snooze happily side by side on the blankets.

Noah and Flick pick up the power kite and walk down to the water's edge to fly it in the warm breeze. Harry does his crossword – uttering many cross words – and I stare out to sea, wondering what I'm going to do with my life, while trying not to watch Flick and Noah laughing and playing together.

Eventually, they pack the kite away and head off to the surf shop. I wonder if Noah is taking Flick to show her, to see what she thinks. Maybe he's asking her if she could see herself living here. If I know Flick, she'd rather saw off her own arms than move out of the city. But I could be wrong. We all have the capacity to change. If you'd told me last week that I would be the type of person who would fall in love at first sight with my best friend's boyfriend, I would have called you mad. Flick might yet give it all up for love and move down here. I know that I would in a heartbeat and the thought frightens me more than I care to admit.

They come back, still all smiles, with a tray full of takeaway coffees and ice creams, which they hand round to everyone. Noah barely glances at me when he gives me mine.

When the sun is starting to tire and sink lower in the sky, we pack up and head home. Everyone's quiet on the journey back. I close my eyes and let weariness overwhelm me. Behind my eyelids the image of me and Noah, standing alone in the cave, a fraction away from my forgetting my wedding vows, is etched for ever. How long will it be before it fades?

As always, Cwtch Cottage is a welcome sight as we pull up outside. Ella and I unpack the sand-encrusted towels and cushions from the boot of their car. I walk the long way round the Bentley to the front door, so that I don't see the dent.

Flick bags the bathroom first and, as far as I can tell, Noah joins her in the shower. I can't even bear to think about it. But, as I'm making tea, the sound of her raucous giggles carry down the stairs. Ella rolls her eyes at me. It seems as if Noah has decided to throw himself headlong back into their relationship and forget all the foolishness in the cave with me. Well, I should be glad about that. I just don't really want to listen to it.

'Christ Almighty,' Harry mutters. He snatches a cup of tea from me and disappears out on to the terrace.

Ella rolls her eyes again.

'I'm sorry,' I say.

'It's not you who should be apologising, Grace.'

Possibly not, but I feel that all the wrongs in the world are somehow my fault right now.

When Flick and Noah are finally finished, I go to see if they've left any hot water. Thankfully, they have. Their bedroom door is closed and still the laughter continues. Soon it will start to make my ears bleed.

Standing in the shower, I let the water wash the sand and salt from my body. In the bedroom, I towel dry my hair and slip on the only dress that I've brought with me. It's long and strappy, the perfect item of clothing for a romantic summer evening. I even smear on some tinted foundation and a lick of lipstick. Let's see what the night brings.

Flick has declared that she's going to cook tonight. The last time I remember Ms Edwards doing dinner for us all, it was a disastrous Thai green curry. We had to forcibly carry her out of the kitchen and take over ourselves to have any hope of getting anything edible at all. Tonight, she's producing nothing more taxing than spaghetti Bolognese and, with Noah's supervision, I'm sure it will be fine. In fact, if I know Flick, her contribution will be to sit and drink wine whilst issuing orders.

'I want you all out of the kitchen,' she announces as I come downstairs. 'I hate being watched when I cook.'

Noah, next to her at the cooker, has a knife poised in his hand. His eyes rake my body, taking in my damp hair and my dress, and I can tell that he struggles to look away. I don't have this effect on men. Not ever. That's Flick's department. And even just a taste of it feels heady. I flush to my hair roots. Noah returns his gaze to concentrate earnestly on the pile of mushrooms in front of him.

'You just want to be able to hide the packets,' Ella teases. 'But we'll know if it's home-cooked.'

'It'll be home-cooked,' she promises. 'Ye of little faith. This is the new me. I'm going to learn how to cook. You won't be able to tell where I stop and Nigella begins. Besides, I have my lovely assistant Noah to keep me on the straight and narrow.' She kisses him heartily on the lips before putting on her apron. I notice that he takes a step back under the onslaught of her attention, but I also notice that Flick seems unaware. 'Just charge your glasses and then clear off.'

We do as we're told. Art and Ella wander on to the terrace and sit at the bench. I think it would be good to allow them time alone together, as she *has* to tell him sometime, so I say to Harry, 'Want to go for a walk on the beach?'

To my great surprise, without any form of argument, he says, 'Yes.'

We leave our glasses on the table and clamber down the rocks. Harry holds out his hands to help steady me and we both kick our shoes off on the damp sand. The sea is calm, the waves lapping gently.

I lift the hem of my dress and walk in the edge of the surf, letting the ice-cold water send pleasing shocks through my toes. It feels good. All my senses are sharp and it's on days like this that I'm glad to be alive.

Even more surprisingly, Harry falls into step beside me as the surf comes up to our ankles. I link my arm into his and, just for a moment, I get a glimpse of how we used to be together.

The seagulls wheel above us as we stroll along, away from the cottage, in companionable silence.

'You look lovely tonight, Grace,' he says.

The simple compliment brings a lump to my throat. It's been so long since Harry has even noticed me.

'I've been a bit of a dick this week,' he says, exhaling a weary breath. 'I don't know what comes over me sometimes.'

I don't like to tell him that his ill-temper is normally directly related to the level of his drinking. But I'm not sure what's brought on this change of heart, so it remains unsaid.

'I'll try,' Harry says. 'From now on, I'll try to be a better husband. God knows you deserve more. You've never done anything to hurt me.'

I think guiltily of the dark thoughts in my heart.

'I feel as if you've gone away from me,' I say. I know because I feel as if I've been away too.

'Things will be different now,' my husband assures me. 'You'll see. No late nights. Work will take second place. We can start to go out again. Have fun.' Harry stops walking and turns me towards him, taking me in his arms. 'I love you,' he says. 'I haven't told you that lately, have I?'

The tears that spring to my eyes block the words in my throat. I want to say, 'I love you too,' but it just won't come.

'We'll start over again.' Harry is burbling away, excitedly. 'It'll be just like old times. We can do up the flat a bit if you like. Get a new kitchen or bathroom?'

Why does he think that this will patch over what's been going on between us? I'm not the slightest bit interested in a new kitchen. Surely he knows that much about me?

What I need is for us to sit down and unpick what's gone wrong. Why do we not want the same things any more? Where has the love we had disappeared to? What if I decide that I want to have children? How would Harry feel about that? I know that it's not on his agenda, but it may now be on mine. Since I found out about Ella's pregnancy, I keep having little visions of myself with my own child. And I like what I see. If I wrap my arms around myself, I can actually feel it and get a rush of maternal love that I've never experienced before. At the moment, I can't even bring myself to raise that with Harry. What if he refuses point blank to have another baby? What if he is absolutely sure that his family is finished when mine hasn't even started?

'Or we could have another holiday,' Harry blusters on. 'Just the two of us. Go abroad somewhere. Wherever you fancy. The Seychelles. We haven't been there. Or what about the Maldives again? We enjoyed our honeymoon there. Didn't we? You can choose. What do you say, Grace?'

I don't want another holiday. This one has been unsettling enough. The thought of just me and Harry being alone together on the other side of the world, with nothing but a five-star hotel and a beach, frankly, fills me with dread.

Thankfully, he doesn't wait for an answer but, instead, crushes me to his chest. I stay there, hardly able to catch my breath.

This should be making me happy. Deliriously happy. Isn't

this what I've wanted to hear? Harry wants to be a better husband. He wants us to try to salvage our relationship. It should be music to my ears. So why do I feel so numb? Aren't I the one who was vowing, just a few short hours ago, to work on my marriage again?

But when push comes to shove, there's still an empty space in my heart and I'm not sure any more that Harry is capable of filling it.

Chapter Fifty-One

Harry is the model husband throughout dinner. He tops up my glass regularly whilst passing over his own. He's not exactly teetotal, don't get me wrong, but he's nowhere near as drunk as he'd normally be at this time of night. He laughs at jokes in the right place and doesn't pick fights with anyone – particularly Noah. It's a long time since I've seen him so relaxed.

Flick's spaghetti Bolognese is quite wonderful and she glows proudly as we praise her, taking all the glory. Despite trying not to, I catch Noah's eye and it's clear that he's the creator of our meal. He smiles wryly at me and my traitorous tummy does backflips.

After dinner, Ella and I offer to clear up. Thankfully, Noah goes through to the lounge with the others and doesn't hang back to help as he usually does. As Ella stacks the dishwasher and I wash up the pans, the sound of their laughter drifts through to us.

'Harry seems particularly mellow tonight,' Ella notes as she

picks up a tea towel to dry the pots and pans. 'And very attentive.'

'Yes,' I say.

'All well with you two?'

I shrug. 'I think so.'

How can I even begin to explain to Ella how I feel?
Normally, I'd talk to her about everything, but this time I have
to keep my own counsel. It would be unfair of me to put her
in a difficult situation with Flick and if she knew how I felt
about Noah, that would be really awkward for her. Plus I
don't really know what has triggered Harry's about-face.
Perhaps he's had a blow to the head or diving off that cliff has
somehow reset his wiring. It's the only thing I can think of. If
you'd asked me yesterday or even this morning, I would have
been sure that we were on the verge of splitting up. Now it
seems as if something has brought Harry back from the brink
and he's willing to try to put our relationship back together.

'What about you?' I ask. 'You and Art seem to be getting on
well too. Did you manage to talk to him earlier?'

Ella shakes her head. 'I wanted to. But I just can't do it,
Grace,' she confesses, voice lowered. 'I've tried but the words
won't come out. It should be so easy to say, but it isn't.'

'How are you feeling now?'

'Tired,' she admits. 'All I want to do is sleep.'

'You shouldn't be on your feet. Someone else could have
taken a turn with the tea towel.'

'I'm fine,' she insists. 'I'll sit down in a minute. In fact, I
might head off for an early night and leave you party animals
to it.'

'No more twinges?'

'A few. But I'm sure it's just the baby wriggling around.' Her hand massages her tummy. 'Nothing to worry about.'

'Take it easy,' I advise. 'I'm sure you could have done without us lot here all week, bickering.'

She giggles at that. 'It's lovely seeing you, Grace. It seems as if everyone is settling down to enjoy the rest of the week. I guess when you introduce a new male into the pack there's always going to be a bit of chest-banging.'

Is that what Harry's problem was? Something as simple as that?

'You've got to admit that Noah is a hard act to follow,' she adds. 'He'd threaten any man.'

'Yes.' Can't deny that and don't intend to. Then before I can check myself, 'Do you think that Flick really loves him?'

Ella avoids my eyes, busily drying a casserole dish. 'As much as Flick loves anyone.'

'Do you think she'll really ask him to marry her?'

'Not if she's got any sense. I think if she goes too quickly with this one, he'll run for the hills.' She puts the dish down. 'You know what she's like. She's full of wild talk that she never carries through.'

I sigh to myself. That's pretty much what I thought. I just hope that she doesn't hurt Noah when she gets bored and the fall-out eventually comes.

Chapter Fifty-Two

We make coffee and take it through to the others. Art jumps
up to serve it and I sit down next to Harry. His arm goes
round my shoulder and he pulls me close, which is most unlike
him.

I can't imagine what has got into him today. Has he somehow read my mind? Did he feel that he had pushed me to the
edge with his drinking and this is his idea of damage limita-
tion?

The love-bombing continues. He strokes my arm and fusses
with my hair while I sit there like a little puppet, wondering
what on earth is going on. I can't remember Harry ever being
like this before.

Across the living room, the scene is much the same. Flick is
curled up on the sofa, head in Noah's lap. She's toying with his
shirt buttons, stroking his chest, running her fingers along his
thighs.

Did she put some sort of love potion in the spag bol? I
wonder.

If she did, then it seems that Noah is immune to it as he looks fairly impassive while she continues her overt exploration of his body. Harry snuggles up closer to me. The same, however, could be said about me, I guess.

Ella drains her coffee – decaff for her – excuses herself and, with a heartfelt yawn, heads off to bed early. Art reaches for the remains of a bottle of whisky that's on the table at his elbow. 'Fancy another nightcap, Harry?'

'Enough for me,' Harry says, holding up a hand. He leans in towards me and whispers in my ear, 'I thought we'd have an early night?'

I don't think that he means to go to sleep. He's clearly been feeling amorous all evening. Instead of feeling pleased or thrilled or getting butterflies in my tummy at the thought of making love, I just feel a cold dread all over.

'You go up without me,' I say, trying to keep my voice level. 'I thought I might have another coffee.'

'Come on, love,' he cajoles. 'You know you can't get enough of my body.'

I flush with embarrassment. What has got into Harry? This is hardly the way to make things up to me. He knows that I'm not one for overt public displays of affection.

What do I do now? I can hardly say no and reject him in front of friends. Besides, the memories of our last sexual encounter are still etched on my brain and I'd hardly call it romantic. Is that simply why I feel so reluctant?

Harry tugs me to my feet. 'I bid you goodnight,' he says theatrically. Then to me, 'Come on, missus. Get up those stairs!'

Much laughing. From everyone but me. And Noah.

300

Unwittingly, my eye catches his and he looks at me with sympathy and something that may be approaching pity. I feel sick to my stomach.

'I don't want you two young lovers keeping us awake,' Flick says, somewhat tartly. Perhaps she thinks that she's the only one who should be letting everyone know each time she has great sex, I don't know. 'Make sure you keep the noise down.'

'Ha ha ha,' Harry guffaws.

With a heavy heart I follow him to the stairs and, with footsteps as weary, I climb up behind him.

Chapter Fifty-Three

In the bedroom, I'm hardly through the door before Harry takes me roughly in his arms. Instantly, I freeze.

'What's wrong?' Harry asks, murmuring into my ear.

I ease him away from me. 'I need to go slow,' I urge. 'Things haven't been right between us for a while and it's going to take time to get back to where we were.'

'I can't think of anything better than starting now.'

So I stand there motionless, detached, while he fumbles with undoing the buttons on the front of my dress. When it's open, he slides it from my shoulders and lets it fall to the floor. I feel awkward standing half naked in front of him. It's as if he's a stranger, not my husband of seven years. If we're going to have a chance together, then I have to get past this. I have to learn to love Harry again and *only* Harry.

He kisses my bare shoulders – something that once would have made me shiver with delight. Now it makes me shudder with revulsion.

Harry's mouth moves on to my neck, covering it with kisses. 'Oh, Grace,' he murmurs. 'Oh, Grace.'

But all I can think is that I don't want this. I don't want it at all. Oh, God, what am I going to do?

As he moves lower, I grip Harry's arms and hold him still. 'I can't do this, Harry.'

He looks up at me. 'Why not?'

Hanging my head, I answer, 'It doesn't feel right. There's too much wrong in our relationship for me to be able to leap around the bedroom with gay abandon.'

'I don't think that you've ever really done that, Grace,' is his curt response. Harry lets his arms fall to his side.

'Probably not,' I admit.

Perhaps it's unfashionable to admit it these days, but I'm not a highly sexual person. I've never been a swinging from the chandeliers type. But do you have to bounce round the bed like the Duracell bunny to be having good sex? Some might say yes. I suspect Harry is one of them. Isn't there something to be said for tender, comfortable lovemaking? I know which I prefer. And I would have thought, after all this time, that Harry would know too.

What I need now is a cuddle, some reassurance. We should talk about the issues between us but, just as Ella finds with Art, there never seems to be the right time. If you're ever going to resolve anything, then you both have to be willing to communicate.

'We need to discuss this,' I press on.

'I don't think we do. There's nothing *to* discuss.'

I stand there not knowing what else to say. If he won't even acknowledge that there's a problem, we have no hope of ever resolving it.

'Let's go to bed,' Harry says with a disgruntled huff. 'I'm knackered.'

Angrily, he kicks off his shoes, pulls off his shirt, tugs at his trousers, while I watch, immobile and struck dumb.

He gets into bed and turns off the light. So, in the darkness, with the room lit only by the moon shining through the windows, I slowly undress and slip in next to him. I know that Harry's awake as there isn't the sound of his customary snoring, but he says nothing and doesn't move towards me. It seems that his attempt at passion is over. Sadly, I'm heartily relieved by the fact.

I lie rigidly in the bed, both of us trying not to touch the other. There are acres and acres of space between us, not just a few inches. My eyes, gritty with exhaustion, refuse to close. Eventually, Harry slides into sleep and his snoring starts. I never thought I'd be so pleased to hear it.

A short while later, Flick and Noah climb the stairs, talking to each other in whispers, and they close the bedroom door. I can't lie here and listen to them. I simply can't. That would be just too much to ask.

So I haul myself out of bed, pull on a cardigan and go downstairs. The kitchen and living room are both in darkness, put to bed for the night. As quietly as I can, I make myself a mug of hot chocolate, figuring that I'm in need of some comfort. I use a pan instead of the microwave so that it doesn't ping and wake the whole household. My feet freeze on the flagstone floor while I wait for the milk to heat. When it's ready, I take my chocolate and tiptoe through to the living room, settling myself on the sofa. There's a colourful home-crocheted blanket slung over the back of it. I pull that down and wrap it around me for warmth. With the fire long gone out, the night air has brought a chill to the room. I nurse my warm mug to me, enjoying the kernel of heat, and stare into the blackness, wondering what I'm going to do with my life. At the moment, I can't see a way forward and yet it seems as if there's no going back.

How can I begin to repair our relationship when I can't even bear my husband touching me any more? The ticking of the old-fashioned wall clock in the silence marks the passing of the night and still no answers leap into my brain.

I don't know what time it is when I hear a creak on the stairs, but I realise that I must finally have dozed off. I wake with a start.

In the darkness I can make out the shape of Ella creeping downstairs.

'Ella?' I say. 'What's wrong?'

'Goodness me, Grace,' she says. 'You made me jump.'

'Sorry. Couldn't sleep.'

'I was looking for you anyway,' she says and, even in my sleep-fuddled state, I can hear the strain in her voice. 'I tried your bedroom door. When there was no answer, I peeped inside. It was obvious you weren't there.'

'Harry and I had a row,' I confess. 'Well, sort of. I needed some time by myself to think.' As she comes closer, I can see that her face is white and scared. I wave my troubles away. 'But it doesn't matter about me. What are you doing up? Are you OK?'

'No,' she says. Her words catch in her throat. 'I'm bleeding, Grace.'

'Oh Lord. A lot?'

'Enough,' she answers bleakly. 'I'm worried that I could be losing the baby.'

She's not the only one. After that fall from the bicycle I'm worried too. 'We should get you to hospital. I'll ring for an ambulance.'

'No phone signal,' she reminds me. 'We'll have to go to the phone box in the village.'

'Damn.'

'Besides, an ambulance will take an age to get here.' Her lip trembles. 'I'm frightened, Grace.'

I jump up and hug her. 'Don't be. You'll be fine. I'll make sure of it. It'll be quicker to drive to the hospital.' Though not equipped if anything goes wrong. What's the worst risk?

'I can't ask Art,' she says. 'He's out cold, drunk.'

'Harry's in no fit state to drive either.' He's not had as much as usual but he'd still be over the limit.

I could drive, I'm sure. I've not had that much to drink – just a couple of glasses – but I don't want Ella to be without me if anything happens while I'm driving. My mind is whirring. 'There's one person who can take us.'

'Noah,' we say together.

I nod. 'I'll see if I can wake him. You stay here. Lie down. Keep your feet up.'

I have no idea if that's the correct advice, but it seems the right thing to do in the absence of anything else. Ella does as

I say. I cover her with the crocheted blanket and tuck it round her.

'I'll be two minutes.'

Tiptoeing up the stairs as fast as I can, heart pounding, I stop outside Flick and Noah's bedroom. Holding my breath, I listen for any noise. The last thing that I want to do is interrupt them when they're hard at it. A gulp travels down my throat and it is the loudest thing I can hear in the silent, sleeping house. I knock gently, but there's no reply. So I knock a little harder. Still nothing.

'Flick,' I call out. 'Flick, are you awake?' Obviously not. 'Noah!' I try. 'Noah.' Still no answer. What am I to do now? I can't stand here on the landing all night, I'll have to go in.

As quietly as I can, I unlatch their bedroom door. Pausing to get my bearings, I creep across the room towards the bed, feeling like some hideous intruder. Flick is fast asleep on her side, hair mussed over the pillow, legs tangled in the duvet. Even in her sleep, she looks beautiful. Noah, asleep on his back, arm slung above his head, is next to her. I inch towards Flick and reach out to shake her arm. She grunts in her sleep and flings me off. I know what Flick is like when she's asleep. We used to be able to hoover around her in the flat and she wouldn't wake up if she'd been out on the lash the night before.

I'll have to go straight to Noah. I tiptoe round to the other side of the bed and, when I'm beside him, I kneel down. Gently, I shake his arm. Instantly, he starts awake and his eyes widen further when he sees that it's me. Before he can say anything, I put my finger to my lips to hush him.

He looks at me questioningly and whispers, 'What is it?'

'Emergency,' I whisper back. 'Ella's not too good. I couldn't wake Flick.'

'We'll leave her. She's had a lot to drink. I'm not sure how much help she'll be.'

I feel bad because I'm sure that Flick would want to know if Ella's in trouble. But if I'm completely honest, I'm also glad that we're going to leave her behind. Flick is hopeless in a crisis and will only panic. If she's drunk, she'll be even worse and the last thing I want is Ella's emergency trip to the hospital to turn into an outing. It will be a much more calm affair if Flick stays here.

'I'll get dressed as fast as I can,' Noah assures me. 'Give me two minutes.'

'Thank you.'

I creep away and go back downstairs to Ella who is, thankfully, still on the sofa. 'He's coming,' I tell her. 'Everything will be all right now.' Already I know that we'll be able to rely on Noah's calm strength to do the right thing.

Sure enough, a few minutes later, he appears in the living room. He's wearing his jeans and a fleece, his hair styled by sleep.

'We need to get Ella to the hospital,' I tell him without pre-amble. 'She's bleeding. We're frightened that she's losing her baby. You're the only one in a fit state to drive us.'

He reaches in his pocket and tosses the keys to me. 'Open up the car. I'll carry Ella.'

There's no way I'm going upstairs again, so I find some shoes by the front door that I suspect might have belonged to

Ella's mum. They're a bit too big, but beggars can't be choosers.

While I'm doing that, Noah has scooped Ella into his arms and is waiting for me. I collect the blanket and rush out to open the back door of the car. Carefully, Noah lowers Ella on to the seat.

Slipping in beside her, I cradle her head as she lies full-length across the seats and I stroke her hair. 'Don't worry, honey. Everything will be fine. We'll be on our way in a minute.'

She clutches my hand as a wave of pain grips her.

'Hurry, Noah,' I urge.

He nods bleakly at me. Then he closes the doors, jumps into the driving seat, guns the engine and we're off. He takes it slowly down the narrow lane so as not to jolt Ella too much, but as soon as he reaches the main road, he puts his foot down.

I look behind us. Cwtch Cottage is still clothed in darkness while we're stealing away in the night.

Chapter Fifty-Four

The Accident and Emergency Department of the hospital looks like any one of a hundred throughout the country. We could be anywhere.

I glance at my watch and see that it's two in the morning. Thankfully, on a week night and out of the holiday season, A&E isn't too busy. At least the place isn't crammed with drunks as they so often are. Clearly there haven't been a lot of fights in Pembrokeshire tonight. Instead, there are just a couple of poorly-looking children who are being nursed by their respective parents while they snivel in their arms, and a chap in overalls with a bad cut on his forehead that looks as if it needs stitches. Other than that, it seems that there's not too much of a queue so I'm hoping that Ella will be seen quickly.

Spying a bank of wheelchairs at the entrance, I grabbed one for Ella. Now she's sitting in it, just waiting for the nurse to come. I hold her hand while tears roll quietly down her face.

'I'll try to find us some tea,' Noah says and he strides off in search of a vending machine. Once again I'm glad that Flick isn't here. She'd be marching up and down, demanding attention and generally winding everyone up. As it is, I can keep Ella calm.

'You'll be fine,' I say to my friend for the millionth time. As it's the only thing I have to offer, I can only hope and pray that I'm right.

'I really want this baby, Grace,' Ella murmurs. 'I didn't realise how much until now.' She sighs tiredly. 'With the situation with Art, I've been largely trying to ignore it. That's wrong, isn't it?'

'It seems a shame,' I acknowledge. 'You should both be celebrating this. Perhaps we should have woken Art.'

'What use would he be to me in the state he was in?' She has a good point. 'Besides it might have been too much of a shock to him to find out like this that I'm pregnant.'

'You're not going to be able to put off telling him for too much longer.'

'I hope to God that I still have that news to break to him.' She strokes her hands lovingly over her bump. 'Hold on, little man,' she whispers. 'Things will be different from now on.'

'It might be a girl,' I remind her and we both manage a laugh at that.

'I don't mind whether this baby is a *he* or a *she*, I just want it to be healthy and safe.'

'I'm sure it will be,' I say. 'I can feel it in my bones and when is Auntie Grace ever wrong?'

'You're a good friend,' Ella says, teary.

'And I'll be a *great* godmother. You just hang on.'

Noah comes back with three cups of tea in plastic beakers.

Sod's law decrees that, just as he does so, a nurse appears in front of us.

'Ms Ella Hawley?'

'Yes.'

'This way, please. Doctor will see you now.'

'Come with me, Grace,' Ella pleads. 'Don't leave me alone.'

I give Noah an apologetic look. 'I'll be waiting,' he says. 'However long it takes.'

So, leaving him with three cups of tea, I push Ella in her wheelchair down the corridor, following the brisk nurse. She shows us into a curtained cubicle and says, 'Can you pop on this gown and jump up there, dearie?'

I'm not sure there'll be much popping and jumping but, nevertheless, when she disappears I help Ella out of the wheelchair and into the hospital-issue gown. Gingerly, she climbs up on to the bed.

I sit at its head, holding Ella's hand tightly and resting my head against hers. She lies, knees up, sighing frequently. 'Deep breaths,' I say. 'Try to stay relaxed.'

Eventually, a doctor appears. I'm assuming he must be the doctor as he's in a white coat even though he looks significantly younger than both of us.

Despite his lack of years on the planet, he has a kind smile and a calm, confident manner. He examines Ella thoroughly, and we explain to him what happened and describe the bicycle accident last night while he frowns at our stupidity. It does sound completely irresponsible that we let a pregnant woman anywhere near a tandem – even though we both judiciously choose to miss out the bit about her coercion and Art being

312

roaring drunk at the time. I hope to goodness that isn't what has caused this. How terrible will we all feel then?

'Any more bleeding?' he asks, feeling her stomach.

'Just a bit of spotting since I left home.'

'Pain?'

'Some when it started, but nothing now. Just the occasional twinge.'

A few minutes later he pulls down her gown again. 'Everything looks fine to me,' he says and we both let out a relieved breath.

'I'm not going to have a miscarriage?' Ella speaks as if she hardly dare utter the word.

'No. I don't think so. But we'll keep you in overnight, just to be on the safe side. Breakthrough bleeding in pregnancy is a common occurrence and, usually, it's nothing to worry about. Sometimes the placenta can lie low in the womb, which can cause bleeding. Sometimes it can be caused by a trauma.' He raises his eyebrows at us both and scribbles on his clipboard. 'I'll arrange for you to have a scan tomorrow and we'll take a good look. You'll have to wait here until we can take you up to the ward.'

'Thank you,' Ella says.

'No more midnight cycling,' he warns.

'No,' she agrees, chastened. I, for one, can tell him quite categorically that it won't ever happen again. I should think after this that Ella will be left with a lifelong phobia of tandems.

'You're going to be a mum.' He pats her hand. 'You need to look after yourself. Rest.'

The doctor leaves us.

'Feel better now?'

'Yes. Baby Hawley lives to fight another day,' she quips and then promptly bursts into tears.

'Hush, hush.' I wrap my arms round her. 'No harm done. That baby's going to be born fit and healthy if I have to tie you down to a chair for the next six months to make you rest.'

I grab tissues from a box on the shelf and stuff them in Ella's hands. She blows her nose on them, heartily. 'I'm going to be the model patient now,' she promises, still sniffling. 'I don't want anything to go wrong, Grace.'

'Of course you don't. Neither do I.'

'I'm sorry to have dragged you out at this hour.'

'Don't even think that,' I admonish. 'Always better to be safe than sorry. It's not as if I was asleep anyway.' When she stops crying, I ask, 'Will you be OK if I leave you for five minutes? I should go and tell Noah what's happening.' It's now past three o'clock. 'He'll be worried.'

'Gosh, yes, you must,' Ella says. 'He's a lovely man.'

'Yes.' I try to keep the longing from my voice.

'How would we have managed without him?' She shakes her head. 'Flick doesn't deserve him. She'll be furious that we've stolen him from her in the middle of the night.'

'We'll cross that bridge when we come to it,' I tell her. 'I did try to wake her but she was absolutely out cold. I'm not even sure that she'll notice he's gone. I just thought she'd make a big fuss and I knew it would be the last thing that you wanted.' I kiss her forehead. 'I'll be back in just a minute.'

I find Noah in the waiting room, two cups of tea down and one cold by his side. He's flicking through an ancient car magazine with a ripped cover.

'Hey,' I say and my heart flips over as he looks up.

His brown eyes are red-rimmed, tired. His chin is dark with stubble and, even in this awful situation, I want to reach out to touch it, see how it feels under my fingers.

'Everything OK?'

'Yes,' I say. 'The doctor thinks so.'

'Thank goodness.' The relief is evident on his face.

'They're going to keep Ella in overnight and give her a scan tomorrow just to make sure.'

'That sounds like a sensible precaution.'

'I'm really sorry that I had to get you out of bed like that,' I say. 'I didn't know what else to do. I was worried that I might interrupt ...' My voice tails away.

'There's nothing going on like that, Grace,' he admits. 'Believe me.'

I feel stupidly grateful to hear that.

'I'm here as Flick's partner, but I'm finding the ... physical ... side of things a bit of an issue. Thankfully, Flick was asleep before her head hit the pillow.'

'You don't need to explain anything to me, Noah. It's your business.'

'But I want you to know,' he says. 'I'm not that kind of guy. I can't just ... Well. You know.'

'I should get back,' I tell him, throwing a glance over my shoulder back down the corridor. 'I'm going to wait with her until she's up on the ward. Are you OK with that?'

'Grace,' he says with a slow smile, 'you do what you have to do. I'll still be here.'

'You have a five-year-old *What Car?* magazine covered in germs to entertain you and cold vending-machine tea. What more can a man need?'

'I can do without my creature comforts,' he says. 'Just so long as Ella is all right.'

'Thank you, Noah. You're very kind.' I find myself choking on my words. 'I'll be back as soon as I can be.'

'Send Ella my love,' he says.

'I will.' And, with that, I dash back to see how my friend is faring.

Chapter Fifty-Five

It takes another hour until Ella is settled on the ward. She looks so tiny in the big hospital bed that I'm loath to leave her alone.

'Are you sure you'll be all right?' The ward is in semi-darkness and I whisper so as not to wake the patients in the other beds.

'I'm fine, Grace,' she assures me. 'Thanks for everything.'

'I hate to leave you.' Her hand is in mine and I can't bear to let it go.

'You've done more than enough. Go home!' When I still look reluctant, she adds, 'I'm tired. I promise you that I'll be asleep before you reach the car park.'

I tuck the crisp, rough hospital sheet around her. 'I'll be back first thing in the morning.' I hesitate before I ask, 'Shall I bring Art with me?'

I'll have to, really. What else can I do? I can't lie to him. He has to know why Ella is in hospital.

To my utmost relief, Ella nods wearily.

'What shall I tell him?'

'He'll have to know about the baby,' she says. 'I know I've put it off, which was stupid, but I really didn't want him to find out like this. What if he wants me to get rid of it?'

'He wouldn't do that.'

'I can't be sure of that, Grace. He's not interested in children at all.'

'It's different when it's your own.' So everyone tells me.

'I couldn't have an abortion. I couldn't before and I certainly couldn't now.'

'I think you're way past that stage anyway, Ella.'

She's three months gone. Technically, I suppose she's still well within the legal limit for a termination. But it's not just some anonymous little squiggle now. It's a proper child growing inside her. I know Ella and her nurturing instinct is just too strong to let Art persuade her to go down that route.

'This scare has made me realise just how much I want this baby. No one will take it away from me.'

'I'm absolutely sure it won't come to that. But whatever happens, you must do what's right for you.'

'I know.'

Ella yawns involuntarily and I take that as my cue to leave. I hug her and say, 'See you tomorrow. Sleep tight.' I put my hand over her tummy. 'Night, night, Baby Hawley.'

'Love you, Grace,' Ella mumbles and, as I walk away, waving over my shoulder, I think she might be asleep by the time I reach the door of the ward.

This time when I get back to A&E, Noah is dozing. There's hardly anyone here now and he's lying out on his back across a row of chairs. His feet are crossed and he has the *What Car?* magazine open on his chest. His face is gentle, contented, in sleep and I enjoy the luxury of watching him for a moment, unobserved, acknowledging that I can never look at him without feeling a warm glow inside. Even with his rumpled hair and his rumpled clothes I could still feast my eyes on him for ever. I sigh to myself and rouse my weary limbs to go over to him.

When I touch his arm, he jumps awake. 'Everything OK?'

'Yes.' Weariness overwhelms me and, without warning, I break down and cry.

Noah is on his feet instantly. He pulls me into his arms and his embrace is warm and oh so comforting. My body shakes against his solid, unmoving mass.

'Hey, hey,' he says, soothingly. 'It's all right now. You did well.'

'I'm just so relieved that Ella isn't going to lose the baby,' I sob. 'I've been holding it all in, trying to be strong for her.'

'It's been a long night,' he sympathises. 'Is she settled now?'

'Asleep already, I think.'

'Then we should go home.' Noah rubs his eyes and glances at his watch. 'Dawn will be breaking soon.'

'I wonder if anyone has missed us?'

He looks at me ruefully. 'I doubt it.'

My eyelids grate over my eyeballs. They're dry and itchy through lack of sleep. 'I'm so tired, I could fall asleep standing up. You must be dead on your feet too.'

'I had a quick doze,' he says. 'I'm blessed with the ability to sleep anywhere at any time. I used to think it was the sign of a peaceful mind. Sleep of the just, I called it. Now I'm not so sure.' He tucks my arm into his and I don't have the energy or inclination to try to move it. 'Let's go.'

Outside the night is lifting already, darkness slowly giving way to the sun. It's forecast to be a hot, sunny day again. Still arm in arm we go back to the car without speaking and when I'm safely ensconced in the passenger seat, I sink back on to the head rest.

'Close your eyes,' Noah says. 'Kick back. I'll see us home safely.'

'Not only am I tired, but I'm starving too.' On cue my stomach rumbles out loud and I manage a weary laugh. 'I suppose it is nearly time for breakfast.'

The car is warm, cosy, its inside battered, worn, well loved. I can imagine that dogs have been in here. It doesn't smell of leather and air freshener like the Bentley. Its scent is altogether more wholesome. Noah's car smells of the land, earthy.

He smiles at me as we swing out of the car park and, to be honest, that's the last thing I remember.

Chapter Fifty-Six

'Hey, sleepyhead.'

Noah's voice breaks into my dream and I force my eyes open. I stretch and look round me, trying to remember where I am.

'I must have nodded off.'

'There are no flies in the car any more,' he teases.

Oh, God, that means I've had my mouth wide open. Attractive. 'Did I snore and drool?'

'Oh yes,' he says pleasantly.

Very attractive. 'Sorry.' I feel myself flushing.

Noah laughs.

I glance out of the car window. 'Where are we?'

'I couldn't face going straight back to the cottage,' he admits, his face serious. 'We're in Broad Haven.'

'We are?' That actually means very little to me as I have no idea where Broad Haven is. But it's information that I really don't feel the need to probe for now.

'Outside a café that's miraculously open,' Noah adds. 'It

must have an insomniac owner. I'm about to go and see if I can get us a takeaway breakfast so that we can sit and watch the sunrise.'

'You are?'

He shrugs. 'You must have pushed my hunter-gatherer button. If the lady's hungry I thought I'd better provide food. Would that make you happy?'

'Oh, Noah,' I say with a tired grin, 'that would be wonderful.' My brain questions for the millionth time why I didn't meet this man years ago. Years ago when I was free, single, available.

'Wait there,' he says. 'I'll be back in five.'

With that he jumps out of the car and sprints across the road to the café.

It's a big, bold place taking the prominent position right opposite the promenade. What it lacks in charm, it makes up for in convenience. The seafront at Broad Haven is possibly the tidiest place I've seen. It's neat, sparse. The guest houses have white picket fencing and look as if they've been freshly painted in regulation cream. There's a row of benches on the uniform paving, one of which might have our name on it. Below the railings lies the broad sweep of pale, golden sand of St Brides Bay, flanked by glorious green cliffs. I'd like to climb up there one day as the view must be spectacular. At this ridiculous hour, there's no one else in sight. But soon the beach is sure to start filling up with windsurfers and families exploring the rock pools.

True to his word, Noah appears five minutes later, holding two takeaway cartons and balancing two polystyrene cups on top. 'Breakfast is served, madam.'

'I thought we'd sit out on that bench,' I say and haul my aching bones out of the passenger seat.

'Excellent idea.'

We walk a few metres along the front and when we're settled, Noah hands me a carton. 'Bacon and egg roll with ketchup.'

'Perfect.'

I get one of the cups of tea too. And a serviette.

The sea air is chilly. As I came out of the house in the middle of the night just wearing a cardigan over my pyjamas, I shiver in the breeze. Noah slips off his fleece and wraps it round my shoulders. 'Thanks.' It smells of him. Of rugged pastimes, woods and fields. I try to inhale deeply and imprint the scent on my brain for the rest of time without him noticing.

I tuck into my breakfast with gusto. The salty air gives it an extra tang. 'I think this egg and bacon is the best I've ever tasted,' I tell him, not caring that there's probably grease on my chin.

The seagulls wheel round us, hopeful of a discarded crumb or two. Not a hope. This is mine, all mine.

We eat the rest of our impromptu breakfast in companionable silence. Then we sit and stare out at the sea, waiting for the sun to make an appearance. I was never a Girl Guide so I can't tell if the tide is coming in or going out, but it's a long way out on the sand. The sky is lightening by the minute. Soon the sun peeps out from its hiding place tucked behind the sea and rises steadily in the sky, washing the world in a delicate shade of pink.

'It's beautiful.' Tears, it seems, are never far from my eyes these days. I let them roll down my cheeks. Gently, ever so gently, Noah dabs them with his serviette. 'This was a nice idea.'

'If I'm honest, Grace, I have an ulterior motive.' He puffs out a breath. 'I just wanted to spend some time alone with you.'

I can't speak. I don't know what to say.

'I know that it's wrong of me.'

Of course this is wrong. It's wrong of both of us. I close my eyes. My soul settles when I'm with Noah. How can I tell him that? Instead, I lean against him and feel his arm slip round my shoulders.

We sit there for as long as we possibly can, not speaking, not moving, until the sun is bold and big, and until we know that our loved ones in Cwtch Cottage will be stirring and we will be missed.

Chapter Fifty-Seven

We pull up outside the cottage and Noah turns towards me. For the last few minutes we sit in silence, warm in the fug of the car and cocooned from the rest of humanity.

Eventually, he lets out a wavering breath. 'OK?' he asks and I nod.

'Thank you.' I don't want to get out of this seat and face the real world. 'Thank you for helping Ella. Thank you for a lovely breakfast.' Thank you for being you.

'Any time, Grace,' he says.

'I have to tell Art,' I venture. 'I'm dreading it.'

'Want me to be with you?'

I shake my head. 'I should do this alone.'

He takes my hand and gives it a brief squeeze. 'Ready?'

I nod. He opens the door and reality rushes in like cold air.

We plod back to the cottage. Noah has his hands jammed into the pockets of his fleece. It looks as if only Flick is up when we get back. As we go through to the kitchen, I can see her out on the terrace. She's still in her dressing gown, but has got a cup of coffee and is puffing on a cigarette, staring out to sea.

Noah and I exchange an anxious glance, then go straight outside.

'Hey,' Noah says as we approach.

Flick wheels round and then recoils when she sees us together. She takes a deep drag on her cigarette and throws it to the ground, grinding it under her flip-flop. Her face is dark, her mouth pursed angrily. 'Mind telling me where you two have been?' she says.

I flop down on the bench next to her. 'To the hospital,' I offer. 'With Ella.'

That takes the wind out of her sails, exactly as I intended it to. I'm not going to mention the extended breakfast that Noah and I shared in Broad Haven.

'Is she all right?' The tone of righteous indignation has gone.

'Yes,' I say, wearily. 'She's fine.'

I don't want to fight with Flick, not over this. It's too heart-breaking.

'I'll put the kettle on.' Noah, probably wisely, disappears while I fill Flick in on the details.

'She was bleeding in the night,' I tell her. 'I came to wake you, but couldn't. You were dead to the world. So I woke Noah up instead and he drove us to the hospital.'

'Shit,' Flick says, suitably admonished. 'I did have a skinful last night. You came to wake me up?'

'Yes.' I shrug. 'You know what you're like. Once you're out for the count, you could sleep through an earthquake.'

She has no argument against that. 'I was worried when I woke up and found that Noah was gone. I didn't know what to think.' For once Flick looks shaky. 'To be honest, I imagined the worst. I thought he'd left for good.'

'I bite down my guilt. 'I'm so sorry. I had to get Ella to the hospital. I didn't know who else to turn to.'

Flick waves away my apology. 'It doesn't matter now. I'm just worried about Ella. I should have been there for her, like you. I'm such a totally crap friend.'

I try a smile. 'She knows you too well to hold it against you, Flick. We managed all right. Noah was a great help.'

'Of course he was,' she says. 'He's bloody brilliant. How is she?'

'Still at the hospital.'

'I should go as soon as I can.'

'I've got to ring and find out what time her scan is, but they're hoping she can come out later on today.'

'The baby's OK?'

'They think so. Apparently, it's not uncommon to have a scare like this, but I don't think her tumble on the bike will have done her any good. It's made Ella realise just how much she wants this child.'

'That's a good thing.'

'Yeah.' But at what price? I cast a glance back at the cottage. 'Is no one else up yet?'

Flick shakes her head. 'Haven't seen either Art or Harry this morning. It's still early, I guess.'

I was forgetting that. It's only just after seven. 'I need to go and speak to Art. Tell him about what's happened.'

'*All* of it?'

'Yes.' Something I'm not looking forward to.

Flick gives a low whistle. 'Do you need back-up? I can do this with you, at least.'

'I think it's probably best if I do it myself,' I assure her. Wearily, I push myself off the bench. 'I'll take him some coffee.'

'I'd take him some brandy,' she says wryly.

It might not be a bad idea.

'Look, Grace, I'm sorry that I snapped at you and Noah. It's just that I don't feel that things are going all that well between us.' She runs her hand through her hair. 'I'm desperate for this relationship to work. *Desperate*. It has to. I can't keep fucking around until I'm fifty. But you seem to get on so much better with him than I do. You're so much more in tune with him. When I saw you together I thought that . . .' Her words tail away. 'Well, I don't know what I thought.'

I do know what she thought and it tightens my heart.

Her laugh is brittle and I flush. 'You're not me, are you?'

'No.' But I think, guiltily, that at this very moment I'm much more like Flick than I'd like to be.

Chapter Fifty-Eight

Noah is just about to pour the tea when I go back into the kitchen. 'I'll give that a miss,' I say. 'I'm going to take Art a coffee. Strong.'

'I'll do it.' Noah fiddles with making Art a coffee so thick and black that you could stand the spoon up in it.

'Think I should put a couple of spoons of sugar in it?' I ask, peering into the cup. 'Isn't that what you're supposed to do for someone who's in shock?' As Art will be as soon as I break this news to him.

Noah adds two cubes of brown sugar and then another two for good measure. He looks at me for approval. I nod for him to keep going and he drops in another two. It will either kill or cure him.

'Good luck,' he says. Then he nods towards Flick who's still deep in thought on the terrace. 'Everything OK out there?'

'Yes.' I pick at my nail. 'She's missing you. You should go and spend some time with her.'

'I guess so,' he concedes. 'If you need me to do anything

else, Grace, just let me know. I can drive you to the hospital later if you want.'

'Thanks. We'll see what happens. I'm sure that Art will want to get over there as soon as he can.'

So, while Noah goes outside to placate Flick, I take the wake-the-dead coffee and reluctantly climb the stairs.

I should probably stop in to see Harry first, but I want to get this onerous task over with as soon as possible. I knock on Art's bedroom door and, from inside, there's an answering groan.

With a leaden heart and a weary sigh, I slip inside. The bedroom smells like a heavy night in a bar. In the middle of the bed, in a tangle of sheets, Art is spreadeagled. I have to smile to myself as he looks every inch the stereotypical hedonistic rock musician. The only thing wrong is that he's in a cottage in Pembrokeshire rather than a city hotel in Berlin or somewhere.

'I brought coffee,' I say, putting it down on the bedside table.

There's an indeterminate noise from the heap in the bed.

I sit down on the edge of the bed next to him. 'And bad news.'

That makes Art wake up. He grunts again and pushes himself up on to one elbow. Art's a good-looking man, but clearly it must take a while for him to settle into the day as, at this moment, he looks every one of his thirty-five years. There's stubble on his chin and, in the light from the window, his increasing smattering of grey hair is highlighted. He's still wearing last night's T-shirt and what I'm assuming are last night's undies. Which is not a good look for anyone. Perhaps the years of drinking and hard living are finally starting to take their toll on him. Maybe there comes a time when the partying has to stop.

'Bad news?' he mumbles.

'Drink your coffee.'

He props himself up now and takes the cup from me. At the first sip, the hit from the caffeine makes him shudder.

I've known Art for years and I'd consider him a good friend, so why am I struggling to break this to him? But then I think that Ella couldn't do it either, so perhaps it's not surprising. I sit down on the floor next to the bed so that my head is on a level with his.

'It's Ella,' I start.

He's wide awake now and, for the first time, he realises she's not in the bed. 'Where is she?' His head spins backwards and forwards as he searches for her. A moment later, he looks as if he regrets it. 'Is she OK?'

'Yes and no.' My heart is racing and I've not had the benefit of strong coffee. I wait until my breathing is steady. 'She's in the hospital, but she's all right.'

'In the hospital? What's happened?' He looks around him, perplexed. 'Was I that out of it last night?'

'It was a pretty heavy session.'

For some of us. Although that's no different from usual.

'Art, there's something that you don't know.' I think of a dozen ways to say this out loud, forming the words in my head, but then I just blurt out, 'She's pregnant.'

That stuns Art into silence. He stares at me, open-mouthed and wide-eyed.

'We thought last night that she was going to lose the baby,' I hurry on. 'Noah and I rushed her to the hospital. They think that the baby's OK, but they're going to do a scan today.'

Still Art is gaping at me.

'Say something,' I prompt.

He rallies himself with a long, low exhalation. 'Is it my kid?'

That makes me smile. 'Of course it is.'

'Wow.' Art runs his hands through his hair. 'A baby, eh? Ella's having a baby?'

'Yes.'

My eyes feel all teary. I'm waiting for the moment when this finally hits Art and he's overjoyed and begins leaping happily round the bedroom.

Now he rubs his face. Instead of the whoop of delight that I hoped for, instead he asks, 'Is this some kind of bad dream? Am I really awake or in the middle of a nightmare?'

'Art?'

'I can't believe that Ella's having a kid.'

'She nearly lost it, Art. That stupid outing on the tandem didn't help.'

'Don't try to lay this one on me, Grace,' he snaps and I'm taken aback. 'Would I have done that if I'd known?' He sucks in an angry breath. 'For fuck's sake, she knows that I'm not interested in having kids.'

I can see now why Ella has put off doing this. 'She needs you, Art. This could be a great thing for both of you.'

'I don't see how.'

'Having a child doesn't have to change your life for the

worse,' I point out. 'The majority of people find it a very enriching experience.'

Now I sound as if I'm quoting from a childcare manual.

'I had parents who were on the road, Grace. They were both moderately successful actors. I spent my time being cared for by dubious housemasters in a hideously expensive boarding school. I just got in the way of my folk's life. If you want children you settle down in a three-bedroomed semi in the suburbs and work at the local building society. Our lifestyle doesn't fit with children.'

'Perhaps Ella feels that it's time she settled down, but it doesn't mean that your life has to be over.'

'What's the point in having a kid or kids if you're never there? I don't want to be an absent dad. I don't want to be a dad at all. I hate responsibility. My job is to look after temperamental musicians. That's enough stress and aggro for anyone. I don't want it in my home life too. Christ, I don't even want a puppy or a goldfish, let alone a kid.'

'You'll feel differently when you see her.'

Art doesn't look convinced. 'Why the hell are *you* the one telling me this, Grace? Was Ella ever going to let me know?'

'I think she was trying to find the right moment.' I daren't even mention that she's actually three months gone and that he's going to be a daddy much sooner than he thinks. 'You guys seem to have been getting on so well on this holiday.'

'She wants to move down here,' he says, waving his hands round the room. 'She loves it. Everything about it. The isolation, the peace. And this cottage, she loves its quaint little bones.'

'But you don't?'

'Do I look like a cottage by the sea man?' His voice is bleak. 'I like the bright lights, Grace. Ella knows that. This whole scene bores me to tears.'

'I thought you were enjoying yourself.' I feel defensive on Ella's behalf.

'It's great for a week, I suppose. But live here? It would be my idea of hell.'

'You guys need to have a long talk about where you're going,' I offer. 'For the time being, we need to get Ella home and rested. She doesn't need any stress now. She really wants this baby, Art. I hope you can support her in this.' This is *your son*, *your daughter* we're talking about, I want to scream. 'She's having a scan sometime this morning. You can call her.'

I don't point out to Art that this will mean a trip to the nearest phone box as that will give him even more reason to complain about rural life.

'I wouldn't know what to say.'

'You'll come over there with me, though?'

He nods, still dazed.

'I know this is a shock, a *big* shock, but you'll get used to it,' I say. 'When she's home and you've talked it through, you'll wonder why you didn't want it all along.'

'If it's such a great thing,' he says, 'then why haven't you and Harry got any kids?'

And that leaves *me* the one stunned into silence.

Chapter Fifty-Nine

I leave Art getting himself out of bed – albeit somewhat reluctantly. I hope that he'll soon be ready to go to visit Ella as I, for one, can't wait to see her. While I wait, I brace myself to take a cup of coffee in to Harry, but when I go back to the kitchen, he's already on the terrace, sitting with Flick. There's no sign of Noah. I want to ask where he is, but don't want to risk making Flick cross again.

I go outside to join them and notice that when I arrive their conversation comes to an abrupt halt, not for the first time. There seems to be a lot of plotting going on. They're probably planning to escape for their next drinking bout together.

Flick pastes on a smile as I sit down. Clearly she's still mad at me for stealing Noah away in the night. 'I'm just telling Harry what he's been missing.'

'Sounds like you've been busy while I've been sleeping,' he says and I can't detect any edge to his voice. He sounds genuinely worried.

'I'm just going to ring Ella now,' I tell them. 'See how she is.'

'You've broken the news to Art?' Flick asks. I nod. 'How did he take it?'

'I'm sure he'll be fine when he comes to terms with it.' I'm not sure at all. 'I'll go over with him to collect Ella if he wants me to.'

'I'll come too,' Flick says.

I don't think that's a good idea, but I keep quiet.

The sun is high in the sky and it's warm on my arms. My bones are aching due to the lack of sleep and it's lovely to feel the heat on them. The waves roll in and out, soothing me with their ceaseless rhythm. The beach looks so inviting and I envy Ella waking up to this remote beauty every morning. How I'd like to stretch out right now down on the sand and catch up on my sleep. Still, I need to phone the hospital and that means a trip to the village to use the phone box. I only hope that it's still fully functioning and hasn't been subjected to the usual vandalism. For a moment I get a glimpse of how frustrated Harry feels out here without his mobile lifeline.

'I'm just going to pop into the village to use the phone box to ring the hospital. Anyone want to come with me?'

Flick shrugs. 'Maybe I should stay here in case Art gets up and needs someone to talk to.'

As I can't be in two places at once, that seems like a sensible plan. I hope Flick can do a better job than I did of convincing Art that becoming a father is a great thing.

'Harry?' He fishes in his pocket and tosses the keys to the Bentley to me. I guess he's not coming either.

'Don't drive it into a post,' he snipes.

I resist the urge to bite back. Worse things happen than having your car crumpled. 'I'll be back as soon as I can.'

Neither of them looks too worried about how long I'll be gone, so I leave them to it.

As I'm crossing the kitchen, Noah comes down the stairs. His hair is freshly washed, he's shaved and he's changed his clothes. I'm wishing that I'd thought to do the same.

'Hey,' he says.

'I'm just heading down to the phone box to ring the hospital,' I tell him.

'Broken the news to Art?'

'Yes. He didn't take it well.'

'That's a shame.' He glances at the Bentley keys. 'You shouldn't drive, Grace. You've hardly had a wink of sleep. I can run you to the phone box, though it won't be in such magnificent style.'

'I hate the car,' I tell him. 'I feel so stupid in it.'

'Then jump into my trusty, if slightly smelly, vehicle.'

I'm very tempted, but sense makes me hesitate. 'I think Flick will be annoyed if I purloin you again.'

'It's a risk I'm prepared to take.'

Oh, damn it. At this moment I'm past caring what anyone thinks. 'Come on then. Let's go.'

So we get into Noah's car and drive down to the pretty village of St Brides. He waits in the car while I go and use a phone box for the first time in many, many years. Thank goodness, I've got a lot of change in my purse. It was about ten pence a call when I last used one, I'm sure. And it's definitely not now.

Finally, I get through to the ward and they let me know what has been happening just before my money runs out. I don't have enough cash to be able to wait to talk to Ella.

Back in the car, I update Noah.

'Ella's had her scan and can be collected later this afternoon. Beyond that, they won't give me any more information, but I'm assuming, as they're letting her go, it can't be bad news.'

'Want me to take you over there?'

'I'm hoping that Art will want to go and that he'll take me with him.'

Noah nods. He doesn't mention our illicit breakfast or what he said to me, and I think I'm glad about that. Instead, he just turns the car around and we head back to Cwtch Cottage.

Chapter Sixty

We pull up in front of the cottage just as Art is coming out of the front door. He's carrying a holdall overflowing with clothes that looks as if it's been hastily packed. Art stops in his tracks when he sees us, his face stricken.

'He's leaving,' I say to Noah and we're out of the car in a flash.

As I run across the gravel, Art clicks the boot of his car open and slings in his bag.

'Art?'

He turns to look at me. 'I'm off, Grace,' he says, flatly.

'So I can see. Where are you going?'

'Back to London. Tell Ella that I'll contact her.'

'You can't do this, Art. At least wait until she comes back from the hospital. I've just phoned them. She can come out later this afternoon. We could go over there together to collect her, just you and me. Then, this afternoon, you can sit and talk things through. I'm sure you can work it out.'

'What's the point? She didn't feel she could talk it through with me before, so why should she now? You seem to be the go-between, so *you* tell her that I've gone.'

'Please, Art.' I tug at his arm. 'Don't leave her like this. It's ridiculous. She shouldn't have any more stress.'

'Then I'm better out of here.'

'What about Ella?' I'm nearly in tears. 'This isn't all about what you want. Don't you care about her at all?'

He opens the door of the Merc and slides in.

I turn to Noah. 'Can't you stop him? Talk to him.'

Noah shakes his head and puts his hand on mine to still me. 'Let him go, Grace,' he says quietly. 'At the moment, she's better off without him if he feels like that.'

Art turns the key in the ignition and the Merc roars into life. My face feels ashen. I can't believe that he's really doing this. Any minute now he'll realise that he's being an idiot and will come with us to the hospital. I want happy ever after for Ella, not this.

Art turns back to look at me, leaning heavily on the steering wheel. His face has hardened. 'Tell Ella . . . ' He stumbles over her name. Then a thoroughly pissed-off sigh. 'Tell her what you like.'

With that he floors the accelerator and, showering gravel everywhere, he spins the wheels, racing off heedless of the bumps and potholes of the narrow lane.

I put my head in my hands. 'Poor Ella. What will I tell her now?'

'You'll tell her that you tried.'

'This is my fault,' I rage. 'I should have handled this differently.'

'You couldn't have done it any other way,' he assures me.

'Oh, shit.'

Misery engulfs me. I look at Noah and all I want him to do is hold me. He looks at me and I know that he feels the same. But he can't because he's not mine, he belongs to someone else, and life is bloody, bloody shit.

Chapter Sixty-One

'Fuck,' Flick says when we tell her what's happened. Which I think more than adequately sums it up. 'What a knob.'

Couldn't agree more. Sometimes Flick has the ability to come out and say just what everyone else is thinking. Most of the time, actually.

'I didn't even get a chance to speak to him,' she says. 'First thing I heard was the front door slamming.'

'Well, he's gone now.'

'Bastard,' Flick puffs.

'I'm going to go to the hospital to pick her up.' I glance anxiously at Noah and avoid looking at Harry and Flick. 'Noah has agreed to drive me.'

Flick stands up. 'We should all go.'

'I think that might be overkill,' I tell her. 'Ella's a bit teary. If we all roll up, it might just upset her.'

'You're right. You should go, Grace. You're so much better at this kind of thing than me.' She sits back down again and drums her fingers on the table. 'What can I do then?'

'You and Harry could run into St Davids, if you want to. We're running low on food and need some more supplies for tonight.'

'If you're willing to take the risk, I'll cook dinner again.'

'That would be great, Flick.' That's a really nice idea and I'm pleased that she's being so considerate. 'I'm sure Ella won't feel up to eating out. She'll want to rest.' I'm going to make sure that she does.

'You should do the same, Grace,' Noah ventures. 'You haven't slept at all. There's time for you to have a quick nap before we have to go.'

'Good idea,' Harry says.

My eyes feel heavy at the very mention of sleep. 'I think I'll get a blanket and lie on the beach.' It seems a shame to waste the opportunity.

'I'll get you one from the airing cupboard,' Harry offers. I'm struggling to cope with the emotional rollercoaster that I'm on. Today you'd think that not a cross word had been exchanged between Harry and me. It leaves my head reeling. 'Then Flick and I will be off and leave you in peace.'

So he hurries off and seconds later returns with a tartan rug. I take it gratefully. He holds my shoulders and kisses me lightly on the cheek. The kiss of an acquaintance.

'Don't run yourself into the ground, Grace,' he warns. 'This is supposed to be a holiday.'

At this rate, I'll need another holiday when I get back to recover from this one. But isn't that always the way?

Then, unexpectedly, my husband strokes my cheek. 'Take it easy.'

343

'I will.' His concern touches me. When he's nice like this, when the Harry that I used to know surfaces momentarily, the old feelings that I had for him come rushing back. 'Thanks, Harry.'

'Come on,' Flick says. 'Let's make tracks.' She kisses my cheek. 'Give her my love.'

'Of course I will.'

Flick kisses Noah. 'Look after my friends,' she instructs.

I see him flush and he nods at her.

So Flick and Harry head off to St Davids together and I get ready to head to the beach to catch forty winks. 'Why don't you come with me?' I say to Noah, throwing caution to the wind. 'We can both catch up on our sleep. I'll set the alarm on my phone.'

'Sounds like a good idea.'

We take the blanket and clamber over the rocks together. The sun is high in the sky and, even though it's a scorching-hot day, the beach is deserted. The lack of parking and the long walk down from the road means that all but the truly dedicated give this stretch of sand a miss. The lure of the ice cream and the teashops, I'm sure, prove too much of a temptation to the families on holiday.

There's a secluded area of sand between the rocks. I lay the blanket down between them, sheltering us from what little breeze there is. I set the alarm on my phone and lie down. Noah kicks off his trainers and he's down next to me, propped up on his elbow. I realise that I'm still wearing Ella's mother's shoes, so I kick those off too. Before we go to the hospital I must freshen up.

On the blanket we're close together, face to face.

'This is nice,' I say.

'Perhaps I should go home too, Grace,' Noah suggests. 'It's making life awkward for you if I hang around.'

'I don't want to spoil your relationship with Flick,' I say.

But *I can't help it* is what remains unsaid. Noah and I are constantly being thrown together and I'm doing nothing to fight it.

'There's no relationship with Flick,' he says. 'I think we've both come to realise that.'

'She said she loves you.'

'I think she *wants* to love me.' He shrugs. 'She wants to believe that this is what she's looking for, but we're completely different people. We'd drive each other mad.'

'Opposites can attract.'

'That's true.' He traces circles in the sand with his finger. 'But not for me. This week has only served to show our differences. I want someone who shares my values, my interests. Flick and I move in very different circles. There's no future for us. Plus,' he hesitates before he continues, 'I might just be imagining things, but sometimes I think I'm not the only one in Flick's life. I get the impression that there's someone else in the background.'

'Really?'

I don't like to say that he could well be right. My dear friend Flick doesn't exactly have the best track record for fidelity.

'You know the type of thing. Secret phone calls. Texts that she hides. Not since we've been here, obviously. I just get the impression that she's keeping something from me.'

'That's just Flick. She likes to be mysterious.'

'Maybe. But I think she's still searching for what she wants and I don't think that it's me. You can't force love, Grace. We both know that.' He gazes deep into my eyes and it's not cheesy. The honesty of it is searing. 'And sometimes you can't stop it even if you want to.'

'I don't want you to go,' I say, mouth dry.

'Then I'll stay.'

We inch closer together on the blanket until our knees are touching.

'Go to sleep,' he says. 'I'll watch over you.'

I close my eyes, feeling the sun on my face and the strength of Noah's presence next to me, and, within seconds, sleep has found me.

Chapter Sixty-Two

The next thing I know is that Noah is shaking my arm gently. 'Grace, wake up,' he says. 'We're late.'

That brings me out of sleep abruptly. 'What?'

'I didn't hear the alarm on your phone, but we should have left for the hospital about half an hour ago. We must have both gone into a really deep sleep.'

'Wow.'

I try to shake myself into an alert state. Reluctantly, I force myself to sit up. My head spins. If anything, I feel worse for the rest. I had clearly gone down, down, down into dreamland and now feel slightly dazed by the shock of being awake.

'Oh no.' Noah looks at me in alarm. 'Oh no.'

'What?' Panic runs through me. 'What is it?'

Then he starts to laugh. He doubles up on the blanket and guffaws.

'Stop it. Tell me what's wrong.'

When he's brought himself under control again, he says, 'Your face.'

'What about it?'

'Half of it is bright red,' he tells me, smothering another laugh. 'The other half of it isn't.'

'You're kidding me.' I touch my cheeks. He's right. One of them is certainly burning much more than the other. Then I look up at Noah and I start to laugh too.

'What?' he says. 'What's wrong?'

'Your face. It's the same.'

Now his hand goes to his cheek. It's bright red too.

Where we've fallen asleep on our sides, face to face in the sun, we've been burned to a crisp. When I glance down, I see that my left arm and leg are the same. Noah has a coordinating right arm and leg. Though the skin on his body is already tanned from working outdoors, it's more difficult to tell. With me, who's used to being cooped up in an office all day, it's not the same. My limbs are the worst possible shade of Brit-abroad lobster and I fear that my face is no better.

'They'll know,' I say. 'They'll know that we fell asleep in the sun together.'

'There's no crime in that, Grace.'

It will make them even more suspicious of us, though. I'm sure that Flick has had enough flings of her own to be able to put two and two together.

'You've made it clear that you want us to be nothing more than friends.' For a moment, he looks sad when he says, 'I can live with that.'

But can I?

We look at each other again and both get a fit of the giggles.

'Don't laugh,' I chide. 'This is bad!'

348

I can't wait to get to a mirror and see what I look like. I'll have to put make-up on, lots of it. By the time I'm fifty I'll probably have skin like a leather purse because of this.

'Do you feel better for the rest?' Noah asks.

'Not a lot. I still feel woozy. But it was nice, anyway.' Before we can get into more dangerous territory, I say, 'We'd better go and pick Ella up. She'll be wondering where we are.'

Noah nods and I fold up the blanket. We're halfway through our week here already and I feel that time is running out for Noah and me. Circumstances have meant that we have been able to slip away from the others with relative ease, to engineer little moments together. That won't be the case once the holiday ends. The only time I'll ever see Noah again is if he's with Flick as her boyfriend, or even her husband.

I watch him, heart aching, as he goes about the very ordinary business of slipping on his trainers. He might say now that he sees no future for Flick and himself, but he shouldn't underestimate her determination. My friend has an uncanny knack of getting exactly what she wants.

Chapter Sixty-Three

Ella is waiting in the main reception when Noah and I bowl in. 'You've not been here long, have you?'

She shakes her head. 'Five minutes.'

'Noah and I fell asleep on the beach,' I explain. 'We were snoozing so deeply that even the alarm didn't wake us. We're much later than we wanted to be.'

'You were up half the night with me,' she points out. 'I can't begrudge you a little catch-up nap.'

Now I feel better for having a few hours of sleep, even if one side of me is probably more chargrilled than the other. I also had a quick shower and changed and, apart from the burned and scarlet bits, am almost human again.

'Oh my goodness.' Ella stifles a laugh as she looks at me more closely. 'You've certainly caught the sun. Did you forget the sunblock?' Then she sees Noah and the stifling fails. 'Oh,' she chuckles, 'you're exactly the same.'

Is it that obvious? I was hoping that my heavy hand with the foundation had disguised the worst of it. Clearly it hasn't. Damn.

I glance down to check that her bump is still in place. 'Everything all right with the baby?'

The expression of relief on her face is palpable. 'Yes. I've been given the all-clear and a stern talking-to,' she says. Ella pats her tummy fondly. 'Now I have to make sure that I put this little lady first.'

'It's a girl?'

'One of the few benefits of an emergency visit to the hospital is that I now know that I have to buy pink baby clothes.'

'That's wonderful,' I say. 'Every cloud has a silver lining. A little girl!' I feel like doing a happy dance round Reception.

'I know.' Ella is glowing. 'It all seems very real now.'

It's not only for Ella that it seems more real now. I can't wait to go shopping with her for baby clothes. And then, from nowhere, for the first time in my life, my heart twists with an overwhelming longing for a child of my own. It's a deep pull of need stronger than anything I've felt before, right down to my core, and it almost takes my breath away. I want a small, chubby body cuddled in my arms. I want the scent of milk and baby powder in my life. I want this fierce, protective sensation that's enveloping me to have a focus.

'Congratulations, Ella.' Noah comes forward to hug and kiss her.

'Thanks. I'm just so thrilled.' She looks beyond us. 'Where's Art?'

Noah and I go from the joy of a second ago to exchanging an anxious look.

Ella's face falls and tears spring to her eyes. 'He's not coming, is he?'

Now it's my turn to shake my head. 'No,' I say flatly. There's no point beating about the bush. I know that Ella will want it straight. 'He's gone back to London, Ella.'

She rocks back, a little unsteady on her feet. Noah catches her under the elbow and holds her. 'Wow.'

'He'll feel differently when you've had time to talk,' I assure her. 'Really, he will.'

What's the saying, 'Hurt me with the truth rather than comfort me with a lie'? I brush the thought aside. I just hope that Art will come to his senses and embrace fatherhood. It will be such a crying shame if he doesn't.

'It's a big shock for him. It'll take time.'

'Did he have anything to say at all?'

'Not really,' I admit. Nothing that Ella doesn't already know. 'But perhaps I didn't break it to him in the best way.'

'I should have done that.'

'Circumstances overtook you, Ella. Don't beat yourself up about it.'

'I knew he'd be like this,' she says. 'I just knew.'

'Let's get you to the car,' Noah says. 'The sooner you're back at the cottage the better. You can put your feet up and we can look after you. Do you need a wheelchair?'

'No,' Ella says. 'I'm fine.'

'We're parked quite near the entrance. It's not far.'

He keeps hold of her elbow as he steers her towards the Range Rover. Her steps are hesitant and she looks so frail that my heart goes out to her. I'm going to do all that I can to make sure that the rest of this pregnancy goes without a hitch, that Ella is blooming with health.

'You're very kind, Noah,' she says as we reach the car. 'I'm sorry that you've been thrown into all our problems. This was supposed to be a holiday for you, a chance for Flick to show you off.'

'Don't worry,' Noah says. 'I feel as if you're all old friends already.' He looks squarely at me when he says, 'Whatever happens, I'm glad that I came.'

'Good.' Ella pats his hand. 'You're a lovely man. I'm very jealous of Flick.'

'I wouldn't be,' he says softly.

But Ella is already climbing into the car and I'm the only one who hears him.

Chapter Sixty-Four

It doesn't take us long to get back to the cottage. I make Ella tea and toast, which she eats with relish. Sometimes it is the best comfort food. Noah disappears to have a walk on the beach, leaving us to our own devices. When she's finished I escort Ella upstairs and, while she undresses, I run her a hot bath. She comes into the bathroom in her dressing gown.

'There's lots of lovely bubbles in there,' I tell her. 'You have a good long soak.'

'Thanks,' she says. 'I can't wait to get in here. I smell of hospital.'

I fix a clean towel for her, draping it on the warm rail. 'Does it feel funny to have a new life growing inside you?'

Ella nods. 'Who'd have thought it would come to this when we were working in the bar together in Liverpool?'

'Life has taken us to some strange places.'

'I feel as if I'm starting a whole new phase,' Ella says. 'Part of me is excited. And part of me is just plain terrified.'

'You'll be fine. I'm sure every expectant mother feels the same.'

'It feels as if I'm having to be a proper grown-up for the first time in my life,' she confesses. 'Once Baby Hawley is born I won't ever be able to just close the door or go out when I want to. I won't be able to lock myself in the studio and paint all day if the mood takes me and not worry about eating or cleaning the house. I'll have someone else who'll rely on me.'

'And you'll rise beautifully to the challenge.'

'I want to stay here, Grace.' She looks round at the solid stone walls. 'Here in Cwtch Cottage, but how can I? Art's right when he says it's in the middle of nowhere. Will it be a safe place for me and the baby?'

'You're less likely to get mugged in the wilds of Pembrokeshire than you are in Notting Hill.'

I try to make light of it. Being here this week has made me realise that this area really is the byword for remote. If Art doesn't come back, will Ella be able to stay here? Shouldn't she be nearer to clinics and shops and civilisation in general? But then out of the window I catch a glimpse of the beach and think it would be the most idyllic place on earth to bring up a child.

'I don't want to go through this alone.'

'You've got me and Flick.'

'But no father for my child.' Her face is sad and tears fill her eyes. 'No grandparents for her to play with. I always wanted to give my child a stable, happy family. The kind of worry-free childhood that I had.'

'Times have changed,' I offer. Tragic though that is. 'Very

few marriages go the distance. We all have different arrangements that we call family now.' I think of Harry's two boys, who are the closest I've had to sons. 'It doesn't make them less than they were. Just different. You'll find a way of making it work.'

'I should go and call Art. Try to explain to him why it all happened like this.'

'Give him a couple of days to mull things over. I don't want you getting stressed again right now. Take some time to recover and get your strength back. These shocks take their toll.'

She sighs. 'You're probably right.'

'I'm *always* right,' I tease.

'Art's a great man,' she says. 'I'm just saddened that this isn't what he wants. I suppose I hoped that when he found out about the baby, he'd be as thrilled as I am. I was worried about how he'd react, but in my heart I didn't really believe that he'd just walk away.'

'Don't dwell on it now,' I urge. 'There'll be time enough for talking in the next few months. He might surprise you yet.'

'He might do,' she concedes. 'Still, enough about me. What about you?' She strokes the hair from my face. 'Something tells me that not all is well in the Taylor household. There's a lot of tension between you and Harry.'

'Tell me about it.' I puff out a ragged breath. 'I feel pulled in a dozen different directions.'

Ella puts her hand on my arm. 'Noah's a lovely man, Grace,' she says. 'You seem to get on very well together.'

'Yes.' I try to keep my voice neutral. 'We do.'

'*Very* well,' she reiterates.

I flop down heavily on the loo seat and Ella sits on the edge of the bath. She takes my hand.

'What am I to do, Ella?' The last thing I want to do is burden my friend as she's got so much on her plate already. 'Harry and I are really struggling in our marriage. I feel like we're worlds apart.'

'And Noah?'

'I like him,' I admit. '*More* than that.' *Much* more than that. 'He's kept me sane this week.' While at the same time driving me to distraction. Funny how love can be. 'But he's Flick's boyfriend. She wants to *marry* him.' I don't add that while Flick might be crazy for Noah, I don't think that the feeling is mutual.

'Flick wouldn't think twice if she was in your shoes,' Ella points out.

'That doesn't make it right,' I counter.

Ella suddenly looks shifty and I don't know why. 'You told me that when it comes to the baby I have to do what's right for me. I could say the same to you about your marriage, Grace. Will you take your own advice?'

'I promised Harry for ever.'

'Sometimes promises have to be broken. He promised to love and cherish you. Does he do that?'

'No. I can't say that he does.'

She looks at the floor. 'Has he forsaken all others?'

'Harry hasn't got time to be unfaithful,' I quip. 'Chance would be a fine thing. He's always too busy at work to do anything else.'

I don't point out that he rarely wants to make love with me these days and, when he does, I don't want to. I don't think Harry's libido runs to other women.

Ella sighs. 'Decide what it is that you really want. Do what's best for you.'

'I will,' I promise.

'Do you love Noah?'

'I daren't even let myself admit it, Ella.'

'Have you talked to him about this? Does he know how you feel?'

'I'm not sure that I even know myself.' The strength of emotion that overtakes me when I think of him has blind-sided me and it seems as if I've lived a lifetime this week. 'We've agreed to be friends.' What else can we do?

Ella frowns. 'If you love him, don't let him go.' She looks directly at me. 'You deserve happiness. Whatever you want to do, Grace, I'll be here for you. You've been strong for me. Now I can do it for you.'

'Thank you.' We hug each other.

I do deserve happiness, but do I want it at the expense of other people's misery? Especially people that I care for. Could I rip up the rule book and throw away my own values in the pursuit of it? Is my own happiness more important than that of others?

Out of the corner of my eye, I see Noah walking barefoot along the beach at the edge of the surf, with his jeans rolled up and his trainers in his hand. Every fibre of my being yearns for him, but he is forbidden fruit.

What *do* I want to do? I think. Only I can decide.

Chapter Sixty-Five

Flick and Harry come back late as afternoon is slipping into evening. I was beginning to get worried about where they were, but it seems I needn't have. They are smiling and laughing as they unload armfuls of carrier bags from the boot of the Bentley. I watch them happy in each other's company, and wonder why Harry and I can't be like that any more.

I've just taken Ella some tea as I heard her stirring. She looks better now that she's had a good lengthy nap, but I didn't want to leave her there for too long as she'll be wide awake tonight.

Noah hasn't yet returned from his walk. He's probably glad to get away from us all for an hour or two and have some peace. I hope he's not deliberately avoiding me.

Opening the door of the cottage, I lift one of the bags from Flick. 'Hey,' I say.

'Christ!' Flick stops dead. 'What have you done to your face?'

'Too much sun.' Not enough make-up.

'I'll say.' Her eyes travel over me and take in my roasted arm too. My legs I've covered up with a long skirt.

'Good trip?'

'Yeah. Sorry we were gone so long,' Flick giggles breathlessly. 'We stopped at the pub in St Brides on the way back.'

No surprise there, I guess. I should have known. I hope to goodness that Harry hasn't been foolish enough to drink and drive, but he does seem marginally less giggly than Flick.

They dump their shopping on the table and I follow suit. Harry kisses my cheek. 'I bought you these,' he says and holds out a bunch of somewhat wilted lemon carnations with the £2.99 price label still on them.

'Thank you.' I assume that I'm meant to be happy that he's bought me flowers, but it seems like a cursory effort. Is this all the value he places on me? They look as if they've been left out of water for too long and are on their last legs. Much as I feel, so perhaps they are a good choice after all. 'They're lovely.'

'Got stuff for stir-fry too,' Flick says. 'Thought it would be quick to knock together, then no one has to spend hours in the kitchen.'

'Sounds good to me.'

'How's Ella?'

'She's spent the afternoon in bed, resting.' I can hear movement upstairs. 'She's just getting up now.'

'Upset about Art?'

'Yes.' Of course.

'Fucker,' Flick says. 'I'd like to give him a piece of my mind.' I think she'd have to get in a queue. Then, 'Where's Noah?'

'He went out for a walk a while ago,' I tell her. 'I haven't seen him come back yet.'

I resist the urge to check my watch as I have been doing every five minutes for the last hour.

As we talk, the back door opens and Noah returns. 'Hey,' he says. 'I was out longer than I meant to be.'

'Had a nice walk, darling?' Flick asks and twines herself around him.

'Great. I walked down the coast to Martin's Haven to see about taking a boat trip across to Skomer.'

Flick looks blank.

'It's a fantastic island, full of seabirds. Puffins, guillemots, razorbills.'

Flick still looks blank.

'It's a unique place.'

She wrinkles her nose. 'I'm taking it that you want to go there?'

'I'd love to,' Noah says. 'Anyone else fancy it?'

Flick shrugs. 'Is there anything else there but birds?'

If I know Flick she's thinking of branches of Harvey Nicks, Selfridges, Liberty's.

Noah laughs. 'No. Nothing but birds.'

'Oh.' Her disappointment is palpable.

'There's one trip a day that leaves early in the morning and comes back late afternoon.'

A look of pure horror crosses Flick's face. 'We'd stay there *all day*?'

'There's a lot to see,' Noah reasons.

'Birds?'

'Sounds bloody boring to me,' Harry says.

'I'd love to go,' I chip in before I can stop it coming out of my mouth. 'If everyone else wants to.'

'We'd have to get down there really early to make sure we could catch the boat. You can't book in advance and there's a limited amount of tickets for each day.'

'*Boat?*' Flick says. 'I hate boats. Unless they're yachts moored at Cannes. How long's the journey? I'm a terrible puker.'

'Not long. About half an hour.'

My friend has gone green already. 'OK,' she says, surprising us all. 'That sounds great.'

Noah is clearly taken aback. 'Excellent.'

Then Ella appears. She looks much better, not so wan, not so vulnerable.

'Sweetheart!' Flick swoops to her and hugs her tightly. 'I'm the one who's supposed to be the drama queen. Emergency hospital runs? What were you thinking of?'

'I'll try not to do it again,' Ella offers.

'I'm sorry I wasn't there.'

'Grace did an admirable job,' Ella assures her. 'And Noah, of course.'

'Noah is a superhero.' The expression on Harry's face shows that he wouldn't necessarily agree. 'You're doing all right now?'

'I'm starving,' Ella says.

'Let's get this dinner on then,' I say. 'Flick has bought stuff for a stir-fry.'

'Mm. Lovely. I'll get started.'

362

'You'll do no such thing, lady!' I tell her, sounding as stern as I can. 'You're doing nothing more strenuous than lifting your knife and fork tonight. Doctor's orders.'

She gives us a resigned smile.

'Noah and I will do it,' Flick says. 'Won't we, darling?'

He shrugs. 'Sure.'

'We make a great team,' Flick says. 'I could really get used to this whole domestic lark. I think it quite suits me.'

Then, just as I think we've got away with it, she stares closely at Noah. 'One half of your face is all sunburned.'

Noah colours up so that both sides of his face match. 'I fell asleep in the sun.'

Involuntarily, his eyes slide towards me and Flick's follow. She frowns when they alight on my similarly roasted cheeks.

'Oh,' she says, puzzled. 'It's just like Grace's face. You look like two halves of one person.'

How can I tell her that's how we feel too?

'Must have been the angle of the sun,' Noah says swiftly. 'Now, what do you want me to do?'

That distracts Flick enough for Ella and me to make a break for it. She and I exchange a glance, but neither of us comments. Instead we both slope out of the kitchen to sit on the terrace, soaking up the last rays of the sinking sun until dinner is ready. I try to bake the other side of my face to match. And we leave Harry hovering around in the kitchen like a gooseberry.

Chapter Sixty-Six

After dinner we retire to the living room. I want this to be a quiet evening with no shocks or surprises. And, preferably, no dancing on the tables. Ella still looks tired to me and I want to make sure that she doesn't have any undue exertion.

'Fancy doing a jigsaw, Ella?' There's a pile of them on the shelves, all covered in a fine layer of dust. Clearly, it's a long time since the jigsawing bug hit the cottage.

'I used to love the rainy days down here,' she says wistfully. 'Daddy and I used to sit all day and do jigsaws.'

'Jigsaws!' Flick scoffs. 'You've got to be kidding me. I've never done one in my entire life. Never. Even as a kid I refused.'

'Then you don't know what you're missing.' I run my fingers over the colourful lids, studying the pictures. I don't like them with too much sky or too many mountains. 'They're very therapeutic.'

'So is a good shag. I know which of the two I'd prefer to spend time doing.'

Only Harry laughs.

As we've got only a couple of days left here, I need to choose something simple with not too many pieces. I don't think I could bring myself to go home if there was a half-done jigsaw that needed finishing.

I pick a gaudy, circular scene that features whales swimming around each other and, for some reason, bright yellow flowers. It's very cheerful, if lacking in any form of artistic merit. I wave the box at Ella, seeking her approval.

'It was Mum's favourite,' she says. 'I think there may be a couple of pieces missing.'

I shrug. 'I can live with that.' It's years since I've taken time to do a jigsaw myself.

'Let's do it in the corner,' she suggests, 'then we can leave it out and finish it tomorrow.'

So we sit cross-legged on the floor, tip out the pieces and start to sort. Even the smooth movement of the small cardboard pieces is soothing.

'I'm bored,' Flick says. 'What can *we* do?'

Noah has been browsing on his iPod and puts on an Ed Sheeran album. The mellow sounds fill the cottage. 'Read a book,' he says to Flick.

'I spend all my working days reading film scripts. I don't read for pleasure any more.'

'There's a whole host of board games here.' Now Noah rummages on the shelves. 'Chequers, backgammon, chess ...'

Flick tuts. 'Do I look like a woman who's had time in her life for playing chess?'

'Snakes and ladders,' he suggests.

'That'll do,' she sighs. 'Can't you get a bloody satellite dish, Ella?'

'I think that'll be one of my next additions,' she answers pleasantly. 'All those long nights with some great films.'

'You forgot to add the word "lonely" to that,' Flick quips and then, as Ella's face threatens to crumple, she adds, 'Oh, fuck. Forget I said that. I'm a silly cow.'

'Here's some sea.' I offer Ella a piece of bright-blue jigsaw to distract her.

'Want to play snakes and ladders, Noah?'

'I'm going to read through this guide book for our trip to Skomer tomorrow,' he says. 'Harry will play with you.'

'Harry?'

'It's a while since I've played. I'm not sure what you've got to do.'

'Christ, Harry, even I can work this one out. You go up the bloody ladders and down the bloody snakes. It says it's for age four and upwards on the box. I'm pretty certain we can cope.'

So while Ed Sheeran softly tells us about his 'Lego House' we collectively jigsaw, read and play board games. The only noise is the occasional slapping down of a counter on Flick and Harry's hotly contested game of snakes and ladders.

While Ella's busy making a whale's face, I sneak a glance through my eyelashes at Noah. He's sitting in one of the armchairs under a reading lamp, the book open on his lap. He's wearing narrow reading glasses and, if possible, looks even more handsome. I have a vision of him in the future, his children around him, immersed in family life. It makes my mouth go dry. It's a scene that I'd like to slip into, sitting at his feet, my head on his knee. Perhaps we'd have a dog too. A proper man's dog, not one of those little handbag things. A chocolate Labrador. That would be Noah's kind of dog, I'm sure. He looks relaxed, content, and when he catches my eye, he smiles over at me.

'We need to cheer this game up,' Flick announces, which breaks the contact between Noah and me. My daydream shimmers and disappears. 'Every time we go down a snake we should drink a shot. What have you got, Ella?'

'Have a look in the kitchen cupboards. There's all kinds of random booze in them. You might have to dig deep. There's an awful lot of strangely coloured drinks of indeterminate origin that my parents brought back from holidays abroad.'

'That sounds like much more fun!'

'If you go down a snake, you've got to do a shot of something hideous.'

Flick scampers away into the kitchen and comes back moments later, arms full of clinking bottles. As Ella said, there is a weird and eclectic selection.

'They're years old,' Ella warns. 'Make sure they're not out of date.'

'They're all out of date,' Flick says, when she's had a quick look. 'How can alcohol go out of date?'

She lines them up next to the board game. From here I can see limoncello, ouzo, schnapps, metaxa, aquavit. There's even a bottle of mead. Combined, they'd make a lethal cocktail.

'Is this wise?' I offer.

I get a look from Flick that says, 'Butt out, Grace.'

So I hold my tongue even though this seems like an accident

367

waiting to happen. I can see myself sleeping on the sofa again tonight.

Flick finds the shot glasses. 'Want in, Noah?'

He holds up a hand. 'Count me out.'

Ella and I carry on with our whales, but I keep one eye on Flick and Harry. The game gets more and more robust as it progresses and they start to knock back the shots. Each one is greeted with a shudder. I lose count of how many shots they down, but the laughter gets more outrageous, the play more raucous. Poor Ed Sheeran is completely drowned out by the noise.

A few more shots and they start to argue vociferously. They drop their voices, but I can still hear them hissing at each other under their breath.

'Play nicely,' I call across.

But the argument just gets louder until Harry shouts, 'You can't do that, woman!'

Clearly drink and board games are a volatile combination. I should have reminded Flick what it was like on the few occasions we played them with Harry and his boys. It always used to end in tears as Harry had to win at all costs.

Seconds later, when Harry knocks the board over and the counters spill on to the floor, I decide it's time to step in. They're just lucky that it's not one of the bottles that has been upended.

'Right, you two,' I say. 'Enough. We need to calm this down.'

'Oh, you're such a spoilsport, Grace,' Harry complains.

I might be, but I've had quite enough excitement for one week.

'You're right,' Flick says, which takes me aback. She's not normally so acquiescent. 'We should stop playing now.' She looks pointedly at Harry for reasons I can't imagine. 'There's something I want to do.'

She weaves slightly as she makes her way across the room towards Noah. 'Attention, everyone!' Flick claps her hands. 'Attention.' Noah puts down his book and, half smiling, regards her over his glasses indulgently before removing them.

Before we know what's happening, Flick drops to her knee in front of him. That certainly gets everyone's attention. Ella and I put down our jigsaw pieces. Harry, white-faced, lets the snakes and ladders counters fall to the floor again.

'Noah Reeves,' she says loudly. In her hand there's a wire top, of the kind you'd get off a champagne bottle, that she's twisted into a home-made ring. 'Would you do me the very great honour of becoming my husband?'

Chapter Sixty-Seven

I don't know who's the most stunned out of all of us. We all stand up, open-mouthed, staring. Harry goes white. Noah flushes scarlet. He looks like a rabbit caught in the headlights.

Flick stays steadfastly in place while the seconds tick by. I want to intervene, say something, anything, to fill this yawning silence, but nothing will come.

There is only one person who can answer Flick's question and, currently, he seems to have gone into a catatonic trance.

Flick, clearly tiring of being on one knee, says, 'Well? Will you or won't you?'

'Are you serious?' Noah asks.

'Deadly,' she says.

I don't think any of us were really in any doubt about that.

He shakes himself, as if waking from a long slumber under a spell, and stands. Taking Flick's hand, he helps her up until they're standing face to face. His eyes are fixed solely on her, without even giving a cursory glance in my direction, when he says, 'I'd be delighted to.'

Flick's face breaks into a grin. 'Really?'

'You're not planning to drive me up to Gretna Green tonight, are you?'

'No. Of course not, silly.' Then she pauses. 'But we could if you wanted to.'

Bitterly, I wonder if she's told him that she's already had one runaway wedding.

Noah holds up a hand. 'We should take our time.' It's only then that his eyes meet mine.

'Congratulations,' I manage.

The word feels strangled in my throat. I need to draw on all my best acting skills to step forward and embrace them both. My body feels rigid, robotic. I should be so happy for my friend, for both Flick and Noah. But I'm not.

She can't be serious about this. They're so unsuited. And what's Noah thinking of? Has he been toying with my emotions all this time? Has he really been in love with Flick all along and is just having a great laugh at my expense? He's been protesting all week that he and Flick are terminally unsuited, so why on earth did he say yes?

Flick hugs me and I might as well be concrete. Then Noah takes me into his arms. Warmth floods through me and it is the closest I think I will ever come to swooning. I keep a grip on myself and move away as quickly as I can. Next Harry steps forward and, he too, looks less than impressed by the turn of events. But then he doesn't like Noah anyway. Although he might find Flick irritating, I'm sure he'll be annoyed by the idea that Noah will now be permanently in our circle of close friends. He gives Noah a cursory clap on the back and, when he looks at Flick, I see with some surprise that his eyes are bleak. Clearly, he too thinks that she's chosen the wrong life partner.

But who are we to advise Flick or to pass judgement on whether or not she's making the right choice? Only Noah and Flick can decide that. Harry and I are hardly walking adverts for *Mr & Mrs*. Flick certainly seems keen to make this work. Come hell or high water.

Now it's Ella's turn to kiss them. 'You make a lovely couple,' she says as she holds them both tightly. Out of all of us, she's the one who sounds the most sincere. But when she faces me again, I can see that her eyes too are troubled.

Flick jumps up and down on the spot. 'I'm going to be married! I'm going to be married!' She throws herself at Noah who, obligingly, lifts her into the air and twirls her round.

I feel numb. I'm watching it all, but I can't believe that it's happening to me. But then, how did I think this was going to end? Did I imagine that Noah and I were going to gallop off into the sunset together? That was never going to happen. I'm sensible, steady Grace Taylor. Whatever fantasies I might have secretly harboured, I'm going to go home with Harry and work on our marriage. I'll be in it for the next twenty-five, thirty-five years. Never entirely happy, never entirely finding the courage to leave. A lot of people live like that, I think. Why not be one of them? Why buy into the fairy tale of fabulous love, of soulmates, of happy ever after? It will only disappoint you.

'I have champagne!' Flick says. 'Let me go and get it!'

I want to say that the last thing any of us needs is more drink, but I'm always the one pouring cold water on her plans.

'I'll go,' Noah says. Frankly, he looks as if he could do with some fresh air.

'No, no,' she insists. 'I'll go.' And, without a backward glance, Flick trips outside.

There's an awkwardness in the room that's hard to disguise. Noah shuffles from foot to foot. So do I. Harry holds on to the mantelpiece, looking for all the world as if he will fall over if he lets go for even a second. Clearly this announcement has knocked everyone for six. I know Flick said that she wanted to propose to Noah, but I never really thought that she'd do it and certainly not now.

'Wow,' Ella says, when it's clear that no one else can find words to fill the void. 'That certainly livened the evening up.'

I try a laugh and it drops into the room like a pebble down a deep well.

'That's enough surprises for me for one night,' Ella continues with a yawn. 'Just a little thimbleful of fizz for me to be sociable and then I'm off to bed.'

The headlights of a car rove over the curtains and there's the crunch of gravel from outside.

'Is that Flick?' Ella asks. 'I hope she's not driving with all she's had to drink.'

Seconds later we hear footsteps across the kitchen. Flick puts her head round the living-room door. 'Look what the cat dragged in!' she says. 'Ta-dah!'

With two champagne bottles in hand, she flings the door wide open and standing there, looking more than a little dazed, is Art.

Chapter Sixty-Eight

Flick opens the first bottle of champagne. Clearly, it has been shaken up in the boot of the car or on its journey in my friend's arms as, when she opens the bottle, it sprays everywhere. She decides to embrace the Grand Prix style of opening fizz and showers us all with it. I try to be joyous and laughing.

'Noah,' she instructs, 'find glasses.' Duly, he disappears into the kitchen.

Art and Ella stand facing each other. He looks like a lost soul. His clothes are crumpled and he's clearly not shaved. The expression on his face is hangdog, worn. 'I've been such a bloody idiot,' Art says. 'Can you possibly forgive me?'

'You don't even have to ask,' Ella says. They step into each other's arms and she buries her face in his neck.

'I got all the way back to London,' he says, voice thick with emotion. 'I pulled up outside the house and just sat there and thought, What the hell am I doing? I turned round and drove straight back.'

Noah reappears with six champagne flutes. Flick splashes the drink into the glasses.

'What are we celebrating?' Art asks, having missed the bombshell of the last few minutes.

'We're toasting our engagement,' Flick says. 'Noah and I are to be married.'

Noah is smiling broadly but, I might be mistaken, I don't think that it's reaching his eyes. He's steadfastly avoiding looking at me.

'Wow. Congratulations,' Art says and lifts the glass he's given.

'Just a tiny bit for me,' Ella says. 'Baby on board.'

Flick ignores Ella's request and hands her a full flute.

'And now we're wetting the baby's head too,' Flick says as she pours one for herself. 'Get it down your necks, folks. Harry and I have been at the lurid liqueurs, so you've got ground to make up.'

'All right,' Art says and his first glass slips down easily. 'To the baby,' he proposes. He and Ella exchange a wary smile. The glasses are topped up again and downed.

'To Flick and Noah,' Flick proposes.

We duly raise our glasses again and echo, 'To Flick and Noah.'

Even the hit of bubbles fails to lift my spirits. It's obviously working well for some people as, moments later, the second bottle is being opened.

I'm concerned to note that Art has moved very quickly from penitent partner to party animal. Ed Sheeran is taken off the iPod and replaced with dance music. The Black Eyed

Peas rock the quiet of the cottage. I'm sure that the ancient plaster on the walls is vibrating. Flick starts to dance and pulls Noah into the middle of the floor. She twines her body round him like a lap dancer and he does nothing to dissuade her. I notice that Harry is giving them both black looks, so I don't suggest that we dance too – not that I particularly want to.

Art pulls Ella into his arms and twirls her round. She's moving tentatively and I get a flash of irritation with him as I realise that he's not in the least taking into account how she feels. Only this morning, she was in hospital having a scan. Only last night did we fear that she was losing the baby.

He might have returned sheepish and repentant, but with the music on loud and the booze flowing, he seems to have forgotten why he's back here at all or why he even went in the first place.

Harry and I are onlookers, detached from the party. It's like having an out-of-body experience. This is all going on around me, but none of it is touching my heart.

Two songs later and Ella is breathless, begging to sit down. She lowers herself into the sofa, looking really tired. I drop down beside her. 'Don't overdo it,' I say. Already it's getting late. 'Why don't you go up to bed now?'

'I might do,' she says. 'Do you think I'll be missed?'

Art is still dancing, glass in hand. He's singing at the top of his voice.

'Perhaps not,' I acknowledge ruefully. 'But you're the important one here.'

'This little one is,' she counters as she cradles her bump.

'No hospital runs in the early hours, please,' I say. 'I want you to have a good night's sleep.'

'Me too.'

'I'm not going to be far behind you.' I stifle a yawn, though I think I'm more emotionally exhausted than physically spent. 'I still hope that we're going to Skomer tomorrow.' Though, with the turn of events, that may have been long forgotten.

Ella lowers her voice, so that only I can hear. 'I guess Art and I will have a lot of talking to do. We'll stay behind and, hopefully, sort things out while we have some time on our own. Wish me luck.'

'You'll be fine,' I assure her.

'Night, sweetie.'

'Promise to wake me if you get so much as a twinge.'

'I will.' She kisses my cheek and then, unnoticed, slips away.

I glance over at Art. He seems oblivious to Ella, wrapped up in his own enjoyment. Harry is now dancing with Flick. She appears to be grinding her hips into his groin. I sigh to myself. I feel as if I'm completely superfluous to requirements.

Noah is leaning on the mantelpiece, draining his glass of champagne. I think it's the first alcohol that I've seen him touch. Perhaps he feels in need of it. Perhaps the reality of a lifetime with Flick is just hitting home.

I can't stand this any longer. It's time for me to go to bed too. Taking my glass and Ella's, I stand and cross the room. 'Night, all,' I say. 'See you in the morning.'

'You can't go now!' Flick tugs at my arm. 'You can't leave me with all these men! The party's just getting started.'

'I'm done. Really.' I kiss her cheek. 'Congratulations again.'

'You and Ella must be my bridesmaids!'

'Of course we will.' A wave of my hand. 'Night then.'

The only person who answers me is Noah. From his little island by the fireplace, he stares at me directly and says, 'Goodnight, Grace.'

'Goodnight, Noah.' But in my head it sounds as if we are both saying, 'Goodbye.'

Chapter Sixty-Nine

It was in the early hours of the morning when Harry finally staggered into the bedroom. He and Flick had giggled all the way up the stairs, tripping and crashing into the walls as they went. I lay still while he hopped around, cursing to himself and pulling off his clothes. When he eventually collapsed on the bed, he was wearing one sock and his shirt – the buttons having proved far too complicated for drunken fingers. His snores are still going strong.

I glance at the clock. Now it's almost five and the sun is streaming through the windows. I've drifted in and out of sleep, listening to the quiet swish of the ocean occasionally punctuated by the sound of laughter from the living room, until the party finally broke up. Thankfully, there's been no call from Ella. So I'm hoping that she had a good night. I'm quite awake and decide that I might as well get up as lie here, my mind in turmoil. At least I can have the bathroom and kitchen to myself before anyone else rouses.

Tea is in order before anything else, so I pull on my jeans

and cardigan and pad downstairs in my bare feet. As I step into the kitchen, I'm surprised to see Noah sitting alone at the table, head in hands. He looks up when he hears me, so no chance to retreat to the safety of my room again.

'Hey.' He nods at the teapot on the table. 'Want some?'

'Please.' I slide into the chair facing him.

Noah gets a mug and the milk and pours for me. We sit on opposite sides of the table, nursing our mugs.

He hasn't shaved yet and his hair is still tangled from sleep. It makes him no less handsome.

'What time did you get to bed?'

'I left them to it not long after you went,' he says. Which surprises me. I thought they were all in for the long haul. 'Flick didn't "retire" till about three.' I knew it was late, but hadn't realised quite how late. 'I think we might be short on numbers for our Skomer trip.'

'You're still planning on going?' That surprises me too.

He shrugs. 'Wouldn't miss it for anything.'

It's doubtful that Harry will be coming to Skomer. If he's true to form, nothing will rouse him from this bed until at least ten or later. The boat to the island will be long gone by the time he's ready to face the world.

'I don't think Flick will make it,' he adds. 'From the way things were looking, she's going to have the most monumental hangover today. I don't think that bobbing about in a small boat will help.'

'You're not going to stay here with her?' That sounds more judgemental than I mean it to.

'No.'

'I don't think Harry will be up for it either. And Art and Ella need to spend some time together talking today so I can't see them wanting to go.'

'Then it's just the two of us.'

My throat tightens. 'Is that wise?'

Noah sighs. 'Probably not, but I think we should go anyway.' He lowers his voice. 'It could be the last time we ever get to spend time together, Grace.' There'll be no cosy little outings together when he's Flick's husband. 'I'm prepared to take the risk, if you are.'

I am quite possibly the most risk-averse person on the planet, but I still find myself saying, 'OK.'

'We have the perfect day for it.' He glances out of the window at the flawless sky and the golden sun that's just emerged. 'There's nothing on the island – other than birds. No café or anything. I'll make us some sandwiches to take with us while you get yourself ready.' The guide book on the table tells me that Noah is taking this very seriously.

'What time should we leave?'

'We'll have to be down at the harbour to buy tickets first thing. We can set off as soon as you're ready.'

There's a lightness in my heart as I quickly grab some cereal and wolf it down. Is it entirely due to the fact that I'm keen to get up close and personal with the Pembrokeshire puffin colony? Or is it more due to the fact that I will be able to escape the others, possibly for the last time, for a few precious hours with Noah?

Chapter Seventy

I take a last glance at Harry, still lying on his back in bed, his arm thrown above his head, snoring. To my shame, I'm glad that he hasn't woken. I'm glad that I don't have to speak to him or have to spend the day listening to him complain. This day is for Noah and me. For me and Noah alone.

I steal downstairs again and find him waiting for me in the kitchen.

Ella's there too. She's swaddled in her dressing gown on the sofa, knees tucked up and holding a steaming cup of tea. She certainly looks a lot brighter this morning.

'Hey,' I say. 'How are you feeling today?'

'Much better, thanks.'

I wonder if it's as much to do with the return of the errant Art as anything.

'Have a nice day at Skomer,' she says. 'Noah's just told me your plans. It sounds lovely. I haven't been there in years. I remember it being fabulous, though. I'm sure it hasn't changed at all. It's a timeless place.'

'Are you sure you won't come with us? I'd love you to.'

Ella shakes her head. 'Art and I have a lot to sort out. We're not out of the woods yet. Not by a long way.' She gives me a rueful smile.

'You'll be fine,' I assure her. 'He came back.'

'I don't want him unconditionally, Grace. That belongs in self-help books, not real life. I have to think what's best for the baby.'

The unspoken words are that someone who still craves a rock'n'roll lifestyle might not fit the bill.

'Want me to stay here with you?'

'No, no. You go off and have fun. We can always do something with Harry and Flick later, if Art and I are still talking. They probably won't want to do anything that requires too much movement. From what Art said, it was a pretty heavy session.'

'There was a lot to celebrate,' I offer. Which makes me wonder why Noah, Ella and I were all missing from the party.

Noah looks sheepish. 'I guess we should be making a move, Grace.'

'Of course.' I bend down and kiss Ella. 'Look after yourself today. Relax. Let Art run around after you and spoil you.'

She rolls her eyes. 'I know that you're ever the optimist, but I think that might be expecting *too* much.'

'Take care, though. Have an afternoon nap at the very least.'

'I will.'

So I shrug on my fleece and pick up my rucksack. Noah puts the sandwiches in his and slips on his boots.

'Right,' he says. 'Let's see what Skomer has to offer.'

'See you later,' I tell Ella.

'Love you,' she says. 'Have fun.'

So I fall in behind Noah and together we troop out to his Range Rover. I look across at him as he opens the car door and he grins at me. And I, for one, have a racing in my heart and a spring in my step that I can't deny.

Chapter Seventy-One

A bright-blue fishing boat bobs into the natural harbour of Martin's Haven, nestled between the cliffs. The long queue on the steps down to the jetty jostles excitedly. We've had a lengthy wait since we bought our tickets from the little stone lodge and most people are getting restless. Me, I'm just happy to be outdoors, alive and with Noah.

As soon as the boat ties up, we file down the stone steps and climb aboard, packed in like sardines for the short journey across to the island. Minutes later, we're cast off again and bouncing about on the waves, the boat riding them with a rhythm that threatens to rock me back to sleep. Only the wind whipping my hair keeps me awake. The waters of the Jack Sound are notoriously turbulent and the little boat throws us high in the air, lifting us from our seats.

Seagulls catch a ride in the slipstream, hanging in the air by the boat's wheelhouse, just above our heads. As we get out into the open sea, elegant black and white guillemots fly alongside the boat, skimming the waves. Noah pulls out his binoculars and scans the horizon.

'Here,' he says and his arms go round me as he holds up the binoculars for me to see them closer. I lean into the solid presence of him and relax for the first time in days.

As we get closer to Skomer, Atlantic grey seals come close to the boat and poke their noses out of the swell. They meander along with us, their big, sad eyes looking quizzically at the strange occupants, before they turn tail and disappear once more.

Puffins are the next to join us, more and more as the landing jetty comes into sight. The cute, barrel-shaped birds look like they shouldn't be able to fly at all. They flap their wings furiously against the air currents.

'This is fantastic,' I say.

'We're not even at the island yet.' Excitement shines in Noah's eyes. 'Just you wait. You're in for a real treat.'

Minutes later, the engines are cut and the boat is roped up at a minute jetty. We wait our turn to disembark, then Noah offers me his hand and helps me out of the boat.

'Back at three!' the skipper says, 'Or you're here for the night.'

So we climb up the steps to the grassy knoll of the island for our first glimpse of the untouched wilderness of the place.

'Wow!' The view is stunning. The sea is a glistening turquoise in the sun, its rays making the waves shine like crystal.

'It's a tiny place,' Noah says, 'just a couple of miles long and even less wide. It'll take us a few hours to walk round.'

As Noah has done all the research and I have done none, it only seems sensible to say, 'Lead the way.'

We fall into step together and he sets off at a slower pace than usual. 'We need to take our time, stop and admire the birds.'

They're wheeling overhead continuously. The lush grass is dotted with the rabbits that flourish here as there are no natural predators for them in this isolated spot.

It's not long before we come to a puffin colony. The comical little birds are rushing in and out of their burrows that honeycomb the ground, their mouths stuffed full of glinting metallic sand eels to feed their hatching young. We're so close that we could touch them, yet they're completely and wonderfully unaware that we're there as they go about their business.

I didn't know that there was a place like this where humans and birds could be in such close contact without conflict. If only humans on holiday could say the same!

I look over at Noah, busy taking photographs of the puffins with their clown make-up and their sad eyes. It's not been much of a holiday for him. Or for any of us. All I wanted was some quality time with my friends and with Harry, yet it seems to have been one drama after another. Don't they say that people row most either at Christmas or when they're on holiday?

Noah finishes taking his photographs and we press on, enjoying each other's company and the wildlife. I'm acting like someone without a care in the world and, for this time at least, my troubles do seem far behind me.

Noah and I share the binoculars to look out to sea, watching the swarms of birds constantly moving to and from the island in search of food. The gulls and razorbills soar majestically up the cliff faces. It makes me yearn to be as free.

We take our time to explore sheltered bays, exposed headlands and rocks that tower out of the sea, a playground for seals. Eventually we come to the Wick, a sheer cliff that drops straight into the waves. The elements have carved intricate ledges into it, making it the perfect nesting place for vast colonies of seabirds, like a block of high-rise apartments. The birds are crammed in so tight that you couldn't put a feather between them. Noah and I sit side by side on the sloping stone to watch and it's as if our arrival coincides with the matinée performance. Below us the sea is as smooth as polished jade, while above it the birds wheel and dive or glide serenely on unseen thermal currents.

Kittiwakes fill the air like flurries of snow, their distinctive call echoing off the rocks.

'Black-backed gulls are the villains of the piece,' Noah explains. 'They eat baby puffins for breakfast and will take a rabbit too if they're given half a chance.'

'Boo to them.'

'Harsh reality of nature,' he says with a shrug.

I feel that I know all about that from this week's events.

'This is a magical place,' I say into the stillness, a wistful sigh on my breath.

We have walked for hours, talking about the birds, the landscape: nothing of great consequence.

'I'm glad we came,' Noah agrees.

He lifts the sandwiches from his rucksack and hands me a tinfoil-wrapped package.

'Cheese,' he says.

'Perfect.'

We eat in companionable silence. He's brought two bottles of Coke from the fridge and we have those too.

Then, as we bask in the sun like the seals below us, I say, 'When do you think that you and Flick will get married?' I try to keep the tone light, but it comes out all wrong.

Noah hangs his head and says nothing. For a while, I don't think he's going to answer me and the silence stretches between us.

Eventually, in a quiet voice, he says, 'There won't be a wedding.' He looks at me bleakly. 'What could I do, Grace?' He runs his hand through his hair. 'I didn't see that coming at all. What would give her any impression that she and I were in this for the long haul? I've never led her to think that. Believe me.'

I do.

'She asked me in front of everyone, all her friends. How could I possibly have turned her down? She would have been so humiliated. But this marriage can never happen.'

'Have you told her how you feel?'

'Not yet. Flick was in no fit state when she finally got into bed.' He shakes his head as if he's trying to clear a troubling picture from his mind. 'What an awful mess.'

'She loves you,' is all I can offer.

'And I don't love her.' He gazes directly at me. 'You know that.'

I twist my hands together, unsure whether I'm elated or distraught. A maelstrom of emotions swirl together and crash in my heart, like the waves against the rocks.

'She's a great girl,' he continues. 'For someone. Just not for me.'

We don't say any more, but I feel certain of what's in his heart. I can hear it in my veins, in my blood. My soul is answering. And we both know it.

'I can't leave Harry.'

'I would never ask you to,' Noah says.

'I'm not that sort of person. I just couldn't hurt him like that.'

'So you'd rather be unhappy yourself?'

'Lots of people go through their lives just getting by. Not everyone lives on a cloud of happiness.'

'Shouldn't they seize it if they have the chance, though?'

'I don't know you, Noah. Flick is the sort of person who runs away to get married, who proposes to someone she's known for only a few weeks. I'm the steady one. The reliable one. I don't have flights of fancy.'

'So you'll go back to London, leave all this behind? Carry on with your work as an accountant? Stay married to someone who's a drunk and treats you with disdain?'

The words sting. 'You make it sound so terrible.'

'Isn't it?'

Yes.

'When we get back to the cottage, I'm going to tell Flick that there won't be a wedding. I'll let her down as gently as I can and then I'll leave.'

My heart wants to tell him not to go, but my mouth won't speak.

'I won't see you again after today, Grace.'

'We could meet up in London,' I say in a rush. 'Be friends. We enjoy each other's company.'

I could get on Twitter and Facebook or whatever, just like Harry. Noah and I can exchange jovial banter about nothing in particular.

Noah laughs. 'I might be strong-willed, but I couldn't do that. I don't want you as a friend.'

'I can't hurt Flick.'

I can't bear the thought of never seeing Noah again either, but I'll get over it. In time. I have to. Flick is my friend and that should count for so much more. And I can't have both. Hot tears squeeze from my eyes and the plaintive cry from the gulls above me is almost painful.

'Don't be sad.' Noah pulls me to him and I lean my head on his shoulder. Clouds cover the sun and I shiver at the sudden absence of warmth. We sit like that, unmoving. 'We'll enjoy the rest of the day together and part as friends.'

I nod as my throat is closed.

Then Noah says, 'Look!' and he points out to sea.

'Where?'

He directs my gaze. I wipe the tears away with the sleeve of my fleece and then see what he's showing me. A pod of porpoise is ploughing gracefully in and out of the waves. Their strong, grey bodies gleam in the sun as they pass the island, purposefully, intent on their destination. The beauty of it takes my breath away.

'That's amazing.' Noah too is almost breathless with joy. 'Where do you think they're headed?'

I don't know. But wherever it is, I wish that Noah and I could throw off our clothes, dive into the waves, leave everything behind and, together, just the two of us, go with them.

Chapter Seventy-Two

Too soon it's time to catch the boat back to the mainland. As we wait in the queue with all the other daytrippers, it seems as if we've already left the magic bubble of this special island and must return to the mundane reality of life.

We sit packed tightly in the boat and bob our way back to the harbour of Martin's Haven. I lean against Noah and he has his arm around my shoulders. I could pretend that he's steadying me against the tossing of the waves, but we both know different.

'I feel as if we're saying goodbye for ever,' I say to Noah.

'It's probably for the best, Grace.'

I think I'm going to be sick and it's nothing to do with the rocking of the waves. 'What will you do?'

'I'll make a new life for myself and you'll go back to yours. I'd like to come back down here, maybe permanently. It's a place that's filled with good memories for me.'

I can say nothing to that. In my heart I wish I was more like Flick. If I was, I'd go back, pack a bag and leave with Noah. I wouldn't look back. I wouldn't give a fig about my job. I wouldn't mind whose heart I trampled on. I would turn my back on my friends. That would be the easy thing to do. So easy.

The harder thing to do is say goodbye to your chance of a dream, to stick to your promises, to honour your commitments. To do the right thing.

But why does doing the right thing sometimes feel so wrong?

We're quiet in the car as we drive back to Cwtch Cottage. For once the thought of arriving there doesn't gladden my heart. I know this will be the end of my time with Noah and he's right, I might never see him again. The thought tears pieces from my heart.

The flowers brush the car as we drive slowly down the lane together for the last time. When we pull up outside the cottage, Noah cuts the engine. We sit and stare at each other in silence.

'We should say goodbye here,' he says. 'It will be more difficult when the others are around. And I'm not sure how Flick will react to being jilted.' He manages a smile. 'I might not get out alive.'

'She'll call you all the names under the sun for a few weeks,' I assure him, 'but she'll move on. Flick always does.'

'And we will too,' he says, 'in time. It's been a pleasure, a joy, to meet you, Grace. You're a kind, warm-hearted and beautiful woman. Harry is very lucky to have won your heart. It's not quite the holiday that I expected, but I feel better for knowing you, for sharing this short time together. In another place and time, I think we could have been very good for each other.'

My eyes have filled with tears, which now splash over my lashes and on to my cheeks. Noah gently traces a finger down them. 'Don't cry for me. Be happy. Enjoy your life. And if you ever find yourself free . . . ' The sentence tails away and he laughs softly. 'I should tell you one time, at least. I do love you, Grace. I loved you the moment I saw you.'

I can't speak. I can't answer. I'm frightened that if I open my mouth, I'll agree to go with him. Anywhere. I want to tell him what he means to me, but I can't. I can't even put my feelings into words, so they will have to remain silent in my heart.

'Dry your tears,' he says. 'We have to go inside. Be brave.'

I gulp back my sobbing and button it down. I am a wife. A friend. These are my roles.

'Ready?'

I nod and Noah opens the car door. With a shuddering sigh, he gets out.

Before he walks to the cottage, before he walks out of my life, I take my courage in my hands and throw caution to the wind. 'Noah,' I whisper to him. 'I love you.'

Noah smiles at me sadly. 'I know,' he says.

Chapter Seventy-Three

We don't use the front door; instead we walk round the side of the cottage and on to the terrace. Out there in the warm sunshine, Ella is alone, lying on a sunlounger in her bikini, dozing, her hands protectively covering her tiny bump.

Noah glances at me and we try to creep past to find the others. But, as we do, Ella's eyes open and she props herself up. 'Hey,' she says with a sleepy yawn. 'I must have dropped off. Have you had a good day?'

'Great,' I say to her. Even to my own ears, I sound ridiculously perky and false. 'Skomer is wonderful.'

'I must go there again, soon, before I forget how special it is.'

'How have you been? Had a good day too?'

'Hmm,' Ella says. 'Yes and no.'

I drop down on the bench next to her.

'Ladies,' Noah says, 'I'm going to leave you to it. I need to pop out to run an errand. I'll catch up with you both later.'

I glance up at Noah. I don't envy him the showdown he has

coming when he breaks the news to Flick that he's leaving. I sigh inwardly. Why does life have to be so complicated?

With that he waves us goodbye and, seconds later, I hear his car pull away. Soon he'll be doing that for the very last time.

'He's going to leave Flick,' I tell Ella baldly. 'He told me today.'

'Wow. She'll be devastated.'

'I know.'

'I thought it was ill advised of her to propose to him, but she was so determined.'

'Don't say anything,' I make Ella promise. 'It's between them.'

'Will he go after that?'

I shrug. 'I think so. But what about you? Have you resolved everything with Art?'

'I did. But not in the way you might think.' Ella sighs. 'He's gone. Back to London again.' She sees my jaw drop but before I can speak, launch in with my commiserations, Ella holds up a hand. 'I'm cool about it. We talked for most of the day, but we just couldn't reach a middle ground. Art still wants to carry on with his band management. He wants to live in London. He doesn't want to be tied to a relationship.' She pauses for breath. 'I want to move here. I want to settle down. I want to give my baby the kind of childhood that I had.'

'Oh, Ella.'

'We've parted as friends,' she insists. 'Art says that he wants to be involved with the child, but I'm not sure how well that will work out. But I accept his position. I don't want to settle for the little he has to give. Baby Hawley and I will be just fine by ourselves.'

'I'm frightened for you,' I admit. 'I don't want you down here alone.'

'I'm looking forward to it, Grace. Honestly, I am. My head's whirring with plans already.' She sounds so excited, but I have a pit of dread in my stomach for her. 'Depending on how the money goes, I'm hoping to keep the flat in London so that I still have a place to stay when I go up there for meetings and exhibitions, but we'll be down here for the rest of the year. It's not the ends of the earth, truly. The village is only a ten-minute drive away. I'm sure there must be some other young mums around somewhere!' She laughs at the expression on my face. 'Don't look so worried. I'm not. Grace, I'm positively looking forward to it. I feel that I've been living under a shadow with Art for a couple of years now. We were pulling in different directions and just didn't realise it. If I'm being truthful, the relationship had long run its course. We'd turned into different people, we just didn't like to admit it.' That sounds closer to home than I'd like. 'I'm better off without him. I'd rather be alone than be with someone who doesn't love me fully.'

She gives me a meaningful look, blissfully unaware of the conversation that Noah and I had just a moment ago.

I hug my friend. 'I want to help you.'

'Then promise that you'll come and visit me as often as you can.'

'Of course I will.'

But it won't be enough. When Ella has her child, I'll want

her round the corner from me. I want to be a big part of her life.

'Come on,' Ella says. She stands and wraps a sarong around her. 'I should make us both some tea.'

'Sounds lovely.'

I want time to think about what she's said and to work out how best I can help her. Despite what she says, I think the reality of going solo with this will be a lot harder than she imagines. How can I be there for her when, physically, there'll be hundreds of miles and two motorways between us?

'Where are Flick and Harry?'

'Hmm. Not sure. They went indoors about an hour ago when I started to doze off, I think.'

How can they bear to be inside on this beautiful day? It's late afternoon now and there's a warm glow to the sky; the sea is shimmering invitingly.

'I didn't see either of them until noon.' Ella laughs. 'They were both looking very fragile.'

'I should think so.' I wouldn't be surprised if they'd both spent all morning throwing up. The pair of them must have iron-clad constitutions. 'Were they cross that we'd gone off for the day without them?'

Ella shrugs. 'I don't think so. They seemed happy enough to mooch about here. To be honest, Art and I walked down the beach to talk so we didn't see that much of them.'

'I should go and see what they're up to.' Find out whether we've been missed or not.

Trooping into the kitchen after Ella, I feel relieved that Harry and Flick aren't there. I peep into the sitting room, but they're not in there either. However, I know it won't last. Soon I'm going to have to face them. I'd like to try to persuade Harry to go for a swim with me later, but if Noah does break his news when he comes back, then I'll need to be around to comfort Flick. She's not going to take this well. I know that she had high hopes for Noah. She thought she'd finally found someone special to love. Poor Flick.

'If you put the kettle on, I'll go and see where Harry is,' I say.

'OK.' Ella smiles at me. 'You look so miserable, Grace. Chin up, sweetie. Everything will work out fine.'

I wish I could be so sure. A huge part of me feels as if I've made the worst decision of my life. With a heavy heart, I make my way up the stairs to find Harry.

Chapter Seventy-Four

I tiptoe along the landing. Perhaps if Harry is deeply asleep, I should leave him be. Wouldn't he have come down when he heard the car pull up? But, as I approach the bedroom, I hear a muffled sound. Seems he is awake after all.

Quietly, I open the door and the sight that greets me makes me stop dead in my tracks.

On the bed, on *our* bed, Flick and Harry are naked. Except that Harry still has his socks on. That almost makes me laugh out loud. Their clothes are scattered at my feet, obviously removed in a frenzy. My best friend is on top of my husband, head thrown back, bouncing away enthusiastically. Harry, eyes closed in ecstasy, moans with pleasure. Flick thrusts her hips harder.

I stand and watch, transfixed. My mouth goes dry, my heart pounds. But I can't move. I can't speak.

'Oh,' Flick says. 'Oh, yes.'

She rides him harder, clearly coming to her orgasm, and Harry grabs her buttocks, digging in his fingers and urging her on. He slaps her rump and she squeals with delight. I feel myself flinch. Her taut flesh is pink with exertion. Harry's face is red and sweating. Harry and I have never had sex like this. Ours is slow, considered, and Harry is invariably on top. He always has time to take his socks off.

They slam together and still I don't move.

Flick shudders against him, grinding her groin into his. She cries out and then collapses on top of him, giggling breathlessly, her blonde hair covering him. Harry joins in the laughter and they cling to each other.

This is hideous. I can't believe what I'm seeing. My husband and my best friend? Harry and Flick? Clearly this isn't the first time they've done this. They are far too comfortable with each other's bodies. How did this happen? How long has it been going on? My brain feels like a pan on the point of boiling over. I want to scrub my eyeballs with bleach. I cup my burning face in my hands and gawk.

I'm frozen to the spot. What should I do? Should I just creep out again and pretend that I've seen nothing? That is what every fibre of my body is telling me to do. If they see me, there will be no going back from this. I don't want them to know that I've been here. So, holding my breath, I start to back out of the open door, praying that there isn't a creaky floorboard in my path.

Then, from the kitchen, Ella shouts out, 'Tea's ready, everyone!'

At that point, Flick and Harry turn in unison towards the open door and their eyes alight on me. Like me, they freeze. And there's a terrible moment where we all just stare blankly at each other.

Flick sits up, stricken. Harry now has his eyes and his mouth wide open. They gape at me, terrified.

My heartbeat returns to a normal level. My confusion turns to a still calm. My anger suddenly floods out of me. I find my voice.

'Now what are we going to do?' I ask.

Chapter Seventy-Five

'Grace,' Harry says. 'This is all a terrible misunderstanding.'

Despite my pain, I have to smile at that. 'I'm not sure how, Harry.'

'She's caught us red-handed having a shag,' Flick snaps. They are still coupled together, though Flick is making an attempt to cover her ample breasts. I wonder for the first time whether they are her own or are those fake too. 'Even I'd struggle to explain that one away, Harry.'

'I suggest you both put your clothes on,' I say. 'Then come down and we'll talk.'

An expression of relief washes over both their faces. Perhaps they think I should stamp my feet, shout, throw things, break mirrors. But I can't. I can't summon up that kind of energy for them.

Like an automaton, I turn and walk out of the room. I go to the bathroom and splash cold water over my face. Looking in the mirror, I can see that nothing has changed. My world has rocked on its axis, but there is nothing on my face to show it. I still look like me. I still feel like me.

While I have been fighting my feelings for Noah, putting my marriage before my own happiness, all the time they have been sleeping together behind my back. Judging by the way they were together, so easy, I'm absolutely sure that this isn't something new for them. How can I have been so blind? How can they have hidden it from me? Of course, I now think of all those furtive looks, the times they've jumped apart when I've stumbled across them in close conversation, and I saw nothing odd. All those late-night calls that Harry used to make, the hours on Twitter, the drinking. Is that all because of this? I thought he had problems at work, was having a mid-life crisis. The last thing on earth that I imagined was that my best friend and my husband were having an affair.

When I come out of the bathroom, there are scrabbling sounds from the bedroom and hissed conversation. Perhaps they're getting dressed whilst having a row under their breath. I can't even be bothered to listen to it through the door. Feeling borderline catatonic, I make my way back downstairs.

'Tea?' Ella asks. I nod and then, when she glances up and registers my expression, she frowns. 'Everything all right?'

'I don't know,' I admit. I'm still feeling dazed. I've got so many thoughts swirling round in my skull that I'm struggling to make sense of them. 'But I think it might be.'

Ella looks puzzled, as well she might. 'Want to tell me about it?'

But as she hands me the tea, Flick comes down. She's back in her shorts and T-shirt, but her face is flushed and her hair is tousled. There's a red rash round her mouth and chin where Harry's stubble has rubbed her. It's clear to anyone with eyes in their head that she has just been thoroughly and soundly shagged. Ella raises an eyebrow in surprise. Flick has the good grace to look sheepish.

'I wondered where you'd got to,' she says to Flick. 'Shall I put some cakes on a plate? Everyone must be a bit peckish by now.'

Not surprisingly, I have no appetite at all. 'Flick and I are just going to have a chat outside.' I dare Flick to argue, but she doesn't. 'We'll be back soon.'

'Is something the matter?' Ella wants to know.

'We have some things to sort out,' I tell her.

'Shall I come with you?'

'If you don't mind, Ella, I think that it's something that Flick and I need to do alone.'

'OK.' Still bemused, Ella says, 'Tea?'

'Not right now,' Flick answers flatly. 'Though if you were offering a double brandy, I'd take one.'

I nod towards the kitchen door and, without offering further explanation, she follows me outside.

We cross the terrace towards the beach, unspeaking, and my mind whirrs as I try to work out the best way to handle this. I thought that Harry had fallen out of love with me through some fault of my own. I never thought that he had found someone else and, if I had, I would never have dreamed that it would be Flick.

Do I know my husband so little? Yes, I think. Perhaps I do.

Chapter Seventy-Six

When we reach the middle of the beach, I sit down cross-legged on the sand. Flick sits next to me, adopting the same pose. There's no one else here but us. At the water's edge, a sandcastle is slowly but surely being consumed by the sea, signalling that a family has been here today, but are now long gone.

Together we stare out at the waves, at the sinking sun. Flick fishes her packet of cigarettes from her pocket and lights one. She shelters it from the breeze while the flame catches, then she inhales deeply.

I'm still thinking of ways to start this conversation, of what I want to say to my friend, when Flicks says, 'I've never really liked the sea. It all looks very lovely, but you can never tell what might be lurking just beneath the surface. It's always made me wary.'

Much like life, I suppose, but it seems too flippant a comment to make in the circumstances.

'It was supposed to be over.' She blows out a stream of

smoke. 'Between me and Harry. I ended it a couple of weeks ago.'

'How long has it been going on?'

'A while,' she admits. 'A few months. Maybe longer.'

'So all the time he was on Twitter, he was talking to you?'

'Yeah. Pretty much.'

'No wonder he was in so much of a panic about getting a signal down here.'

'I'd said I wasn't coming. How could I? Who in their right mind would want to come down here and play gooseberry with you lot? He'd been trying to text me to find out if that was still the case. And, because I couldn't ring him, he wasn't aware of Noah. It was a terrible shock to him.'

It must have been.

'Do you love him?'

'Harry? I've tried not to,' she says. 'God only knows I've tried. But I just couldn't help it, Grace.'

I say nothing, but I can certainly identify with that.

'I didn't want this to happen,' she continues. 'The last thing I ever wanted was to hurt you. Harry and I, well, it started out in innocence, then it got out of control. You know how it is?'

I should say, 'No, I don't.' But I do. I could see it happening so easily.

'You're my friend,' she says softly. 'My closest friend. You, Ella and me, we're like sisters. I love you.'

I want to say that she has a strange way of showing it, but how can I be so judgemental when I was a hair's breadth from doing the same thing to her? I could take the moral high ground and think that Noah and I never actually did anything physical, but is that really what adultery is? Does the physical act actually matter? Surely it's more to do with what's in your heart that shows whether you are betraying your loved ones or not?

'Harry and I are like two peas in a pod,' she says. 'We have a laugh together.'

As he and I never can now.

'But you and *Harry*?' I sound stunned. As, indeed, I am.

'Oh, Grace,' Flick's voice is bleak. 'How can I ever begin to say I'm sorry?'

I feel I should rail and shout, get out what I'm feeling inside. But how can I do that when I'm not even sure what I feel myself? I'm dazed. Reeling even. But there's also a numbness inside me. I feel no anger, no pain. I could rake this every which way, but what good would it do? I don't want there to be recriminations. Harry and Flick are in love. These things happen. I should know.

'Say something,' she urges. 'Tell me to fuck off or something, for Christ's sake.' Flick takes a last drag of her cigarette and stubs it out angrily in the sand. 'I wasn't even going to come this week. Ella was desperate for me to be here, but how could I? Art and Ella would be loved-up, I thought. And how could I watch you and Harry playing happy families and me be on my own? Again. But when I met Noah, I thought that I could do it.'

It seems ridiculously optimistic.

'Noah's a great guy. I've tried so very hard to love him, Grace. It would be so much easier if I did.'

'You asked him to marry you, Flick.'

'Oh, God.' She puts her head in her hands. 'I'm such a fuck-up. I don't even know why I did that. It was seeing you and Harry together and then Ella with her baby. I felt that nothing good ever happened to me. I'm just fickle, flaky Flick. No one takes me seriously, I'm just here to provide the fun. I wanted something good for *me*, Grace. Is that so awful?' She starts to cry and wipes the tears away with the back of her hand. 'I thought that if I was with someone else, then Harry would have to accept that was the end of it. That it would all be fine.'

'Does Harry love you?'

'I don't know. He thinks he does. When I told him that I was really going to try to make this work with Noah, he was distraught.'

'That was the night he went missing in the storm?'

It all seems so very clear now. Why else would he have risked his life in that weather if there wasn't something gut-wrenchingly important behind it? All that flirting, that feigned fondness, it wasn't done to win me back, it was all a sham to make Flick jealous. I feel such a fool.

She nods. 'He's a stupid twat.'

I can't help a half-smile at that. You can tell when it's true love with Flick.

'I'd told him again that we couldn't be together. How could we?' she says. 'Then, when he went off like that, I thought I was going to lose him.'

'Me too.'

'I realised then that I still wanted to be with him. Silly old duffer. But you're my best friend, Grace. I couldn't go on sneaking around behind your back. I have tried so hard to end it with Harry, but I can't.' She turns to me. Her face is blotchy, her eyes red. 'So, as you said, "Now what are we going to do?"'

'Oh, Flick,' I sigh.

'I'll go away. I'll never speak to him again. I'll never darken your door. I'll emigrate.' She sobs. 'Just tell me what I can do to make this right with you, Grace.'

'I wish you'd told me, that's all. So that I didn't have to find out like that.'

I glance back at our bedroom window, the one that overlooks the beach. I wonder if Harry is watching us now, trying to lip-read our conversation. The vision of Flick and Harry joined together will stay with me for a long time.

'When we were running round together at university breaking hearts, who knew that it would come to this?' A tear runs down her cheek.

'You were always the one who broke hearts, Flick. That was never me.' I'm not the destructive kind. I'm the picker-up of pieces. Perhaps that's my role now too. I check that my pulse rate is settled. I check that my heart is content. Then I say, 'You should be together.'

That makes her start in surprise.

'If you love each other, then you should be together.'

I could fight for Harry, but what would be the point? We might limp on for another year, maybe more, but where's the joy in that? Perhaps I've learned from Ella that forcing a relationship, trying to make someone stay with you when they'd rather be with someone else or be somewhere else, is like trying to push water uphill. There's a way forward that doesn't have to involve conflict and pain. What's the point of Harry and me trying to patch things up when, actually, all we both want is out?

'Harry's packing now,' she admits. 'I think he wants to leave here as quickly as possible.' Typical Harry. When it comes to the important emotional stuff, he hates confrontation. 'I expect he thinks that Noah will want to lump him.'

'He's not like that,' I offer in Noah's defence.

'I know. He's a great bloke. He will make someone a fantastic husband.' She rolls her eyes at me. 'If you're into birdwatching.'

This would be the time to tell her. To come clean and admit my feelings for Noah and his for me. I could tell her that Noah never wanted to marry her and that he was coming back to break it off with her. But my mouth remains shut. I wonder, would I be hurting much more about this if I hadn't met Noah this week? But while I can't rant and rave at them for their affair, I can't bring myself to be so magnanimous either. I was going to sacrifice any chance of happiness with Noah, and put Flick's feelings first because she's one of my very closest friends. It seems that she didn't afford me that same courtesy. But then I know what Flick's like. I just hope for Harry's sake that she makes a go of their relationship and doesn't get bored with him after a few months. If I'm brutally honest, I don't hold out great hopes for them. I think that very soon Harry won't be enough of a challenge for Flick.

'This isn't just a fling for me, Grace,' she says. 'I know what you're thinking.'

'If you're going to take my husband, Flick. I want you to love him. I want you to love him for ever.'

'And I'll try,' she promises. 'This time, I'll try. I'll try my very hardest. We're just so right together, Grace. You must see that.'

In some strange way, I can.

'I wouldn't risk our friendship if I thought this wasn't for good.'

She sounds so sincere that I really want to believe her.

'Despite all this, I'd dearly love it if we could still be friends.' She sniffs. 'I couldn't bear not having you and Ella in my life. When Ella has her baby, she's said that she wants us both to be godparents. Could we do that together, for her?'

I watch the ebb and flow of the waves. What do I do? Cling on to the ties that bind us, the bonds of friendship, or let them be pulled apart by the tides? Our friends define us. Sometimes they are our biggest strength and sometimes our biggest weakness. Do I accept that Flick will always be Flick and that her behaviour really shouldn't surprise me? If I have loved her for so long for who she is, why should that change now?

Do I give Harry and Flick my blessing and try to repair our relationship? I've had great times, great years, both with my husband and my friend. If I turn my back on them, wave them goodbye and cut them out of my life, I would be wasting all those precious years. I take a deep and steadying breath. I look at Flick, at the pain on her face, and I can't do it. To me she's still that troubled young girl at university, the one who does her best but invariably falls short. I realise that I'm stronger than her and it's up to me to make this work.

Perhaps I won't ever feel quite the same about Flick again. There'll always be a wound in my heart that she's caused, with a sticking plaster over it, but we've been through a lot together. Do I want that all to be for nothing? Can I put our friendship above this betrayal? I hope so. I'm sure it won't be easy but, at the end of the day, I don't want to see her or Harry miserable in their lives. If they can make each other happy, then they should do it with my approval.

Sighing to myself, I nod. 'I think we should try.'

Flick puts her arms round me. 'Thank you, Grace.' Her tears soak through my T-shirt. 'I feel so ashamed.'

'Just make this relationship work,' I say. 'That's all I ask.'

'Harry and I can't cause all this upset for nothing. I'm going to give it my best shot.'

'Love him,' I say. 'Cherish him.'

'I will, I promise you.' And I do believe in my heart that Flick really means it this time.

'We'd better go and speak to Harry.'

'He's probably thinking that you've hit me over the head with an axe and are now burying me in a shallow grave.'

'Then he doesn't know me very well.'

But perhaps the point is that I haven't known myself very well either. That could all be about to change.

Chapter Seventy-Seven

As we go back inside, arm in arm, Harry is coming down the stairs with his holdall. He looks as if he's dressed hastily as his shirt is buttoned up all wrong. The clothes that he's stuffed in his bag are spilling out of the top. Panic seizes him when he sees us.

Ella is sitting at the table, flicking through a magazine. She looks up at our entrance, glances at Harry and then back to us. Her pretty features settle into a frown as she says, 'Would someone like to tell me what's going on here?'

'There's no easy way to say this, Ella.' Flick takes a deep breath and then launches into: 'Harry and I are lovers. Have been for a while.'

Ella's mouth drops open. Harry's does too.

'We're going to try to make a go of it,' Flick continues. My husband looks quite dumbstruck by this announcement.

'You and Harry?'

'Are you really so surprised?' Flick asks.

'Yes, I bloody am!' Ella says. 'What about Noah? Yesterday

you were marrying him. Even for you, Flick, that's moving on quite quickly.'

'Obviously there'll be no wedding now.' She sighs. 'I guess it was a long shot anyway.'

Ella turns to me, her face dark, perturbed. 'How do you feel about this turn of events, Grace?'

Resigned. Elated. Crushed. Liberated. Frightened. Excited.

I settle on, 'It's a lot to take in.'

'I bet it is. How could you, Flick?' Ella snaps. 'To one of your own friends? To Grace? We arc closer to you than your own family. What were you thinking of?'

Flick looks as if Ella has slapped her in the face.

'I've given Flick my blessing, Ella.'

'Really?' She stares at me, amazed. 'Count yourself very lucky, Flick. If you'd had an affair with Art, I'm not sure that I'd be feeling so gracious towards you both. I'm not that happy with you anyway. I asked you if there was something going on between you and Harry. You swore that there wasn't.'

'I know,' Flicks says bleakly. 'I feel like a total shit. And so does Harry.'

'But not enough of a shit to end it?' Ella fumes.

It's clear from his expression that Harry wants the ground to swallow him up and I see him for the person he's become, not the person I married.

'I'm sorry, Grace,' he mumbles.

'I'll get over it,' I assure him. 'But I think you should both leave now.'

'I haven't packed yet,' Flick says.

'Then go and do it.'

Without protesting, Flick scampers upstairs.

'I'll walk you to the car,' I say to Harry.

He seems about to kiss Ella, but thinks better of it. Perhaps he feels that the gesture would take him just too close to her and that Ella isn't in any mood to forgive and forget.

'This has been a lovely holiday,' he says. Really, he does.

'You must come back again soon,' Ella says sarcastically.

But you know, strange as it may seem, I can actually envisage a time when it might be possible for us all to be together again. I can't see the six of us having a holiday at Cwtch Cottage in the near future, but with a huge amount of goodwill we might build our bridges in time to attend Baby Hawley's christening.

I follow Harry out to the Bentley, with the big dent in the back. I wonder now whether this shiny monstrosity was bought in an effort to impress Flick. He gazes disconsolately at his damaged car but, frankly, I'd consider that the very least of his problems at the moment. He drops his bag on the ground.

We look at each other and it's like staring at a stranger. I can hardly believe that I've spent so many years of my life with this man. In a short space of time, he's turned into someone I don't recognise.

'This is a terrible business,' he says without meeting my eye. 'I realise that, Grace. I'm most dreadfully sorry. I could have handled it so much better.'

He couldn't really have handled it much worse.

'If you can move your stuff into the spare room before I get back,' I say, 'that would be very helpful.'

'Of course. Of course.'

'You can buy me out of the apartment,' I carry on.

'You don't want it?' He looks taken aback by that.

'No,' I say.

I'm going to take this opportunity to change my life and already I feel quite light-headed with the thought of it. I shouldn't be afraid though; if Ella can embrace change, then I don't see why I can't. I should see this not as the end of something, but as an exciting new start. But Harry doesn't need to know all this. Not yet.

'You'll be all right, Grace,' Harry says, sounding slightly disappointed. Perhaps I was meant to fall apart but, at the moment, I feel stronger than I have in a long time. 'You always are.'

'I hope she looks after you, Harry.'

In truth, I don't know if having a hot meal on the table every night is as important to men as having hot sex. With Flick he'll have a much better chance of the latter than the former. Still, Flick's shortcomings in the domestic department aren't really my problem. Harry has made his bed and he'll have to lie in it.

'We had such high hopes, didn't we, Grace?' he says sadly. If I'm not mistaken there's a tear in Harry's eye. 'And it's all turned to dust.'

I don't like to contradict him, but I *still* have high hopes, with or without a man by my side.

Thankfully, just as Harry and I are beginning to be awkward with each other, Flick arrives. She's towing her wheelie case through the gravel, her sunglasses perched on the top of her

418

head, looking as if she'd be more at home in Puerto Rico than Pembrokeshire.

'Hey,' Harry says.

Flick keeps her eyes on the ground. 'Hey.'

He takes her case and puts it in the boot. Now they're both uncomfortable and it's time to make myself scarce.

'Well,' I say, 'good luck.' At least one of them is going to need it.

Flick bursts into tears. 'I'm sorry, Grace. So sorry. Can you forgive me?'

I nod. 'You're not waiting to tell Noah yourself?'

She shakes her head. 'You do it,' she begs, and adds, without a trace of irony, 'You're so much better at this kind of thing than me.'

I can't tell her that Noah will more than likely be relieved that he doesn't have to broach the subject himself. I wonder where he's gone. His errand has kept him away for only a short time, but he won't believe that he's missed so much.

She pulls me to one side and lowers her voice. 'He loves you, Grace.'

'Harry?' I cast a glance at my red-faced husband who is fussing in the boot.

'Noah,' she corrects. 'I've seen the way he looks at you. And you both love all that outdoors and nature stuff. If he doesn't love you yet, then I'm sure he soon will. But perhaps you know that already.' So it seems that Flick wasn't entirely unaware of our attraction. 'You're better suited than he and I ever were.'

We are, I think. Yet for you, to preserve your happiness, I

419

was prepared to turn my back on him to go back to my old life.

Harry is now hopping about awkwardly. It's clear that he's anxious to be gone from here, to forget about me as fast as he can. If Harry can just walk away without any explanation, then he will. Would he ever have left me if I hadn't walked in on them and caught them red-handed? Would he have carried on with the affair when we got home and made me believe all along that there was something wrong with me? Would he have let me pass up this chance of finding real love? The only reason he wanted to make a go of our marriage was because he thought he'd lost Flick.

Suddenly, I can feel anger rising inside me, bubbling up like a spring. I wish he'd just leave. Now. I'm trying to do this amicably, but my patience does have its limits. 'You should both go.'

'You can't let us leave like this, Grace,' Flick says. 'I can't bear to see you simply stand there. Say something. *Do* something.'

Then something snaps inside me. Flick's right. There *is* something that I need to do.

'Could you just wait a moment?' I say. 'I won't be long.'

They both wait, bemused, while I stride back to Cwtch Cottage. I open the front porch and inside, after a little rummaging beneath the growing pile of coats, I find what I'm looking for.

I march back across the gravel, purposeful. Like the dolphins swimming across the horizon at Skomer, I'm focussed on my goal.

'Grace.' Harry's voice wobbles. 'What are you doing with that? Put it down. Be a love.'

Flick says nothing.

'Grace!' Harry shouts now. 'Don't do this! You know you'll regret it!'

But, do you know, I don't think I will.

I glance at Flick, but she says nothing, does nothing.

'Grace! Nooooo!' He lunges at me, but he's too late to stop me.

With all my strength, I raise the golf club in my hand high in the air and bring it down, full square, on the bonnet of Harry's beautiful Bentley. I let out a cry of splendid release as it sails towards its target. The metal crunches satisfyingly beneath my blow.

Harry leaps towards me. I whirl the club at him and, quite wisely, he leaps back. 'Flick, do something,' he implores. 'Stop her.'

Flick stays where she is. So I climb up on to the bonnet and hear Harry squeaking in dismay. The golf club is planted directly in the centre of the roof and then I climb down again. Perhaps I don't look my most elegant, but I get the job done.

'Grace!' Ella is shouting now. She's clearly heard the noise of crumpling bodywork and has come to see what's going on. 'What are you doing?'

She runs up to our little group, but Flick holds her back. 'She's doing what she needs to do, Ella.'

I move to the side of the car, set up my swing – I did have a lesson or two many moons ago, but golf was never going to be my game. I slam the club into the driver's door, caving a spectacular circular depression in it. I feel years of anguish, frustration, emptiness, my attempts at perfection, flooding out of me.

'Oh, God!' Harry is running up and down, tugging at his hair. 'Oh, God!'

Somewhere in my rational mind, the thought comes to me that I shouldn't smash the windows as I still want them to be able to drive away. So, instead, I move round the Bentley, taking a swing at each of the panels.

'Oh, my car,' Harrys laments. 'My poor car!'

I hack three lumps out of the lid of the boot, which, let's face it, wasn't in pristine condition to start with. With my last bit of effort, I take out the panels on the passenger side. Flick watches impassively.

Harry dives towards me again.

'Leave her,' Flick snarls. His face darkens but, with a protesting shout of 'Aaaargh!' to the sky, he obeys.

And then, to be honest, my anger is spent. My arms ache and I let the club drop to the ground. My breathing is heavy. That really was quite hard work.

Harry darts backwards and forwards, inspecting the damage and making strangulated sounds of anguish.

'Next time,' I pant, 'get a less stupid car, Harry.'

I think he might spontaneously combust with impotent rage.

When my breath is steady again, I turn towards Flick. She's grinning at me. 'I would have done the same thing.'

'I know.'

'Better now?'

'Yes,' I say. 'I think I am.'

'Do you think we're going to be all right?'

'Yes.' I sound ridiculously bright. 'I think we are.'

'I love you,' Flick says. She gives me a brisk hug and kisses my cheek. 'Harry, get in the car!'

With a long and lasting howl of pain, Harry does as he's told. With a hefty yank, the crumpled door creaks open and he hurls himself into the driver's seat. Flick opens the passenger door, which drops on its hinges. I have to help her to close it. She fusses with getting comfortable. As I step away to pick up the golf club again, I see Harry cower behind the steering wheel, his hands over his head.

'She's finished,' Flick snaps. 'Don't you know anything?'

With shaking hands, Harry starts the engine.

Flick lets her window down. It jams near the bottom and won't go any further. She peers over the top of the glass. 'I'll phone you.'

'Leave it for a few days,' I tell her. 'I need time for this to settle.'

'How will you get home?'

'Oh.' Hadn't actually thought about that. 'I can probably come back with Ella.' Or Noah. 'I'll fix something up.'

'Can we go now?' Harry asks tentatively.

'Yes,' Flick says. 'We can go.'

And there's a look that travels between them: a mixture of relief and disbelief that they have come to this. But there's love too in their eyes. A lot of it. It seems genuine and warm. I've never seen either one of them look like that before and I realise

423

that I'm glad of it. I hope they make it. I hope they'll be happy together.

It's my time to go. I hold up my hand to wave and bite down on my tears. I hear the crunch of tyres on gravel, but I don't turn round. I don't look back. I keep walking forwards, towards Cwtch Cottage and the future.

Chapter Seventy-Eight

Ella is waiting for me, arms open wide. She folds me into her embrace. Despite her tiny size, her strength comforts me.

'I'm exhausted,' I admit as we walk back to the cottage. Taking a golf club to a Bentley has left me physically and emotionally spent.

'What came over you?' she says. 'It's not like you, Grace.'

I manage a smile. 'That's exactly what I wanted to hear.'

I don't want to be the woman who does the right thing, who always wants everyone's approval, who is always perfect. I want to be ruled by passion and fury, joy and rage. I want to act on whims, be led by impulse, be unpredictable. Maybe this is just the start.

For too long I've been in the role of the girl who plays nicely with the other children. They're the ones who get put upon all through life. They're the ones who sit degrees that they don't want to take, do jobs that they hate, marry men that they don't love with all of their hearts, with every fibre of their being. I feel it's time to dump that Grace. It's time I did what *I* want to do.

'I think if I was you,' Ella says, 'I'd have wanted to plant that golf club into both of their heads.'

I chew my lip. 'I feel quite bad now.'

'You shouldn't,' Ella assures me. 'I'm sure you've hit Harry where it hurt most.'

He certainly was very fond of that car.

'Actually, I don't feel bad at all.' A slightly hysterical giggle escapes my lips. 'I think that has probably just saved me years of therapy.'

Back in the kitchen, I flop down on to the worn sofa and let out a heartfelt 'Ouf'. Like this sofa, I feel as if all the stuffing has been knocked out of me.

I'm trembling on the outside, but inside there's a core of calm that I never even knew I possessed.

'You're going to have a medicinal brandy,' Ella insists. 'Even though you don't like drinking.'

'I think there are certain occasions that warrant it,' I concede.

Ella roots in a cupboard until she finds the dregs of a bottle that has escaped from Harry and Flick's drinking games. She pours me out a small glass.

'Did you know, Ella?'

I wonder if Flick has confided in her and whether she chose to keep the secret.

'No,' she says and I believe her. 'Although I did begin to suspect that there was something fishy going on. Even for Flick, she's been behaving strangely recently. She told me that there

426

was another married man on the scene, but that's nothing new. I never suspected it was *your* husband. Then I thought I caught a glimpse of them kissing at the beginning of the week when we went to Portgale beach. They pulled apart quickly and Flick, as usual, made a big joke of it. I couldn't be sure. It made me wonder, though. Flick looked extremely shifty. But then you can never quite be sure what Flick's up to. I asked her if anything was going on and she assured me there was nothing between them. I took her at her word. Maybe, I should have told you.'

'I'm not sure that I would have believed it.'

'No offence, Grace, but the last person on earth I'd imagine her with is Harry. He's far too staid for her – and for you. It won't last.'

'Maybe Flick will change,' I offer. 'I hope so.'

But, as part of the new me, I'm not going to worry about their happiness. That's now very much up to the two of them.

Ella hands me the brandy. I sit and sip it, gratefully. The smooth warmth feels comforting. I don't know if it's a myth that you should give brandy to someone in shock, but it certainly seems to be hitting the spot. And that's another thing that has instantly shifted in me. I no longer need to feel responsible for someone else's drinking habits – excessive or otherwise. All I have to look after now is me. If I have a brandy, I don't have to worry that it will start Harry off on a drinking session. If I want to open a bottle of wine, I know that it doesn't then have to be drained to the bottom in as short a time as possible. I can enjoy it at my own leisure or not.

Ella sits down next to me and we cuddle up together. 'Do you know what you'll do?'

'I'm not sure.' How can I even begin to tell Ella about my hazy, crazy plan as I haven't even had time to fully formulate it myself yet? 'I only know that I can start all over with a blank page. I think it's time to turn my life around. I've been stuck in a rut with my job, with my relationship, with how I run my life in general. If it's done nothing else, then this has jolted me out of it.'

Everything that I used to think mattered doesn't any more. I may not like what Flick has done, but I can't help but admire the way she goes all out for what she wants. At any cost.

'I want to try to use it as a fresh start.' Harry and I aren't short of money and I can't imagine that he'll be difficult about dividing everything. There's nothing I want from the flat, so as long as he can give me my fair share, I'm happy just to walk away. 'I've told Harry that he can buy me out of the apartment. I'm sure he'll want to. He loves it there.'

'Where will you move to?'

I give her a watery smile. 'I'm thinking here,' I admit.

Ella's eyes widen. 'You're kidding me?'

'Why not?' I shrug. 'This could be a complete new start for me. What's to hold me in London?'

'Your job?'

'I haven't thought it all through properly yet. It's just rattling round in my head.' My brain feels as if it's got a million bees buzzing in it. 'But I think I'm going to give in my notice on the partnership too,' I tell her. 'If there's one thing this week has taught me' – and I feel as if there have been many lessons – 'it's that life is too short to spend it doing something that I hate. I'm still young enough to turn it all round, do something else. I don't want to be an accountant for the rest of my life. It bores me to tears. I'd like to do something outside, work with nature.'

I have no idea in what capacity, but the trip to Skomer island with Noah made me think that I have a lot more to offer than my ability to juggle figures so that people can cut their tax bills. I could volunteer in some capacity to get experience and I'd have many more opportunities down here than in London, that's for sure.

'With the sale of my share of the flat, I'll have some money behind me, so I won't have to find work immediately.' If I'm careful, it could last quite a while. I'm not like Flick, I don't have to buy all the latest designer gear. I could give all that up quite easily.

'Now I'm excited,' Ella says. 'If you're going to do this, Grace, you *have* to come and live here with me. Please tell me that you will.'

'I was hoping you'd say that,' I confess. 'I've been really worrying about you, Ella. I didn't want to see you here alone with a new baby. If I can be here for you through that time, then I really want to be.'

She hugs me tightly. 'You are the best friend a woman could have.'

'I think if we're together, then it will be a better experience for you both.' I can also help with babysitting duties when Ella wants to get back to work. I'm getting all broody just thinking about it.

A thrill of excitement runs through me. I'm sure that my partners will let me work out my notice at home. Which means that, in theory, I can be back in Pembrokeshire within a matter of weeks. Harry can sort out the details on the flat. It's the very least he can do, after everything he's put me through. It's bizarre, but already he's in the past tense. Perhaps adrenaline is helping me to deal with this or maybe I'm just stronger than I think.

'It'll be like being room-mates again,' Ella says.

'It won't,' I assure her. 'Those gauche, optimistic girls have long gone. We're successful, mature women. Maybe we've been unlucky in love, but we've got our act together now. This is a new phase in our lives. And we are going to smash it!'

'I'll drink to that. Well, I would do if I could!' She licks her lips covetously. 'God, that brandy looks good. But I don't think that someone would forgive me.' She pats her bump fondly.

'You can inhale mine,' I tease, wafting the glass under her nose.

We both laugh and then my laughter turns to tears that I can't stop and Ella gets me the kitchen roll to weep into and holds me, rocking me in her arms on the sofa. She cries too.

I cry for what I've lost and for what I might be about to find. For the end and the beginning. And when, eventually, my tears run dry, Ella and I cuddle up to each other again.

'Oh, Grace, did you ever think we'd come to this?' she says, twirling one of my curls in her fingers. 'I thought by the time we were this age that we'd all be settled down with reliable husbands, 2.4 children each and an Aga. Funny how life turns out.'

'Hilarious,' I say and that sets us off laughing and crying again.

In the middle of this, Noah walks into the kitchen.

His face is sombre and he frowns as he says, 'Have I missed something?' He flicks a thumb towards the road. 'I'll swear that I've just seen Harry and Flick driving away in the Bentley and it was absolutely covered in dents.'

That sets us off again and we laugh until our sides ache, while Noah waits patiently for us to calm down. When we finally stop and blow our noses and wipe our eyes, he says, 'I daren't even ask. I'm frightened I might set you both off again.'

Ella eases herself from the sofa. 'You two should go out on to the beach for a stroll and you can fill Noah in. I'm going to make a start on dinner. I don't know about you, but all this emotion has given me an appetite.'

I'm starving too, now that Ella mentions it.

'All what emotion?'

I link my arm through his and lead him outside. 'Quite a lot has happened while you've been away, Noah.'

Chapter Seventy-Nine

He holds his hand out to me and we scramble down the rocks, on to the sand. The tide is coming in. We slip off our shoes and walk along the edge of the surf, letting the cold water gently wash over our toes.

'Want to tell me what I missed?' he says. 'It looked as if someone had taken a baseball bat to the Bentley.'

'It was a golf club,' I tell him.

He raises his eyebrows at that.

'And I was the one who did it.'

Now he stops in his tracks and stares at me. 'Isn't that slightly out of character?'

'For the old me,' I agree. 'But maybe not for the new me.' We walk along some more and I kick at the sand. 'Harry and Flick have gone back to London.'

'I'm assuming they didn't go just as friends?'

'No.'

Noah blows out a heavy breath. The sun is low in the sky, its rays fanning out across the water. Gulls cry overhead.

'So there *was* someone else all along. I suspected as much.' He rubs his stubble. 'I just never thought it was Harry.'

'Me neither,' I say flatly.

'What did they do? Did they just come out and tell you?'

'Not quite.'

The images of them bouncing around on the bed replay for me. It makes me squirm inside and I think it may have put me off sex for life. It would have been so much easier if they *could* have just told me about it.

'I caught them in a compromising position, you could say.'

He shakes his head. 'Wow. That's bad.'

'It was something I'd have preferred not to have seen.'

We walk on and I don't know what else to say. Noah picks up a few pebbles and skims them at the sea, but his mind isn't on it and I can tell that he's deep in thought. I push shells into the sand with my toes.

When he turns back to me, he says, 'What happens now?'

'I'm coming to live down here,' I tell him. 'Ella and I were just talking it over. I'm going to give notice on my partnership at work. As soon as I can, I'm going to move in with Ella. I want to be here when she has the baby. I'm really looking forward to helping with her. When they are both settled, perhaps when the winter is through, then I can start to look for a job.'

He looks at me, stunned, as well he might. 'You sound as if you're OK with this.'

'It's not the terrible blow that I might have imagined,' I admit. 'I'm trying my best to accept it.' I cast a sideways glance at Noah. 'After all, I don't feel entirely guilt free.'

'You should. You've done nothing wrong. Quite the opposite,' he insists. 'You were prepared to give up your own happiness so as not to hurt Flick or Harry. Doesn't seem to me that they've done the same for you.'

'In some ways, I feel as if they've done me a favour. Does that sound stupid?'

'I think it sounds as if you're a very understanding person.'

'I am trying to be.' A sigh. 'I don't want to lose Flick. Whatever she's done, I'd like her still in my life at the end of it all, if we can manage it. She's my best friend. I love her dearly.'

Then I remember that Noah's very firmly in the centre of this maelstrom too.

'How are you about Flick?'

He still looks bemused. 'It's not what I expected, but I'm not sorry either. I was coming back to tell her that there wouldn't be a wedding, that we couldn't be a couple. I was fully prepared to have to ride off into the sunset and never see you again.'

'You won't have to do that now,' I tease.

'No.' He exhales a long, shuddering breath.

We walk on along the beach together. It's so peaceful and isolated that I can't imagine tearing myself away even just to go back to London to close the files on my old life. I feel as if I should always have been here, that my life will start in earnest only when I am.

We reach an outcrop of rock, near to the place where we found Harry on the night of the storm. It all seems such a long time ago now. Noah sits down and I find a spot next to him.

'I've been busy too,' Noah says. 'While your life has been

crashing around you, I've been trying to sort out mine.' I wait patiently until he starts to tell me what he's been doing. 'I went back to the surf shop and had a long talk with Callum.'

This is music to my ears.

'We've agreed on a price for the shop,' Noah says, breaking into a grin. 'All I have to do is fix up the finance when I get back. Callum wants to go to Australia as soon as possible, so we're trying to sort out a deal where I come down here and work alongside him until he goes. Then he can show me the ropes and, hopefully, the transition will be smooth.'

'Oh, Noah,' I say. 'That's fantastic news.'

'I can hardly believe it,' he admits. 'It's just like a dream come true.'

'Maybe if I'm down here too, then I can help you.'

'We'll see,' he says. 'It would be great. But that's not what I need from you, Grace. I don't need you to fix me or help me out. I just want to be with you for who you are. I want to love you, that's all.'

Hot tears prickle my eyes. Perhaps I no longer have to be the person who looks after everyone else. That woman is going to be hard to let go of, but I'm definitely going to give it a try. I slip my hand into his. It's warm and comforting.

'Do you want us to have a future together?'

'Oh, yes,' I say. 'More than anything. I'm glad that we'll be both starting out here, building a new life.'

'It's more than I could have hoped for,' he says.

'Me too.'

I move close to him. The breeze from the sea picks up and Noah folds me into his embrace, protectively.

Who knew that, when we agreed to come on this holiday to this little cottage by the sea, it would be anything more than a short break to recharge my jaded batteries? I never thought that I would watch my marriage unravel and fall deeply in love, probably for the very first time. Or that I would say good-bye to my old life and look forward to starting a brand-new one with Noah by my side.

He strokes my wayward curls from my face and, gently, tentatively, for the first time, his lips find mine. They're warm and sweet, laced with the tang of sea salt. And they taste just as I'd imagined they would.

Acknowledgements

To Owen and Sharon, Craig and Hem, Ann and Ash, Dave and Sue and, of course, Lovely Kev – my companions on our holiday in a cottage by the sea. Always fun. Thank you for undertaking the more extreme parts of my research. I will never forget parking in the potatoes, Gully, the peregrine falcon, the puffin nuffin' or, indeed, the shag.

'We're all Going on a Summer Holiday'

My Summer Holiday Memories
by Carole Matthews

When I was a child my holiday involved a week away in this country. I was brought up near Liverpool and sometimes we used to go as far afield as North Wales, over an hour's journey away! Once we went to Tenby, which was deemed to be so far that it required an overnight stop on the way. It was a happy time of sitting in a steamed-up car, drinking tea from a thermos flask and, generally, looking at the beach through the rain and the whooshing windscreen wipers. Sometimes we went to my Auntie Elsie's static caravan in the Lake District and thought we were terribly posh.

My parents' love affair with holidays in the UK ended when we went to Butlins one year and there was an outbreak of chicken pox. We came home the day after we arrived, when the fold-down bed I was sleeping in folded itself back into the wall with me still in it. The trauma stayed with me for many years.

Then, The Overseas Family Association sprang up and we saved all year round to go to New York to visit my mother's sister who had moved out there many years earlier to marry an American. My mum had to have special permission to take a month off work as we were going so far.

We all had new clothes for the journey. Finest crimplene, of course. The six-hour flight felt like it was taking us to the other end of the earth and my dad sat through it all, buttoned up in his suit, tie and new shoes. At the other end, we 'took it easy' for days to get over the terrible affliction of jetlag.

It seems like another era. We jet all over the world at the drop of a hat now and I'm still not sure what caused the change in our travel habits. What has happened in the intervening years? Has international travel become so much cheaper? Has the world become a smaller place? There seems to be nowhere too remote to visit now. Or have our expectations simply increased with time? Was it simply the lure of visiting somewhere with unbroken sunshine that did it?

I look back to that first trip to New York. It was like a step into the unknown. America was a country that was truly very foreign to us. A strange land, indeed. McDonalds – years away from opening in the UK – seemed exotic and glamorous. How funny that years later we think nothing of going to the Big Apple for the weekend or even for a business meeting. I know it as well as I know London. Six hours seems like a mere hop, skip and a jump. Jetlag now only kicks in when we've done twenty hours or beyond.

Another example. My first honeymoon was to a caravan in Sheringham, Norfolk. We went mad and had a fortnight away. It rained torrentially the entire time. Ten years later and my second honeymoon – and second husband – we had an extravagant three weeks in Hawaii. And not nearly as much fun.

My hen night – both times – involved a few drinks at the local pub. Now the 'Hen Night' – and indeed 'Stag Night' – can involve an entire party of two dozen or more going somewhere exotic for a week. A weekend to a European city is, at the very least, *de rigeur*. Barcelona and Prague are, for better or worse, hen and stag weekend meccas. Subsequently, the honeymoon needs to be that much grander to compete. The current must-go-to destinations include the Bahamas, Bali and Bora Bora. Bognor Regis and Bournemouth rarely feature on anyone's list.

My own travel has also become increasingly more exotic over the years. When my partner, Lovely Kev, and I first met, he whisked me away to five-star luxury in the Maldives. I spent a week on a sunlounger, never without a colourful drink in my hand. It was fabulous. It was also all smoke and mirrors. Now I'm lucky if I get a tent. Ever since then we have embraced 'adventure' holidays with gusto. This usually finds me up a mountain somewhere, with a backpack and walking boots on.

We've walked the Great Wall of China, puffed along the Inca Trail to Machu Picchu, white-water rafted in Nepal and scaled Himalayan peaks. We've camped in the Maasai Mara with lions roving round the tent and cycled the western cape of South Africa. We went to see the amazing wildlife on the Galapagos Islands, somewhere that you don't get to without huge effort. It involved four flights and over six and a half thousand miles of wearying slog. Our latest and most fabulous trip was to Swedish Lapland where we slept in a wilderness lodge, went husky sledding and saw the Northern Lights, all in temperatures of minus 36 degrees. And it's all been brilliant. We have memories that will stay with us for ever. But now I don't care if I never get on another long-haul flight in my entire life.

What should be a glamorous, or at least, a pleasant form of transport has been made into something truly hideous by every single airline company. The queuing, the random security measures, the interminable hours waiting in crowded terminals, the cramped seats. Then there are the delays due to fog, volcanic ash, snow, sundry super storms. I start to shake with anxiety the minute we book a flight now.

So the last few years we've gone back to our roots and have taken several holidays at home. The first one was to Cornwall and I'd forgotten how beautiful that part of our country was as I hadn't been down that way in over twenty years. We had a glorious week. The sun blazed down on us and we surfed on Newquay beach. Holidays at home were, we decided, the way forward! It seemed silly to have seen so much of the world when there were huge gaps in the places we'd been to in our own country.

Since then we've made sure that we've had at least two weeks of our holiday at home. We've been to North Wales – which hasn't changed much since that fateful Butlins trip – to the Lake District, Derbyshire, Dorset, Suffolk and Scotland. Beautiful Pembrokeshire was, of course, the rugged setting for this book and it's still such a wonderful, remote place. I feel as if I've come full circle and am rediscovering what this lovely country has to offer. We can just throw everything – and I mean everything – in the back of the car and go. No weight limit to worry about, no having to take off coats, belts, shoes, watches, etc, every few paces. In the time that we'd be sitting stewing in the airport, we could be halfway to our destination in familiar comfort.

Mind you, we still have our moments of sitting in car parks looking out wistfully at the beach through the mist and rain. There are some things about British holidays you just can't change.

Carole's Q&A with her readers

What sort of holiday would be your ideal holiday? Beach? City? Countryside? Active? Lazing around?
Maggie Hill, Salisbury

Any of the above! Until last year, I wasn't very good at doing the lazing around type of holiday. The trouble is if I'm lying on a sunlounger, I start to think of stories in my head and then I want to be off and tapping away on my laptop. So it was always better for us to do something that was very active, which is why my holidays usually see me halfway up a mountain or white water rafting. I must be slowing down in my old age though as we had four days lazing around a swimming pool on our last trip and I relished every minute of it.

If you could go on holiday with anyone, alive or dead who would it be with? (Besides Lovely Kev)
Cheryl Fayers, Ipswich

You know, there's no better holiday companion than Lovely Kev. I'd hate to go on holiday without him. He's very solicitous, carries my bags, helps me up mountains, removes creepy crawlies from rooms/tents. I couldn't manage without him and we always have a great time. Plus I'm blessed with a lovely group of friends – the ones who we went to Pembrokeshire with. Every year we try to have a week away together. We all like the same sort of things and we can have such a laugh doing absolutely nothing.

Tell us your most memorable holiday moment with a friend.
Jasmine Aherne, Cardiff

When Lovely Kev and I first got together we went on holiday to the Maldives. I was slightly alarmed to see that the island we were staying on was little more than a patch of sand. There'd definitely be no escaping each other! I wondered whether that would put our new relationship under pressure when, in fact, we had a lovely time together. Then one night we were sitting out on the beach. In front of us the sun was setting, dolphins leaping across the horizon while behind us the moon was rising, the stars glittering like diamonds. It was a really magical moment. And, sneakily, I used it in *A Minor Indiscretion*!

Do you have a bucket list for things to do whilst you're on holiday, like do you plan what you do beforehand or do you just go with the flow?
Gilly Coventry, Rayleigh

Because we go to far-flung places where solo travelling can be challenging, we quite often go on an organised group tour. When you only have a limited amount of time it can really take the strain out of travelling. The downside of that is that we very rarely do our own planning now. Sometimes, we even get on the plane before we read up on what we're supposed to be doing on the trip. But we're both laidback people on the whole and tend to go with the flow. I've come to accept that you can't possibly do every 'must do' on a holiday when you're only there for a short time.

What was your favourite holiday, Carole and Lovely Kev?
Sam Clarke, Oakham

We've been fortunate to take so many trips that there are many highlights. We've been to the Galapagos Islands which is a very special place. We stayed on four different islands and the diversity of wildlife is just amazing. One day we swam with baby sea lions in the wild which was a unique experience.

More recently we did a trip to Swedish Lapland, which was research for my next Christmas novel, *Calling Mrs Christmas*, and I think that was the most stunning place I've ever been to. We stayed in a wilderness lodge with no electricity, absolutely in the middle of nowhere and it was magical. The trees covered with snow are like beautiful sculptures. We had a go at cross country skiing, snowmobiling and dog sledding, which was the most wonderful fun. We also built an igloo but did baulk at sleeping in it! One night was spent in the world famous Ice Hotel, which is a fantastic experience. The temperature plummeted to minus thirty-five, but we still stayed outside – in arctic suits! – for four hours watching the most magnificent display of the Northern Lights. I'd go back there in a heartbeat.

What's the worst holiday experience you've ever had, and why?
Donna Turner, Halifax

We finally reached Machu Picchu in Peru after four days of hard walking and sat down, happy and tired, on the grass overlooking the site to take in the magnificent view. I was bitten all over the back of my legs by tiny no-see-ums and every single bite became infected. My legs swelled and they were agony to touch. Luckily we had a doctor on the tour and he gave me the name of some antibiotics and I trotted off to the chemist to buy them. You can buy literally *any* medication over the counter in Peru and I was extremely glad of it, otherwise I think I might have scratched my legs off.

One of the best bits about holidays is tacky souvenir shopping! What's the worst (or best depending on your point of view) souvenir you have ever bought?
Sarah Diment, Ringwood

We've bought so much tat over the years that we've now put a stop on it and rarely bring home souvenirs. Something that looks vibrant and wonderful in the African plains just doesn't sit well in a minimalist home in Milton Keynes. Believe me we know! We did crack one year and brought back a stuffed toy mousse from our trip across the deserts and canyons of America. Lovely Kev saw him sitting on a shelf in the supermarket and he looked really sad and forlorn. Despite the fact that we were camping and our bags were fit to burst, we bought him. He now sits on the desk in my office and is much happier.

Where in the UK has been your favourite place that you have been on holiday?
Shona Shaw, Dumfries

We've only recently got back into the swing of holidaying in the UK and there's so much of this country that we don't know. The theory was to go to lots of far flung places while we were fit and young! Now that flying is such an awful experience, I really appreciated being able to just get into the car and go. We've been to Cornwall, Dorset, Suffolk, Derbyshire, Wales and the Lake District and have loved them all. I think this year we'll return to Keswick in the Lakes. We're keen walkers and it's an area I'd like to explore more. I thought that Keswick was a really lovely, little town with some nice cafes and restaurants.

Do you think that the dynamics and 'rules' in a relationship and in friendships change when people go away on holiday together? And why do holidays sometimes make or break relationships?
Julie Louise Phillips, Telford

I think when friends are 'hot housed' together on holiday their flaws and faults tend to be amplified. You might usually spend a few hours with them over dinner or for an afternoon, but we don't usually spend day after day with friends. I think the danger is that you feel you have to spend all the time together and then tensions can be created. We've found that the key to group holidays is to also have some time on your own or to go off and do things in smaller groups and come together in the evening. We had a great holiday in Cornwall a few years ago with ten friends, but the logistics of getting that many people to agree what to do and where to eat is quite challenging. It helps if everyone is prepared to compromise a little.

I think relationships sometimes struggle on holiday because you're out of your normal routine and you don't have the mechanics of daily life to distract you. It was on holiday that I realised my marriage had ended. We had a great time during the day when we were playing golf with other people but, at night, we turned into the couple who sat at the table opposite each other and had absolutely nothing to say. That was a horrible realisation.

Have you ever been arrested or got into trouble with the police whilst on holiday?
Jontybabe JB Johnston, Brook Cottage

A few years ago I was invited to go to the big, annual chocolate festival in Perugia, Italy, as *The Chocolate Lovers' Club* had won an award for the Best Chocolate Book of the Year. We'd taken lots of samples of good British chocolate in our cases to share with our hosts and my Italian publishers. When we arrived at Perugia Airport, there was a drugs dog – a massive, fluffy Alsatian – who excitedly pinned a man off our flight to the ground and bounced all over him. I said to Lovely Kev, 'That dog needs to go for a long walk,' and we both had a good laugh.

Then we went through Immigration and went off to wait for our luggage. Everyone else slowly disappeared with their bags until we came to the realisation that our cases hadn't appeared. We were getting a bit worried when, suddenly, the door burst open and two armed officers and the very bouncy drugs dog came in carrying our suitcases. Our hearts sank. This was never going to be a good sign.

We were escorted to a windowless room and one of the officers threw open the suitcases. 'Where is the cocaine?' he said while the other man glowered at us and the dog leaped around.

'There's no cocaine,' I explained. 'We have a lot of chocolate, but no cocaine.'

They were unconvinced and stripped every single thing out of our cases, even emptying our toiletries all over the counter.

By this time our hearts were pounding and our palms were getting very sweaty. We were very worried that they'd soon be reaching for the latex gloves. The dog bounced some more.

When they finally pulled out our stash of chocolate, he pounced on it. The officers exchanged a worried look. The dog barked and wagged his tail a lot.

'You are very lucky this time,' the officer said and gestured with his gun that we should repack our case.

We did so, very quickly, and we legged it out of there as fast as we could. I even resisted the urge to give the dog a bit of chocolate on the way out.

What would be your five staple things to take on holiday if the luggage was limited, and why?
Sharon Viant, Bournemouth

Years ago we went to China for three weeks and were only allowed to take 10kg of luggage including a sleeping bag. That needed very careful packing! I always have to take my iPod for entertainment on long journeys or for lying on the sunlounger. I think I'd struggle to do without my Kindle now – the joy of taking all those books on holiday! In terms of clothing it would have to be flip-flops and a sarong. I can't live without mascara either.

On a girly holiday in my twenties I discovered that one of my friends slept wrapped tightly in a sheet with her arms crossed

across her chest like she was an Egyptian mummy. Very disconcerting. Have you ever discovered any disturbing and previously unknown facts about a friend whilst on holiday?
Jodi Mountain

A similar thing. My friend and I shared a room for the first time and I was a bit alarmed at how little she slept in given that she knew someone else would be in the room. Also she was the most untidy sleeper! She ended up tangled in her sheet with her head at the bottom of the bed. She was also in the middle of a torrid affair and spent the entire night texting her man in between bouts of wrestling her pillow and snoring loudly. I didn't get a wink of sleep and I'd never share a room with her again.

Is there anywhere in the world you would like to travel to and why?
Marcella, Kingston

I keep looking at cruises in Antarctica. I'd love to go down there and see some of the wildlife – whales, polar bears, penguins. We'd have to fly across the Drakes' Passage though as, apparently, it is one of the roughest crossings in the world and I am the world's worst sailor. Every year I get a brochure for it and every year I pass out when I see the cost. It is most extraordinarily expensive. And it frightens me how often the words 'weather permitting' appear in the blurb.

Where did you go on your first school holiday and which teachers went with you?
Carol Galvin, St Helens

The first school holiday I went on was on a coach tour to London when I was in primary school in St Helens. The only teacher I remember being there was Mr Gleeson, our lovely headmaster. The best part of the trip for me was going to Hampton Court for the day. I was mesmerised by the stories of those naughty Tudors and it's given me a life-long love of that period.

When on holiday are you always looking for a new story for your books or do you take a break?
Pauline Curson, Norwich

I have long given up trying to have a complete rest on our trips! My mind is too much of a busy body. The minute I'm not fully occupied, I start to think about stories and travel is so fabulous for throwing up ideas. We quite often go on group holidays as I love group dynamics and it's great to meet people from totally diverse backgrounds – we've met every type of person from train drivers to forensic scientists. There's always someone who I can call if I'm stuck for a fact or two.

With this book, *A Cottage by the Sea*, the idea didn't come to me until I was back at home, but I'd obviously been absorbing the wonderful scenery and setting as somewhere I'd like to write a future book.

If you enjoyed *A Cottage by the Sea*,
you only have to wait until October
for Carole's next bestseller,

Calling Mrs Christmas

Join Carole Matthews as she takes you on a romantic and
emotional rollercoaster ride in this wonderfully festive read.

EXCLUSIVE!
Read on to enjoy the first two chapters!

Chapter One

Perfume ads on the telly. First it's Charlize Therone strutting and stripping her way through some mansion until she's wearing nothing but J'Adore and an alluring smile. Next it's Keira Knightley over-acting 'fun' for Coco Mademoiselle. Finally, for Chanel No. 5, it's the stylised Red Riding Hood advert with the best-looking wolf you've ever seen that's been doing the rounds for years. When, and only when, these luscious advertisements grace our screens, it's at that moment you know that the giddy, helter-skelter run down towards Christmas has finally begun in earnest.

All three of these advertisements have been screened in a row and it's barely mid-morning. I missed a lot of the ads last year. All of the daytime ones. I hear myself sigh. It's a bad habit and I've been doing it a lot lately. This year, as I am an unemployed, redundant couch-potato, I am running the entire gamut of Christmas commercialism. It's the first week of October and already Stacey and Jason are extolling the virtues of Iceland's pre-prepared party food.

There is much laughter, much over-indulgence in these adverts, much that is red and gold and glittering. Which is all very lovely. I'd usually buy right into it. Except there'll not be much partying at our house this Christmas. Very little, if any, party food from Iceland – or elsewhere – will be bought. Our table will not be replete with festive delights. Our Christmas tree will not be surrounded by half a ton of presents. It will be a big contrast to last year. I stop the next sigh that threatens to escape.

'Budget' is the watch-word of the moment. Closely followed by 'cutbacks'. Last Christmas we had a great time. As is expected, the table groaned with food, the booze flowed, we force fed ourselves an excess of Quality Street. All the usual things. Wonderful. But last year I had a job. This year, I don't. And there's the rub.

This Christmas, any tightening of the belt will be entirely down to our dwindling finances and not, for once, caused by the calorie-overload of the festivities. I have now been out of work for a grand total of eight months, four days and, checks watch, three hours. And it's fair to say that no one seems to be missing the great contribution that Ms Cassie Smith, age thirty-five, of Hemel Hempstead in the fair county of Hertfordshire has made to the cut-throat world of commerce.

I switch off the television and stare at the walls of the flat. This place has become my prison and my refuge all at once. I hate being trapped in here all day with nowhere to go. Yet when I get the chance to go out, spread my wings, I'm now frightened. My heart pounds, my mouth goes dry and my palms sweat at the thought of stepping out of my comfort zone. Do you think that's how budgies feel? Do they desperately want to fly free, but as soon as that cage door is open, they freeze? If it is then I feel so sorry for them. I used to be sure of my place in life, but my confidence in myself has dwindled just as fast as our meagre savings have.

My job, I have to admit, wasn't fantastic. I grumbled about it a lot. To anyone who would listen, really. But, my goodness, how I miss it now. I would give anything to be complaining about hauling myself out of bed on a frosty morning, scraping the car windscreen, blowing on my fingers to keep warm, muttering about the crap office coffee. Instead, when Jim gets up for work, I simply turn over and go back to sleep. No need to get up. No need to rush. No need to do anything. No need to be here at all.

I worked as a secretary and general dogsbody for a small engineering company specialising in component design and fabrication. The price I paid for daydreaming in school. But I was good at my job, efficient. People liked me. I was a dedicated and diligent dogsbody. I could turn my hand to anything and frequently did. Sometimes it felt as if I was running the flipping place. Jim and I went to my boss's house for dinner. Three times. He opened champagne. I always went that extra mile, my boss said. He said I was indispensible. In fact he said it the very morning before he called me into his office and told me that from the end of the week, I would be surplus to requirements. Not enough people, it seemed, needed components designed or fabricated.

I push my misery aside and phone Jim. Just the sound of his voice can pull me out of a downward spiral. His mobile rings and rings. My other half, for his sins, is a prison officer based in the Young Offenders' Unit at Bovingdale Prison. He can't have his phone with him when he's on duty, but I'm hoping that I might catch him on a break when he tries to go out to his locker if he can, snatching a few minutes to listen to his messages and look as his texts. He never used to go out to his locker during his shift when I was at work because I never used to have time to phone him during the day. We did all our catching up on the evenings when Jim's shifts allowed us to fall exhausted on the sofa together. Now I spend my entire life on the sofa – primarily alone – and Jim is conscious that he's my lifeline to the world, so he checks his phone as often as he can.

As I think it's about to go to voicemail, Jim picks up. 'Hi, love,' he says, sounding harassed. 'A bit busy right now. Just got a call on the radio. Can I ring you back later?'

'Yeah.'

'Was it anything important?'

'No. I'm just bored.'

'Okay. Catch you when I've got a spare mo. Love you.' He hangs up.

'Love you,' I say to the handset.

And that's the trouble when you're not busy. Everyone else is. I switch the television back on. The John Lewis advert. Something sentimental to have you reaching for the tissues as usual. The Argos ad. Then Boots who seem to be trying to guilt mothers into excess present buying. No wonder vulnerable heartstrings are stretched to breaking point. Soon everyone but me will be wrapped up in Christmas. A time when all sensible spending goes out of the window and everyone racks up the debt on their credit card to pay another day. Well, we can't do that this year.

To be honest, I didn't particularly worry when I was made redundant. I wasn't exactly overjoyed as I thought I'd done my best for the company and I thought they were happy with me. But I thought I'd get a job really easily. I'd waltz straight into another company who'd love me and appreciate me more. Who doesn't need secretaries? What sort of company doesn't have a dogsbody on which to dump all their most depressing and unwanted tasks? Who doesn't want someone to molly-coddle and care for all the staff and their various crises. An office angel. I assumed that the local paper would be filled with opportunities for someone of my skills and experience. It seems that I was wrong.

Chapter Two

I stare at the clock. Nearly ten minutes have passed since I last looked at it. Still Jim hasn't called me back. In fairness, he has a very busy job. Jim, unlike me, works in a growth industry. No shortage of customers in Jim's company. No chance of anyone saying that there isn't enough demand for *his* skill set. The Young Offenders' Unit at Bovingdale is already overflowing and there's a steady stream of thieving, drug-dealing, car-nicking, house-breaking kids that they can't even begin to accommodate.

But no matter how much I hate being unemployed, I couldn't for all the money in the world, for all the tea in China, do a job like that. My Jim is a saint amongst men.

We've been together for five years now, meeting in a less than salubrious bar in Watford just after my thirtieth birthday and just after I'd decided that true love would never find me. There he was, standing with a pint of Magners in his hand and, for me – for both of us – it was love at first sight.

Sometimes, you just can't put your finger on what causes

that strength of attraction, but you know that it's there. It's not that Jim's an oil painting. I wasn't bowled over because he's a dead ringer for Matthew McConaughey. He doesn't have that kind of movie star looks. His hair is cropped close which makes him look a lot scarier than he actually is. From his time in the army, he's got tattoos on his toned biceps. A heart and a rose entwined on one side. A skull with flowers growing through it on the other. Between his shoulder blades there's a colourful phoenix and I love to trace the outline of them on his skin when we're lying in bed. He's stocky, not that tall, has a face that's too pale as he spends his working days locked inside and we haven't had a sunny holiday in years. But my Jim has the kindest eyes you'll ever see. They're soft, grey and always have a twinkle in then. He smiles much, much more than he frowns. When it comes down to it, Jim's just an uncommonly nice guy and it radiates from every pore he possesses. Everyone adores him. Me included. Jim is the epitome of the word 'solid' and, since the day I met him, I know what it is to be loved, to be cared for.

By the end of our first week together – a week where we saw each other every night – we'd decided to move in together. Just like that. No ifs, no buts. I knew instantly, instinctively he was The One. I'd had a few relationships in the past, but no one had ever made me feel like Jim did. It wasn't that he showered me with flowers or diamonds. Quite the opposite. Present buying, isn't Jim's forte. He isn't romantic in a showy way at all, but I watch him sometimes when he's making me some toast or a cup of tea. I see how much care he takes. He's knows that I like my toast well done with loads of butter right up to the edges of the bread. He frowns in concentration as he makes sure that the jam is spread really thinly, exactly like I do it myself, and that it's cut in triangles not sliced straight across. He puts his feet on my side of the bed to warm it before I get in. He opens doors for me, walks on the traffic side of the pavement and pulls out my chair in a restaurant. To me, that's love. It's not roaring down the street in a Ferrari, it's not sky-diving out of a plane with an 'I LOVE CASSIE!' banner trailing behind you. I think it's the constant, quiet things that tell you that it's real love. And I feel that I am very loved.

My Dad cleared off when I was young. I barely remember him, but something like that leaves it's mark and I've always felt wary about getting too involved with men. I always expected them to let me down and, invariably they did. It got to the point where I hardly dated at all, didn't really trust men. With Jim it was completely different. This might sound mad, but it was like finding the other half of myself. From day one, I knew that I could trust him with my life, that my heart would never be mashed by him. And, if that sounds corny, then so be it. He is truly my soulmate.

We can sit for hours just reading together or walking through the woods. There's never any drama with Jim, I don't have to worry about where he is or who he's with. Jim isn't one for nights out on the lash with the lads, he'd rather be at home with me than anywhere else. And that's all I want too. Just to be with Jim. We're content in each other's company. We don't need the high-life, we're happy exactly as we are.

If it wasn't for Jim, I don't know how I would have survived the last year. He's been my only brightness, always there with the right words to cheer me up or knowing when a well-timed bar of chocolate would lift my spirits. When I was made redundant, I thought I'd take a couple of weeks off, have a bit of a rest. A 'career break' I laughingly called it. After all I'd been in work constantly since I was sixteen, there was no rush to find something else. I'd been given a month's salary as a pay-off. Yeah, thanks for that.

Then, when I'd caught up on the ironing and the flat was so spick and span that it looked like Anthea Turner had been through it and I'd watched all the films I'd been meaning to watch but hadn't got around to, I applied for jobs. There weren't as many of them as I'd expected and some, I felt, just weren't right for me. I was surprised when, having sent off a rash of my splendid CVs, I only got one interview. Even more so when I didn't get the job. I thought the interview had gone so well. Seems that I was wrong about that too. After that setback, a little bit of panic set in. I catalogued all our DVDs and old CDs alphabetically and then applied for more jobs. This time I was less choosey. Got one interview. Got no job. And so it went on.

I signed on. Was given Jobseekers' Allowance, went on a workshop which showed me how to present my CV properly and then applied frantically for anything that there was with the word 'vacancy' attached to it. Still no luck.

When the spring morphed into summer and I was still terminally unemployed, I began to lose my nerve. The few interviews I did have went badly. A lot of firms that would normally employ secretaries seemed to have embraced an age where managers did their own donkey work or they made use of university graduates who had a degree, thirty grand's worth of debt and were desperate. Instead of 'unpaid slaves', they called them 'interns' and insisted the posts were great and necessary work experience for their CV. But whatever it was, it meant that people like me – who actually wanted paying – went down to the bottom of the pile.

I don't mean to sound sorry for myself. But I am. Very sorry. I don't want to be like this. I look at the television, at the snowy scenes, at the promises of unfettered festive happiness, at the excessive consumerism and I want to be part of it. I love Christmas. I want to embrace all of its tacky indulgence. It's my time of year. Perhaps sometimes, I let myself get a bit carried away – Jim said the flat looked like a flipping winter wonderland last year – but it's supposed to be like that. I don't want to be thinking of getting a meagre Tesco Value chicken rather than a big, fat Kelly Bronze turkey. We can cut back on presents, that's no hardship. It's the little things that make Christmas special. But I don't want to miss out on the atmosphere.

This is the only difficult part of my relationship with Jim. We never have enough money. We might not like the high-life, but we've never actually had the money to try it. Funds are always tight. Even when I was working we didn't have a lot left to splash around, now it's a terrible drain on us. Our desires are fairly modest, but I feel as if I've been on a budget since the day I was born. We don't want for much but, sometimes – just sometimes – it would be nice to treat ourselves without having to count every penny. Surely Christmas is one of those times?

I don't catch what the advert is for, but there's a mother on television, dressing the Christmas tree, two mop-haired children and dog from central casting at her feet. Presents are piled around the tree which sparkles brilliantly. A beautifully set dining room table replete with ravishing food is in the background. Carols soar to a crescendo and Daddy comes through the door to his perfect family and his perfect Christmas. A sigh rises to my throat. Surely there must be someone out there that needs extra help at Christmas? Doesn't everyone try to run round doing ten times more than they normally do? There *must* be a role for me out there? My ideal job, my *raison d'être* is organising stuff. What a shame that I can't get paid for celebrating Christmas! Then something inside me clicks and the most brilliant idea hits me like a bolt out of the blue. A grin spreads over my face. I could be a part of this. I don't have to sit here on the sidelines and let the joy of Christmas pass me by. I can embrace the commercialism and bring in some much needed extra cash. I can do something about it.

My mind is whirring with the kernel of an unfocussed plan when the phone rings. Jim's at the other end. That means it must be his lunchtime and here's me, still in my pyjamas. Well, all that's about to change. No more slobbing around the house feeling sorry for myself, I'm going to launch myself back into the world with a vengeance.

'Hey,' he says. 'Sorry I couldn't speak earlier. I was on my break, but something kicked off. It's total madness here today.'

It is total madness where Jim works *every* day. While we're talking about money, they don't pay him nearly enough for the stress he has and what he has to put up with. That's another one of the reasons why we're still renting this tiny flat and both drive clapped out cars. I want to do my bit. It's not fair on him. I want to get out there again in the big, bad world of paid work. I don't want our life to be like this, constantly living from hand to mouth. I hate having to accept benefits from the government just to get by. We're young, we're resourceful. We shouldn't be in this situation. I know can do more. And know I might just have a plan as to how.

'Are you OK, Cassie? Still bored?'

'No,' I say. I can feel myself beaming widely. It's as if a terrible fog has suddenly cleared from my head. A light bulb has gone ping-diddy-ping in my brain and it's burning brightly. I let out a bubbly laugh, a sound that I'd forgotten I could make. 'You'll never believe this,' I tell him. 'But I have just come up with *the* most brilliant idea.'

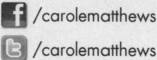